The Wicked Skill

Sartorias-Deles Books

Historical Arc

"Lily and Crown"
Inda
The Fox
King's Shield
Treason's Shore
Time of Daughters (two volumes)
Banner of the Damned

Modern Era

The CJ Journals
Senrid
Spy Princess
Sartor
Fleeing Peace
A Stranger to Command
Crown Duel
The Trouble with Kings
Sasharia En Garde

The Rise of the Alliance Arc

A Sword Named Truth
The Blood Mage Texts
The Hunters and the Hunted
Nightside of the Sun

THE WICKED SKILL

Sherwood Smith

BOOK VIEW CAFE

Book View Cafe

Published by Book View Café
304 S. Jones Blvd., Suite #2906
Las Vegas, NV 89107
www.bookviewcafe.com

ISBN: 978-1-63632-061-8

I fix mine eye on thine, and there
Pity my picture burning in thine eye ;
My picture drown'd in a transparent tear,
When I look lower I espy ;
Hadst thou the wicked skill
By pictures made and marr'd, to kill,
How many ways mightst thou perform thy
will?

But now I've drunk thy sweet salt tears,
And though thou pour more, I'll depart ;
My picture vanished, vanish all fears
That I can be endamaged by that art ;
Though thou retain of me
One picture more, yet that will be,
Being in thine own heart, from all malice free.

John Donne

Sartorias-deles
Sartoran continent
with parts of Drael, Toar,
and Goerael
Geranda and Sky Island
not represented
Goerael
Bereth Ferian
Drael
Roth Drael
Wnelder Vee
Everon
Imar
Erdrael
Danara
Narad
Chwahirsland
Mearsies Heili
Enaeran
Sles Adran
Shiovhan
Alsais
Colend
Marloven Hess
Vasande Leror
Sartoran Sea
Eidervaen
Sartor
Sarendan
Norsunder Base
Toar

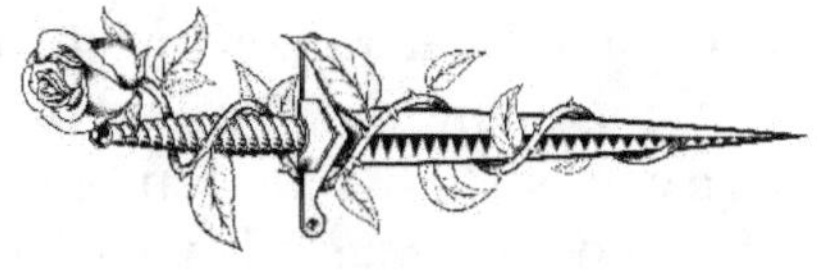

ONE

This summer interlude I have the honor to relate is a story of revolution and of romance. It is a story of two young kings without thrones. It might be said that is a story of revolution by rose, and a story of revolution with no roses.

This is also the story of a shopkeeper's daughter who once saved the world, then went away to learn who she was. It is a story of trust and betrayal; it is about the different faces of love, and it is about the sovereignty of music.

I invite the reader to follow me, for a short time, away from Sartorias-deles and to its sister world, Geth-deles, forever circling the sun Erhal opposite one another.

In this world, made up of uncounted islands in a world-spanning sea, we come to a very small island midway in a set of archipelagos, where a one-person boat has just skimmed into the tiny harbor.

"Sister Orchid is back!"

Word spread from the ten-year-old girls weeding in the garden to the white-haired eldest reading reports at the other end of the rambling building

The place: an old and famous mage school exclusive to those who identified as women, built centuries ago above a quiet bay on an island on the world called Geth-deles, opposite to Sartorias-deles in circling around the sun Erhal.

The time: afternoon, as rainclouds departed.

Prospective students left their names at the door; over the past few years a medium-tall, reed-slim girl who now appeared to be somewhere in her mid to late teens had worked her way up the ranks to become the current Sister Orchid.

The young gardeners paused to watch Sister Orchid bring her sailboat to the end of the floating dock and tie it down one-handed. She swung her baldric over her unbandaged shoulder, and patted her rapier into place with nearly five years of unthinking habit. Gazes raked over her oval face dominated by large eyes so light a brown they looked golden in most light, framed by tousled wheat-colored braids swinging against her hips, thence to the arm in a sling.

Questions semaphored between the girls—would Sister Orchid be promoted to become the new Sister Sandpiper, or would she be sent to seclusion for being two months late, and where had she been, anyway?—until called to order by the supervising elder sister, who added, "I'm certain we'll find out soon enough what happened. Once we finish our weeding."

The quicker ones got the hint and began to yank weeds with new vigor as Sister Orchid slipped inside the heavy outer doors, relicts of wilder days.

Sister Orchid crossed the outer court, encountering more friends among the students, young and old, but no one impeded her as she walked down the tiled halls cooled by breezes off the tended waterways, the hiss of her sandals the only noise.

By the time she reached the office of the Eldest, the senior staff had agreed on who would remain to interview the late arrival.

The three women sat on cushions as Sister Orchid entered and put her hands together in the gesture of respect all Ones extend to each other, youngest candidate to the eldest, their chief. The three mirrored her greeting, and the oldest indicated the cushion placed before them.

Sister Orchid unslung her baldric and set it aside, her pack next to it, before sitting cross-legged with the unconscious grace that characterized her. A wince tightened her features as her elbow in the sling jogged against her knee, indicating that the wound in her shoulder was fresh.

"I apologize for the long silence," she said—tired enough that a slight trace of accent rounded her vowels. "I dared not trust magic communications. It was compromised. And I couldn't find any Sister Ones to pass word through."

The eldest leaned forward, hands on knees. "Word might have been impossible—we all know that events can overtake one—but rumors have reached us of duels, manifold inquiries still being prosecuted in four different courts of appeal, and the smoking ruins of a government?"

"All that in two months?" The middle mage, she of the salt and pepper hair, straightened upright. "I am astonished you were not gone two years."

The youngest said, "Of course it would be you, the best student we've had in generations."

The eldest sat back: neutrality, surprise, eagerness tempered with flattery. How would this brilliant young sister respond?

Sister Orchid dropped her gaze to the arm curled against her. "Anyone who'd been sent to that particular Sister One at that particular time would have done the same. Or better," she breathed, suppressing the instinct to touch her throbbing shoulder.

"Were you then a messenger or a catalyst?" the eldest murmured, white brows raised.

Many prospective candidates who had longed to join the exclusive, prestigious and powerful mage school could not encompass the training that channeled the instincts of competition and self-importance into acting for the good of the group, but that had never been the wounded girl's problem. The self-denial of her early childhood had nearly driven her to self-immolation.

Long, dark lashes framing those thoughtful golden eyes lifted. "I *had* to act. Fast. There was no one else, and you train us in covert movement as well as in defense."

"You fought the assassin yourself?" the eldest asked.

"Yes."

The girl before them—not born on Geth—had soared up the levels from beginner to advanced in all subjects and skills, faster than any student in memory, and in certain regards she was advanced beyond some instructors.

But, the eldest reflected, in crucial ways she was still so very young.

"We would like to think so," said Sister Clematis, she of the salt-and-pepper hair, "but we all have strengths and weaknesses. Not every sister, sadly, would do as well against a trained assassin." She looked puzzled. "And yet, from your words, that would seem to have been your first encounter, two months ago. But you move as though the wound under that bandage is quite fresh."

"It is. The assassin I disarmed with no blood shed, and is in trial now. This wound is from another duel, one I lost two days ago." The golden eyes shuttered as memory gripped viscerally: the brush against her ear of soft hair that had never known weather until recently, the accented whisper, *I'm sorry, but my orders are clear. And I had none about you.* Then the lightning-fast feint and the cold/hot shock of honed steel sliding deep into her shoulder. "I could not save a friend's brother from being taken by Norsunder."

"I am sorry to hear that, and I share your grief," the eldest stated mildly. "But we are waiting for your summary of previous events."

Out it came, in exemplary concision, as the girls were taught: no false modesty or coy self-effacement, no brag. Simply — or dauntingly — a series of events beginning with a spoken message that led to the rescue of a guild chief who'd reported evidence of embezzlement. After that, the fight to disarm the assassin, whose thoughts during the duel had revealed clues to a secret cadre poised to overthrow what turned out to be a corrupt government. This government, she had discovered, was busy dividing among themselves the vanishing treasury of an island group, while inventing a naval crisis to cover their actions.

The naval crisis — a pirate attack orchestrated from within the government — led to a harbor battle that ranged up into the capital buildings. All headlong events, each propelled by the revelation of secrets requiring instant decision, action, reaction, all accelerated by the intensity of emotion, because there is always a human cost.

"... and then I was taken to meet Daumnek-Pol Leteur, leader of the sea guild defenders, whom the government had been blaming for attacks, treason, and insurrection, but in my interview I discovered that he had spoken the truth all along."

Sister Orchid brushed fingers over her high forehead. "So I, with the Sister One, facilitated a meeting between Leteur and the guild representatives. And when everything was settled, or so I thought, a friend begged me to track his brother in the mental realm . . . and, well, that led to the encounter I lost . . ." And she forced herself to detail how she had lost.

The eldest remained silent, scarcely heeding those details. She already knew most of them. She listened to

Orchid's assessment of what she'd been taught, until the well-meaning questions, exclamations, and praise by the other two began distressing Orchid, whose voice quieted to a near whisper, her expression of calm belying the tightness of her posture.

When Sister Orchid's fingers drifted up to touch one shoulder, the eldest waited for a natural pause, and spoke up at last. "Perhaps we might return to this discussion after Sister Orchid has had a chance to recover a little."

"Excellent idea," Sister Clematis said. "Orchid, dear, I want you to know that the rest of your cohort is eager to embrace you among them again as soon as you are ready."

The eldest saw that kindness, with that undertone of eagerness, was almost more than Sister Orchid could bear, and refrained speaking as she led the way to the wing where girls and women who, for whatever reason, required the benefits of seclusion. Here, Orchid was left in a pretty infirmary room overlooking the smaller waterfall, and the eldest returned to the flow of duty.

But never was Orchid far from her thoughts. By nightfall the sister on duty reported that Orchid had a fever, and needed an infusion of fever-weed; another sister, recovering in the next room from a heavy cold, soundlessly moved rooms during the night, disturbed by the muffled sounds of weeping carried in through the open windows.

The eldest was aware that her hope that the quiet security and tranquil atmosphere of the community would draw Orchid out of herself was just that: a hope. In most, she would take that peaceful reintegration for granted. This mage school was the world's oldest, female exclusive by tradition, and few of those who traveled long ways to be considered for candidacy were accepted.

By rights Sister Orchid ought to have remained at rest for several days to a week, but after a second sleepless night, she presented herself early outside the interview chamber, and such was her reputation among the others that the small group there waiting all agreed she ought to go first.

The eldest shut the door, and even closed the window, though early as it was, it promised to be another warm, humid day.

Sister Orchid sat across from her, then said, "I want first of all to express my gratitude. You took me in though I was older than the seedlings usually are, and I didn't speak the language, and . . ."

The Eldest raised a hand, smiling. "My dear, you needn't retail what we both know. Speak what is in your heart."

"I need . . . I need to go home," whispered the distraught girl so close to womanhood. One might even have said that she should have been over that threshold by now, but cleaving to childhood had been one of her emotional defenses. Even though, by her own admission, she had a young daughter left behind on Sartorias-deles.

The eldest reflected on that, then returned her gaze as Orchid continued, "For a little while. To recover." A touch to the shoulder. The words came quickly, uncertainly, a protest or defense, though no one argued—outside of her head. "I love it here. I'd love to stay through seabird level. Or even mountain bird." That was the highest level of Ones training, the sisters taking names for mountain birds as they prepared for either dealing with world affairs or remaining to teach.

"We both know that you are capable of that, and more," the Eldest said. "It is our earnest wish that you will find your life's path among us."

Sister Orchid's eyes lifted, the gleam along the lower lids gathering to spill over in silent tears. "I love this place. The people," she said. "But I think . . . I think I need to be home. For a time." She bent forward earnestly, the braids she had never been willing to cut a silent emphasis to her words. "Cath—Dak's brother—he is what you call Marsh mad, that is, he is very powerful on the mental plane. At least as strong as I am. Lyal was sent to capture him."

Here, Sister Orchid indicated her bandaged shoulder. "Lyal was trained as a knife fighter on Aldau-Rayad. Norsunder captured him and made him into an assassin. If Cath's at Norsunder Base on my world, well, I feel I ought to go after him." She shivered in memory. "Or at least tell the mages what I learned. And I know we don't talk about our outside families, but there's my daughter . . . It's been almost five years."

"My dear girl," the eldest said kindly. "You needn't convince me. If you feel you must go, then you must go."

"I would like to come back. And study more. You—all of you—have taught me so much! I was such a disaster when I arrived."

"You were never that." The eldest smiled. "You simply needed to learn the difference between self-discipline and self-punishment. A new environment gave you the opportunity to replace old habits with better." She gestured toward the door. "As you know, it is our custom to celebrate one going out into the world, if that is your wish."

"No." A quick shake of the head and a thumb surreptitiously wiped tears. "It's so . . . so permanent. And it would hurt so much, to say goodbye. I would rather you tell anyone who asks that I cherish you all, but had no wish to disturb the peace that has meant so much to me." Her voice caught.

The eldest rose. "It shall be as you wish."

Sister Orchid walked with the eldest to the storage room where new arrivals left the belongings they brought with them. She hadn't much. The clothes that no longer fit she donated, and took only the transfer token that would bring her back to her world.

The eldest took her face in her hands and kissed her forehead. "Remember, my dear, you are always one of us." Then let her go.

The flash of magic transfer, seen from outside the room, brought Sister Clematis in. "I wish we could have kept her."

"I know." The eldest sighed, still watching the floor where the former Sister Orchid had stood, as if she could bring her back by will. "In so many ways so advanced—far beyond any of us in the mysterious realm of the mind, and equally formidable in other skills." The eldest touched her head, and her right arm. "But here." She touched her heart. "After so many years hiding away on her world in the form of a child, and so new to physical maturity, I fear that . . ." She let the fear drift unspoken.

Sister Clematis said, "It would have been so much better if she could have gained some emotional experience here, within our safe walls."

"Yes," the eldest murmured, then breathed, "And because of who she is in her world, I am afraid that she will not find any safe walls awaiting her."

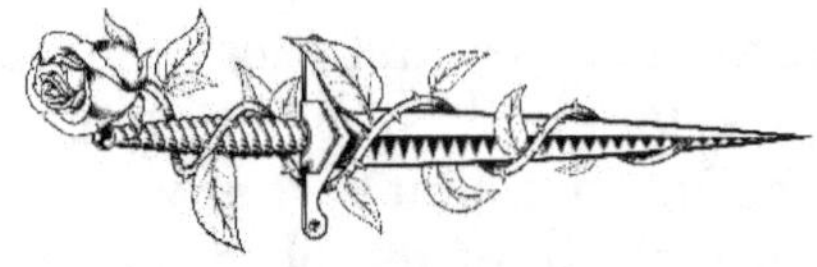

TWO

T hey turned away, and began to discuss which girl was ready to be the new Sister Orchid as Liere, already regretting leaving behind that name, and the person she had become, endured the magic transfer from world to world.

A flash of light, the sense of being flung down a long tunnel, and after nearly five years, she was once again Liere Fer Eider, standing on the soil of Sartorias-deles. Liere's eyes stung, her throat hurt, but neither ached as much as her heart. Was it the familiar scents — not only the late autumn blooms in the garden, some of which also grew on Geth, but the smell of the air itself? How to define it? Autumn leaves, late wildflowers, a trace of wood smoke, and sedge, and the strange winds off the Ghost Lakes. After nearly five years, the familiarity of that mix of scents actually hurt.

This was her home world, beloved and yearned for.

But this *place* wasn't home.

Liere looked around the moonlit garden. Bereth Ferian was as beautiful at night as it was during the day. She gazed at the indistinct blue reflection of the single moon in the tall windows of the state wing, and wonder-ed if those windows were still framed by the stylized acorn scrollwork popular earlier in the century, when the building had been renovated for the twentieth time. Maybe there'd been a twenty-first renovation while she was away. The thought made the palace seem even less like home.

The air was also quite chilly, something she had for-gotten, living for nearly five years in a much warmer climate.

She breathed in, bringing up her core warmth, then walked briskly to the residence wing, while in the dream realm her daughter Lyren-Sartora sensed presence.

She was too well-trained to ignore it. She sat up and reached for the dagger that lay on her nightstand as her door opened to a tall, slender silhouette, who spoke. "Lyren?"

"*Liere?*" Lyren-Sartora exclaimed.

"I'm home, Lyren."

"It's Lyren-*Sartora* now." This was no little girl's voice. Lyren-Sartora sounded precise, assured. Twelve going on twenty-four.

Liere leaned down to hug her daughter, whose familiar scent, part sunshine and part blossoms, sparked an anguish worse than the stab wound in her shoulder, a pain that had no limit or definition.

Liere fought to steady herself, and indicated the dagger hanging slack in Lyren-Sartora's hand. "Was that a hint? Or were you really expecting Norsunder to attack?"

Lyren-Sartora had grown—of course. Liere laughed unsteadily as she let go. "I feel obliged to point out that any Norsundrian assassin sneaking in would probably grab it and use it on you first."

Lyren-Sartora bounced out of bed and reached for her robe. "Pooh! As if I wouldn't smell a Norsundrian five days' ride away." And then, with airy mendacity, "I thought it might be Mac joking me, or Yanli—she loves sneaking up on you, and when you jump, she chortles and says *Yer lazy!*—" Lyren-Sartora stiffened, shoulders up as she eyed Liere's silhouette. "Is this a visit, or what?"

"I . . . I don't know." Then Liere said quickly, "If you're angry with me for going away, I don't blame you." Liere drew a deep breath, embarking on the con-versation she'd imagined so many times. "The first year, we weren't permitted communication outside of emergency. I knew that I would hear if you were in danger. And I knew that others were taking better care of you than I ever did. Or could. And then, well, I kept remembering how we kept quarreling before I left."

"Quarreling," Lyren-Sartora repeated. Even in the weak light she make out pain in the shifting shadows on Liere's face, and in the tightness of her quiet voice.

The knot of resentment inside Lyren-Sartora eased enough for her to reach for balance. For truth. "No, I was being a brat. Mac and I both were. We thought ourselves so smart. Until you left, and Siamis said he'd feel sorry for me only when I'd examined the reasons why you had to get away." She waved a hand, as if dispelling stale air.

"Siamis," Liere repeated, thrown back in memory: once an enemy, then everything changed—and Liere retreated to Geth. "*You* weren't to blame," she said, and the old guilt pulsed through her, sour and unsettlingly familiar, as if those five years had never happened. "The truth is, I was incompetent as a parent. I can always say I was too young— blame the Child Spell—but even if I'd let myself age physically I don't know that I would have been any better. Not the way I was here." Liere touched her forehead. "So I left. You could say, I ran."

"You had to be away. I get that." Lyren-Sartora's tone was steady.

"You do? I'm not sure *I* really do, yet."

"Arthur said that you weren't escaping us so much as escaping others' expectations. You kept telling me, ever since I was little, that you hated being Sartora, and I figured out that it's because Sartora wasn't a real person, she was this story girl, a great heroine, and you didn't want anyone to see *you* and be disappointed. But you felt this duty to try to be her anyway." Lyren-Sartora spoke quickly—for she, too, had been planning conversations for a very long time.

"And failing to be her," Liere said, her voice low. "Always failing."

Lyren-Sartora had imagined her own instructive and lofty wisdom enlightening Liere once she did return, bolstered by her firm foundation of moral superiority. She had never envisioned the *hurt* of true remorse, and shifted uncomfortably. "Are you hungry? I am. At least, for hot chocolate. I got the habit from the Mearsiean girls, chocolate in the middle of the night."

"I'll join you," Liere said.

Her tone sounded artificially brisk, but that was all right. A miracle had happened. Lyren-Sartora had Liere back. She didn't want any talk about failures. She tied her robe around her, fingered back the loose curls esca-ping from her long, heavy night braid. "If anyone's out and about they'll have to put up with my night robe."

"You have guests?"

"We, Liere," Lyren-Sartora said over her shoulder as she led the way out.

This was not her home. But Liere was not ready to say that yet, for if it wasn't, what was? "We have guests, then?"

"A pack of herald archivists and scribes, mostly. Arthur is making his library, you know. Right now that means translating a lot of old Venn runes, and other equally ancient and boring stuff. Erai-Yanya's been here helping Arthur a lot with wards, while Mac and Yanli are over at the mage school. I've helped by staying out of the way."

The ironic tone was new. But what one expected from a girl turned twelve.

"My family?" Liere asked, feeling her way cautiously.

"They left South End. After your father died. They settled in some town called Belann, in Imar," Lyren-Sartora answered. "They're perfectly safe. And yes, I did my duty and visited them for the memorial."

"My father died? What happened?" A fresh sense of guilt overwhelmed Liere—though she could not identify the source. Her father had made it clear how much he despised her, and it wasn't as if she had caused her father's death or could have done anything about it.

"It happened *ages* ago. He got into a violent quarrel with the neighbors over their Flower Day petals blowing in front of the shop, and how they were responsible for sweeping them up, and the neighbor said he wasn't responsible for the wind and your father was in the middle of threatening to drag the neighbor before the town council when he clutched his heart and fell down dead," Lyren-Sartora said, without a trace of regret. "I did my duty and went to the memorial, for Grandma Elen's sake. When I told her you were on another world going to school and should I find a mage to send word, she said no, it was the best thing for you. So . . ." Lyren-Sartora spread her hands, a gesture both graceful and unconscious.

Guilt pulsed again through Liere. "I will have to visit my mother and explain."

"Do! Grandma Elen will love to see you, I'm sure, but she's busy with the grandchildren in Belann. I don't go back because I'm not a Fer Eider. I love the name Sartora because it's a part of you. You were given it, or earned it, and *you* never felt like a Fer Eider. I *know* you didn't. I knew it even before I could talk. So I added Sartora to my first name, as it brings us together."

Liere sighed as they walked downstairs. "I was such a

disappointment to my father."

"Everyone and everything was," Lyren-Sartora said. "Did you know he'd dragged various neighbors before the council more than twenty times? Always over stupid things, like his insisting the neighbors should be sweeping once an hour in front of his shop because the wind blew their dust over. One of the cousins told me."

"I know." Liere shuddered at the memory of family dinners presided over by her father, who used that time to criticize his children for the tiniest infraction. It had been a relief when he ranted about the neighbors, the town council, the government, or the weather instead. "But I've come to see that it's a mistake to turn your back on kin. One thing I learned so far away, they're a part of you."

They reached the kitchen, and Lyren-Sartora clapped the glowglobes on. Both blinked in the sudden light, and both pairs of golden eyes widened, amazed at the changes in the other.

Liere had become *beautiful*. Lyren-Sartora, intensely sensitive to all kinds of beauty, stared, stunned, then worked to take in Liere's features as separate elements: wheat-gold hair the exact shade of her eyes, and long! Instead of hacked off close to her head with a knife, the way Lyren-Sartora remembered it. High forehead in a perfect oval face, long, tapered fingers, graceful feet in sandals, slender wrists that didn't look frail only because somehow — somewhere — Liere had developed smoothly feline muscle tone in the arms above those wrists.

Liere stared at her daughter, who was Liere's sister Marga all over again. No. That wasn't right, either. Marga, she of the dark curls and the smiling blue eyes and the dimpled face and form, resembled Lyren-Sartora, but Lyren-Sartora's coloring was far more vivid than any of Liere's pale siblings, and her thick, shining, waving dark hair was tinged subtly with gold-glinting ruddy strands, unlike that of anyone else in the family. Those winged brows above her golden eyes — those did not remind Liere of any of the Fer Eiders, whose brows were mostly colorless and straight. That high, fine dark arch, so easily quirked into irony or laughter, that be-longed to some unknown ancestor.

"You're different," they both said, and laughed.

Liere sat down on the prep table, as Lyren-Sartora set a

shallow pan of milk over the banked fire. "Five years were bound to bring changes. Why don't you tell me the latest news among our friends?"

Lyren-Sartora plopped in a chunk of chocolate and began to stir the milk. "Who first?"

Liere wasn't ready to introduce Senrid's name quite yet. Not after years of silence, following a not-quite-argument. "Who's had the most changes?"

"Who hasn't? Well, maybe the Mearsieans, who haven't lifted the Child Spell. Were you here when Aurora was born?"

"Yes."

"Oh, then you definitely will find them pretty much the same. And Aurora isn't always there. She visits a lot with Crystal Ingrid, not surprisingly."

"Who is Crystal Ingrid?"

Lyren-Sartora's brows arched in surprise. "Senrid's daughter."

Senrid? "You don't mean Senrid Montredaun-An? Had a child?"

"How many Senrids do you know?" Lyren-Sartora chortled as she poured the steaming chocolate into two cups, and dunked the pan with a quiet hiss into the cleaning bucket before hanging it back up, still dripping. "I take that back. You must have met *millions* in Marloven Hess. I know it's a traditional name, and someone told me those Marlovens aren't very imaginative when it comes to names. You didn't know about Crystal Ingrid?"

"Crystal seems imaginative for Marlovens," Liere observed. "How did it come about? And when? Recently?"

"It must have been about the time you left. Perhaps right after, since you didn't know. She's four, almost five. It happened at an alliance gathering, where Senrid said he might as well collect all the good advice at once because he was going to try the Birth Spell."

Nothing had prepared Liere for how much that news . . . hurt.

As Lyren-Sartora went on to describe this gathering, and who was there, Liere examined a sense of shock that was so strong it almost felt like betrayal. But no one had been betrayed. Of course life had gone on while she was away. It was that last conversation, before Liere left Sartorias-deles. She remembered attempting to scold Senrid out of the idea of having an heir by Birth Spell, using her own failure as example. But he'd done it anyway. And she hadn't known about it.

". . . then little Carl Delieth said, 'Her name is *Crystal Ingrid*,' and Senrid gave her this odd look."

"That's where the Crystal came from?" Liere groped about mentally, trying to find in these surprising actions the Senrid she'd always known. Thought she'd known.

"Oh, I think Carl picked 'Ingrid' from his mind. Perfectly ordinary Marloven name. I think she stuck in 'Crystal', which was her favorite name. I think everybody was surprised when Senrid went along with it, though I noticed for a long time he called her just Ingrid. But everybody else uses both names, and he got used to it, I guess. Isn't it good?"

"Good?" Emotional vertigo made Liere reach un-steadily for the noun behind that good — the child? The names?

"The chocolate! You don't like it?"

"It's very good." Liere blinked at the cup in her hands, and quickly drank some, then reached for another subject. "Siamis is still here?"

"Less often, now." Lyren-Sartora heaved a dramatic sigh. "Mainly to see Yanli, now that she's in the mage school. And he comes sometimes to add to our Dena Yeresbeth lessons, which are easy, and to oversee self-defense, which isn't. I hate it. I loathe getting sweaty, and even bruised. But Roy and the rest of Detlev's gang, when they are here, go on and on about how Norsunder Is Going To Come, hoola loola loo. They make us practice."

Liere's neck tightened at Lyren-Sartora's careless tone. Her thoughts arrowed straight to beautiful Cath, Dak's brilliant, musical brother, Cath of the perfect face and the lighter-than-corn-silk hair. And her failure to save him. Liere breathed that out, too. "Detlev's boys?" she said, striving for neutrality. "Running tame here?"

"Some of them. They don't come to train *me*, it's Yanli and Mac, but I get swept into it too. Vana insisted on being the one to teach us to ride properly. David teaches those defense lessons I mentioned. Roy and MV argue on and on about magic with Arthur. They all argue about history, and then I run to the library to read up on that, because I hate not knowing." Lyren-Sartora gave an airy shrug. "Then they're off again. Who knows or cares where? Let's see, who does that leave? The twins in Everon, and the Selennas, where Ian is doing really well, and he has a new cousin . . ."

Lyren-Sartora talked on, but Liere's attention slid again as she looked around the grand kitchen, so clean, with pans of rising dough set out under cloths for baking in a few hours.

So familiar, unchanged, and yet not home. How did you decide a place was home? If she wasn't home here, where was home? It seemed that horrible house in South End no longer belonged to the Fer Eiders, and she didn't even know where Belann was.

Silence brought her attention back; Lyren-Sartora gazed at her with that ironic smile again. "I just realized that you're not listening."

Liere drank off her chocolate. "Because I just realized I'm more tired than I thought. Though it was morning on Geth where I was, I haven't slept well."

Lyren-Sartora narrowed her eyes. "There's a bandage under that sling. Looks fresh. What happened?"

Liere shook her head. "One thing I've learned is, battle stories are boring, especially about people no one knows, and problems no one has any interest in."

"Just like the old Liere," Lyren-Sartora exclaimed. "Oh, I flew on a horse made of lightning and freed the world from enchantment, but that will just bore you —"

Liere blushed, knowing that Lyren-Sartora was right. "Do you want to hear about my failure then?"

"A Liere failure or a real one?"

Liere let that stinger slide. "This does not have a happy ending. The result is, I need to talk to the southern mages about someone who might be a prisoner at Norsunder Base."

The skepticism arcing Lyren-Sartora's expressive brows faded, and she looked away soberly. "No, don't tell me if it's got a sad ending. I think you ought to visit Atan. She can tell you about Norsunder Base. I know she has people watching it from a distance."

"'Atan.' So she's still Atan, even though she reversed the Child Spell before I even left? She's not become Queen Yustnesveas V of Sartor?"

"To *us*, she's still Atan."

Liere did not want to argue, so she didn't ask Lyren-Sartora to define that complacent "us." People's hierarchies could be a tricky subject at any time, the rules for who was included in a circle and who wasn't, could be invisible to others, and it was especially fraught when these invisible rules overlapped with the privileges and traditions of rank. Add that to the fact that Sartor was the oldest kingdom in the entire world, and Yustnesveas-who-preferred-Atan the last living member of the oldest ruling line, and yet Lyren-Sartora was clearly comfortable with her private name. Comfortable with yet another ruler of an enormous kingdom.

Liere said, "We were never even remotely friends. Isn't that kind of presumptuous, to assume she'd even have the time for me?"

Lyren-Sartora shrugged one shoulder. "Tsauderei doesn't move around much anymore, that's what everyone says. If you want to get to the mages in Sartor who watch the doings of Norsunder, I think you ought to begin with Atan, who speaks most often with him. Or I will. I can write to her." Lyren-Sartora gave a little toss to her head. "She gave me the spell to her own private notecase, that nobody else opens but her. And I *love* visiting there. It's the most *interesting* palace in the world."

Liere did not miss Lyren-Sartora's blithe assumption that wherever Liere went, they would go together.

"Thank you," Liere said.

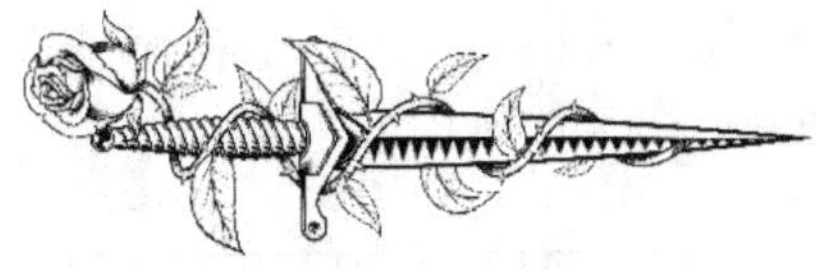

THREE

At the beginning of this record I have the honor to lay before you, I promised two young kings. Before I can introduce the first of them, I am obliged to bring to the reader's notice his setting, along with an individual who, if not the most prominent member of his regency council, certainly is the most ambitious.

Though Sartor is the oldest kingdom in the world, it is said (even by others besides the Colendi themselves) that Colend is the most stylish. In its center, where two rivers converge, is its most beautiful city, Alsais. And central to the city, the jewel in the crown, lies the royal palace.

In the wing that houses the most prominent of that kingdom's nobles during the spring and summer months, the Count of Ariath surveyed the breakfast tray, then flicked her fingers in dismissal, for she did not want servants hovering about while she spoke to her daughter Talian.

"It would be best," she said as soon as they were alone, "if you were to be found practicing your singing this morning."

In the old days, regarded by many as the height of Colend's formal elegance, the Hour of Stone—the old Rising—required the entire court to gather to await the monarch, in full courtly array. These days, more than half the time the young king was still abed at the Hour of Stone (sometimes all day, Talian had made it her business to discover) but the regency council was always gathered by that Hour at the Chamber of Lilies to hear and adjudicate. And the rest of court used that hour to call upon one another, exchanging news and views, making music, or speaking informal invitations to delights planned for the remainder of the day.

Talian's mother had raised her to believe that true melende—*royal* melende—comprised not only honor and style, it required control. A future queen, the count had repeated since Talian was old enough to talk, *must* embody royal melende. Here they were, at the Hour of the Deer, breaking the night's fast so that they could reflect upon the day to come and ready themselves without the undue haste that was not consonant with the *melende* expected of her rank.

And the first thing Talian heard was that she had to waste a morning playing music on the off-chance someone might come by to hear her. "Someone." There was no chance the king would. She thought her irritation well hidden, but her mother lowered her eyelashes in rebuke.

Talian suppressed a sigh, opened her hands as she bowed her head a little in a pretty gesture of apology, then said softly, "Honor me with enlightenment, I beg: if the king is too busy with his current dalliance, or mourning over an older one, will he have time to call to hear me singing?"

There. She'd come as near as she dared to the root of her dissatisfaction. But older people, Talian thought with the world-weary experience of two whole years at court, could be so oblivious.

The count was not oblivious. She saw no reason, yet, to inform her daughter that her own hire in the king's private wing gave her a detailed report every single morning on everything he saw the king do and say on the day previous.

Further, she knew very well that her daughter—like too many of her peers—harbored romantic notions about that young dreamer of a king (she would not be so disloyal as to think him a fool), pretty as he was. She knew that Talian had tried, once again, to entice Shontande to her boating party the week before. Alas, with no success.

The count turned her hand over, gesturing Rue, and though she regarded bluntness as an error in taste, they were alone, and she needed Talian to comprehend. "Shontande is not going to *marry* Niate Dazci. He will not marry *any* Dazci. We on the regency council would never countenance it, and I believe he is aware of that. Those young men he replaced her with may be regarded as mere toys. One of them even an uncouth foreigner! Ah-ye." She flicked her fan. "He ought to know what he owes us socially. I have made it abundantly clear that we would welcome a call. And when he does, it behooves you to be discovered comporting yourself as a future queen would."

Talian put her hands together in the peace, but her bow was no more than a dip, a gesture of neutral acceptance, and her lower lip betrayed the slightest droop of sulkiness.

The count eyed her. "Surely you do not pay attention to mere dalliances on his part, with persons we deem of no consequence? Do you not wish to be Queen of Colend one day?"

Talian made a business of choosing between a golden sunblossom and a pale blue raindrop pastry, to hide her face. It was true that Shontande's affair with Niate had scarcely lasted two weeks before he took up with the dashing Ikais and that wild fellow from Locan Jara. Aware of her mother's regard, she abandoned the pastries and again made the peace, palms placed together before her heart, and bowed over them, as graceful as a swan.

Her mother's mouth relaxed incrementally. "Then you must carry yourself like a queen, and be seen as one not merely by our . . . let us be merciful and call him distracted . . . yes, our distracted young king, but by the entire court."

For the third time Talian made the peace, thinking, *Here it comes. Mother has a plan.*

The count had a number of plans, few of them spoken. Her soft voice was complacent as she said, "I have exerted myself to make certain that you are one of this year's Music Festival judges. Any callers who chance by at the Hour of Stone are to find you singing. You have a fine voice, and everyone knows that Shontande loves Pereis Ada's compositions. It would be well for him to come upon you singing these."

Talian bowed her head submissively and finished the tart sunblossom pastries, which she knew her mother did not care for, but they were very much in fashion.

Her mother critically observed her tapered fingers and neat manners, her beautifully groomed hair, a good shade of blonde that as yet needed no arts of the colorist as it would complement the king's own entirely natural auburn. Impeccable hairline, with the little peak between the brows that emphasized a flawless heart-shaped face.

Pride and dissatisfaction unsettled the count. Talian was perfect in every way. Beauty, brains, birth. She'd been carefully tutored to have excellent taste, and she had memorized all the court protocols a queen would be expected to know before she turned fifteen. Once she reached the age of interest, her lovers had been carefully screened so that no political enemy of the count might be lurking in the background for daily reports.

When Shontande had demanded dueling masters after those dreadful Marlovens had visited, the count had seen to it that Talian trained as well. He showed an interest in the language of flowers, and Talian had tutoring in flowers. When he bought a barge for the canal, Talian was taught graceful poling. Her dancing lessons had begun when she first learned to walk, almost before. Perhaps it had been an error in strategy to make certain that Talian was first among the boy's playmates, resulting in her being regarded in some wise as a sister?

Such thoughts were irrelevant. Talian was *not* his sister. As long as no bright and beautiful princess popped up from some neighboring land, Talian had an excellent chance of becoming queen; Ariath might be a small county, but at least the count was on the regency council, and she would exert all her considerable influence to veto anyone else, until Shontande woke up to his duty.

Which, after all, lay in the far future. It would be gratifying to have a betrothal settled, but decade-long troths were no longer the fashion. And the count had no desire whatsoever for change. As long as the council was unanimous when Shontande foolishly jibed against the benign harness of their collective wisdom, their will prevailed, because everyone agreed that unanimity by its very nature reflected the good of the kingdom. And he was smart enough to agree with that—which moral suasion always weakened his troublesome attempts at interference. At least these attempts at interference had lessened over the past five years—and ceased altogether over the past two. Let him wander among the roses, enjoy the delights of theater and music, and at night, indulge his passions. That was expected of the young.

Everything, in short, was perfect as it was.

A betrothal could wait.

Talian finished her last pastry, dusted rice powder from her fingertips, then said, "I will of course do as you say, but I beg leave to point out that on every side we are told that the Alsais Music Festival judges are supposed to be unknown, and chosen regardless of rank."

"Mere persiflage, my dear. *Nothing* important is regardless of rank in court. Or unknown," said her mother. "And who can choose musicians who properly reflect the glory of Colend but its court?"

Talian smiled at her mother, and her mother smiled back.

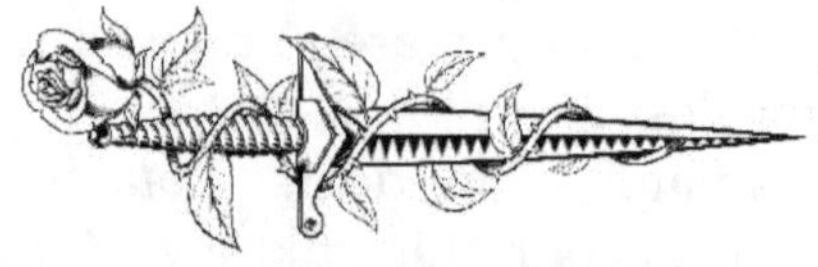

FOUR

Having introduced to the reader one of the young king's chief adversaries, I shall proceed with his subsequent actions.

The time was midway between Hour of the Deer and Hour of the River, as the royal palace's courtiers began their leisurely morning—those who had not been up all night, retiring at the Hour of Repose before dawn. Pages and lower ranking scribes crossed the palace grounds, the guest wing, and streamed over the little bridges to the noble houses on the other side of the Crown Skya canal.

One of these pages made her way to the royal residence wing, passing the herald-guards, whose gazes swept and dismissed her as familiar. She stopped at the outer salon, where the duty scribe had been sitting since the Hour of the Bird, first after Daybreak, in order to gather all communications sent to the king's attention.

The page and the scribe made the peace to one another.

"The Count of Ariath," the page stated, "bids me insist that his majesty sign off on this first of all." Having delivered the message that was intended to instigate that social visit previously referred to, the page effaced herself.

The duty scribe sketched the peace to the page's back, and set aside the list of judges for this year's Music Festival for the chief scribe to deal with. This was the sixth item that the king must sign off first, and here they were, the Hour of the Deer scarcely half over. But the chief scribe—appointed by none other than the Duchas of Altan (second of the young king's chief adversaries)—was skilled at balancing importance of sender against importance of content.

The chief scribe appeared a precise quarter before the

Hour of the River to take up the priority items and the growing stack of invitations, reports, and other private notes. He was already mentally composing the first portion of his daily report to the duchas about every bit of correspondence, public and private, that reached the king's chambers.

He touched the little silver bell at the side of his desk, which summoned the inner chamber page. When the page glided in, the chief scribe asked without much hope, "Any stirring?"

"Still quiet," the inner chamber page whispered, as if he could be heard in the bedchamber two hundred paces off, with its doors closed.

The chief scribe sighed, and used the rest of that quarter-hour to sort the communications in priority order so that the duty scribe could list them all for the daily record. Five more messengers arrived to hand off sealed scrolls on fine paper before the carillons rang the Hour of the River.

The chief scribe exchanged questioning looks with the duty scribe, whom he had trained himself — though he did not know that the duty scribe, with ambitions of his own, reported in secret to the Count of Ariath every day.

They were both thinking that there ought to be signs of stirring by this time, even if the king had been carousing in the crane-dance chamber all night. The king and his paramours would send out for something to drink, surely, at which time the chief scribe could insinuate a polite message about the urgency of council affairs. Even if the king ignored that, the chief scribe would have discharged his duty with the reminder.

The last of the quarter-hour slipped through the sandglass, followed by another. A third.

The Hour of the Stone — the traditional Hour of the Rising — when the monarch officially rose for the day, and historically could be visited privily by inner council and courtiers with pleas, passed, as usual, with no notice: anyone with privy business would, of course, be gathered in the Chamber of Lilies over in the state wing, where the regency council met.

The chief scribe looked in despair at his desk, knowing that the councilors would be expecting a message by the end of the hour, and once more summoned the inner chamber page, who arrived with the chief valet. The inner chamber page's long jaw lengthened in assumed solemnity as he said, "Not a sound. I even sent the kitchen page to tap at the door and call out to ask if any food or drink were desired. Nothing."

By noon, whispers had turned fierce. No one wished to disturb the king, whether he was in the crane-dance chamber with guests or in his bedchamber by himself. Though no favorites had emerged from either, deepening the mystery.

"You saw all three go in last night?" the chief scribe asked, again.

"Yes." The chief valet spoke for the inner chamber page. "We sent in a tray of Algyran bluewine and fresh strawberries, as requested. The door has been closed ever since."

Everyone turned to the chief valet standing by the door in thin-nosed self-righteousness, meager lips folded in a semblance of concern. He had been chosen by none other than the unctuous Duchas of Gaszin (would-be third adversary), to whom the valet reported in person every evening on the king's private activities and conversations.

The chief valet gave a curt nod to the third valet. "Open the door. Without sound. Collect any laundry you find, and report back to us."

The third valet had no one to pass this duty to, and so perforce he crept to the double door — to find it locked. He returned to report that.

The servants, all except the kitchen page connected in secret to either of the Duchases Altan or Gaszin or to the Count of Ariath, looked at one another. The first valet said to the kitchen page, "Try the chamber of cranes."

"I dare not contravene the chief steward of the royal kitchens." The kitchen page bowed over pressed hands pointed downward, the duty-peace, which also conveyed reserve. "I am expressly forbidden to venture into any private chamber without direct royal order."

The others regarded the kitchen page with hidden irritation: though he was the lowest there, as well as the youngest, orders surmounted their convenience. They all knew he was unassailable, though it was now nearing the Hour of the Wheel.

Even after two days of carousing, the king was usually awake by this time — and in less than an hour, he would be expected at the Exchequer to seal in royal blue the amended tax requests, which the regency council had been negotiating (fiercely, the chirps said at the Hour of the Bird) with the city merchants' council and with the river guild since New Year's Week, which in turn would permit the elite among the nobles (to which all of the regency council and their extended families belonged) certain privileges. Midsummer would be here before anyone knew it, and everything must be settled before the king ceremoniously handed over the Letter of Permission that released the money to pay for the preparations for the Music Festival.

While the royal wing staff were arguing these facts well known to all, each—mindful of what report they must make to those who paid them in secret—attempting to gain moral ascendancy over the others, the only one who noticed who was missing was the third valet.

"Where's Bee?" he asked the kitchen page, as their superiors carried on in low tones all the more fierce for their repression.

The kitchen page glanced around, then turned his hands out.

Quiet as the question had been, it still caught the ear of the first valet, who expressed his rising ire by a quelling frown toward his underling, and an ominously toned, "Your interruption, I trust, appertains?"

The third valet bowed so low his pale hair swung over his skinny shoulder. "I beg pardon of all for my disruption, but I perceive that Scribe Keperi is not among us. I wondered if he might have had orders from his majesty."

The chief valet said with justifiable sarcasm, "A blind man is not sent off like some page."

The kitchen page reddened at that dismissive "some" but kept prudent silence. *I chose you to venture into that den of snakes surrounding our king because you are quick and quiet*, the chief kitchen steward had said. *The only one of those slitherers I'd trust is the blind one. And he keeps himself to himself.*

The chief scribe bowed. "If you will honor me with a slight correction, there is, in fact, a precedent. The king has from time to time dispatched Scribe Keperi with the occasional personal message, when he wishes one directly spoken."

They knew that, but these spoken messages had traditionally been trifling, a request to meet at the salle for sword practice to the king's cousin Nashande Desentis being the most common, and in the past year or two, invitations to various lovers for impromptu gatherings. The staff were all used to Scribe Keperi's constant, quiet presence, in case the king should summon him. Bee Keperi almost never spoke, so it was easy to overlook him — since he couldn't see you, it was easy to assume he didn't hear you either, so quiet he was — but now his absence seemed significant.

The chief valet turned to the chief steward of the inner chambers, who met his gaze, and withdrew from under his livery robe his keys of office. When the latter made a slight sign, as if handling a transfer token, the chief valet thought, impossible — they were careful to notice every object the king touched from the time he stepped from his bath. And the council had expressly forbidden any magic transfer tokens ever to enter the royal chambers. He said, "Wait here."

They did, but all ears strained to follow the nearly noiseless hiss-hiss of the steward's slippers as he fitted the key into the bedchamber lock, then slid the door open no more than a finger's width. He closed the door again, and returned. "The king," he whispered — though he could not have said why — "is not there."

"Then he is still in the crane-dance."

The chief valet, lips tightened into a white line, went round to the servants' entrance and listened well before he unlocked the door to the crane chamber. He found a room empty not only of individuals, but any signs of a night of pleasure, barring only the empty bluewine glasses sitting on the tray, and the bare platter on which strawberries had been served. Everything else was undisturbed, as if a toast had been drunk, and the strawberries consumed, directly before departure.

"Search the entire royal wing," the chief steward ordered. As he made the official report each evening upon the safety and comfort of the king, the chamber servants were nominally under his command. Everyone, even the scribes, dispersed to search the chamber of blossoms — seldom visited by a monarch who was rarely ill — the bath chamber, the library, the study, the inner salon and the outer, the wardrobe and dressing room — all were empty.

The king, in fact, was gone.

Magic transfer of course.

But who was to be blamed for this laxness?

They divided again, this time to search for clues to his whereabouts in the kitchen, laundry, and the royal wardrobe annex, where the king normally never ventured, many already forming alibis, and some constructing reports that would point away from themselves.

Finally the chief scribe dispatched the kitchen page to seek Scribe Keperi. That duty, the page could also have refused, but he had been hoping for an excuse to get away. The rest of the royal wing staff was still turning over the extensive royal wing—painstakingly replacing everything as they found it—as the Hour of the Quill rang musically in the background. When the kitchen page returned, the staff gathered in their own antechamber, where they knew they were never overheard by those they served.

"Did you find Scribe Keperi?" the chief scribe asked.

"I did." The kitchen page made a general peace as he spoke. "Scribe Keperi—wearing his blues—presented himself to Lilies at the first peal of Quill."

The chief scribe wrinkled his nose at such temerity. "Blues" indeed! Vastly inappropriate idiom for the formal livery only worn at direct royal command, and exclusively for important occasions!

But he forgot that when the kitchen page went on, his dark gaze deliberately diffuse as he firmly hid his gratification. "Scribe Keperi spoke orders directly from the king, beginning with a list of people he had selected as judges for the Alsais Music Festival. There were other commands, which he said were being delivered to the appropriate location at the customary time."

The staff listened, stunned.

"Where is the king?" the first scribe demanded.

"I have repeated everything I was told," stated the kitchen page. "And now I am to return to the kitchen." He made a last peace. *Report and get out of there*, his chief steward had said.

His departure was unnoticed as everyone in the royal wing spoke at once to his or her neighbor, mentally preparing self-exculpatory reports for those who paid them in secret. They stopped talking when they heard a tick-tick sound on the marble floor outside their antechamber. The chief scribe signaled for silence, then all drew back as Scribe Keperi himself opened the door, a tall young man, his red hair a stylish contrast to the blue of his scribe's robe.

His vague gaze moved over their heads as he turned his ears from side to side, then he set his walking stick unerringly inside the door in its usual place, and made a profound peace. "I am ordered by his majesty to deliver the following message to the servants of the royal wing, having first presented four proclamations at the Hour of the Quill . . ."

While Bee Keperi, his voice utterly neutral, gave orders dismissing the nest of regency council spies — that is, the royal residence wing staff — with a promise of a year's pay and excellent recommendations, on the other side of the palace, at the Chamber of Lilies, the regency council sat in stunned contemplation of the four proclamations lying before them.

For the Duchases of Altan and Gaszin respectively, maintaining a veneer of calm over boiling fury required all their focus. The saturnine Duchas of Alarcansa, who enjoyed baiting those two greedy hypocrites almost as much as he enjoyed thwarting the tiny Count of Ariath, biggest hypocrite of them all, hid his amusement.

The silver-haired Elder Duchas of Desentis suppressed a smile, but she was worried, too. Alone of them all, she loved her grandnephew-by-marriage for himself. Which was the sole reason why, elderly as she was, she attended these exhausting council affairs as frequently as she could.

The Count of Ariath was equally furious, but her thoughts were entirely bound up with ways to counteract these attempts at wresting Colend's welfare from those (as she frequently referred to herself and the other council members) who labored the most for the good of the kingdom.

Since no one spoke, Alarcansa leaned forward, and made a pretense at musing over the demands. "So we're to pay our back taxes, we and all those we saw fit to excuse must pay as well. We're to hand off royal communications to Scribe Keperi, who will oversee this year's judges for the Festival. Nashande, heir to Desentis, to oversee the replacement of the entire company of royal wing herald-guards by the king's return." He leaned back and tapped the beautifully written proclamations in celestial royal blue. "I believe that is even his royal hand. Wager, anyone?"

The Count of Ariath turned to the elderly duchas. She made the most formal of bows, and restrained her hand from turning her palm out in the shadow ward. "I beg leave to ask of her grace why she might not have informed us of these tidings, that we might have circumvented this rash act?"

"If I had known . . ." The thin, elderly voice trembled. "I should have at least discussed it with my grandson Nashande. As he has been traveling this past week, I have not heard from him. Perhaps there is a letter. I shall return home, if you will all pardon me." The Elder Duchas of Desentis rose, made a dignified formal peace, and departed—having avoided mentioning which home.

"We must find the king," the count enunciated in her carefully cultivated melodious voice, the duchas already forgotten. "And counsel him to wisdom before the situation becomes any more inharmonious to good order."

The Duchas of Altan, big and handsome, relieved a part of his ire in ringing the little bell to summon a page. When she appeared, he said, "Require Scribe Keperi to present himself before the council at his earliest convenience."

The Duchas of Gaszin, equally tall though thinner, his back still straight in spite of his age, betrayed nothing of his irritation at Altan's assumption of authority, beyond a thinning of his lips. The order was pertinent, whoever spoke it. But scarcely had the page departed when the carillons rang the Hour of the Seal, at which hour contracts were traditionally signed.

A herald page appeared to announce that Scribe Keperi was back. The regency council awaited the scribe, who, still dressed in the formal livery of the king's service, tapped his way in, bowed in the peace, and said, "His majesty King Shontande has entrusted me with a last communication to the former regency council. I am to inform you that by tomorrow at the Hour of the Bird the heralds will proclaim all that has been thus furnished to the council for reflection upon in private. With his majesty's thanks for your service, he declares this council disbanded. Your last requirement is to consult the exchequer heralds on the subject of ten years of back taxes that the kingdom is owed."

The Duchas of Altan's already deep voice dropped to nearly a growl as he said, "May one inquire the whereabouts of the king?"

"The king," Scribe Keperi said, "has accepted an invitation from Queen Yustnesveas Landis to make a state visit to Sartor."

The (officially former) regency council stared at one another as this thunderclap resounded through their heads. He was escaping—that is, leaving Colend? For Sartor? To discuss *what? Why?* And how had he gotten away? No one would have permitted a transfer token into that wing of the palace. As for his own studies of magic, they had put a summary end to those years ago, and had monitored his every breath from waking to his reported slumber at night ever since. He couldn't possibly have gained knowledge of transfer magic himself!

Whereupon Bee Keperi, as ordered, gently delivered the *coup de grace*: "He will return once the council has complied."

Ariath stared at Altan, who waited for someone else to ask the question that lay heavily in the air: what if he didn't? Surely he would not dare miss opening the Alsais Music Festival, which Colendi rulers had done for over a century! He couldn't possibly. Could he? Though there were much older festival days, this particular one was known for being the single time the king interacted directly with the people. Therefore anyone who took his place would in effect be claiming the kingship in the eyes of the populace.

He wouldn't *dare*.

But until today, they would have sworn he wouldn't dare try any of the astonishing, maddening changes they had already heard that day.

The Count of Ariath waited for one of the men to betray a lack of melende in demanding answers of this presumptuous scribe. Altan and Gaszin eyed one another in mistrust, their rivalry going back to the first day the rest of court accepted them as regents. A response required melende—honor, and manner—as whatever was said at such a disastrously momentous an occasion would assuredly be repeated at Hour of the Bird by the abominably vulgar gossip-mongers called "chirps."

The Count of Ariath held her breath until the Duchas of Alarcansa threw his head back and laughed in delight. He'd begun to wonder if that boy would ever wake up. And he had, oh yes he had. An unambiguous coup, and not a leaf stirred, a weapon raised, or an angry voice. The Count of Ariath could not forbear a single glare shot in his direction—mirrored by Altan and Gaszin—but Alarcansa only laughed louder.

"Whatever else you can say against him," the Duchas of

Alarcansa declared to the three furious leaders of the council, "you have to admit that boy has style." And he walked out, still laughing, the panels of his summer robes swaying with his long stride.

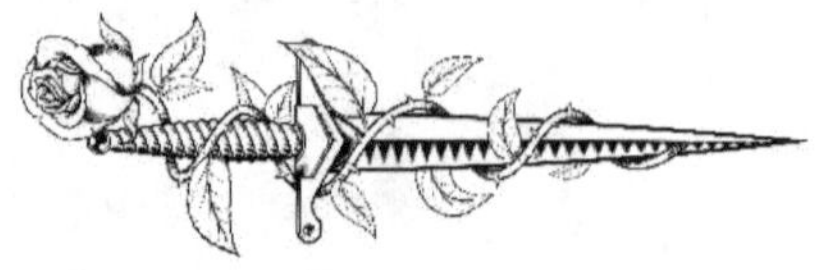

FIVE

That same day, while Colend's royal city reverberated with the astonishing news, Liere slept in. She then spent the rest of the day and most of the night delving in the archives for information on Norsunder Base before falling into a brief, troubled sleep. Later the next morning, when Arthur—tall now, still snub-nosed, blond hair darkened to light brown—saw Liere at the dining table with Lyren-Sartora, he stopped short, considerably startled to see a stranger there. Stranger?

Lyren-Sartora crowed in triumph, "Surprise! Look who's back!" Then she scowled. "You know that's Liere, right?"

"Of course," Arthur said, and spoke words of welcome.

It was Liere who smiled uncertainly. It was odd, seeing Arthur now so tall, the bones of his face a young man's. Stupid to think five years had only changed her! Arthur turned to introduce the cluster of archival scribes coming in behind him to join in the midday meal, then he asked about Geth. "I know only that Cath was taken by Norsunder. Dak studied with us a couple of years as we compared magic methods," Arthur said, looking down at his hands. "He sent a message to me from Geth-deles a couple days ago, hoping I had a way to investigate the Norsunder Base, but I had to tell him that I don't know any more than he does."

Liere steeled herself. "What Dak didn't tell you, I guess, is that I was the mage who lost Cath."

Arthur's wince and turned-away gaze brought Liere's failure back afresh. She said, "Lyren-Sartora and I are going to Sartor to follow up, as soon as possible." And to Lyren-

Sartora, "You mentioned something about possibly writing to Atan?"

Lyren-Sartora scowled her way. "Anyone else with a knife wound in their shoulder would take a week or two at least."

"A knife-wound?" Arthur exclaimed, his fork clattering to his plate. He peered at Liere as if trying to descry the wound.

"I'm fine," Liere said. "But Cath isn't. I need to find out whatever I can."

Lyren-Sartora rolled her eyes—an expression that had earned her age-mates among the sisters on Geth extra garden time for reflection—but then said, "I thought you'd say that. So I *already* wrote to Atan. She said to come any morning, as long as it's before she has duties."

Liere and Arthur both thanked her, then, mindful of the silent scribes whose gazes shifted between the speakers, Liere turned the subject to the plans for the new library, an entire wing of which was to be dedicated to books sent over by the Venn.

Arthur launched into a description of his visit to the Land of the Venn and his meeting with King Kerendal, who had introduced him to his young sister Erenlara. "She's a year or so younger than Lyren-Sartora, but she reminded me of you, Liere," Arthur said. "So serious and studious. Kerendal told me she's been that way since she was a baby—and she wants to come here to study our magic, after she masters theirs, as she will be his chief mage one day, what they call the Eyes of the Crown, Erama Krona. We want to get the translations going both ways. We've got mage students learning Venn and Old Runes as fast as they can . . ."

Liere half-listened, a little disconcerted by the side-long, blushing glances from many of the scribes. She had spent nearly five years in a place with no mirrors. When she was sent on her courier mission, the variety of startled, sidled, covert glances brought home the truth of the prediction that she had once overheard when she was small: *She'll be beautiful one day, you'll see.*

As a child who was invariably scolded every time her father noticed her, and teased unmercifully by her eldest brother, that prediction had acted on her as a threat. People *stared* at other people they thought beautiful. She'd longed to be invisible, as only then would she be safe.

That longing, intensified by her gnawing sense of her own inadequacy as Sartora the Girl Who Saved the World, had terrified her into clinging to the Child Spell, wearing only old clothes until they actually disinter-grated, and every time her hair had gotten long enough to her to run her fingers through, she'd hacked it viciously, usually with a knife. It wasn't until she escaped entirely to Geth that she was able to comprehend that making herself into an anxious eyesore had had the opposite effect of making her invisible. She had learned on Geth to accept who she was: she had refrained from cutting her hair, though the Ones' island was in a very warm part of the world, as a reminder of her determination to make peace with herself.

If she needed to be invisible, there were ways to achieve it simply and effectively. Practicing those ways once her two-day courier trip stretched into a protracted adventure had been satisfying—until the very end.

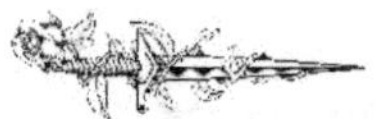

Eidervaen, Capital of Sartor

Bereth Ferian and Sartor were at opposite poles of the world: Bereth Ferian and Sartor's capital, Eidervaen, lay on a nearly straight line north to south. Morning in the one would be morning in the other, the sun autumnally distant in the southeast when Liere and Lyren-Sartora left, and spring bright where they appeared.

When they recovered from the transfer, Lyren-Sartora watched Liere eagerly as Liere studied the Destination chamber, three walls of which were plain blue-white marble. Liere's gaze rested on the fourth wall, which had been divided into three long panels, a gilt sun crowning the middle panel, its rays slanting outward and down through all three. Highly stylized fire dragons wound in a sinuous curve up the outer panels, their open mouths reaching up toward the sun.

How Lyren-Sartora loved beautiful things, as well as graceful, harmonious ritual! But as Liere studied those dragons, Lyren-Sartora remembered how Liere had displayed no interest in decorative arts, even avoiding it as much as she had avoided attention. Lyren-Sartora suppressed her disappointment in Liere's lack of admiration and awe, and, before a page could enter, quickly said, "Rel's door or the public entrance?"

"What's the difference?"

"Rel's door is the servants' back entrance. The other one, you get pages, and second circle bows, and see all the art on the way."

"Rel's door," Liere stated, as Lyren-Sartora had expected. Then she added, "I wouldn't mind seeing the art, but without the ritual."

Lyren-Sartora hid a sigh. No one understood how much she loved the grace of it, the order, how it all fit together like a living dance. "Rel's door it is." She added with a slight air of self-importance, relishing her pose as guide, "They're giving us time to recover from the transfer. We can leave before the page gets here."

Liere followed her, glancing around the oldest palace in world as Lyren-Sartora led the way to a discreet door partly hidden by flowering shrubs. On Liere's first visit, she'd been intimidated by the weight of age. Everything had been strange, daunting, incomprehensible. After her years on Geth, with different influences and history, Liere saw her familiar world anew: the clusters of threes, the twined symbols.

Lyren-Sartora was distracted by the crowds of work parties in an area that was usually quiet. Everywhere, it seemed, people polished, painted, clipped, and scrubbed.

"I've never seen it like this," Lyren-Sartora whispered, as Liere ducked around three burly men carrying a rolled up rug. How very stylized were these swooping lines of the intertwined flowers painted high along the walls, deceptively simple in design yet compelling in form. Hidden symbols. Liere would have to delve into history and uncover meanings.

Sartoran buildings were designed to maximize winter light on the north side, the cool gardens and pools to disperse summer light and heat on the south side. An old woman appeared in the doorway giving onto a tiny court, her habitually grim expression lightening when she saw Lyren-Sartora. "Ah," exclaimed Steward Gehlei.

Liere remembered when she'd been afraid of Steward Gehlei, who had once been a guard and risked her own life to save the last Landis princess as a helpless infant. Now she just looked tough and old, much like the elders among the Ones on Geth-deles.

"Go on up. They are having breakfast. You'll be welcome," Steward Gehlei said.

"They?" Lyren-Sartora asked.

"Julian turned up yesterday."

"Ooh! Julian's back!" Lyren-Sartora exclaimed, and ran on ahead.

Steward Gehlei gave Liere a startled second glance that made plain her lack of recognition as Liere followed Lyren-Sartora up the worn stairs to the queen's private suite. Liere suppressed a strong wish that it would always be that way. Time to live down her past, and make a new one.

"I smell sweet-berry muffins!" Lyren-Sartora ex-claimed, bursting without ceremony through the glass doors of a small sitting room onto a terrace, where tall Atan sat with her cousin, Julian Dei—who appeared to be fifteen or sixteen. "Oh! And I brought Liere. She's back!"

Julian jumped up, a golden belt of linked disks briefly glimpsed at the waist of her plain, worn traveling clothes. A livid cut down one side of her face was clearly still healing. The sight of it made Liere's shoulder twinge.

"Where have you been?" Lyren-Sartora exclaimed to Julian, as Atan looked past Lyren-Sartora's tall, graceful companion in search of poor, scrawny, nail-bitten Liere. Then her gaze snapped back to those big golden eyes.

Liere, who had been wondering if she was expected to bow or not, gazed as Atan's protuberant, droopy eyes widened. *"Liere?"*

"In the flesh, Queen Yustnesveas," Liere said.

"Oh, please call me Atan. It was my mother's heart-name for me, you know. Yustnesveas, that impossible mouthful, is saved for the throne downstairs."

There it was, the private name, but without any of the invisible traps of exclusivity. Liere let out a breath of relief as Atan went on, "Liere, what a great surprise to discover you are back! Please, sit down. I know Gehlei will bring extra plates. I hope you two are hungry."

"Thank you." Liere let the impressions flow: Atan was very tall, and broad through bosom and hips. She wore over a silk shirt and loose trousers a simple robe of deep, deep blue, edged with fine gold embroidery. Her brown hair was braided in a complicated coronet.

Her bony face would never be beautiful—few Landises were, especially those who inherited those distinctive protuberant eyes with the droopy under-lid, and the dark, straight lines of brows—but the clean line of her jaw, her broad forehead, the humor and intelligence of her expression, made her handsome.

"It's good to see you again," Atan added, thinking, *You had the Deis in your background. Somewhere. Sometime.* Atan tried not to stare at the astounding change in Liere. The stiff, stick-thin child with the unhealthy, hacked-off hair and unkempt clothing had altered so astoundingly that only those eyes were recognizable. In fact, Liere looked very much like those rare portraits of what through the centuries had been termed Golden Deis. "Your journey was useful?"

Liere smiled. "You knew where I was."

Atan glanced at Lyren-Sartora and Julian, chattering as they leaned against the balcony, then said, "I asked Arthur up north there in Bereth Ferian. He told me that Detlev, of all people, sent you to Geth-deles, to some school that trained mages to fight villains. Imagine, the king of villains recommending a place that teaches one to fight villains."

Liere opened her hands, palm up, aware as she did that she was using Senrid's gesture. "It is true. I take it that . . ." *You still don't trust Detlev.* ". . . he hasn't managed to overcome his past?"

Atan shrugged. "Does a villain ever overcome his villainy? Especially centuries of it, a great deal of it described in a wealth of detail in my archives fifty steps away."

"Has there been more villainy?" Liere asked.

"No." Atan's straight brows twitched. "That is, that I know of. There are always rumors. If something terrible happens somewhere, and the culprit is not immediately apprehended, inevitably the next thing we hear is that Detlev must be behind it. Or one of his boys." She gave a short sigh. "I haven't seen any of them. I know he's got some sort of house somewhere on the north coast beyond my western border, but he keeps himself to himself."

"I'm surprised he's even that obvious," Liere said. "Surely Norsunder is angry about his leaving. You'd think they'd be after him."

"So I once thought. Sveneric—did you ever meet Detlev's

strange little boy? Sveneric told Tsauderei that Norsunder would rather wait, and strike in their own time and way."

"Well, that's sufficiently nasty. What about Detlev's gang of killers?"

Atan's smile quirked. "I haven't heard Detlev's boys called that since, oh, the last time I saw Tahra of Everon."

Liere reflected on the fact that here she was, in the realm where mention of other kingdoms' monarchs was like family gossip anywhere else.

Servants appeared with corn cakes and a pot of honey-butter, eggs with sprinkled cheese, and slices of fresh fruits. The two younger girls descended on the trays, piled up their plates, and withdrew again to the balcony, where they were busy whispering.

"May I ask your advice?" Liere asked softly, and at gesture of invitation from Atan, said, "I lost someone on Geth. Came home because I think he might have been taken to the Norsunder Base south of your border. Did you ever meet Dak? It's his younger brother."

"Dak?" Atan repeated, then, "Yes! Arthur used to bring him to study with Tsauderei. I didn't know he had a brother — oh, wait, that little boy who played the flute so beautifully, that time we were on Geth-deles? I'm truly sorry," she added, her tone heartfelt. "I'm especially sorry as there is nothing we can do. We have wards up along the southern border, but know little of what goes on at Norsunder Base. You'd have to go to Detlev or Siamis for that."

Liere thanked Atan as she helped herself to some fruit, using her arm as little as possible. She'd left off the sling, and already her shoulder ached. She glanced up, and caught a narrow-eyed look from the Sartoran queen. Dropping her hand into her lap, Liere said with a tip of her head toward the earnestly whispering girls, "Could Julian and Lyren be plotting something?"

Atan accepted this diversion. "Julian got herself mixed up in some sort of civil war in one of those kingdoms along the opposite coast of the Sartoran Sea, and insists that Norsunder is somehow involved. *I* don't think so. No magic is practiced anywhere in that segment of the continent, and no one else has reported any marching armies or dark-magic wielding conquerors settling in. Sometimes I think people bring up Norsunder anytime there is trouble. My skepticism annoys her, of course."

As Liere ate a grape, she glanced at that livid scar on Julian's cheek.

Atan followed her gaze. "She was almost killed, which might be why she is seeing Norsundrians in every shadow."

"Um." Liere poured out the lovely Sartoran steep. The steam smelled like the first blooms of spring. How she had missed it! "Could that belt have anything to do with it? From here it looks like real gold. It has to be worth a fortune."

"Worth a fortune and with a great deal of magic on it," Atan said, her voice low. "But she insists that the belt has nothing to do with the Enaeraneth matter." Atan's mouth curved. "As for my own news, I will have you know that we're about to experience a first, after many centuries: the mysterious, seldom-seen Shontande Lirendi of Colend is coming to Sartor for a state visit."

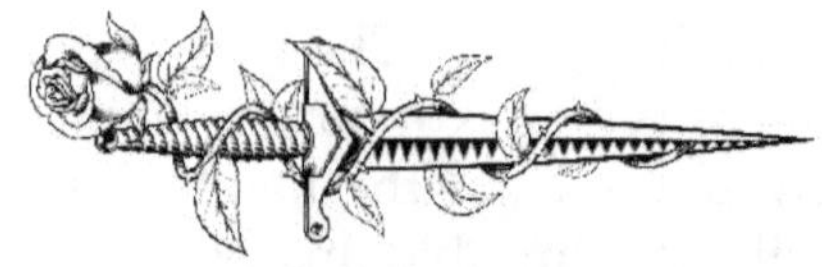

SIX

In this chapter, continuing from the previous, I have the honor of introducing to the reader the outsider's perspective on the situation of our story's second young king.

Liere exclaimed, "Shontande Lirendi of Colend? I thought rulers don't go outside their borders, unless it's by magic transfer."

"This one is going to."

"Is that the purpose of all the polishing downstairs?"

Atan chuckled. "Indeed it is."

"Have you ever met him?"

"No. Senrid met him some time ago, I understand. Thad Keperi knew him well, before his sister was killed, back in the alliance days. I don't think anyone else has met him. He's been kept strictly sequestered by his regency council. You're welcome to stay here, and when he arrives, pull on some velvet, come in through the front door, and make your four bows."

Liere faced away from the younger girls, so she could not see Lyren-Sartora's disappointment as she gave her head a shake. Hiding her instinctive loathing of courtly ritual—which surely a Colendi would be expecting from waking to sleeping— "Maybe someday, but after I find my place in the world."

"Good enough," Atan said equably. Liere hadn't changed completely, then. "What are your plans, once you consult with the mages about Norsunder Base? Going off to visit Senrid, of course." And she was about to mention the meeting she was very shortly to depart for, when Liere glanced away, her brow puckered.

Liere was trying to find words for the turmoil inside her. Foremost was guilt, but she had to acknowledge the unsettling sense, very near resentment, that clung to the news that Senrid had had a child while she was gone. No! Not resentment. Never that.

Atan's eyes narrowed. "*Not* of course?"

"Oh, I will! But not right away," Liere exclaimed, and then scrambled to explain away whatever it was Atan had seen in her face. "Senrid was always my friend. Is my friend. We talked about everything together. Without the least fear, or having to defend ourselves. Until one day. It was not long after Detlev came over to our side."

"Ah." Atan gave an appreciate laugh. "Senrid does have a tongue."

"But we didn't argue," Liere insisted. "I gave him what I now suspect was very bad advice." Liere gestured around her, indicating the world. "Which I discovered he did not take. So, I don't know, I don't think I'm ready to visit him yet. Does that make sense?"

Atan tipped her head. "Do emotions ever make sense?"

Liere smiled back, gratified that Atan talked to her like a peer, but at the same time, this kind of talk was unnerving in a way that had nothing to do with knowing how to scan a room for possible enemies.

"Did I hear Senrid's name?" Lyren-Sartora asked, coming up on one side. And then, without waiting for an answer, "You said you went to some school on Geth-deles. It sounds like a school for spy mages. Well, how about some spying?"

Liere's instinct was to deny being trained as a spy, and to refuse to poke her nose somewhere she didn't belong. Lyren-Sartora was showing interest, even eagerness. "Where, why, and what?" Liere did her best to sound interested.

Julian pushed forward. "It's Enaeran, a kingdom on the other side of our sea. Why: I think Norsunder is sniffing around. What: find out if they are, and either get rid of them, or come back and get my dear cousin to listen, because she won't listen to me."

Atan sighed. "Julian. You know I listened. I listened long and long, but you still haven't any evidence, and what could I do if you'd found it? We have no legation there. Enaeran never renewed the Eidervaen Protocol when Sartor returned to the world. I think they were involved in a civil war, or had just ended one. Another one."

"I know, I know," Julian declared, flapping her hands in annoyance.

Atan finished patiently, "Kingdoms without magic are usually that way because the government does not trust mages. I can't send an official envoy from the Mage Guild into a kingdom that has no relations with us, and did not invite us."

"You could send *us*," Lyren-Sartora burst in. "Liere can be your envoy! And I'll be her assistant." She danced on her toes. "It would be such fun! I'd love to do it!"

"But Julian was badly hurt there," Liere began.

Julian shook her head. "That was an accident, during the fighting. Which is over. With your Dena Yeresbeth" —she tapped her forehead— "all you'd have to do is go and spend a day or two sniffing around in a way that I couldn't." She whirled away, the coin belt faintly jingling as she dug through some letters on a side table. She pulled up a folded map, which she flicked open.

Liere stared down at the exquisite drawing. The Sartoran Sea, roughly wedge shaped, cut in to a point above Sartor. Enaeran lay above the thickest part of the wedge, a large kingdom next to another large kingdom called Sles Adran, the two bisected by a considerable river into which smaller rivers and streams from both kingdoms emptied. Mountains bordered Enaeran to the west, with Senrid's Marloven Hess somewhere off to the other side. The inner portions of both kingdoms were plains, meadows, and farmland. Artificial lines south of both, slicing east and west, represented treaty-established borders that blocked the big kingdoms from sea access, evidence of long-ago ambition and war.

"I think I remember being in this place," Liere said slowly. "The capital was, um—Shee . . . Shee-ya-vhan, I believe it was."

"That's Shee-OH-vhan to the natives," Julian said. "Shiovhan."

"All right. The ruler was older, and quite imposing."

"King Alored, that would have been," Julian prompted.

An image flickered in Liere's mind from long ago: a big, loud-voiced man with lemon-yellow hair and wide-spaced white teeth. He'd laughed a lot, but Liere remembered feeling both intimidated and condescended to, even though it was she who had released the Enaeraneth from Siamis's enchantment. All she remem-bered of the queen was a vivid memory of a sour mouth, and the impression that she was a lot older than the king.

"Well, King Alored and Queen Mara were killed in civil war," Julian said. "She was poisoned—all the factions were together in hating her—and the king was supposedly killed in a duel, though some said it was a duel with about six duelists all at once. Then two sets of relatives claimed the throne."

"Sounds awful," Liere said, still staring at the map. "You believe Norsunder caused this civil war? From your description, it sounds more like a faction fight."

"No. Or maybe at first. There are, or were, maybe still are, people who want to do away with monarchy altogether. The poor in Shiovhan joined for a time, until it still didn't get them anything worth having."

"The guilds would hate losing their influence, especially in trade towns," Atan said.

Julian cast an impatient look at her royal cousin. "They had problems, too. The poor wanted everybody to have a say, as well as food and a roof, and that only the rich ought to pay taxes. Others felt that only guild members and merchants—people who actually paid taxes—could vote on taxes. They were arguing it out in the middle of all the fighting until one of them enlisted the help of the king of Sles Adran to stop the fighting. The Adranis came in to keep the peace, and then wouldn't get out again."

"Uh oh."

"That's when I got there," Julian said, and frowned at Atan. "You mages worry about kingdoms with magic, but I think *they* can take care of themselves. Who's watching out for these kingdoms with no magic, if Norsunder is sniffing around?"

"Themselves?" Liere asked.

Julian whirled away, her arms crossed, her shoulders tight and angry.

"Julian, I wasn't being flippant. Isn't that what sovereignty means?"

"Exactly," Atan said. "And Sartor is not an empire. Without leave from the Enaeraneth, we cannot interfere there."

Julian shook her head stubbornly, her friend Jaydi's pleading face clear before her eye. "An empire invades kingdoms and tells them what to do. We ought to *help*."

Liere rubbed her finger along the carved edge of the table, rapidly considering and discarding replies. This was not the time to get into an argument about diplomacy, sovereignty, and foreign interference, especially when she herself felt so ignorant about such patterns in her own world, after her years of studying Geth's.

So she said only, "You found chaos, then, in Enaeran? And?"

Julian scowled, struggling between lingering resentment and her promise to Jaydi. The latter won. "Right now the trouble seems to be mainly between King Bartal of Sles Adran and the one branch of the royal family, not direct descendants but cousin to both the old rulers' families. He's descended from a second prince who had, as traditional, changed his name when he married a powerful duchas. Their family name is Marsael."

"That's an old Colendi name," Lyren-Sartora said. And when the other two looked at her in surprise, she said, "I heard it once when visiting Tahra. She had Carl and Jessan memorizing all the principal families they are connected to."

"Well, anyway, Adon Marsael started styling himself Adon-Marsael, n'Elsarion — *the* Elsarion. 'Na', or the en sound before a vowel, meaning 'The.' It's a kind of title for head of the family."

"Bartal na Shagal," Atan murmured. "King of Sles Adran."

"That's right," Julian said. "They all do it like that there, royalty, nobles on down. I was told that Adon was 'na Marsael' — the only one left, after the fighting — but Elsarions have been the rulers in Enaeran for centuries. Since they split off from Sles Adran. And so he took back the royal family name, you could say. Somehow he got the Adranis to leave the capital, though there's still fighting on the border."

"Tell her the rest," Lyren-Sartora urged.

Julian was quite happy to. The words poured out of her, amid many side-glances Atan's way. "I stayed with some people who turned out to be part of an underground group, who helped me to the southern border. With — it's rumored — the former king's son at its head. So he'd be the *real* n'Elsarion.

Only he'd been disinherited, see, right before the king was assassinated, and everyone had thought he was dead. And there's a price on his head."

"You didn't mention that part," Atan exclaimed. "Why?"

"Jaydi, this street boy, vows that Prince Andri was accused of something he didn't do. His followers are mostly made up of leftover nobles' sons and daughters whose estates have been taken away, thieves, former apprentices, and people with no homes. Like Jaydi."

Atan's expression betrayed what she thought of this prince with the price on his head, and a gang of dispossessed and possible criminal followers. "Perhaps we ought to rethink this idea."

Julian said flatly, "When he helped me out, Jaydi asked me if I'd ever seen a Norsundrian, and how would you know them if you saw them?" She grimaced. "I tell you, it gave me the chills, how close he listened, and then he wouldn't tell me why! He was too scared. And he's a street boy, and you know how tough they can be!"

"We can *help*," Lyren-Sartora stated. "*Nobody* sniffs out the stench of Norsunder better than us! If there's one thing I've been harassed about from Roy and the others, it's that. And Liere, you are better than *anybody* with Dena Yeresbeth!"

"I wish I were." Liere sighed as she took in Lyren-Sartora's adamant expression. Her hand crept to her shoulder, then dropped. It was true that she could listen on the mental plane, because most people did not use mind-shields. But she had shied away from Siamis's offer of training.

However, she had learned a great deal on her own, far from the pressure of being Sartora, the Girl Who Saved the World. If she went to Enaeran, where no one she knew practiced magic or had diplomatic relations, she would be just as anonymous as she had been on Geth-deles—and in her own world. The notion of testing the rest of her training without the horrible expectations of "Sartora" beckoned. As she turned to her daughter's painfully expectant face, she knew she risked losing Lyren-Sartora's respect if she refused for what would sound like timorous reasons.

"Just one day," Lyren-Sartora pleaded. "We go and listen." She tapped her head. "Then come back."

"The fighting really has ended?" Liere asked. "I don't want to walk into the middle of someone's civil war." *I already did that, and look at me now.* She rubbed her shoulder.

"No civil war." Julian waved off the very idea. "As I said, the only fighting's up north, along the border."

Liere said, "But I don't have the wherewithal for that kind of travel."

Atan spoke unexpectedly here. "Liere, Lyren-Sartora, I have a meeting imminent, one I cannot easily rearrange. if this is really a matter than can be easily resolved with Dena Yeresbeth, I can accredit you as an envoy. There is even a budget for such. You know magic, which saves me from having to go to the Mage Guild over this matter. You and I would be the only ones knowing you are there, though of course if they want to test your credentials, I'd back you. And you could always take one look around and decide to transfer out."

Liere studied Lyren-Sartora's pleading face. "All right. If you think it would help." Her reward was Lyren-Sartora's bright smile. "But there is my first quest to resolve before we address this one. And at any sign of danger, we leave. Understood?"

"Of course," Lyren-Sartora scoffed. "I don't even like danger!"

SEVEN

Part of ridding herself of the Sartora notoriety meant no expectation of any of the intimidating privileges of those horrible days.

To get started on her quest to save Cath, Liere had assumed that Atan would send her to the mage guild scribe desk, where she would be passed along from waiting room to waiting room until she reached an assistant or mage student with sufficient knowledge to answer her questions about Norsunder Base.

But when a bell rang, Atan exclaimed, "Already! I must go. First, Liere, are you going to Enaeran as yourself?"

Liere recoiled. "No. That is . . ." She reddened. "I will go as myself. But no Sartora. Or even Fer Eider, in case someone knows it."

"Do you want a new name written onto the accreditation letter?"

Liere's lips parted, then she pushed her hand away. "I might forget. I can go as Liere. It's common enough."

"Especially in the present generation. Very popular name. I can give a Sartoran form of your family name, Feriadar, how's that?"

"Perfect."

"Second, to your question about Dak's brother, write to Tsauderei. I can tell you that the Sartoran Mage Guild isn't going to be able to help you much. Anything having to do with Norsunder crosses my desk, and I read it first thing. We know little of what goes on at that base — Tsauderei is the best informed."

"Tsauderei?" Liere repeated. "Write? Is he still in that valley?"

"Yes, but he's very frail. Rarely leaves his cottage. But he keeps up with world events as much as ever. Here is his sigil. Go ahead and use my private notecase. I'm afraid I cannot be late. Those I meet are as busy as I." She stopped there, willing to say more if Liere asked, but Liere gazed down at the desk as if she scarcely heard.

Very well then: Liere would visit her old friends when she was ready.

Atan left her there with pen and ink, so, as Lyren-Sartora and Julian chattered in the background, Liere wrote to Tsauderei. She received a note back almost immediately, written in a shaky but legible hand:

Welcome home. I can't help you with anything concerning Norsunder Base or its Beyond. My advice: consult Detlev. Tsauderei.

He included another sigil, which Liere assumed had to be a way to reach Detlev. Feeling very peculiar—five years ago she would have never guessed she would be in this situation—she pulled a new strip of paper off the stack on the silver tray, dipped the pen used daily by the queen of the oldest kingdom in the world, and wrote:

Tsauderei gave me this sigil. I am back from Geth, and need to know if there is a way to rescue someone I believe taken to Norsunder Base. Liere Fer Eider.

She sent it off, then stared at Atan's notecase, wondering if Detlev would approve of the changes in her, as behind her, Julian's and Lyren-Sartora's voices rose and fell, an occasional word distinct: "Barban . . . wanderers . . . Dtheldevor . . ."

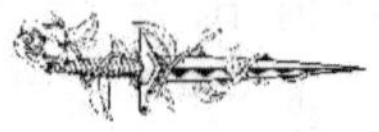

Detlev's House, Western End of Sartor, to Eidervaen

While Liere sat there suspended between question and lingering echoes of the old dread, at Detlev's house, David, who was currently in charge of what served as an unofficial relay desk when Detlev was not in residence, opened a beautifully written note, then exclaimed, "Shontande Lirendi is *what?*"

His voice echoed out the window overlooking the terrace on which several people sparred, with and without weapons.

Most ignored him, but two heads turned, then a short time later Adam and Curtas appeared in the doorway, both sweating profusely, weapons still gripped in their hands.

To the question in their faces, David flicked the scrap of paper and said, "Missing. Word is rippling out through the scribe world."

Though Curtas had not seen Shontande for years, he blanched under his tan. Smearing back a tangle of short, curly light brown hair, he said, "Yeres?"

"How?" Adam asked, his mild brown eyes wide. "Yeres and Efael are both warded from Alsais. Ever since Efael killed the old king."

David read off the note. Adam's expression cleared. "He gave out orders through Bee? Sounds like he's finally shrugging off that soul-sucking regency council."

David leaned perilously on the back two legs of his chair, hands behind his head, one bare foot propped on the desk. "And took a step away. He doesn't want a fight over the throne."

"He'd hate that," Curtas said.

"Fighting isn't stylish," David said derisively. "A Colendi get mussed? The horror!"

"You couldn't be more wrong if you studied for a year." Curtas gave him a disgusted glance. "I'm at liberty. I'm going to Colend to see for myself."

"You?" David dropped the paper on the desk. "They'll kill you on sight. Style or no style."

Curtas gave his head a shake. "The only one who'd recognize me would be Shontande. And he's not there, right? And Bee Keperi."

"Bee is obviously there," Adam said, leaning in the doorway, his cloud of curly brown hair spangled with sweat. "Though of course he wouldn't *see* you."

"Smell you, maybe," David cracked.

Curtas ignored him. "The Keperis know I wasn't there when Noser murdered their sister. It's guilt by association. Thad must be with Shontande. I'd be worried if he wasn't. Surely one of the Keperis will give me a listen, after all this time." He ran back down the hall. Adam followed.

David was about to call Curtas back—tell him not to be stupid—but the notecase pinged again. Exasperated, David took out the new note and his exasperation sharpened into annoyance when he saw Liere's name at the bottom. He tried to breathe it out.

He knew the absurdity of Sartora the World Saver was not her fault, but to him, back then at the intolerant age of fourteen, her behavior afterward was definitely her fault. Her anguished pose, from bitten nails to hacked off hair and war refugee clothing, begged for pity and attention while she bridled and moaned variations on *Don't look at me, I'm not worthy!* And she'd carried on like that for years.

He hadn't given her a thought after she vanished from the world around the same time he and the boys left Norsunder for good. It appeared she was back. It was difficult not to read into her short note that she was still expecting everyone to drop their own lives and rally around her again.

Let Adam deal with her. He had more patience, and . . . yes. The sand had run out. His watch was over. Just in time. He sent off a transfer token to Liere and turned the glass; the desk, and everything on it, was now Adam's problem.

David bolted down the stairs, and called to Adam, who was stashing his weapons in the rack, "The desk is yours."

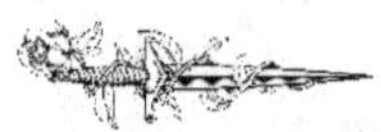

In Eidervaen, Liere sat motionless at Atan's balcony breakfast table in a turmoil of ambivalence. A quiet tap in the notecase startled her out of her reverie. She opened it to find not a note, but a transfer token.

She took it out, then glanced at the girls, at that moment leaning over the parapet to watch the swans in a fountain below. Atan had vanished on her appointment, but apparently Julian had no duties. It seemed that Atan had kept her promise not to make her a princess — and five years had not changed that.

Liere glanced at the two girls, and wondered if Lyren-Sartora, who was so smart, and better educated than many adults, was also going to end up wandering the world. Lyren-Sartora was clearly at ease in this palace setting, as she was in Bereth Ferian's palace. She'd spent twelve years living like a princess, except even princesses had duties. Guilt wrung through Liere; she ought not to have left her.

Lyren-Sartora swung around, brows aslant. "Liere?"

Liere smoothed her expression. "I'm going to consult about Cath."

"Tsauderei?" Lyren-Sartora asked, tripping forward in her fine, tailored linen travel tunic and trousers. She really did have a princess's taste.

A fresh surge of guilt harrowed Liere. This trip to Enaeran could be a chance for them to get to know one another, without the distractions of familiar friends and places—after which they could have a serious talk about Lyren-Sartora's future. "Not Tsauderei," Liere said, forcing a bright tone. "Detlev's house. And if they have a definite trail, I'm going to have to follow it first, before going to Enaeran."

Lyren-Sartora's expressive brows furrowed, but she said, "If it's to save someone from Norsunder, of course."

"Want to come along?"

"No." Lyren-Sartora's smile vanished, and here was the eye-roll again. "I see enough of *them*. All they'll do is harass me—have I been practicing the warmup, do I do my Dena Yeresbeth drills, hoola loola loo."

"Stay here. Let's go visit Hinder and Sinder," Julian suggested.

"In the morvende geliath?" Lyren-Sartora clapped her hands.

"That's where they are." Julian laughed.

"Oh, let's!" Lyren-Sartora turned back. "We'll meet back here when we're done." She waved at the balcony as if the palace belonged to her.

Liere was left with nothing to say, so she said nothing as the girls vanished inside in a patter of feet, leaving Liere alone on the balcony. She quickly penned a note to Atan, laid the note down, put the golden notecase on top so it wouldn't blow away, then used the transfer token.

She'd been to Detlev's house once, not long after he'd taken up residence. In those days it was new, the stonework fresh, with shady silver-leafed argan trees in huge pots at the edge of a broad terrace. The stones of this terrace were patterned in interlocked loops of threes, like the maze behind Atan's palace. Liere turned in a slow circle. Was it merely a random pattern that pleased the eye, or was there some meaning behind it?

Light rain cooled her face and hands as scanned the terrace, attention drawn by a pair of young men, one blindfolded, sparring with bare steel. She knew that exercise. More surprising was the spurt of, ah, not quite resentment, but she had to admit to annoyance, that Detlev's boys were clearly very familiar with an exercise that only those with the highest level of training as well as mental skills were permitted to learn. She'd had to earn her way to it, and had this past half-year struggled to get her mind to cooperate with physical senses. The fast, expert blows from the blindfolded blond made it clear they'd been at it for years.

She turned away and headed for the doors, taking in the tall, shady trees as rain rustled in spring leaves.

At that moment, inside the house, Adam laid aside his pen.

He couldn't trust his hands to the exacting requirements of forgery so soon after a hard practice with swords. Leef's life depended upon his not making an error. Just as well there was a new arrival—and he was now on duty.

He wiped his inky hands and ran down the stairs as Liere stepped through the open doorway, the breeze catching ribbons of silken hair the exact sheen of ripened wheat, and blowing a plain robe around her straight, slender figure.

Adam paused on the last step. Beauty would always catch his eye, whether it be in human form or in any other. "Liere?" Adam asked.

"Adam," Liere exclaimed, taking in the deep dimples on either side of Adam's mouth. He had changed so much. He was taller than she was, and thin. The lineaments of his face were those of a young man, but his guileless, sweet smile was the same that she remembered in the round-faced boy.

She exclaimed, "The last time I saw you, you had a broken leg." Remorseful at how self-involved she'd been then, she hastened to add, "I'm glad it's better now. You never did tell us what happened?"

Adam's happy smile of welcome smoothed into blandness, but before he could speak David—sensing Adam's reaction as a comet flash across the mental plane—broke off his bout and loped across the terrace toward the doorway. He shot through the door before Adam could frame an answer, and Liere turned, startled at his sudden appearance. It took her a heartbeat or two to recognize him; he, too, had grown: he appeared to be eighteen or so, quite tall. Liere had had little interaction with him. All she remembered was that sleepy light brown gaze, but it wasn't sleepy now. He looked annoyed.

On the mental plain he shot the thought at Adam: *I shouldn't have left her to you. I'll deal.*

To which Adam responded tranquilly: *It's no trouble.* And, bypassing her question entirely, he said to Liere, "Who needs rescuing at Norsunder Base?"

Liere shifted her gaze between them, sensing that she had really blundered somehow, more than her well-meant question would seem to warrant. Thrown off-balance, she spoke carefully. "I don't know that Cath is actually there." And once more, she gave her report about Cath, confining her defeat by Lyal to a single line. When she repeated what he'd said about orders, the two reacted subtly. After five years among people without Dena Yeresbeth, she was so used to being the only person who could communicate on the mental realm that she nearly missed the signs.

Then David said, "If there's no evidence he's at the Base, as likely he's been hauled off to the Beyond. Especially if he was nipped for Yeres to play with."

His light tone stung Liere. "I feel responsible," she explained. "I lost him. There has to be something we can do, and you have the most experience."

David's soft voice conveyed sarcasm as effectively as any loud sneer. "We?"

Our side, she was going to say, but the words died unspoken as Adam shot David an amused glance: *Let me handle this before you turn an awkward moment into a continent-wide feud.*

Too irritated to trust his voice, David whirled the tip of his sword in a tight arc that took in Liere and in effect tossed her to Adam: *All yours.* And he retreated to the terrace, where he picked up the blindfold he'd cast aside.

"I failed to rescue him. I want to make that right if I can," Liere said.

Adam responded, "Were you aware that there have been incidents?"

"Incidents?" Liere repeated.

Adam said, "Yeres of Norsunder has been . . ." *Seducing.* ". . . collecting boys for mind control experiments."

Sickened, Liere said slowly, "The rumors were vague, but nothing about a woman who might be Norsundrian. Dak told me there was a minstrel. Very skilled —"

"That might be Connanre of the Host." Adam looked away, his expression pained. "Collecting them for Yeres. Boys in late teens, no older than twenty. Smart, handsome. On the periphery of power, you might say, but no one in the world's eye. Your Cath might be one of these. I'm sorry if he is. But Yeres hates the prospect of aging more than anything, so there's a likelihood that Cath is in one of Norsunder-Beyond's outer, ah, call them holding areas, where time is suspended. Or even off world, though she would be in time's flow again. Definitely not at Norsunder Base, where she rarely goes."

Liere tried to suppress sharp disappointment at this news. She'd thought if anyone had all the answers, and the means to act, it would be Detlev, or failing him, one of his gang. But she had to try. "Didn't one of you get in and out of the Beyond, a year or so before I left?"

"Roy did." Adam looked apologetic. "And that egress no longer exists."

"Norsunder. Connanre. I didn't know that name. More of them coming into the world, after centuries of silence. That can't be a good sign."

"No," Adam said.

"What's going on?" she asked.

Adam hesitated. Either he explained it all — which would require years — or nothing. The fact that she did not know what questions to ask indicated how relatively little she understood about Norsunder's recent movements. And we might be effectively blindsided as well, which might lie behind Detlev's recent silence, he was thinking. "That's what many of us are trying to determine," he said. "The important thing here is that there really is nothing you can do, right now, for Cath, short of going to the Beyond."

Liere recoiled, aware that she would probably not be ready for that even with ten years of training. Which these boys had had, she reminded herself.

Her eyes stung. Her shoulder ached. David's derisive gesture with the sword evoked her old feelings of failure. She had been about to explain her prospective Enaeran errand — and ask if they had any advice — but the words would not come. They clearly regarded her as the same incompetent mess she'd been before she left.

But. She'd accepted this envoy mission to Enaeran to

prove to herself, as well as to her birth world, that she wasn't an incompetent mess. "I understand," she said, pleased her voice came out brisk. "Pardon my interruption, and thanks for the information. I'm glad that someone is aware. And doing what they can." Her voice husked, so she stopped there.

She laid their transfer token down on a side table, pictured Atan's balcony, and murmured the transfer magic to take her back to Atan's balcony.

Her note was still there, flapping in the breeze.

Liere folded up the note, stuck it in her pocket, and sat in one of the empty chairs to recover, and not merely from transfer reaction.

She had never assumed that while she was gone, everyone on Sartorias-deles had frozen in place until her return. She'd come back expecting to find everyone different, but it seemed the same did not hold true for her. Adam's patience, which she suspected arose out of pity, David's tension that found expression in scorn—those were for the Liere of the old days. For *Sartora*.

That sick sense of defeat wasn't just because she had been warned off going after Cath. It was the way David had shooed her away as though she were merely an annoying distraction.

Liere walked to the balcony and looked out, seeing anew the swarms of busy workers repairing street stones, trimming trees, polishing windows inside and out. Atan, her household, and her city, from high degree to low, were frenetic in preparing for the visit of the Colendi king—which meant she and Lyren-Sartora were an added nuisance while Atan was already busy.

But there was another job she *could* do. The Ones had taught her that the best anodyne for failure was to get right back to work.

She left the balcony, and asked the first page she encountered for directions to the scribe guild.

By the time Lyren-Sartora returned from her visit to the morvende, and had finished describing the trip to the hot springs in the caverns, and the echo-singing, Liere had nearly everything planned.

"We'll return to Bereth Ferian," Liere told Lyren-Sartora. "I visited the scribes, and found an old courier Destination on the outskirts of the capital city. What we need to do is prepare our guises."

"Guises?" Lyren-Sartora's eagerness altered to delight. "I want to go as a visiting princess! Wouldn't that get us more information quicker? Everyone always wants to please princesses, especially in pays!" She clapped her hands together.

Liere looked down, hiding her sharp reaction of dismay. It was just a wish, not a declaration of future intent, and even if it had been, Liere had lost any authority she'd ever had, even before she left for Geth.

But one thing she'd learned there was that authority was not a moral absolute: when she was ten years old and people had called her Sartora, they'd expected her to somehow make herself responsible for ridding the world of villains because of that one time she'd happened to be in the right place at the right time, with the right ability. On Geth, she'd finally been able to truly comprehend that such assumptions didn't mean she *was* responsible.

Freed of the yoke of guilt, she had learned how to be responsible for specific tasks. It was Sister Orchid who smiled at Lyren-Sartora as she said, "What do you see going on below?"

Lyren-Sartora turned in a circle, her expression puzzled. "Everyone is making ready for the King of Colend's visit."

"Exactly. What is he going to see when he arrives in kingly state? How life here usually is, or is he going to see what the Sartorans want him to see?"

"Is that wrong?" Lyren-Sartora asked warily.

"Not at all! It's just as it should be. The Sartorans are honoring him by making sure he sees their city at its best. But doesn't our visit to Enaeran have a different purpose? Aren't we supposed to see what is truly there, not what the Enaeraneth want us to see?"

Lyren-Sartora's eyed widened. "Oh! So we're *spies!*" Her tone suggested that this was even better than being a princess.

"If we go without drawing notice," Liere said, "then we have a better chance at seeing what is truly there."

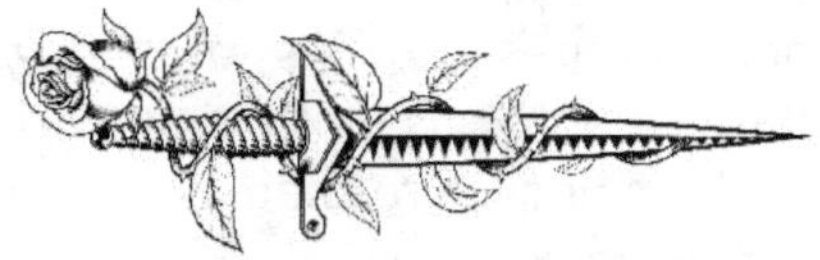

EIGHT

Athanarel, royal palace in Remalna-city, Remalna

Meliara Astiar, Queen of Remalna, had never been so glad to see the candle change from gold to green. Why did it seem that the later summer arrived, the fiercer the heat? The sky curved overhead, bright as a metal bowl by the morning candle-measure called First Gold, and so Vidanric, the king, had moved open court to the earliest hour, a change in the schedule that everyone had hailed with relief.

Even magic couldn't keep the rooms cool, through Meliara had learned the spell to pull air from high above down to the level of the ground, which created breezes. But it seemed that the warm air reached all the way to the stars, because the breezes she labored to bring down did not furnish much relief.

"Or maybe I'm not going high enough," she was saying to Vidanric as they followed the last of the courtiers from the throne room. She paused and cast a look over her shoulder at the enormous goldenwood tree whose smooth-barked branches reached up nearly to touch the ceiling, which had had to be raised to cover the tree. Some of the heat was due to the dome of paned glass they'd built so that the tree would not be denied light and air. Sun streamed down, catching dust motes with such brilliance the sparkle hurt the eyes.

"I hope you're toasting as much as we are," Meliara addressed the tree. "No, I hope you're toastier."

In the eight years since Flauvic Merindar had been transformed into a tree after he'd tried to take Remalna's throne, Meliara had spent considerable time airing her opinions to his silent branches and leaves. Daily, at first, while the throne room was rebuilt around Flauvic's topmost reach. Less often as the years slipped by, and her time was taken up with her share of the chores of ruling, plus magic studies, plus her share of child-raising, as both she and Vidanric had promised they would not leave their children completely to nannies and tutors to raise.

"You still talking to poor Flauvic?" Vidanric asked.

"Of course," Meliara stated. "You never know if the Hill Folk might up and change their minds one day, and reverse that spell. If they do, then he will have had plenty of things to think about."

Vidanric laughed silently, the well-trained courtier's laugh that Meliara had once hated, because it implied a self-control she'd never had, but now she loved the soft sough of his breath, and the way his eyelids seemed to smile.

"And, no doubt, plenty of retorts piled up," Vidanric said. "Assuming he can even hear you."

"That's what I don't know," she admitted as she bumped shoulder and hip up against him, and he slid his arm around her. "The more deeply I get into my studies, the more I'm discovering just how little we humans understand about magic, and time, and form. Life! He may never be human again. That tree might be his form for the rest of his existence."

The hot breeze from the terrace brought the smells of dust, dry grass, and a faint whiff of horse from the stables; she swallowed a couple of times, suspecting why her innards were unsettled. Eh, early days, and while a possible third child was as exciting and wonderful as the other two had been, the idea wasn't as new. She might as well wait to be sure. It could just be that honey-nut roll she'd swallowed down too quickly. "But if he is, he will be the most well-lectured tree in history."

"That he will," Vidanric acknowledged. "I find the idea quite satisfying. But we've a more immediate requirement; Flauvic is going to have to wait."

"Doing what he does best," Meliara agreed—then scowled at the floor when she remembered that it was War Conference Day. She said in a sprightly voice that didn't fool Vidanric for a heartbeat, "I'm so glad your meetings seem to be so successful. You're having them more often, aren't you?"

Vidanric took her hand, saying nothing until they'd

reached their suite. Then he smiled down at her, question in his eyes. "I thought you were reconciled to these meetings."

"I am," she said stoutly. She knew that it was quite reasonable for the meetings to take place in Remalna. Officially it was a sort of midpoint, meaning that no one had to endure a very long transfer, but actually it was considered neutral ground—none of the monarchs of mighty countries who hypothetically attended was either summoned or summoning the others. Remalna was so small that even the most suspicious of kings could hardly think that it was claiming ascendance over the others.

Meliara secretly found it hilarious that monarchs of huge kingdoms came to tiny Remalna, which probably would fit right into their capital cities, with room to spare. "Truly. I was flattered and delighted to host the Queen of Sartor here that first year—twice! The Queen of Sartor, in Remalna! Of course nobody knew it, but I'm *not* the type to want attention from those snobs in Sles Adran, where I happen to know she's never been."

Vidanric nodded solemnly. "Very true."

"And it's never been any trouble, especially since a lot of them stopped attending." Meliara thought of that odd white-haired teen from another continent, and the king with the scarred face from Erdrael Danara, and that huge heroic-looking Rel who sometimes came with Queen Atan. But he'd been missing the last few times.

"I like Queen Atan. Very much. And I like Jilo, whether he's a king or not. I even like Senrid—as long as he's not talking up that horrible school for our boys." Here she included Russav and Tamara's son, who spent at least half of his time with them, as Russav traveled for Vidanric, and poor Tamara was the first to admit that fiercely as she loved her offspring, she was not very good at being a mother.

"Senrid knows there is plenty of time yet to discuss the prospect of the academy. And the boys will have a say as well," Vidanric reminded her.

Meliara groaned, because she knew what those two boys were going to say. If she'd let them, they'd be off to Marloven Hess tomorrow. "It's just that it seems strange that with you meeting more often, there are even fewer of you. I thought that the prospect of Norsunder attacking would make them *want* to talk about ways to ally and to resist!"

Vidanric remained silent, his mind going straight to Bartal na Shagal of Sles Adran, smooth as a snake, and how he had listened intently until he understood that the conversations were theory and not practice. Though the man had been pleasantly urbane, Vidanric had found some of his questions suspicious—and so had Senrid. Since these were mere suspicions, and not facts, he kept his reservations to himself. "They all have their own reasons for not returning. Or not coming at all."

"I know. The Marlovens' reputation. A lot of them wouldn't set foot in King Senrid's evil lair lest they not come out, I get that. History is a hard thing to ignore, and the Marlovens' history seems to be pretty much a lesson in *Don't be like this*. But they don't even want to listen to him coming *here?* That is just prejudice! A subject I'm an expert at," she added a lot less heatedly, and cast a worried look up into his face. "I'm glad you are a part of it, but oh, Danric, I really thought we were done with war. Galdran was enough for a lifetime."

His smile vanished. "I agree. As you know. But Norsunder is not offering us a choice."

The bells rang the candle-change. Vidanric kissed her and went off, leaving her in charge of their children; Meliara knew she ought to get her bad mood well away, as rumor had it King Senrid of the Marlovens could read minds. It was time for horseback riding, Meliara decided. That would keep her out of sight, and hopefully out of mind.

While she went to the other wing to fetch the children, Vidanric got his most trusted servants to clear the area around the tower study, which he'd had furnished with a low round table on which could be spread maps of the Sartoran continent, markers, and plenty of paper. Around the table he'd placed comfortable cushions.

Senrid and Jilo arrived first, spaced out so that the transfer magic did not cause that warning hot-metal smell.

Meliara passed the Destination tiles as the two recovered from the transfer. When you saw people in their late teens once or twice a year the difference could be startling. In the two years Jilo had not come to the gatherings, he'd shot up a hand, skinnier than ever. Senrid had grown more slowly, the bones in his face sharpening. He'd always had a compact build on the slim side, and that still held true. He was solid muscle, but not of the bulky sort. Marlovens tended to be shorter and lighter in build overall, Vidanric had told her after she first met Senrid, and discovered that he was not built like Rel the traveler, the way she'd imagined. Vidanric had read somewhere that Marlovens being shorter was a result of their ancestors being plains riders who depended on speed, which meant less burden on a horse's back.

Whatever his ancestry, Senrid was not at all what Meliara had expected of a king. His blond, wavy hair was worn short over his collar in what she was told was the Marloven military style, his clothing invariably a white shirt over uniform trousers tucked into blackweave riding boots. Jilo was so lanky his clothes flapped, or that might be due to his hunched posture, his thin, bony, pale face habitually lowered so that most of what you saw was a messy nest of unkempt black hair.

Usually Atan was first, as the hour was the same in Sartor as it was in Remalna. But everyone knew she had a very demanding court and council. Not to mention the Sartoran Mage Guild, which was supposed to be detached from politics, but Meliara had gained the distinct impression that what Atan considered detached, and the guild considered detached, differed.

Meliara passed through the door, the children hirpling about her regardless of the heat, and they headed for the stables.

In the tower, Vidanric summoned cool drink and eatables, knowing that Jilo always loved these. The food and drink had arrived all the way from the kitchens before Queen Atan of Sartor turned up, as usual a couple of ancient records in hand. "I am so sorry I'm late," she said. "Unexpected visitor." She turned to Senrid as spoke, and hesitated—but as usual, forgot a mind-shield and her thoughts were loud with a roil of emotions. He caught the name Liere before he shut her out.

Atan pressed her lips together, then said, "Rel just got back from visiting his father, and got swept up by the city guard." She brandished the books. "After what you've been saying about city fighting, I went and looked up two eyewitness accounts of fighting in Eidervaen. One is very early, when the entire city was behind the first walls."

"Siege," Senrid said, his expression giving no clue to his

thoughts. Liere was back, and no communication? His awkward blunder five years ago could not possibly still rankle. Could it? Liere was no grudge-holder. But five years could change anyone. With an effort he set that aside, and recovered the previous subject. Right, street fighting. Sieges. "As long as you've got food and water as well as high and thick walls, force is on your side. Inert, but there."

Atan tapped the record, from which a faint whiff of mildew rose. "So it was. They held out until a duchas came to their rescue. But the second one was written after two districts spilled beyond the old walls, and the second set of walls had yet to be raised."

Senrid said, "If you like, I can read those and write up some commentary."

"I hoped you would."

"If we only have an hour, then let's get right to it. I thought we ought to talk about patrols, from both sides, attack and defense . . ."

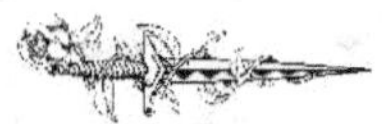

The evening bell had rung when Rel entered Eidervaen's royal palace through the back door. He cut through the servants' and pages' halls, exchanging greetings with his friends among the staff, then emerged into the hallway across from Atan's summer parlor.

The sun had nearly vanished beyond the western mountains, shafting ochre brilliance slantwise across the shaded balcony outside the parlor. Rel, drawn at first by the light, observed the coruscant ribbons of potential magic curling lazily through the air, gathering in streamers around the taller of two figures at the balcony wall.

He stepped through the open glass doors, out of habit blinking away the distractions of the streamers. He recognized the smaller, girlish figure as Lyren-Sartora, who visited Atan from time to time. His eye was caught by her companion, her fair hair gilt in the setting sunlight. She was dressed plainly in dark brown over light blue, which complemented a body of cambered grace: the curve of neck to straight shoulders, the concave arc to tiny waist contrasting to the convex curve of hip tapering down long legs whose shape the soft fabric hinted entrancingly.

"Lyren, and—?"

"Lyren-*Sartora*," the smaller figure said impatiently, as both turned. "Oh, hello, Rel!"

Rel blinked, scarcely hearing *Lyren-Sartora*. He stared with deep appreciation at that slender, graceful figure whose sun-bright fall of hair ruffled in silken locks as she stilled. Familiar golden eyes widened. He knew those eyes. Didn't he?

"Rel!" Liere exclaimed, her gaze going up and up as Rel stepped onto the balcony, the top of his thick, blue-black hair barely clearing the lintel. He'd always been tall as a mountain and nearly as broad through the chest, but he seemed even taller and broader since Liere had seen him last.

She also remembered him as old, and though if anything his strong-boned face seemed even more rough-hewn, his dark eyes so deep-set they appeared shadowed, somehow he wasn't *old* anymore. The eight years' difference in their ages had blurred into irrelevance, underscored by appreciation— attraction—that startled both. Rel was a young man, and she had become a young woman who appreciated young men.

Rel—with more experience—recovered in a heartbeat, snuffing utterly his mild appreciation of her form as he said easily, "Welcome back, Liere. I understand you were on Geth?"

"Yes," she said, thinking that Rel looked more like a king than any king she'd met.

"I don't know if you remember, but I spent some time in Geth-deles," Rel said—easy subject— "a year or two before you went. Where did you stay?"

Liere recovered her scattered wits, and went on to discuss places and people Lyren-Sartora had never heard of, which made her impatient. "Where's Atan?" Lyren-Sartora asked as soon as she could get a word in edgewise.

Rel broke off his commiseration about Cath, with whom he had spent some time—and had found very odd. "My guess is she's stuck in an interview she can't get away from. Probably concerns Shontande Lirendi's prospective visit. Have either of you met him? I never did."

"Nobody has," Lyren-Sartora said, arms crossed. "Except Senrid. I remember Senrid telling Arthur once that Shontande Lirendi was surrounded by spies."

"Are you staying to meet him?" Rel asked.

"No," Liere said. "Actually, we were about to leave. We're merely waiting to thank Atan for the visit. And I think she mentioned something about an envoy letter, though if that puts her to too much trouble, we'll do fine without—"

The door opened inside the parlor. Rel went in and returned a moment later. "There's a page here, with what looks like an official letter. As Atan sent these rather than bring them, I suspect she's going to be stuck for a while yet." He held out the tray containing the scroll tied with gold and purple ribbon as well as two other items.

Lyren-Sartora bounced up and down. "That's for us! And she gave us a golden notecase!"

Liere glanced down. "And a letter of credit." Which she would never use. She was far too frugal, and too scrupulous, for that. But she appreciated the gesture. "Rel, please convey our thanks."

Atan showed up some time after they left, and walked straight into Rel's arms. He tried to kiss the tension from her forehead as she said against his collarbones, "Half of court is already trying to figure out who will rule and who will reign. Can you believe it?"

"I take it they have you married off to Lirendi?" Rel asked, his quiet laugh a rumble in his chest.

Atan pressed her ear against the linen fabric of his shirt, delighting in the fremitus. "Mmmm, do that again."

"What?"

"Laugh."

His laugh deepened as she snuggled against him. "That's so much better," she sighed. "What a terrible day! They have me married off in one breath, but in the other, go on so self-righteously about how they have burned all their Colendi lace and will never again wear Colendi silk. It's going to be a very hot summer if we're all in velvet."

She lifted her head, twined her fingers in Rel's, and they wandered inside, and to the private supper that the servants had been waiting to lay out, word having run ahead as Atan at last crossed from the state wing. "I can deal with court. What I find more oppressive is the, oh, deliberate weight of moral superiority in the different guilds getting petitions up signed by every single musician, and instrument maker, in the entire country."

"This is all about the Music Festival," Rel said.

"The *Sartoran* Music Festival. For *centuries*. We want it back. Some feel we need it back." Atan turned her head, her gaze earnest. "And everybody is thinking that their fashion changes, their high talk, their moral superiority will cause the Colendi to bow and say, yes, while you Sartoran were removed from the world we took it over, but now that you are back among us, we relinquish this festival once again to Sartor, where it belongs."

"And—pardon my ignorance—but you can't simply start holding it again?"

"Two Music Festivals at Midsummer? The same prize?" Atan threw up her hands in mock horror. "The truth is, a great deal of the income from it in the old days was from the Colendi, who made it a fashion to travel here. Of course they won't come if they are holding their own. There is no way around the unpleasantness and awkwardness that would result. No, we need a graceful gesture restoring it to us. And many are hoping that Shontande Lirendi is coming to do just that, though I wonder if he's coming more as an escape from that regency council of his."

"Well, then, sic the court on Shontande Lirendi," Rel suggested. "He's a Colendi. They're supposed to be experts at eeling out of diplomatic boxes."

"Slithering," Atan said, thinking of the Colendi ambassador Vardathe Gaszin, whom she thoroughly hated. "Before I do that, I have to *get* him here. Properly. Honorably. Maintaining our historic dignity, as we might very well lose it all if the fanfares and flowers aren't just right."

Rel knew that tone: she needed to vent to a safe, sympathetic ear. "You know where I was?" she asked, bumping her hip against his. "With the Heralds of Etiquette and Revelries. A quarter-hour meeting that stretched to two hours, as *he* insisted that as we'd never had a Colendi ruling monarch here, we ought to salute him with Colendi custom and shower him with flower blossoms, and *she* said that we'd had Colendi royalty coming all the time to the *Sartoran* Music Festival, back when it was properly here—true, though no kings of queens, or at least, after they were crowned—and that we ought to go back to the old ways as a reminder of what we lost. And round and round we went, until I began to wish that Shontande Lirendi wasn't coming at all."

"Speaking of." Rel kissed her hand before dropping it, and they sank down side by side onto the long chair. "I almost don't want to tell you that the border patrol has been reporting word of a Colendi entourage gathering in Bais-on-the-Shore."

"Entourage? *Gathering?*" she repeated. The Herald of Etiquette had been right. State visits between monarchs weren't the fashion anymore. When Peitar Selenna of neighboring Sarendan had visited, he'd come by magic transfer, without so much as a single servant. Somehow she'd assumed that Shontande Lirendi would ride in with Thad Keperi, a guide, and maybe a servant or two hauling his hair ribbons and nail paint.

Rel, seeing her expression, said, "This is the king of Colend we're talking about. The Colendi don't do anything slapdash. I suspect they would consider it a terrible insult, to themselves and their notions of melende, if not to us."

"How many?" Atan asked, hands to the sides of her face. "We'll need to house them. The Colendi don't have their state houses here anymore. I took care of *that* the year that snake Ambassador Gaszin made it clear Colend was keeping the Music Festival. Now I wish I hadn't been so mingy." Her voice rose, and he heard the incipient panic in yet another problem.

"Wasn't mingy. They didn't own those houses. They'd been granted them by your ancestors, for the duration of the Music Festival. Which is no longer here." Nothing he said was new, of course, but hearing the facts in his calm voice reassured her. "As for housing the entourage. We're already preparing for that, between the guard barracks, and Gehlei dispatched a royal page in formal livery to ask how many rooms Gaszin has in that magnificent embassy residence. He took the hint. By the time Shontande Lirendi actually gets here, we'll be ready."

"Good." Atan sighed. "At least we've still time. I received a note last night that Shontande had left his capital and has begun his royal progress through Colend. If he's going to ride in from Bais, then that gives us extra time." She raised a goblet, then set it down. "Bais. That's a harbor west of Onekhaer, which is still infested with bandits, isn't it?"

Rel shook his head. "Not so many, these days. But I've sent word in your name to furnish some hardy border riders as escort and guides. I figured you'd want that."

"Thank you." Atan's expression cleared in relief. Then tensed again. "In my name. I hate that, the pretense. I wish the court would accept your leadership. The city guard has never been better organized. Or the border. And everyone in Sartor, it seems, except my first circle, knows that it's due to you."

"Oh, they all know," Rel said. "It's just the ambitious ones who want to make certain I remember my place. Which is why I will be with the guard, and not in your court, when your guest does arrive, so none of them will be able to give in to the urge to remind me." In other words, he did not want to be around as ambitious first circle nobles did their best to pair Atan off with Colend's young king.

But Atan, who knew him better than anyone else, understood the unspoken question, and muttered, "I cannot imagine marrying anyone but you."

Rel said nothing. Legally he could only be consort, never king—an officious courtier, jealous that Rel had never looked her way, just last year had tracked down the exact law that forbade commoners being crowned.

The irony was, Rel's mother had been a princess from Chwahirsland, one of the oldest and most powerful kingdoms on the continent. But no one knew that outside of Rel's father, the mage Mondros (noble-born himself, though disinherited)—and Prince Kessler, the single surviving member of the Chwahir royal family besides the evil old king.

Atan didn't know. Rel was not certain he would ever reveal the truth. Certainly not while the evil Wan-Edhe was still ruling Chwahirsland so abominably.

"We have tonight," he said, leaning over to kiss her. "How did command class go today? Did Senrid give us an exercise? Old Tansaree sent a note begging me to include him if there is."

Atan rubbed her aching temples, and forced her mind to shift. It still surprised her that the gray-haired Duchas of Tansaree, who had been badly wounded in the old war before the enchantment, had altered so much: he was now one of the strongest supporters of the war games Rel had been running with various duchal home guards.

"We talked about patrols, and then he did give us an exercise," Atan said. "I wrote down the conditions of the game."

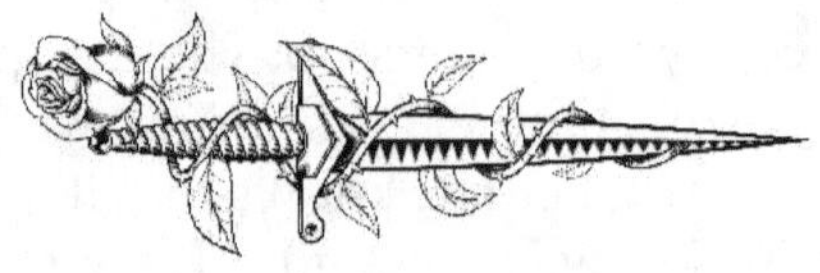

NINE

To Lyren-Sartora's astonishment, Liere insisted on remaking donated clothing herself before they could go anywhere. Thoroughly exasperated — and impatient to start their adventure — Lyren-Sartora had first thought she was joking, then she realized she had never heard Liere crack a joke.

"Liere, there are *tailors* to do that. If you can't find anything that fits in the donations trunks. Tailors are fast, and they know what they're doing."

"I'm not fast," Liere said, "But I know what I'm doing. I made my own clothes while on Geth. More to the point, I haven't any earnings with which to pay a tailor."

Lyren-Sartora spun around, trying to find words to express her annoyance with Liere's ridiculous scruples. "In case you never noticed, there's no lack here. The mage school brings in plenty, and so does the library, even if there weren't already *piles* of wealth going back to the federation days."

"But it is not mine." Liere breathed against the familiar stomach-churn of the old anxiety, but she spoke with an appearance of calm conviction. "I'm an adult now, and that means paying my own way in the world. And it would be dishonest to use Atan's envoy stipend before we even cross the border into Enaeran."

Though Liere's calm was largely assumed, it was convincing enough to fluster Lyren-Sartora. To her, Bereth Ferian was home, and home didn't charge you money. Well, maybe Grandfather Fer Eider would have done that, but he was gone. And anyway, she loathed thinking about adult life if it meant grubbing for money, and was Liere going to start hinting that she ought to start making her own clothes, or apprentice to a tailor or a baker or some such boring thing?

"Tell me when you're ready," Lyren-Sartora said airily. Though she couldn't resist adding over her shoulder, "If you still want to take along somebody who gets her clothes made."

As a parting arrow it fell far short, and she sensed it, which sent her stamping off to the stables, where she rode herself out of her temper. Lyren-Sartora's moods were as mercurial as the weather. She relished riding out into the brisk cold air, with, crisp, fresh-fallen snow squeaking under the horse's hooves. Though it soon clouded into a sleety gray, Lyren-Sartora returned with the sunny conviction that Liere was always going to be Liere. Though she'd changed on the outside, she hadn't on the inside, so Lyren-Sartora might as well accept it, and keep herself out of Liere's way until she was ready.

And in a sense, she was right. Liere said nothing out loud, but she wanted her shoulder wound to heal enough that the scabs would hold and every movement didn't hurt. Sewing as she mentally practiced magic was as good a way of passing the time as any, and evenings she could scout the archives for any histories about an area she was completely ignorant of, other than where it lay on the map.

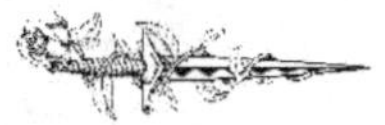

Alsais, capital of Colend to Colend's border

Before I have the honor of introducing the young king Shontande Lirendi to the reader's notice, we must pay a brief visit to the Colendi regency council to see the result of the royal order to retire.

They debated behind closed doors into advanced hours, but remained sharply divided, which perforce permitted the royal heralds to read out Shontande's declaration for the requisite three days. Thus the people of Colend learned that their young king was ready to assume his throne.

During every one of those days, the three prime movers

of the council were uncertain enough not to act on their own. Each waited for one of the others to move first, so that they could gauge reaction, and support or regret (a diplomatic way of saying abandon) as suited them best. But none had. The Duchases of Altan and Gaszin glared covertly at each other, mentally forming contingency plans, and both narrowly watched the Count of Ariath, who everyone knew was the most ambitious of all.

The Count emerged from the shock of betrayal by that young fool Shontande to a firm conviction that Colend needed *true* leadership. She had been trained from childhood to marry a king—who had gone mad, and who'd had a son without choosing a queen.

She knew what to do now. But how to accomplish it with grace?

On the third morning, after the last reading, she saw only one way to recoup the natural order. It was not going to be easy, and it would make a permanent enemy of the young king, but if he could be folded gently yet firmly back into their benign governance, he could sulk as much as he wished without risk of any further harm.

"We must think of Colend," she enunciated as she daintily adjusted a bracelet on her wrist. She paused as the movement and the words gathered the council's attention. Then she brushed her fan over one side of her chin, then twirled it in the gesture of Rue, saying sadly, "What I feared most might lie behind this abrupt . . . awkwardness."

She raised her eyes in well-practiced sorrow, and saw enlightenment lift Altan's fine brows, and smooth Gaszin's perturbation. "After all, he is so like the former king," he murmured, his fan held at the angle of Regret.

From a lifetime of habit nobody would utter the term *insane*, but the context was understood. Except who was going to try for that throne without the safe acclamation of a crowd? A wrong move would be so very permanent . . .

As they watched each other narrowly while pretending not to, their missing king sat on a woven rice-straw mat at a small, unvarnished wooden table inside the common room of a traders' inn on Colend's border, before him a bowl of egg-drop soup simmered with fresh shallots and a dollop of white wine. Being tired from little sleep was perhaps not the ideal circumstances for reviewing one's plans, but necessity—he had decided the year previous, when he first put this plan into motion—was king of the abstracts.

Shontande's second-cousin appeared, damp brown hair damp tied back, riding clothes plain though well made.

"Good morning, Nash," Shontande said, touching his fingertips together.

Nashande Desentis mirrored his salute and dropped cross-legged opposite Shontande. He poured out some fresh steep as he said, "Ikais and Jessan really gone?"

"Last night, after you retired," Shontande said.

"Excellent fellows," Nashande commented, his broad hands open in a gesture of honest regret. "Fun to ride with. Jessan especially."

Not for Nashande the studied gestures that made silent irony of courtly compliment or observation. He said what he thought, his expression mirroring his emotions.

"Ikais is curious to find out what the chirps are saying in Alsais." Shontande added wryly, his voice pitched low, "Now that the entire kingdom has heard my wishes. Jessan said it was time to see for himself what the new peace treaty between Khanerenth and Locan Jora means for his family, but I suspect he was surprised that he was not called to defend them." He did not give voice to his further suspicion that Jessan was secretly disappointed; he'd been trained to captain border patrols, and his was not a nature for the slow traditions of rice farmers and silkworm breeders.

Nashande touched his fingertips together, his expression sober. "Jessan said he doesn't believe the treaty will hold. Though he likes the new king, even though he's a Merindar."

Shontande said, "Peace is a new idea in Khanerenth."

"Not custom." Nashande's handsome, honest face sobered. "We've got it as custom, if not conviction. I think I should ride for home now. You'll move faster without a party."

The creak of the stairs caused both to look up as Thad Keperi came down to join them, after a morning of writing letters. He'd bathed before dawn; his ruddy hair was already dry. He paused to scan the room. This inn did not even have private parlors. Shontande had been specific about that, choosing places that the ordinary trader favored.

Thad's scan took in the two at the back table, noble and king, both dressed for riding. Shontande had been firm from the beginning about the importance of traveling as common traders; though Thad admired Shontande without reserve, he also knew that Shontande had never spent a single day not surrounded by luxury and an army of servants. He had had private misgivings about this plan, both its wisdom and its success after a few days of what a noble would consider hard living.

And yet there they sat in company with a party of male wagon drivers, a traveling tinker, and four female upholsterers from Sarendan hoping for better work in Colend. It was plain that Shontande and his cousin had been kept waiting for their food, in favor of the larger tables.

To Thad, they stood out. Nashande was good-looking in a regular-featured way, but Shontande, many had said all his life, was a throwback to Mathias the Magnificent, the single Colendi emperor. He was always going to draw attention; before she was murdered, Thad's sister Karhin had been fascinated by Shontande, who'd been maybe thirteen at the time, and she nearly four years older. He wore the clothing that Thad had chosen for him: undyed linen shirt and riding trousers, covered by a robe of brown raw silk, much as a prosperous merchant would dress. No paint on his nails, his hair simply pulled back. Though he had been trained in court movement and mannerisms, Thad was relieved to see that somehow Shontande had learned to sit, and to move, without drawing attention. But nothing would ever hide the symmetry of his features, or the harmony of his vivid coloring.

Thad recognized with a spurt of hilarity that the sneak peeks on the part of other customers were not those for a king, but simply for a very pretty young man; what he did not recognize was that Shontande, in consciously setting aside the training of a lifetime, was mirroring Curtas, from all those years ago.

Thad stepped into the room, raising no interest in his travel-worn courier clothes. As he approached the little table at which Shontande knelt and Nashande sat cross-legged, he suppressed the habit of protocol, only touching his fingers briefly together in the polite greeting everyone used, and sat down at Shontande's right. "Want the latest news?" he asked.

"Is there . . ." Shontande turned his hand over in the Colendi sign for regret, easily interpreted as *Is there trouble?*

Thad brushed his fingers over his heart in reassurance.

"Then break your fast," Shontande invited. "Whatever is going on can wait. Unless it's good news that can be summed up in a sentence?"

Thad raised his hands in the shadow ward, which prompted an ironic smile from Shontande, and a sigh from his cousin.

"Thought it would be too easy," Nash muttered, as a harassed young waiter brought over a heavy tray of food and set it down with a bang, the utensils on the stack of plates clattering. Neither Shontande nor his cousin reacted to this piece of rudeness that would be grounds for instant dismissal among palace staff.

As Thad waited for the other two to serve themselves first, he suppressed the impulse to scan for eavesdroppers. His younger brother Bee had taught him to listen to the quality of voices, as well as their direction. A drop in tone, a pause, usually indicated shifting awareness. There was none: the talk from the table of drivers stayed otherwhere focused, buzzing below the lighter hum from the upholsterers at the other large table.

Thad filled his plate with blue raindrop pastries, thin-sliced melon, and shirred eggs, then murmured, "So far, the council is going on as if nothing happened."

"Which they can do as long as Uncle Donais holds the herald guards," Nashande muttered.

"They did issue two covert decrees this very morning. The note arrived half a heartbeat before I was going to shut my notecase for the day."

"Let me guess." Shontande sighed. "Find me, and constrain Bee."

Thad cast him a glance of mild surprise as a low rumble of thunder reverberated through the building. The wagon drivers cursed, and one exclaimed, "At least the cider is good here. Looks like we're in for a stay."

"You are correct," Thad said to Shontande, forcing his verbs to friends-on-equal-footing mode, though instinct screamed at him to choose the subject-to-monarch formality; it was nothing in Shontande's manner that demanded it. Thad was self-aware enough to recognize that his desire for the customary habits of speech and manner was a longing for right order. Talking to Shontande as if they were equals somehow underscored the possibility that Shontande could shrug off kingship altogether and go adventuring on his own, leaving those greedy, corrupt regents holding the kingdom they so badly wanted to rule outright.

Thad wrenched his thoughts back. "Bee's contacts among the lower scribes warned him. Neither runners nor herald-guards will find him. Nor will they cut off his access to news."

"I thought he would be the next target once they accepted that I'd slipped their leash," Shontande said in an undertone. "Next they'll surely send out personal scribe runners, while they watch each other to see who dares try for the throne."

Nashande chuckled deep in his broad chest. "Runners who will run through every town, looking for a king galloping down the road to Sartor."

"Looking," Shontande said, "for the sort of parade and pomposity their chiefs use themselves when they travel. It should protect us for a time, though it won't last past my being recognized by the one or two who have actually seen me."

Thad touched fingertips together, understanding this oblique hint that Shontande meant to stick to his plan of traveling through Colend via byroads, talking to Colendi as another Colendi, and not as a king. Thad should have seen it from the outset, how easily Shontande would adapt despite the luxury of his silken prison. Back in the old days, Thad and Curtas had sneaked to the lonely palace at Lake Skya and often found Shontande on the rooftop, in shirtsleeves despite winter ice and summer heat, practicing archery, sword drills, and fan fighting. He had made friends with them, though one was common and the other the child (so he'd hinted) of thieves.

Thad was not the only one to take the hint. "Ah-ye!" Nashande set his cup down and fisted his hands on his thighs. "I keep forgetting myself. You know me. I blurt out what I think, and I'm bound to ruin things, if you want to keep on with your disguise. Perhaps I ought to ride back to the city."

Nashande loved the conspiracy. It had disturbed him for years to see his cousin mewed up by the regents, and he knew his elders felt the same. But he did not love stopping to smell retting flax, or stare at silk worms munching leaves, while people nattered on about their lives as if they were world events. That sort of thing he had to deal with when making the yearly round of the family duchy. He regarded listening to the people of Desentis as part of his duties, for he could actually talk to his family about this or that problem, but the leddas-gatherers of Altan, and the canal polers of the south, and so forth? He'd had enough of listening to problems he couldn't fix. "You might need me in Alsais," Nashande added hopefully.

"Thank you." Shontande touched his palms together, knowing that Nash would inevitably be the regents' third target, but if Nash wanted to go, he should be free to go. "For your company, and for the horses."

Nashande flashed a brilliant grin. He peered upward as he ran to get his travel pack; if the wind was right, he clearly intended to outride the storm if he could.

"Where to from here?" Thad asked, wanting time to plan the route and to establish a new relay among his trusted scribe contacts.

Shontande lifted his crudely fashioned cup and gazed past the fragrant liquid of pale greenish gold as he contemplated the journey so far: he had ridden alongside a curving river, observing flax bundles retting in the water in side streams; he had listened to the farmers singing as they worked the rice fields along peaceful canals gleaming blue in the sun. He'd shared the midday meal with farmers, tinkers, traders and travelers, listening to their talk, complaints, victories, sorrows, and wishes.

He'd trotted past kitchen gardens backed by rising hills full of silk trees in full bloom, seeing people weeding, picking, tending: he had never known that green beans grew on vines, twining up poles as gracefully as the finest inlay on his tables at home, but sweet beans did not so grow. Gardeners, given ear, had been glad to discuss their vital work, and what those seasonal rounds did to shape their view of the world.

He had talked about planting songs with a young boy sent to gather a pail of eggs from a broad yard where chickens roamed about, pecking and muttering. He had witnessed people singing different many-versed melodies as they tented fulled wool in the summer sun.

The evening before, he'd walked freely about a marketplace before closing at the Hour of the Cup, seeing actual Stringers in the flesh, who with deliberate ceremony measured all kinds of commodities, their scribes writing everything in ledgers, then copying the trade for each party involved. He'd listened to passionate bartering about the quality and price of corn, the exchange every bit as ritualized as courtly banter.

He'd listened to a glassmaker instruct a new apprentice, and he'd overhead two of the upholsters talking over embroidering techniques with the gravitas of diplomats in treaty-making. And that morning, before anyone else in his party woke, he'd watched bakers putting the morning bread into brick ovens.

His ever-evolving plan was twofold. He needed to know if the Colendi people wanted him as king. And he needed to hear what they thought. In both situations, he wanted them to have the freedom of choice. Who would obey his wishes? He had not expected cooperation from the council. Were the commons content to live under the council rule because that was what they were used to?

He looked down at himself. Though the rough-woven shirt was itchy, and the scuffed boots unmercifully chafed feet used to court slippers, he meant to keep on exactly as he was: what he was learning was more precious than mere gems. And it was worth the blisters.

"As for where next. Why don't we," he murmured with a wicked smile, "tour Ariath?"

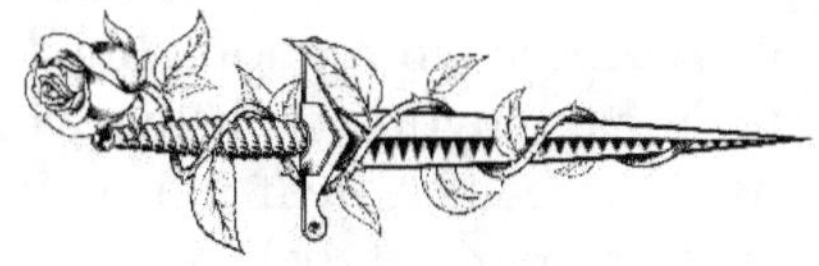

TEN

Liere felt Lyren-Sartora's absence as a reproach, but she stuck to her plan, sewing by day, and reading about the history of the diplomatic Eidervaen Protocol by night, until the day she could lift her sword and (slowly) perform the Ones' morning drill, without the scab breaking. Her shoulder still hurt, but she could live with that. At least it was mending.

She went to breakfast, and when she saw Lyren-Sartora, she said, "Are you ready to go to Enaeran as envoys?"

"Of course!" Lyren-Sartora exclaimed, her arched brows slanting in a mock frown. "I packed *ages* ago! My trunk is right by my door."

"Then open it and repack. Two changes of clothes at most. Plain as possible, because I can embellish them with illusion magic if we need it. Or we can return here if we have to get more clothes. I've made transfer tokens in case we need them."

"Ugh. Transferring that far *hurts*. Why can't we take a magical carryall?" Lyren-Sartora asked. "We have two. The one Arthur made for me puts an entire closet into no-space. My trunk will go easily."

"That much magic can be traced by someone testing for magic. Like Norsundrians," Liere said.

"Oh!" Lyren-Sartora cocked her head, considering that. "But if we have illusions on us, won't they trace those?"

"Illusion magic is too flimsy for tracers," Liere said. "That is, you could put together tracers for it, but it takes too much effort as illusion is all over most cities."

"You're thinking of theatres, after all that civil war."

Liere said, "Stage illusionists make plenty of money on the side selling illusions to anyone who asks. Think about how much illusion you see, and ignore, like false lights over eating houses and inns. Anyone with the wealth to pay for them get illusions to embellish their places to draw custom. Nobles add illusions to parlors, ballrooms, courts, gardens, and fountains as part of entertainment. Nobody troubles to put tracers out for those."

"That's true! I mean, about both: they do it, and I don't pay much attention."

"What I do will be subtle—nothing more than adding trim of a design that we see around us. I'll make my eyes dark, and add some shading to my face, so we don't look so obviously like we're related. Such flimsy magic would never trip a tracer. And we'll go unnoticed."

"Make me older!" Lyren-Sartora exclaimed, with the exuberance of twelve. "This is going to be fun."

The Destination Liere had chosen brought them to the edge of Shiovhan, in a rundown district destroyed during the old civil war. It was an unpromisingly dreary introduction to their first diplomatic mission—though Lyren-Sartora looked around with intense interest at the fire-blackened remains of a row of stone houses, the narrow lancet-arch windows gaping darkly.

They walked out onto a road that once had been good, but weeds tufted up between the flat gray stones, some cracked, others missing altogether. Liere looked away from the houses, which had once probably comprised an outpost of some sort, and glanced to the east. As she'd surmised, meadowlands stretched out, with clumps of trees here and there. The air smelled of early summer grasses, and a little of horse. Surprisingly, it reminded her of Marloven Hess.

Liere had put illusion over herself, adding shadows to flatten her nose, recede her chin, and dull her hair. Lyren-Sartora was startled at the difference, but she shrugged it away. This was typical Liere, like the plain clothes, and not wanting to meet the mysterious Shontande Lirendi, king of Colend, because she hated dressing up and courtly ritual.

"Make me a teen," Lyren-Sartora said. "Then I can pretend to be a scribe student. Nobody notices those."

She was short for a teen, but Liere obligingly added a bit

of shadow to Lyren-Sartora's cheeks and chin, as Lyren-Sartora exclaimed, "Do I look older? How much older?"

"At least fourteen or fifteen," Liere said, with generous intent.

That made Lyren-Sartora happy—people took you seriously when you were older, and fifteen was very old. Then they set out walking northwards, toward the jumble of rooftops on the skyline. The buildings vanished for a time, leaving dusty fields. The old gray stones had even vanished, leaving a road of hard dirt that must be a mire in rainy weather, unless mages came along regularly. But Atan had said that they had no resident mages here, and hadn't hired anyone from the guild since the troubles began.

A long, dusty, hot march later, they encountered paved road again, equally neglected, and entered the jumble of buildings outside an ancient, half-crumbled wall, the visible portions covered with chalked and white-washed slogans and politically-motivated cartoons. Most of the city was built of the same mellow golden stone that comprised the greater portion of the buildings in Marloven Hess.

"Doesn't this remind you a little of Senrid's city?" Lyren-Sartora asked, looking around in surprise. "Not as nice. Though it seems funny to call Senrid's big castle-town 'nice', but you know, some of it really is."

Liere peered under her hand. "These stone buildings here are all flat-sided. They don't have those old arch carvings above the windows, or the stylized raptor carvings under the roofs that they have in Choreid Dhelerei."

Lyren-Sartora snapped her fingers. "That's it. And some of these houses have a lot of wood." She pointed. "I don't remember seeing anything built of wood in Choreid Dhelerei. All stone."

"Maybe the weather isn't as violent here, protected as it is by the border mountains," Liere said, looking west. The city blocked the horizon where she expected the border mountains rose. "And there's a lot more forest, which means the Wood Guild permits a lot more use of wood."

"How did you know that?"

"I studied the map."

"Oh. I guess I could have done that, but I thought it would be more fun to let everything be a surprise." Lyren-Sartora skipped a couple of steps.

"Those mountains to the west are the Ghildraith range, and beyond that the plains of Nelkereth, and beyond that is little Vasande Leror, which shares its border with Marloven Hess. There was a lot of back and forthing between the Marlovans and the Adranis in the past . . ."

Liere halted, wondering if she was talking a bit too much about the Marlovens, who were far away on their side of considerable mountains. She shifted the subject. "Some of that rockiness seems to extend this far, from the looks of that ridge to the north. I see two types of stone around us, the gray underfoot, and the sand-colored stone."

Lyren-Sartora shrugged with an air of distraction, far more interested in people then geography. She scanned the wooden houses jumbled together, gapped here and there with burned ruins, many patched with brick and gray stone and warped wood. Houses that had escaped fires sported window boxes, and most were painted either goldenrod — a shade akin to that building stone — or else bright colors like sky blue.

Liere couldn't help comparing what she saw with what she remembered of Marloven Hess. Shiovhan was different enough from Choreid Dhelerei, which was still a defensible citadel. This city had sprawled beyond its walls in a way that the tidy, wary Marlovens would never have tolerated.

As they walked toward the city center, Liere noted guard posts at intervals among the ruins, tattered banners hanging limply in the still, hot air, the device on them difficult to make out after seasons of weathering. People moved about on horseback or on foot, wagons pulled mostly by slow, patient oxen. Few coaches. Most of the little side streets winding toward the city walls looked too narrow for a coach to pass along. That, too, reminded her of Marloven Hess, where everyone rode.

Differences? Well, no Marloven uniforms, of course. Some of the people wore long tunic shirts that laced in the front, sashed at the waist, loose pants stuffed into riding boots or high mocs. V-fronted, cap-sleeved armored or ring-reinforced vests of varying lengths — some to the tops of boots — worn either over or under the sashes, and here and there people wore robes of varying degrees of decoration. Even the most raggedly dressed had at least a cudgel thrust through their sash or strapped over a shoulder within easy reach. Everyone wore brimmed hats warding the brilliant sun of early summer, and all but the shabbiest of those hats were tied with some bright color around the brim, sporting feathers or ribbons as streamers.

Equally they all, at least in this part of town, looked down at heel, the seams and hems worn. Liere added small touches to the illusions on their own sensible riding clothes, noting with approval the way Lyren-Sartora mimicked the walk of a girl of about fifteen or sixteen.

The other main difference? Those scrawls and drawings on walls and fences. Liere had never seen any kind of markings on walls in Senrid's city. But from what she knew of Marloven Hess's history, when Marlovens had internal problems, they struck fast and hard, without advertising their intentions.

The more crowded the streets, the more Liere noted wariness, not quite tension in eyes and hands around them. Shops gradually began looking more prosperous, the walls newly scrubbed or painted. Nearly all had armed bravos lounging at the doors, male and female — all looking tough.

The only oddity was the sets of four small plinths in the middle of market squares or circles of the sort where in other places one usually found wells or fountains. These stepping-stone-sized plinths appeared to mark off a square within the greater square or circle. They were maybe ten to twelve paces across.

She didn't see any wells or fountains. That is, she occasionally spotted what once had been fountains, but they were dusty-dry, a few filled with dirt and planted with beans climbing dustily up poles. There were other hardy kitchen-garden crops, like turnips and cabbages. As for those odd squares of plinths, no one stepped between those markers, but walked around them even if a square lay directly in their path.

Liere and Lyren-Sartora passed yet another and entered an adjacent street dominated by a pair of riders in dusty battle tunics of dull midnight blue. The pair bristled with weapons, forcing their way through the crowd by trotting down the middle of the street. They left angry glares and muttering in their wake, some raising the backs of their hands in a rude gesture.

One of their horses snorted and dropped a steaming load. Liere watched for a wander to appear and wand away the waste, but no one did. And yet the street was not filthy. She paused under an awning.

"Why did we stop?" Lyren-Sartora asked.

"I want to see if the wand guild is still operating here."

"Of course they would be," Lyren-Sartora began, then faltered to a halt. Her eyes widened, then she said, "Are we going to stand here all day to watch for that?"

"No," Liere said. She was tempted to magic away the waste, but that wouldn't solve the larger problem. She turned her head, and noted that the two armed riders also avoided the plinth-marked square. Then they vanished up another street.

"Let's go," Lyren-Sartora begged.

Liere agreed, mind proliferating with questions about magic in governments. They'd walked another four blocks when Liere spotted a disgruntled youth in the guards' dark blue riding along on a donkey. He leaned out and waved a sword, no, a wand, and magic scintillated. A mess on the street vanished.

They had a few wanders here, though he didn't wear Wand Guild colors.

"I'm thirsty," Lyren-Sartora said presently. "Should we pick an inn and listen to the talk while we get something cool to drink? Maybe we'll hear something about Norsunder."

Liere thought that unlikely, but she was thirsty, too —

Her nerves flashed as she caught a mental echo, a brief, intense image of herself as seen from behind. Someone had scanned her on the mental plane, then shielded. She side-eyed the thick market-crowd, but encountered no return gaze.

"All right," she said to Lyren-Sartora, her voice low, the language Sartoran. "We need hats, then a place to stay. You pick. I want to listen to the people around us." She hesitated, then decided she might sound pompous if she explained that she wanted to get the gist of the local language so she wouldn't have to depend on the Universal Language Spell.

Lyren-Sartora glanced around, intensely curious after Liere's stiffening and her fast glance at the passing jumble of strangers of all ages. She met the eyes of a few urchins, who eyed her back. A couple ragged girls whispered as they stared at her, then they turned around, braids swinging, and vanished into the crowd.

You can often learn the truth about what's really going on from the street urchins in any city, Julian had said. And who better to get urchins talking than another one?

Lyren-Sartora made the gesture to end the teenage illusion on her as she and Liere walked down a slight rise onto a street with newer paving, bordered by more prosperous-looking houses with iron-work balconies. No slogans or scrawls on any walls here.

The street gave onto a circle with another dry fountain in the middle. This circle didn't have plinth squares — though Liere spotted four rough granite spots marring the flagged pattern, as if plinths had been battered down to ground level. Vendors passed the spots, hawking their wares, singing or shouting.

From the circle four streets led off. Three inns vied for custom, and street vendors hawked wares. Liere bought hats from a tired-looking vendor more or less her age, then Lyren-Sartora picked the inn that had a tiny garden in front, with round tables at which people sat and watched the market-day travelers go by. Good smells emanated from it.

"Here," she said, then wrinkled her nose at the floppy hats Liere had chosen — both dun colored, and plain. That much was exactly like the old Liere! Lyren-Sartora decided that if she had to wear a hat, she'd at least decorate it with flowers, as had some of the girls on the streets.

Liere jammed her hat on her head. It shaded her face, giving her a sense of added camouflage. She approached the innkeeper, doing her best to mimic the local accent as she inquired about a room. The man brightened at once. Despite the considerable crowd, it appeared they had plenty of rooms — the crowd was all local, there to socialize. Travelers were few.

The room was small, and still hot from the bright sun. A bed entirely filled it, with a palm-sized, cloudy mirror on the wall at the foot. Hooks on the back of the door took their travel packs. At the end of the hall was a cleaning frame, apparently shared by all. They stepped through — Liere holding the hat out so the magic would get inside and out — felt the snap of dust and sweat vanishing, and made their way back down into the hot, crowded common room.

Lyren-Sartora soon had a headache from the heat and noise. The food, when it came, was good, except the punch was warm. If they'd had a basement cooling spell for their liquids, it had worn out; maybe the war had kept any passing house-mages from coming around to renew. Lyren-Sartora loathed the taste of warm berry-and-citrus juice.

Worse, it was too loud to talk, not that Liere even tried. Someone played music, but it was too hot and crowded for dancing. As for Liere herself, she just sat there staring at everyone who came in or went out, for what seemed hours and hours.

Lyren-Sartora was glad when they retired, the noisy common room diminishing to a dull roar beneath their feet.

"Did you find whoever scanned you?" Lyren-Sartora asked as she sank on the bed. "Was it a Norsundrian?"

"No." Liere frowned, considering. The contact had been too brief and clumsy to characterize, someone with no training but a lot of mental energy; the scan was more like a stinging slap in the mental realm, though with utterly no malice. Curiosity only. But at least she had begun to master the patterns in how the local language had diverged from Sartoran, and some of the Enaeraneth idiom.

"When are you going to start asking?"

"I'm not," Liere said. "The moment you mention Norsunder, people start speculating why, including about whoever asks. And though most are perfectly innocent, we don't want any real Norsundrian hearing that we're looking for them. We'll not mention Norsunder." *Until we have to,* she amended silently to herself.

Lyren-Sartora threw herself on the bed, and let out a squawk. "Straw mattress! Ugh!"

They thumped and kneed the mattress into a semblance of flatness. "At least the straw seems to be fresh," Liere pointed out.

"And will be hotter than hot to sleep on," Lyren-Sartora retorted. "And if we roll together into the middle, we'll boil. This is getting stupider by the hour."

She's twelve and I just returned, Liere thought, setting her pillow on the floor and stretching out. She had slept on dirt often enough of late, and insistent memory threw her back to sleeping on the forest floor with Senrid when they ran from Siamis. This was marginally better.

Lyren-Sartora thought: *She's old now, acting like a grownup. Of course she picked the ugliest hats. Well, we're together for the first time in practically five years.*

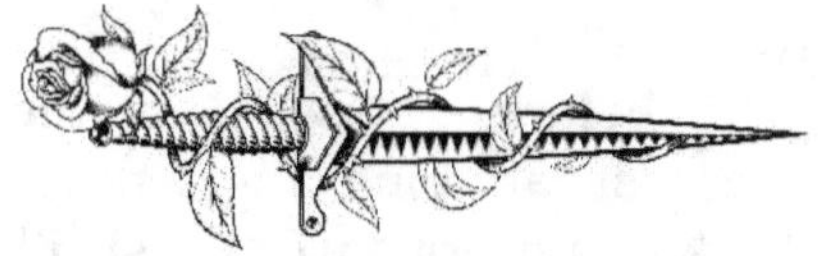

ELEVEN

It is time to introduce the second young king to the reader's notice. Though both Shontande Lirendi and Andri Malcolin Elsarion share certain similarities—born into the rank of crown prince, fathers assassinated, both in anomalous positions and at large—there the similarities end, as we shall see.

The next morning Liere rose early and walked through the cleaning frame. She did a few stretches, careful of the still-aching wound, then used the tiny mirror to redo the fading illusion over her features.

As soon as Lyren-Sartora woke, she dashed through the cleaning frame with the heedlessness of youth. They left the inn, finding the morning air humid, but a breeze had kicked up. Liere clamped her hat down onto her head and squinted through swirls of dust.

They bought fried bread from a street vendor, and ate as they walked. Gradually the street narrowed, the buildings on either side as patched as the clothing of the passers-by. Liere began to get a sense of the city: the farther away from the river one got, the poorer the houses. There did not seem to be any canals carrying water to everyone. But poor or prosperous, most everyone was armed.

Liere said, "I can't figure out why the streets slant so oddly. I understand the better areas lying along the river, but why do these streets slant off that way?"

"I don't want to climb up and down that hill in the heat," Lyren-Sartora said. "Unless we have to. Do we? Do you think that's where the royal palace is?"

"Possibly. Let's try it, and if we see or hear nothing of use, we can try somewhere else in the kingdom."

"But Julian made it clear that whatever was going on was right here in the capital. Everywhere else it's little trade towns, or even smaller villages."

"We can always—"

Liere stopped. Before a row of weather-beaten small shops, a crowd was fast gathering, angry shouts rising. People began shoving back as a furious woman shrilled, "Stop! Stop the thief!"

A man's roar joined, "Pickpocket! Stop him!"

A few people tried to give chase, frustrated by those gathered to see the entertainment, until an angry shout rose from the other direction, "The snouts!"

The crowd surged, Liere and Lyren-Sartora jostled hard as people tried to ram their way through the solid mass of bodies. Liere leaped up, spying a brawny pair on horseback, both wearing the dark blue tabards over blackweave armor. The woman wielded a stick, smacking the heads of those who got in the way. Her companion, a man with a fierce moustache, cracked a whip. People screamed where the whip lit.

Another surge. In the other direction, a carter hauling barrels blocked traffic. Riders milled about.

"Get the thief!"

"Pickpocket! I was robbed!"

"We'll be trampled!"

Someone elbowed Lyren-Sartora in the back, nearly knocking her onto the cobblestones in the path of a white horse with brown spots, but the yellow-haired rider expertly wheeled the horse aside, leaving Lyren-Sartora sitting on the ground gaping up at a young man with long blond hair, his face shadowed by a battered broad-brimmed black hat. A scruffy small boy rode behind him.

The boy pointed past Black Hat. "There's the pickpocket!"

"I see him," said Black Hat, nodding to two raggedly dressed young men, who ducked expertly through the milling crowd, each carrying a sliver of mirror. As Liere watched in fascination, they leveled the shards so that sunlight lanced across the eyes of the guards' horses, causing them to plunge and turn away.

"Elsarion forever!" the boy shouted.

"Not while we're catching a pickpocket," replied Black Hat with a quick grin as he used the horse to cut across the path of the pickpocket, then swung out of the saddle and tossed the reins to the boy.

He wore a sword, but didn't pull it. Instead, he caught the thief by the wrist. The crowd surged, as the pickpockets' victims struggling madly to get closer. Liere reached down to give Lyren-Sartora a hand, but could not take her gaze from Black Hat a few paces away, who bent to whisper in the thief's ear.

It was pure instinct to listen on the mental realm.

"Not these people. They have nothing," Black Hat said into the terrified thief's ear. "If you have to steal, take it from someone who can afford it."

"And get brained by bodyguards?" the thief retorted. He was skinny, ragged.

"Not Marsael House," Black Hat replied. "South side. Upper windows. Next to the oak."

"Clear the way!" a voice of authority bawled from the other direction—the guards had regained control of their horses, and the man cracked his whip over the heads of the crowd. "Clear the way or the next will take out your eye!"

Black Hat let go of the thief, who backed away, eyes wide—leaving the two purses he'd taken in Black Hat's hand. The victims burst through the onlookers, and the young man tossed the worn, flat purses to them, then swung back into the saddle, eyes searching the crowd for that brief impression he'd gathered: slim as a candle flame, moving with the distinctive walk of someone trained in weapons, the annoying flicker of stage-magic about her face. Making herself look younger? No, that body was already young, and he frowned, though instinct insisted it wasn't *Her* in some guise.

There she was. She raised her head and their gazes met.

Liere's breath caught.

Lyren-Sartora watched the boy, who sighed loudly as the robbed people clutched their purses close and vanished into the crowd almost as fast as the thief had. She noticed that Liere had stilled, though the crowd pushed around them, try-ing to get away from the guards forcing their way toward them. Lyren-Sartora tugged on Liere's arm. "We better move!"

Liere didn't hear. Between one heartbeat and the next the world narrowed to that hazel gaze locked onto hers.

Every nerve shocked into sun-brightness.

Generously curved lips grinned, bracketed by deep dimples to either side. The young man lifted a hand in casual salute, and turned the horse away, long straw-yellow hair under the black hat flapping on his back.

He vanished up an alley on the opposite side of the street as the guards rode up, scattering people right and left. Most of the crowd had melted away; with the purses restored to their owners, the crowd's intent had swung abruptly, uniting against the guards. They began to disperse in all directions, hiding weapons inside vests and robes or under shirts, but a few lingered with arms crossed, watching the guards with stony expressions as one guard shouted, "Where's the thief? Speak up, rabble, or we'll take you all in as conspirators!"

Lyren-Sartora and Liere backed under the awning of a saddlery, Lyren-Sartora watching the crowd, and Liere the after-image: long corn-yellow hair framing a bony face under that hat, white shirt, threadbare long black vest sashed with sun-faded green, riding trousers, battered riding boots. His clothes were as worn as those of the crowd around them, the only anomaly a diamond in one ear. He wore a sword on a baldric, knife hilts winking in the tops of the boots.

More guards in blue battle tunics rode up, waving sabers and halberds. "Break up! Go about your business!"

"I think he saw me," Liere said softly.

"Who?" Lyren-Sartora blinked. "And we're standing right here."

Liere meant that he'd seen past her illusion, but she wasn't certain about that, or about anything, except the unsettling sense that she had stepped onto a path to find it giving way, leaving her tumbling mid-air.

She reached for sense. That wasn't a contact on the mental plane. In fact, it was the exact opposite: he'd had a rigid mind-shield. The only person in the entire crowd — the entire city — whose mind was shielded. *Elsarion*, the boy riding behind him had shouted. Wasn't that the name of the former royal family?

"Come on. I don't want to be here if they start swinging those sticks around." Lyren-Sartora tugged Liere's arm.

And while Lyren-Sartora led the way and Liere blindly followed, three streets away, Andri Malcolin Elsarion flicked a look at one of his followers. "Bran," he said. "Follow the two foreigners. See where they go."

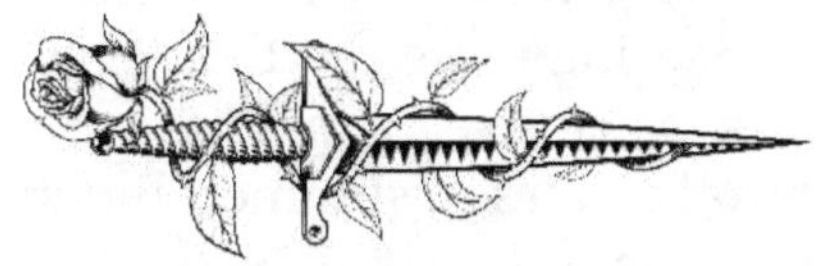

TWELVE

For the first time in Talian Ariath's life, the established order she had taken for granted . . . wasn't.

The only thing the count said to Talian about the regency council's resistance to the king's proclamations was a mild drawl at the end of breakfast several days after the king went missing, "I find the vulgarity of the lower orders distressing. Wearing red roses during the hours of trade! As if anyone wished for their uninformed opinions. If nothing else this discreditable display proves that Colend will only exist in peaceful community when we expel the gossip-mongers and quiet their lies."

"Gossip-mongers." That was the term that Talian had grown up with, though she had seen and despised the papers posted in windows by certain booksellers early each morning at the Hour of the Bird, called "chirps." She'd avoided them, for how could those of lower rank get true facts about court except third-hand? The truth of Colend's important people was properly and formally propagated at the Hour of Stone by heralds, and less formally at other times through trusted channels.

But many in court were talking behind fans about these chirps, as well as wearing roses, or rose color. These the count derided, yet she said nothing about the teal-hued lily theme at the ball the Duchas of Altan threw for the court, or the blue-green lily decorations on the barges for the Ranflars' wedding celebration a couple days later. And she always wore at least one cyan-shaded robe, or embroidered lilies, cyan ribbons, or all three.

But Talian was beginning to see red everywhere. It *couldn't* be spreading! She was simply more aware of such a vulgar, obvious color. And yet Talian couldn't quite convince herself she wasn't seeing more red than cyan. At least not in court, which was of course of primary importance. Most nobles wore neutral shades in summer. But among the lower orders, red had become the fashion: public transport barge polers wore embroidered roses on their hats, red ribbons instead of cyan had been worked into window displays, and even bakeries (especially those located across from the booksellers who posted the chirp papers) served pastries with tiny twists of red icing that everyone knew represented rosebuds, symbols of renewal.

Or, welcoming a new king.

It seemed to be understood by everyone, from the youngest garden weeder to the furious Duchas of Altan that violence (which everyone knew denied melende) would only achieve moral superiority for the other side.

"The Duchas of Altan looks toward Thorn Gate," Talian observed to her mother—feeling very grown up at using the old symbol instead of unrefined statement. The word *anger* was nearly as uncouth as the word *no*.

"What I observe," the count corrected in her smoothly modulated lilt, after a long enough pause that the entire carillon of the Hour of the Deer had rung, "is his contemplation of Silver Willow." The slight emphasis on Silver was a reproach. Why? Everyone knew that the Gate of Silver Willow symbolized not just mourning or regret but *disappointment*, and the silver implied unassailable moral superiority.

The count wiped her fingers delicately, as if wiping away an inapt subject, then said in her council voice, "It grieves us all to observe pusillanimous tendencies in our young king." She indicated herself and Talian with a well-considered, gracious gesture that meant privacy.

But this conversation wasn't private. That is, her mother was repeating what the council was saying to everyone, in various ways. Talian understood then that she was being *managed*, as the council managed court. Her mother had taught her this precept, that for peace and order, court and Colend needed to hear only what the council thought best, after due consideration. For the first time in her life, Talian tested the idea that what the council thought best might be a separate thing from the truth. If so, what was the truth?

Her mother went on, "The Duchas of Altan and Honor Donais have put themselves to considerable hardship by sending their runners to locate the king and assure his safety."

Talian opened her fan in acceptance. "I understood the king was going to Sartor . . ." She let the sentence drift, her eyes downcast.

"So we were informed. If the folderol from that noisome scribe can be trusted. He certainly cannot. No one can find him to question more closely about the king's whereabouts and safety. Very suspicious." The skin under her mother's eyes tightened and Talian began to suspect her veneer of complacent conviction. Then her voice smoothed again to the musical court cadence. "One might applaud our king's desire to establish him-self among his royal peers, but alas, not in such a way that brings little credit to Colend. Our ambassador was as astonished as we."

Talian remembered that the ambassador to Sartor was an old relation of the Duchas of Gaszin.

The count's fingers gestured Rue. "Honor Gaszin ought to have been approached first, to handle the communication between the Sartoran queen and ourselves, especially in so historic an occasion. Our king — well-intentioned as he is — truly requires our guidance."

Our guidance, not *my* guidance; Talian suspected that her mother had tried, and failed, to gain leadership over the council. They were still poised in a mutually dis-trusting balance, united by the conviction that to disband would lead to a disaster not to be contemplated.

Talian bowed in the peace, because her mother's tone made it clear that this subject, too, was ended, now that she had had her final say. Though Talian was left with even more questions. She went off to get dressed, venting her frustration by rejecting all the clothes her maid offered.

"Pure silk in this heat will kill me." A sharp sigh. "Moth-gauze is still *silk,* and three layers of that will be stifling. Those trousers are wrinkled. Green is vulgar — I've seen merchants wearing aprons in that shade. Bring me something . . . eggshell blue."

The silent maid went away with armfuls of floating fabrics, and Talian shut her eyes. Blue, the royal color, though of course no one wore the royal shade of pure, celestial blue. But light blue was comforting. It was her color, the next thing to a royal color. If she was expected to become queen someday, then the regency council ought to be including *her*, too, by telling her the truth. And not managing her, as they did the rest of the kingdom.

And the king.

That thought was so startling that she retreated to the chamber of blossoms under the pretext of a headache, and as she breathed essence of lavender and citrus, she considered the question.

First, who now comprised *they*? The Elder Duchas of Desentis no longer attended council meetings, nor did the Duchas of Alarcansa. Talian's mother had said the first was delicate in health, no surprise at her age, and about the second she had flicked her fingers in the shadow-ward while saying, "Perhaps he feels the need to attend to his duchy."

If her mother's hints were true, someone was using the king to make a power play. This mysterious conspiracy might even be keeping him prisoner somewhere. If Honor Donais really had sent out all the herald-guards to find the king, what if he didn't want to come back? That sounded deliciously sinister.

But what if there were another truth? Talian had discovered by careful listening that Honor Marith Desentis, commander of the border riders, had not acknowledged the council's orders to search, find, and secure the king. Apparently she was in some obscure area between Colend and Locan Jara, out of reach of communications. Considered as a lone fact, it wasn't significant. But when you put that together with the elder duchas no longer attending council gatherings for the first time ever — the duchas and his latest consort staying in Desentis, and his son Nashande riding around somewhere in Colend at the height of the court season . . . The entire Desentis family appeared to be elsewhere.

That was odd.

She was still mulling these questions when Nashande Desentis unexpectedly showed up at a minor poetry reading.

Talian had almost sent her regret: the family was of minor importance, and poetry readings were not fashionable these days. But there was Nashande, dressed in layers of gray with a single layer of dark red, visible at the front, cuffs, and hem beneath his over-robe, and a single hairpin of silver, the only ornament a ruby. The ruby of roses? Impossible. Nashande was as empty-headed as he was handsome.

Before they'd gotten through the first round of poems, the Duchas of Gaszin showed up, then the Duchas of Altan in company with Talian's mother, both wearing overrobes embroidered with cyan lilies of a stylishly dark shade. Talian knew her mother had not intended to come, so word had to have spread fast. Why?

They sat there applauding lightly as an old courtier recited yet another dull paean to Martande Lirendi, the first king of Colend. It wasn't until the poem was over, and Talian was startled out of her reverie by the light tap of fans in approbation, that she began to perceive she had missed some kind of signal. Something in the poem, judging by the looks she caught between the Duchas of Altan and her mother—and the flash of light along her mother's jewels, that meant stiffened posture—had perturbed them.

She sighed. No guessing now. Instead, she eyed Nashande. Back when they were all court children together, Nashande cheerfully did anything anyone asked, especially by his royal second-cousin. Talian decided that she and her old playmate were going to have a chat.

But she wasn't the only one with the same intent. In the break for refreshments, the nobles made their way to Nashande's side. Talian listened from behind her mother's straight, silk-covered back as Nashande said, "I don't know where my cousin is. I've been riding cross country, training my new racers." And he went on to describe each of these new animals in tedious detail until the poetry reading resumed.

The guests sat down again, but afterward, it was more of the same, to which Nashande returned the same answers. Sometimes the same words. Stolidly, without the puzzlement that Talian remembered when they were young and certain others would talk past him, or play pranks that left him bewildered—though only when Shontande was absent.

So much repetition convinced Talian that Nashande had rehearsed those words. Which meant he had prepared to be questioned, even though he'd left Alsais at least a week before the king went missing. The older people seemed to accept his answers, but they didn't know Nashande the way she did.

The next day, at the Hour of the Wheel, Nashande turned

up for the garland hunt, wearing peach and chestnut, simple sporting pins holding his hair. No meaning in any of that. He always came to events that had to do with riding. He was so very predictable. Ever since they'd reached the age of interest, Nashande had flirted with all the girls, Talian the most. Not that it mattered. Her goal was royal blue. But Nashande didn't need to know that right now.

During the ride, she let Nashande catch up to her, and when he looked over at her, she smiled. He smiled back, blushing, and her smile increased to real mirth, though he did not know the cause. He only felt the effect.

He was thinking, *at last*, for he liked her best of all the girls. She rode very well—she did everything well. He smiled to see her finally smiling at him.

And she was thinking, *This is going to be easy.*

Shiovhan, capital of Enaeran

After another night in a stifling room, and another day wandering about, Lyren-Sartora was showing signs of restlessness. The shadows began to lengthen as Liere and Lyren-Sartora climbed the ridge.

Liere was learning that if Lyren-Sartora asked a question, she listened intently to the answer, however long it might be. But if Liere made any observation that could be conceivably regarded as lecturing, Lyren-Sartora twitched impatiently and changed the subject as soon as she could.

Liere reminded herself that she'd abrogated her rights as parental authority when she left for Geth. Lyren-Sartora had many more competent parental figures in her life. She had early reached that age of wanting independence: it was only the young who held their youth cheap, declaring things like, "I'm very mature for my age," and "People think I'm a lot older than I am," in a tone of self-gratification that she had never heard in any adult.

Liere noticed that Lyren-Sartora's attention stayed on a cluster of excited youngsters more or less her age as they followed a pair of loudly dressed teens toward one of those plinth-marked squares up ahead. When Lyren-Sartora exclaimed, "Liere, I think they're going to fight a duel!" Liere only nodded, rather than admit she had no interest in duels. She welcomed the chance to catch her breath. Though the daylight had begun to fade the heat was still stunning, and her shoulder throbbed; she still hadn't regained her strength. On Geth she had run all the way up steeper climbs than this ridge, after a strenuous day of work.

Lyren-Sartora was watching intently as the teenage boy and girl swaggered into the plinth-marked square. They loosened their weapons, the feathers in their broad-brimmed hats floating and bobbing. Lyren-Sartora listened to the watching youngsters shouting the names of their favorite. Liere noticed that other teens had taken up positions at either end of the adjoining streets, watching outward as most of the older folks in the market square carried on their business.

A woman carrying two heavy baskets paused, yelling, "If you pinch-brashes bring the snouts gowping on us, I'll break your pissy sticks m'self."

The teenage boy made a loud fart noise, and the girl mockingly saluted the woman, who stamped on by, the fabric flowers on her hat jiggling at every step as she muttered under her breath. Meanwhile, a ring of spectators, mostly teen and younger, had gathered to watch.

The teens squared up to one another, and began circling, feinting, attack and withdraw. Lyren-Sartora clasped her hands, her avid attention on the crowd as well as the duelists. Liere watched a few passes, observations streaming: the two were reasonably trained, but not well, too busy trying for flourishing than for finesse; they wanted to win, but the drive was not hatred, as a part of their attention was on their audience.

Wider observations: the old plinths, mossy on the sides that got less sun. Dueling square markers? She recollected that in some areas the plinths had been level-ed to the ground. This fact, plus the young guards doing sentry duty at the street corners and the threat by the basket woman, indicated that dueling was now forbidden.

Liere turned back to the duelists. The girl probably had a couple years on the boy, though he was taller, and her skill was somewhat better. Both were breathing like bellows; she saw three openings for a deadly strike, which either they didn't see or wouldn't take, then in a quick feint-and-bind the girl caused the boy to stumble, his blade swinging wildly, and she poked him in the butt.

He whirled, yelping an outraged, "Ow!"

"I'm satisfied," she declared, and turned her back.

"I'm not, you muck-sucking—"

"You," she cut in scornfully, "challenged *me*." And she turned to the cluster of youths watching. "I won, right? First blood?"

"Show us your butt, Chass," one of the watchers hooted, to general laughter.

As the boy slunk away, limping and cursing loudly, Liere watched the crowd break up, a familiar face slipping away in the opposite direction.

She recognized him from the foiled theft the day previous: brown of hair and skin, a cowlick at his right temple, snub nose. The sentry at the street saluted him with a casual wave. They knew one another.

"That was fun! I *hoped* she'd win. She has a much better hat, and she was funny. He was just loud." Then, in a fretful tone, "It's late, and I'm hot, thirsty, and tired of walking. Let's find a place to stay." Lyren-Sartora tugged Liere toward a promising inn on a broad street along which many of those riders in midnight blue patrolled alertly.

Liere tested her ability with the Enaeran language while getting a room. This place was an improvement in that they were able to get two beds—though they were narrow, the mattresses again stuffed with straw.

Liere and Lyren-Sartora descended the worn stairs into the trapped heat of the main room. The area outside was roofed, and marginally cooler in the slow-moving breeze. The girls squeezed at a corner table meant for one. A hot meal sounded terrible, so they ordered bread-and-cheese with greens. At least this place's cellar lay under a cold storage spell of some sort, for the cider was wonderfully chilled.

Lyren-Sartora turned her attention to the people around her, as Liere listened on the mental plane for signs of Norsunder, though she remembered Black Hat's mind-shield. And his eyes.

Lyren-Sartora sighed. No one her age was around, except for a couple of ragged beggars. That meant all the other young people were busy, either as apprentices or some other training. She didn't want Liere nagging about that, so she listened to the adult conversations while Liere sat there, her eyes distant.

When the innkeeper trod heavily to their table to remove their empty cups with a clatter in a not-so-subtle hint to free up the table, Liere blinked.

Lyren-Sartora poked her. "Did you hear what the people behind us were saying? About Adon-Marsael Elsarion?"

"No. What?"

"Some think he's going to be the new king, and others hate him, and think he's worse than the old king. Tomorrow morning he holds open court. Anyone can come, anyone at all. That crabby woman sitting behind you was going on and on about it to those other two people. You didn't hear her?"

"I was listening here." Liere touched her brow.

"To what, if you didn't hear her?"

"For Norsunder."

"I could have told you there isn't a whiff of their stench."

Liere looked down at her hands, and sidestepped the matter of Black Hat. "The language. I like to learn languages, and not be dependent on the Universal Language Spell, which so often has gaps, and never truly keeps up with idiom. I listen for rhythm and so on."

"Oh." Lyren-Sartora mentally shrugged; that was typical Liere. Why not depend on the Universal Language Spell? That's what it was there for, right? "Well, why don't we go see this Adon-Marsael Elsarion? We're supposed to be envoys, and it sounds like he's the government."

Liere stiffened. Listening on the mental plane was somewhat like drifting through fireflies winking in patterns, until a brilliant golden light lanced across the firmament. Toward her. But when she reached, it vanished — shut tight — portcullis slammed. All in less than a heartbeat.

"Liere?"

Liere forced herself into physical awareness. Noise, heat, the impatient landlord hovering with customers lining up at the door, waiting for tables. "All right."

They left. At the tavern across the way someone was hanging out paper lanterns as musicians gathered, plucking and tooting to ready their instruments. Lyren-Sartora pressed into the circle to listen as Liere fell into reverie, subliminally aware of the music, wild and aban-doned, mournful and longing. Memory evoked images: Dak, tender and tentative, her first trembling essay beyond what had been until then a locked door . . . Lyal's beautiful dark eyes, his silky hair as he bent over her, close as a kiss, then drove his knife into her shoulder.

She pressed her fingers against the healing wound and swayed, alone in her own world until the music stopped at last, and there was Lyren-Sartora, eyes drooping.

"Let's sleep," she said, yawning. "I danced so much my feet hurt!"

"All right," Liere said.

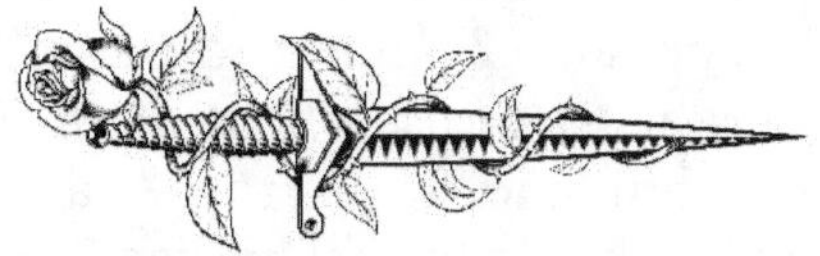

THIRTEEN

When Enaeran's younger generation of nobles were children, before civil war smashed the royal court both figuratively and literally, Martande Eldias's peers had teased him for his pretentious Colendi first name — handed down from his grandfather, whose mother had been Colendi. It didn't help that the principal part of his family was Adrani, or that he was small and skinny, with doe eyes that all the old people thought were so adorable, and said so before the disgusted ears of their progeny.

He learned early not to show any reaction at the shrill, derisive "Mar-r-r-TAUN-dah!" — mangling his name with the hard "r" instead of the light Colendi trill, and grunting that "ah" at the end instead of the breathy "eh." He'd hated that, and he'd hated court, preferring to hide in the royal archive reading whenever Andri wasn't there to fend off his tormentors. Or he lurked in the kitchen, fascinated by the process of turning dusty vegetables or dully glistening fish into delicious food. It was Andri who had shortened his name to Marten, animal nicknames being common and acceptable.

This was life until the night many noble families woke to the crashing of mobs into their ancestral houses, the roar of flames, and the shocking discovery of dead parents surrounded by dead private guards. That is, in the houses where the private guards hadn't led the attack.

The latter situation was most common among the worst bullies Marten had had to endure, and when afterward Marten observed the angry ghosts of those courtiers drifting around the ruins, including those of his own parents (who had been indifferent to him in life), he began to contemplate the effect of spoken as well as hidden anger, and how it spread from one to another.

He still hadn't come to any definite conclusions, because though many of his worst tormentors had been the younger siblings of bullies or came from horrid parents, not all were. For example, there was Andri, whose older sister had been carelessly mean to him and whose royal parents were hated by many. Andri had always fought bullies, even when he was a weed not much bigger than Marten, like his friend Gared (son of the Master of Horse), in training to be a royal bodyguard. Until Andri was imprisoned by his royal father, he had done his best to protect Marten. Gared was the oldest of them all by a couple of years—perhaps it was his influence that kept Andri from being like his parents? How did influence work? Marten could not remember ever *choosing* to let someone influence him.

Marten had prowled early that morning for greens less withered than usual when Bran turned up in the tiny, cluttered courtyard below. "Marten, Gared's not back yet from martial arts drill upriver. Andri needs you to take a look at some foreigners."

It was Andri's order that they offer a meal once a day for everybody who turned up. Marten had to admit that the gatherings seemed to bind Andri's disparate friends and followers together in a way that mere words wouldn't, though perhaps it was only simple hunger. He set aside his basket, picked up his hat, and clambered down the ivy-covered trellis next to the window.

They slipped between the much-patched buildings of their hideout and into the already shimmering heat of the streets. "Foreigners?" he asked. "Why foreigners?"

Bran lifted a shoulder, tipping his dashing curly-brimmed hat slightly to ward reflections of the sun from the windows they passed. Marten pressed his more modest hat on his head, and smiled at the watchers at windows and roofs as they left their turf and crossed into the mercantile borough. Bran watched for danger. Marten noted which ghosts lingered, and where. It was always odd when living people walked right through them. Some ghosts seemed to be aware of that, and others not.

Bran began using alleys and side streets as the city guard was out, as usual, and the Marsael private guards among them might recognize Marten. They slowed at a corner, where

Bran's sister Elies waited, hefting a cloth-covered basket full of fresh-baked rolls from the fragrant smell. She flicked a glance at a pair of girls walking toward the royal road. "They just left their inn."

Marten turned his attention to the two who stood out not just because their clothes were different, but the older one by her walk, and—he sighed. "I was trying to figure out a different way to cook tomatoes. You interrupted that just to make me toil through the heat to look at a new flirt?"

Andri drifted up to join them, wearing a green hat patched with gray pulled low over his face. The hat looked like a horse had stomped it. All three cast looks around for signs of guards or lurking spies.

"New flirt?" Bran repeated doubtfully.

"What?" Andri asked. His gaze shifted, and Marten sensed sharp interest beneath his easy tone when Andri said, "The older one. No weapon, but the way she walks. And she had magic on her to hide her face."

"You mean she's even uglier than that?" Bran asked, eyes wide.

"Opposite," Andri said.

Everyone knew how to blink away the illusion magic store keepers used to lure custom, as well as the illusions players employed on the otherwise bare stage. They blinked away the blur around the elder girl's face, then Bran and Elies gasped. Marten whistled softly.

Then Elies sighed. "Andri, how many flirts have you already got? Why are *we* following another one? *You* can do that!"

"It's something else," Andri began, and when three pairs of eyes turned his way, he knew he was treading dangerous ground. He had to protect them all from *Her*. So he sidestepped the real question and offered a reasonable alternative. "Wondered if she was going to walk into a Challenge Square."

"Now that duels are illegal?" Bran asked with a skeptical eye-roll.

Marten was silent, aware by subtle hints of glance and tone that Andri was being evasive. The deposed prince had always talked freely until right before the series of murders he had been blamed for, every one of the victims someone he knew, or had visited recently. When those happened, he stopped talking for a while—even disappeared. When he came back, he was quieter, tense, wary, and he rarely stayed with them anymore, though it was he who had chosen their main hideout. And there were times when he turned up moving as if he'd been in some kind of fight, though there were no cuts or bruises evident.

Like last night. Marten glanced under the hat, noting the bruised shadows under Andri's eyes. He always looked like that after one of his disappearances.

All four watched the foreigners vanish into the crowd.

"She's definitely got the walk of a warrior," Bran commented. "Made it easier to follow her."

"More like a dancer," Elies said, hand shading her eyes.

"She's trained," Andri murmured. "I wonder how much. Who by. And why she's here, disguising herself with magic to make herself look chinless and flat-nosed."

"She's looking for someone, I'd say." Elies gave a sharp nod.

"Looking for trouble?" Bran asked, more to get some kind of reaction from Andri.

Andri said nothing.

Marten broke the silence. "I only caught that one glimpse before they turned the corner, but I believe their eyes are the same shade as well as the same shape. I would venture a guess they are related."

Bran rolled his eyes. Who cared if possible trouble was related or not? But he liked Marten, even if he was a bit like a cat, sometimes staring at things no one else saw, so he stayed silent.

"And there they go toward the royal road." Andri rubbed his jaw. Then flicked a questioning glance at Elies. "Mind taking over?"

"Someone else will have to take my turn helping at cook duty." Elies gloated openly—they all knew nobody but Marten liked to cook, but Andri would not let them dump all the cooking chores onto amiable Marten. Especially when Andri needed him for spying: Marten drifted between the court and the city worlds without being noticed, and he saw everything.

Andri eyed Marten. "You cooked the last two days."

"I really don't mind," Marten said. There was no use explaining that chopping, scraping, and cooking food, its textures and aromas, were all so very reassuringly real. Especially on days when the ghosts were as bright as the living and he had trouble discerning which was which.

Marten held out his hand. "I'll make pies. Easy. Won't need help. Is that basket for us?" The scent of fresh-baked rolls made his mouth water, and he recollected he had not eaten breakfast. "Is there any flour?" he added, thinking of the aromatic sweet-basil he'd liberated from the palace kitchen garden. That would be splendid in a cheese and tomato pie.

"Devea traded a pot for a bag of flour this morning," Elies said. "And of course we've tomatoes."

"We always have tomatoes," Bran muttered; their vines had produced like mad, this time of year, and the results went bad fast in the heat, so whatever the cooks made got stretched out with tomatoes.

"There's a little wine left over," Marten said. "And I found some herbs."

Andri said to Elies, "If that pair goes to the open court, I want to know everything."

"All right." Elies handed the basket to Marten. "Do you want to me keep a distance?"

"Yes. No. If they spot you, be friendly. Helpful. Suggest Genda's at Brydon. And anything else you can learn without raising suspicion."

"Got it," Elies said. "And Genda could use the trade." She took off in the wake of her quarry.

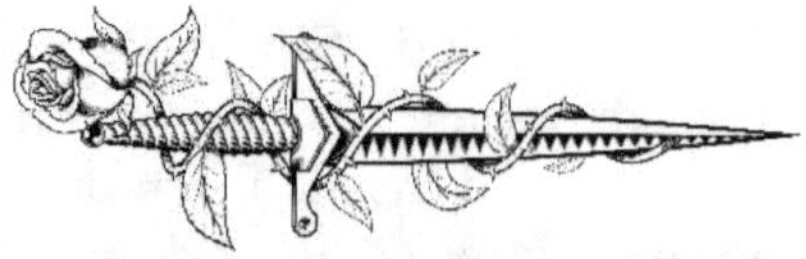

FOURTEEN

Liere and Lyren-Sartora had started up the last of the switchbacks zigzagging up to the top of the ridge. As Lyren-Sartora walked, she noticed Liere glancing at angled windows. Lyren-Sartora did as well, at intervals of fifty steps apiece, and each time the crowd was different except for a young woman wearing a green bodice and dashing wide-legged trousers gathered at the ankle.

"I think we're being followed," she said to Liere in Sartoran.

"Yes. Have been. Since yesterday. This is a new person." A glance of respect. "Siamis taught you to be observant about such things?"

"Well, it was Mac, actually." Though David had trained him. But Mac was the one Lyren-Sartora had listened to.

Liere gave her a distracted smile as she noted a party of armed guards overseeing some glum workers with heavy rock-breaking tools smashing plinths in a pretty patterned square surrounded by what appeared to be expensive shops.

Lyren-Sartora tried a mind-scan, hearing nothing but the scramble-jamble of multitudes of inner voices, and walking at the same time gave her vertigo. That and the heat were not a pleasant combination, so she closed her inner ear, saying, "You think we'll hear something about Norsunder from this maybe-king Adon-Marsael Elsarion?"

Liere opened her hands. "I don't know what to think."

"Well." Lyren-Sartora heaved a martyred sigh, and neither spoke until they topped the ridge at last, affording them a distant glimpse of the river below the falls. Then they turned up a grand, tree-line avenue, and began passing two story houses that overlooked the river, some still fine, others gutted and dark. "I just hope we're not being let in for a lot of boring speeches. If we are, Atan had better be grateful for the fine spy job."

The two hastily moved aside as a cavalcade of guards in blue battle tunics rode by, gear clattering. Lyren-Sartora veered and began walking under the shade of the intermittent trees, Liere with her. The curving avenue gave way onto a broad flagged street marked off with alternating statuary and potted flowering trees. As they turned onto the street, they spotted fountains plashing from elaborate statuary.

The flag-stoned street broadened, fountains frequent. The stones were patterned, but it was too crowded to see the patterns, only that they were well tended. The buildings beyond the statue-and-tree borders were three and four stories tall, the windows arched. The girls followed a sizable crowd past a statue of some king on a horse, now pitted and hacked, and beyond it, the border widened into a massive half-circle parade ground before the biggest palace either of them had ever seen.

The immense size recalled Senrid's royal castle to mind, built to house (or prison) numerous relatives, or clan leaders, plus their armed retainers. But this one was not a castle, in that it had tall, glassed windows, and instead of a sentry walk along the top, a slanted roof with dormer windows. It also featured gardens in all the courtyards (just visible through some of those larger archways), and a massive parade ground in front, with a patterned brick carriageway leading to the biggest arch, directly below a fancy balcony from which kings must have been giving out proclamations for centuries.

"If you can rule this palace, why bother with the rest of the country?" Lyren-Sartora asked with a laugh, staring around. "How many windows across the front, do you think? A hundred? And it looks as if there are even more wings out back! But a lot of those windows are smashed. It's going to take an entire army to fix them."

When Liere didn't respond, Lyren-Sartora glanced her way, and caught her frowning ahead, one hand rubbing up and down the other arm.

Liere was searching on the mental plane again. She knew she was becoming obsessive, but she argued with herself that scanning was part of her current mandate. That comet could be anyone. And even if it was the surviving Elsarion scion, that told her nothing about what kind of person he might be.

Lyren-Sartora poked her to get her moving, and they joined the shuffling, overheated crowd of petitioners and gawkers being funneled by armed stewards through tall carved doors, and down woven rice stalk mats over the patterned marble floors into a great hall lined at either side by pillars that supported long galleries above.

Of course a great crowd was already gathered, tightly packed and impossible to see past. They shuffled into a vaulted throne room with a gallery running around above, halfway between marble floor and high carved ceiling.

By standing on her tiptoes and bouncing, Liere glimpsed a dark-haired man seated on a dais at the other end, but she couldn't see much more than that. Lyren-Sartora saw even less. To either side pillars obscured discreet doors set into the walls at intervals. Aware of their shadow, and of the guardian stewards managing the crowd, she gave in to temptation, and nudged Lyren-Sartora: *See yon doors?*

Lyren-Sartora glanced out of the corner of her eyes: *Servant halls?*

: Shall we?

Liere backed up a step, and then took a step sideways, Lyren-Sartora—intrigued—following. Liere began marking the attention of their shadow, and each time her head turned, Liere took another side-step. The people crowding in around them pressed forward to fill the space. Side-step, back. Side-step, back. Side-step, back.

Ahead they heard the rise and fall of voices. Servants in subdued gray-blue livery and light gray caps stood along the pillars, but not all of these paid attention to the crowd; a few gossiped with one another, and a young fellow with a quantity of red hair brushed over his shoulders stared into space, blinking and yawning.

Liere selected the two whispering together. When she sensed the shadow's attention peering in another direction, she quickly cast an illusion, a semblance of the golden-white marble pillars and wall. Careful to make no noise—the illusion would only work as long as no one looked right at them—they scurried to the nearest door and slipped inside.

Liere banished the illusion, forgetting the one on her face as they ran up the empty stairway to a narrow hall. This ended at a landing with another door to the gallery. They slipped in and eased up next to the first pillar, directly above the chatting liveried guards. Now they could both see and hear. The dais was bare, fire scorching where a throne must have been. Adon-Marsael sat in an ordinary chair placed to one side of the dais, as if he wasn't quite ready to assume that royal spot.

Adon-Marsael was a tall, powerfully built man wearing a long, embroidered vest silver on pale blue silk, belted with linked gold in an overlapping leaf pattern, a fine shirt embroidered with matching pale blue, and contrasting blue trousers embroidered with silver, his manner very much that of the noble. His complexion was dark, his glossy long hair blue-black. He had a strongly marked nose, and a generous, curving mouth that was immediately familiar in its cut. Oh. Of course. The laughing young Black Hat, who Liere was fairly certain was Prince Andri Elsarion.

". . . of course I regret the continuation of the fighting." His voice was low, his drawl courtly.

The girls stared down at Adon-Marsael. Ostensibly he was speaking to a matronly woman obviously wearing her best summer robe, who, by her stance, was the current petitioner, but the lift of his head, the pitch of his voice, was meant for as much of the group as could hear.

"And you are not alone in mourning friends and family. But until Sles Adran agrees to restore the natural borders, I fear that people along the borderland will continue to raid, and the Adrani will then punish us with reprisals."

"You can stop it!"

"With what? All of my late cousin's commanders are dead, and as I said previously, the army is largely run now by its own field appointees. Brave they no doubt are, and fiercely loyal to Enaeran, but as yet few will accept orders outside their own friends with whom they trained. I am endeavoring to reestablish the chain of command."

He ended on a weary note, conveying the sense that he'd said this before, many times. The woman fidgeted with the cuff of her sleeve, and when Adon-Marsael brought his fine-cut chin down in a smiling but definite dismissal, she dropped a quick, awkward curtsey, and vanished back into the crowd.

People clamored to be next, but when they tried to push forward, the blue-liveried guards kept them back until Adon-Marsael gestured toward a tall, grizzle-haired man. "Have you any recent reports on the fighting up round Ovaish?" the man asked.

The reply was detailed, and incomprehensible to Liere and Lyren-Sartora. Liere studied the huge midnight blue banner hanging above the empty throne space. The banner featured a gold crown made of three stylized lilies worked into the center—the same device seen on the tabards of the patrol captains riding about the city.

The petitioner backed away, and the crowd began jostling to be picked next when a voice echoed through the vast room, "When are you crowning yourself king? And after that, when come the triple taxes that ruined *your* land?"

The voice cracked on the last word; it came from the gallery across from the girls. They spotted a skinny boy of sixteen or seventeen sitting on the edge of the marble balcony, swinging bare feet over the long drop. Ancient murals of kings and heroes framed his tousled head, and above those, the carved and gilded wooden ceiling.

Lyren-Sartora watched the boy, but Liere transferred her gaze back to Adon-Marsael. One well-manicured hand gestured very slightly. Two of the liveried guards—these ones with the bearing of trained warriors—bowed and vanished through the door to the stairway on the opposite side of the throne room.

"War with the Adranis ruined my land," Adon-Marsael said to the crowd, his voice pleasant and humorous, "as it has far too many others'. As for the taxes, which I no longer collect, what remains of my treasury pays the guardians' salaries—until it runs out."

Voices murmured at this.

"You might say I am paying for what peace we have left. What are you paying for, my anonymous young friend who apparently is too superior to wait in line like everyone else?"

He was definitely speaking to the crowd by then, as halfway through this melodious, even-tempered speech, the boy flipped his feet around, and ducked through a door a heartbeat before a host of guards streamed out of another door and spread along the gallery. They split up and began trying all the doors.

Below, the interviews went on, most of them personal, about people or places that meant nothing to the girls, until distant bells caused a restless shifting and susurrus of murmurs through the crowd.

"I believe we are finished for the day," Adon-Marsael said in a tone of regret. "The rest of you, leave your petitions with the scribes."

The liveried stewards began firmly to urge the angry, muttering crowd back as three young scribes brought out small writing tables, paper, pens, and ink. Adon-Marsael rose, nodded politely, and took his leave through a side door beyond the line of liveried guards. Some petitioners lined up to talk to the weary-looking scribes. Others turned around and began shuffle out again, everyone talking.

"Scribes, tchah! I know what happens to those petitions — straight into the fire."

"My uncle says, you give your name, and next thing you know, the snouts knock on your door and it's off to the mines."

"Or the fighting!"

"What's the use of . . ."

"My brother told me . . ."

". . . triple taxes . . ."

Liere said, "Let's move before the searchers decide to look on this side."

Liere and Lyren-Sartora tried their service door, and hearing another set of voices below, they veered and ran up another, narrower flight of stairs, which gave onto a hallway. Double doors stood open to a vast empty room with a beautifully patterned ceiling mural. Sunbeams slanting in through round windows bathed marble pilasters in muted tones of gold, lighting lazy dust motes to pinpoints of fire, and illuminating tapestries depicting heroic faces and situations.

"I love royal courts," Lyren-Sartora sighed, twirling around. "Everything about rulers and courts is so *fascinating!*"

"Because?" Liere prompted.

Lyren-Sartora turned around again, the light touching her golden eyes. "Because of the art, because one person can effect changes for so many others. What makes the others go right along with it? How — when — does a person get that whatever-it-is that makes others follow?"

"You love power?" Liere asked, smiling at that ardent face.

"Nope." Lyren-Sartora wrinkled her nose. "I just want to know how it works. Like, how does Detsie get everyone to do things his way? I used to think it was by killing everybody who dared to say no, but Mac and the others all scorned me. And it's true, they aren't dead." She sighed. "Of course I still loathe, despise, and detest him," she added quickly, lest her interest be misinterpreted.

Liere smothered the urge to laugh. "Of course. Detlev wouldn't have it any other way."

Lyren-Sartora sniffed. "You can stop making fun of me any time."

Liere smothered a laugh as they left, and found another set of very high, ornate doors. One opened onto a library. Next, a very formal parlor, all in rose marble and gilt furniture. Then a smallish ballroom also made of white-gold marble, with gold and blue arabesques around the fine carved wood of the ceiling.

On and on, all empty, even of servants. The place was enormous, and a lot of the rooms down one wing showed fire scorching and looting damage; these rooms were not only vacant of people but of furniture. When they came across one that contained not just the nasty smell of old fire but brownish stains and smears, they retreated.

"I'm surprised no one's cleaned that up," Lyren-Sartora said, casting a troubled glance back.

Liere whispered, "Maybe it's left that way on purpose."

While they were taking their tour upstairs, Elies ran back and forth in the brilliant mid-afternoon heat, furious with herself as she scanned each of the hot, tired people who emerged slowly from the throne room. How could she have lost those two? She and Bran were the best at shadowing!

Her only consolation was that the foreigners would have to come out the way they'd gone in: every other entrance and exit had a pair of heavily armed snouts—Marsael private guards—dressed in the dark blue of the old guard.

Ah! There they were.

Elies saw them at the same moment Liere saw her. Their shadow's face changed from relief to a forced friendliness; Liere did a quick scan, sensed no harmful intent, so she scrupulously kept herself from delving further, and waited as the erstwhile shadow approached them. "I can't help noticing foreign garb. We don't get many visitors in Enaeran. Do you have family here? Or do you need a guide?"

"We're traveling," Liere said, testing her ability with this new language.

"Oh? Where from?"

"Different places," Liere said, forestalling Lyren-Sartora about to say, *Sartor.*

Lyren-Sartora shot Liere a puzzled glance as Elies said eagerly, "Oh! Well, if you're staying, I ought to warn you against sleeping out tonight. There's thunder in the air. And you better not try along the river. The dockers take a stick to interlopers."

Liere sensed her question, and answered it. "We have coin."

"Oh! In *that* case, my aunt's sister used to be in service here in Brydon, and she and some of the old staff rent out the staff wing, not far from here. It's cheap, and it's almost as good as staying in the royal wings with the nobs! The front windows overlook part of the city, and the back balcony gives you a great view of a part of the royal gardens, where they used to hold balls. In fact, I hear that there might be one tonight."

Lyren-Sartora turned expectantly to Liere, who hesitated, tempted to send a mental tendril, but knowing she ought not.

Elies, misinterpreting her hesitation, said, "It's cheap. Not much travel anymore, what with all the trouble." She lowered her voice. "They could use the trade." She added, "And you'd get your own bed. Which is better than I can say for some of the places on the south side o'town, away from the river."

Lyren-Sartora had listened with growing impatience. She understood that Liere was being cautious in her answers, but really, how much danger could there possibly be? Flashing an impatient glance Liere's way, she said, "The friend who recommended we visit said people were nice. Especially a boy named Jaydi, who told her all about the city, she said."

Elies's mouth rounded. "Oh," she said, and both Liere and Lyren-Sartora felt her recognition of the name: they caught a vivid mental image of the short boy riding behind Black Hat on the white and brown horse.

"I'm Elies. I'll show you the way," she said brightly, and led them through a neglected garden to a plainer wing of the palace: made of the same sandy stone, no carved decoration, smaller windows, and a plain door. They entered a foyer with a counter, everything scrupulously clean.

Elies said to the older woman behind the counter, "New custom for Genda," and she, too, faded back.

Liere paid for a room with two beds. She was halfway up the stairs when there it was again, that sense of lightning striking on the mental plane, only there was no pain, just this intense awareness. Too ephemeral to be a contact—at once too powerful and too clumsy, and yet able to hide identity.

It left Liere intensely self-conscious, nerves sensitive to every shift in the air, a feeling that faded slowly as they reached a room on a long, plain corridor. It contained two narrow beds, and it overlooked a terraced garden with half an adjacent palace wing beyond, exactly as Elies had said.

Lyren-Sartora put hands on her hips. "I meant to ask where we can get a meal. I think I'll run down and ask."

Liere knew she was being told, not asked for per-mission. She smiled, and when the door closed, leaving her alone, she sat cross-legged on one of the beds, closed her eyes, and slipped into the mental plane to search for that odd contact. Because it had been reaching for *her*.

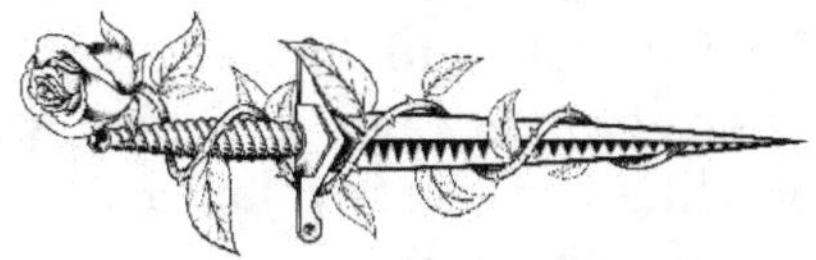

FIFTEEN

The sun had set behind the western mountains bordering Enaeran, leaving Shiovhan shadowed in the long blue twilight of summer, when Elies passed the last of the sentries watching from upper windows and tiredly slumped into the ramshackle row of houses that they had taken over as their headquarters.

The smell of sweet-basil and wine sauce floated through the much-patched walls, and she rejoiced that Marten was cooking. He was by far the best of them at it. Though they used an outdoor bake oven, even getting near it on days like this made her gasp for air.

Not surprisingly, she found nearly everyone gathered in the main room, sitting either on the floor, the cold hearth, or perched all over the sagging sofa that still smelled faintly of fire; some of the boys had pulled this and other furnishings out of a burned nobles' mansion. At a glance Elies saw that, true to her promise, Devea had managed to secure them a block of cheese.

Andri had clearly arrived shortly before she had, as usual via some torturous route that kept him from being seen by too many. "Elies," he said as Marten handed him a ceramic bowl covered with a plate. "What did you find?"

Marten said from the doorway, "Both of you. Eat first." He handed Elies another bowl. The tomato pie retained a bit of warmth, enough so that the melted cheese had not congealed. She wedged in beside Devea, who shifted one of her generous hips. Elies dug her spoon into the bowl, her mouth watering. Then she became aware of silence.

She looked up. Everyone was waiting. She dropped the spoon and sighed. "They seem to be travelers. But somebody sent them. Some girl — the small one said 'she' — and Jaydi's name."

Several of the older bows whistled and crowed. Jaydi, sitting along the far wall with his scrawny brother and a couple of the other younger boys and girls, scowled as Bassl hooted, "The girls like you already, Jaydi, and you don't even have anything to offer them. Woo, are *you* gonna be hot!"

Jaydi heard that tone in the elders' voices that meant kissy stuff, and scowled at the laughter. "You're all stupid," he yelled. "I don't even know who you mean. C'mon, Skinner."

Gangling fourteen-year-old Skinner got up and slunk on his younger brother's heels, as he always did, and Elies went on to report the very little she'd learned. She'd just finished saying, "And so I took them to Genda's," when a shrill voice cut through from the outer room:

"Vec's dyers got Gared trapped."

Andri was the first up, the others a heartbeat behind. They stampeded for the door, some pulling weapons still on them, others racing to fetch theirs.

Andri halted in the doorway, arms braced, feet apart. When everyone stopped, ramming into a pack, he said, "No wild mob. Gared taught us better than that!" He glanced at the skinny girl with short flyaway hair. "Fronsa. You lead. Bassl, you and Kizka take partners around to flank . . ." He issued orders — outlining a familiar drill that they had practiced many times.

They ran silently after Fronsa, who fled lightly down a moldering alley behind the equally moldering buildings that they had cobbled together into their primary HQ.

They flowed over two fences, across a street, and then shouts and clangs drew them into what had once been the dyers' guild square, weakly lit by the second story windows of weather-beaten, neglected buildings, with twilight fading unnoticed overhead.

Most of the younger members of Andri's gang paused to watch the amazing — and daunting — sight of Gared fighting off no fewer than six of the former apprentices that made up Vec's gang.

Elegant, handsome Bassl and scrawny, nervy Ratface, who had earlier been yelling insults from the throne room gallery, each charged the assailants at Gared's either side.

Andri took in the situation at a glance, as someone pointed at him and shouted, "It's him!"

"Get him!"

"He's worth—"

"*Now!*"

A rush of assailants from the shadows charged into the circle. Andri waded in, mostly using the flat of his blade and the knife hilt. He'd seen at a glance that Gared wasn't going for the kill, and his attackers were plainly trying to bring him down alive. The fight was hard and fast; exhilaration made Andri laugh, and he scarcely noticed blows as he whacked, kicked, and smacked his way toward the leader of this ambush.

He brought up sword and knife, and the big, hulking fellow slashed a wicked-sharp scythe at Andri.

Andri whipped up his sword in a block. Two clangs and clashes added to the noise, the scythe went flying. Andri's assailant backed to a wall, clutching his bloody hand as Andri whipped up his blade and held it across the fellow's neck.

"I warned you, Vec," Andri said.

"Hey, why are you even *here*," Vec snarled.

"I'm all over the city."

"This is between Gared and us."

"What hits him hits me," Andri said. "Hits us *all*. Why can't you see that keeping us divided makes the snouts' control easier? You're doing their work for 'em."

Whereupon the real issue came out, half a snarl and half a wail, "They got Nanthalin! They got Nanth, they dragged him away today, and now the shit-eating soul-suckers got *both* my brothers. Gared said, no more attacks on the snouts, back off, and we did, and we're gonna give 'em Gared in trade. Fair's fair!"

By now both sides were slowly lowering weapons, Vec's group aware of their leader pinned against the wall with a blade across his throat, one hand dripping blood, splat, splat, splat.

"They got 'em both, and now they're dead—" A tall, sharp-jawed prentice snarled.

"They're not dead," Andri stated, lifting his voice so everyone could hear—even the ones hiding on the wall, and both sides' sentries on the roof.

"How do you know?" This was a grim-faced girl of

maybe fifteen, arms crossed, body rigid with distrust.

"I don't. But I know the new orders," Andri said. "Fronsa heard 'em."

"That's right," Fronsa said, voice shrill with conviction. "I was *right there* at the snout-yard, watering the horses as I listened."

The dyers watched their leader. Vec didn't argue, just breathed hard, blinking rapidly against tears of fury and a sense of helplessness.

Andri said, "What was Nanthalin doing? He *didn't* walk into a challenge square?"

Vec's eyes shifted. "No! He and a couple of the boys were down at the Running Deer, and they mighta been yelling stuff. Just being funny. Everybody does," he said defensively. "Snouts rousted 'em, and the boys got off but Nanth fell." He didn't add *dead drunk*, but everyone heard the words anyway. What else would they be doing at a dockside tavern?

Andri lowered his sword, wrenched his baldric back around from where it had become twisted, and rammed the sword into the sheath.

"So how do we get them back?" Vec's voice cracked. "Everyone says, if you go to the lockup, they grab you, too!"

"You, yes. But not if you send your granny or gramps or a six-year-old sister with the bribe coins." Andri turned to face the square full of people. "Adon-Marsael is trying to convince the city he's rescuing it. That means he's not likely to start executing people for much less than outright murder—for now." He waited for the curses and spitting to die down. "I think he's sending anyone who can hold a sword to fill in up north, where the fighting is still going. Or worse, off to the mines."

"What if you're wrong," Vec muttered.

Andri said, "Then come find *me*. If you want a fight, we'll find a place." He lifted his head. "Hear that? What you want to wager at least half a dozen nosers sent off messengers, and here come the snouts, hoping to round up a fresh supply of bodies for the mines?"

He was right, and sooner than anyone had expected. The sound of rapid footsteps echoed off the stone buildings not far away.

The crowd split in five directions.

Andri's gang went high, climbing to roofs and running

along ridgepoles until they reached the farther street. Then they dropped down into a chicken yard, scattering poultry as they ran across and vaulted a fence, then retreated back to safe territory, watched by sentinels at windows and roofs.

As soon as they returned, Marten helped to pass out bandages and salve. Gared looked the worst, except for a cut over Devea's right eye. She let Marten bind a cloth around it as everyone reviled against the dyers and the guard. Gared waved off the salve—he'd been training in the guard court since he was five, and was used to nicks and bruises.

Those who eked out a living as water carriers left, as they had to be up well before dawn. Devea and a couple of trusted others got ready for their stints as roaming sentries; before she slipped out the door, she paused and shafted a glance from heavy-lidded eyes over her shoulder at Andri, her lips curved in invitation. Expectation.

He flashed her a grin and raised a hand, meaning later. She laughed and vanished.

The last of the youngsters were sent off by a short nod by Gared to clean up after the meal, the boys, with their stronger hands, to start the day's laundry setting in vinegar and salt with the last of the dish water. They groaned, but it was the groan of habit.

Left alone at last, Gared said to Andri, "Why're you on this side of town? Thought you were northside."

"It can wait. Listen, a couple of foreign girls came into town . . ." Andri paused, remembering those large golden eyes. Usually you didn't see eye color five paces away, much less fifteen. But he remembered hers clearly, the impact of her gaze rippling along his nerves. "I had Elies decoy them to Genda's—"

Gared said, "Heard it from Marten." Despite the scars he'd gotten from the ferocious training to become a royal bodyguard, the expression on his square, even features was habitually mild. Now his upper lip lengthened, betraying his uneasiness. "Two?"

"One of 'em is Jaydi's age. But the other . . ." His expression turned wry. "Don't fret. I won't get burned twice."

Relieved, Gared said, "What about Vec?"

Andri picked up his dish of congealing pie. "What else?" He twirled his fork. "Have to break Nanthalin out, of course. Vec is never going to see past the next watch change, but most of his flock were waiting to hear what we were going to do. Did you see?"

Gared carefully fingered a bruise. "Nah."

"Who's on duty?" Andri spread his hands, dish in one, fork in the other. "Can we wait?"

Gared sidled looks up and to the side, reluctant to pass on what he'd learned that day from his cousin in the palace guard. But he knew Andri. Knew there was no help for it. "There's a bounty out. They need bodies for the mines. And Talipin and his snakes are on duty."

"Talipin!" Andri's eyes widened, bright and mad. "What could be better!"

Gared didn't waste the breath pointing out that "better" would be lying low. "Even if they don't see us, we'll get the blame."

"And? What's Cousin Adon going to do? Add to the price already on my head? Any more will make him look ridiculous."

Gared gave his head a shake. "Talipin is looking for any reason to get a shoot on sight order." And when Andri shrugged, Gared gave up trying to be reasonable. Being reasonable hadn't done much for them so far. "I'll put a team together." Speaking of unreasonable; Gared stopped and glanced back. "What do you want to do about the foreign girls?"

"Nothing." The humor leached from Andri's face, his gaze diffuse. Then his mouth tightened and he added, almost inaudible, "Yet."

Gared dipped his chin in a brief nod, stopped in the next room to round up the rowdier youngsters who had water duty in the morning, and Andri watched them argue, complain, but comply, loving their tattered ferocity. Even the ones he and Gared had had to thrash—especially the ones they'd had to thrash—knowing that superior strength had been the only semblance of order in their lives so far.

Gared vanished to get a rescue team, and Andri gulped down his long-cold pie, shut his eyes and reached.

To find a smooth wall hiding identity and intent.

He opened his eyes and grinned. The game was on.

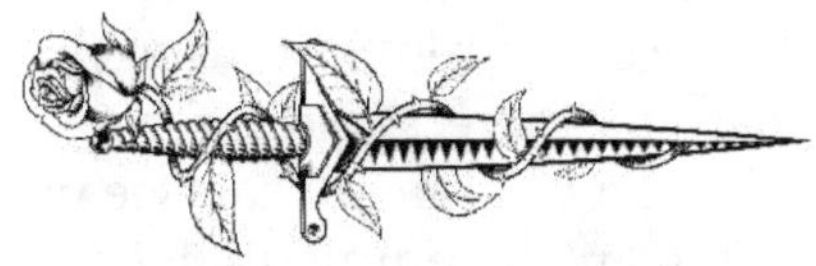

SIXTEEN

Lyren-Sartora discovered that meals could be bought downstairs. Twice daily everyone gathered in what clearly used to be the servants' mess, sitting at long tables. "Don't let's sit together," she whispered to Liere on entry. "That way each of us can listen to different people."

Liere obligingly sat at the other end of a table from Lyren-Sartora, who noted that the youngest person there beside herself was fifteen or so. She hoped her illusion magic made her look fifteen, and tried consciously to act older.

Liere noted people clumping into distinct groups. As they downed their soup full of spring vegetables and bits of pepper-fried fish, she listened to the talk. Some were old servants, working their way back into the palace as Adon-Marsael's people labored to restore order. Others were leftovers from the Liberty days. They and the former servants maintained a tense neutrality; Liere gathered from a terse comment that any signs of violence would result in summary closing of the building. Then there were the very few who paid to stay, mostly out-of-towners agog at actually staying in the palace.

After the meal, Lyren-Sartora ran off to explore, Liere following more slowly. There wasn't much to see until they got upstairs to their floor, and discovered a balcony at the end of their hallway. This was the promised view over part of the royals' garden, where it seemed a party had begun.

Paper lanterns hung from the trees, lighting up the part of the terrace that they could see. The strains of music carried on the heavy, humid air, as people dressed in summer robes danced in and out of view, twirling and dipping, their silks fluttering. Liere sniffed in the scent of cedar, and wondered if the candles inside the paper lanterns had been scented. No glowglobes in sight, a reminder that magic was largely unused here, except for the basic spells everyone knew.

"A garland dance," Lyren-Sartora exclaimed. "Sartoran style!" She turned to Liere, holding her arms out limp-wristed. "Care to join me? Nobody can see us!"

Liere did not want to admit that her shoulder ached abominably. "Too warm," Liere said. "I think I'll turn in."

Lyren-Sartora shrugged, and twirled about on the balcony, light as a butterfly, her steps perfectly timed as Liere walked back to their room, once again sat cross-legged on the floor, and sent a mental tendril out to search for that elusive awareness.

Nothing. She leaned her back against the bed and spread her awareness over the city. It had surprised her to discover that this was difficult for many with Dena Yeresbeth, that coinherence manifested differently in people, just as tastes and talent did. She could not remember a time in her life when she was not able to sense others on the mental plane, somewhat like gazing down from above on thousands of colored lights. Her awareness swept over them, catching the surface thoughts—most, especially in the lower part of the city, busy putting out bowls and pots, every available receptacle, in hopes it did rain.

That was odd. The city lay next to a river.

Lyren-Sartora returned presently, and was soon deep asleep, but Liere lay awake, puzzling over what she'd seen so far. She fell asleep without coming to any conclusions, and moved restlessly in worry dreams as thunder smashed overhead.

When they woke, Liere said, "Let's plan the day."

Lyren-Sartora crossed her arms. "I want to explore the palace. I saw pages my age." With a mutinous look, "You know how much people my age talk."

Liere hesitated, acutely aware that Lyren-Sartora could take off at any moment, and there would be nothing Liere could effectively do or say. She didn't like the idea of Lyren-Sartora running about on her own in this violent kingdom—

No, she knew better than that. Enaeran was made up of people, like any other. It's just that civil war seemed to have made a certain level of violence seem everyday. But Lyren-Sartora had been trained in self-defense, and Liere had given her the means to transfer away entirely.

Meanwhile, this was a palace. Wouldn't people be more likely to be on their best behavior? "Very well. But try to stay unnoticed, all right?" And at another mutinous look, "Only until we get a feel for the place. A plan. We'll make as big a splash as you want once we do have a plan."

Lyren-Sartora smiled sunnily, and submitted to illusion magic to change her face.

It was two nondescript girls, one young, one a little older, who drifted about that day. Lyren-Sartora was confident that if she found age-mates, she'd find out everything going on in the country, including whether or not Norsunder was about—but then she had spent her entire life among people of rank and influence. It was a revelatory experience for her to overhear just how small were the interests of others her age.

Liere was walking about when a gaunt woman with gray hair skewered tightly into a knot approached one of the servers. She said abruptly, "Let me ask before that Liberty . . . person Genda thrusts her snout in." The word "snout" came out with a heavy, ironic twist. "You work here. If a body is seeking work, where would she go?"

"Palace steward," was the short reply from Genda's cousin. "I happen to know that the palace steward is hiring pages."

She was mulling that when she and Lyren-Sartora meet that evening. Liere told Lyren-Sartora what she'd overheard.

Lyren-Sartora scowled. "You want us to become servants? What if I see a sinister spy lurking around and I can't follow them because I'm stuck washing dishes? They don't even have dunking buckets here. You have to scrub!"

"We're envoys, remember? But it seems that the palace is desperate for help."

Lyren-Sartora's expression cleared. "I know that. I went by the kitchens today, while the bread was being kneaded, and heard some of the pastry prentices crabbing about how they had to do extra running because there weren't enough pages. So I asked someone about pages, and tried to be boring and unnoticed," she added quickly. "Asked how they get hired, and if they get to wait on the throne room. She said, not likely! She said The Elsarion is getting pages from the nobles, and they have to learn palace ways. But they are definitely short-handed."

They went down to dinner. As they entered, they spotted a knot of people whispering. Liere caught, ". . . broke into the prison. They say half the prisoners got away!" before someone saw her and Lyren-Sartora, and the group broke up.

Liere passed by, keeping her gaze averted, but she sent a tendril back, catching an eager mind behind the whispered words, "Who was it, did they say?"

A self-important answer, from a mind that relished being in the know, "They didn't catch anyone, and the raiders all wore masks. But *we* can guess."

And because she was listening on the mental plane, Liere heard the thoughts clear as whispers, *Prince Andri the Assassin*.

She chose a seat at random, aware that she had three goals now: one to explore the city to find out why people had been so desperate to put out receptacles for the rain, and two, to learn more about that prison break. Were those political prisoners or criminals, what did their capture reveal not just about them, but about the community that had taken their freedom?

Thirdly: Prince Andri the Assassin?

SEVENTEEN

County Ariath, Colend

Shontande stopped his horse, and sat very still, eyes closed, head slightly tipped back.

Thad looked around, not quite worried. He wouldn't know how to defend them if there was danger. Anyway, surely Shontande wouldn't sit with his eyes closed like that if he heard some kind of stealthy attack approaching.

Thad breathed in the heady, sweet aroma of linden trees in full bloom, clusters of tiny bell-shaped flowers hanging amid the heart-shaped leaves. All around him the sky-scraping trees rustled in a slow, humid breeze, but below that he felt more than heard a thrum so subtle he could not identify it. He found it curiously com-forting.

Shontande spoke. "Do you think the Chwahir Great Hum was inspired by bees?"

"Bees?" Thad repeated, startled.

Shontande lifted a hand, palm up as he gestured toward the trees around them. "Can't you hear them? Hundreds — thousands of bees."

Of course. *That* was the thrum.

"I suppose it's possible," Thad said slowly. "If they hum on a single note. I have no idea what the Chwahir hum sounds like."

"You probably know, having been scribe-trained, that our Lirendi lily is not a sword or dagger, whatever anyone says. It's actually a bee."

Thad had not known that. History had not been his subject, back when he was a careless youth longing to be on the road instead of confined to a desk. It was his sister Karhin who had loved history. All these years later any reminders of his sister caused a ball of ice behind his ribs. But Shontande, prisoner in a silken cage, had briefly met Karhin once before she was stabbed by one of Detlev's boys. So he said nothing.

Shontande sensed the shift in Thad's mood, wincing inwardly, and the subject dropped. From among the tall, straight trunks emerged a rotund, white-haired man whose green robe was edged with the sun-faded yellow of beekeepers. He was accompanied by young people in green, one holding the rope of a sturdy horse that drew a long, flat wagon. Behind this parade walked a pair of older members of the wood guild, clad proudly in brown.

They ignored the road, bent on a path only they could discern. As the wagon was gestured to a halt, all parties conferred, then the apprentices directed to remove dangerous basal sprouts from a couple of linden trees. Longer consultation was required about the removal of a drooping branch.

The pruned wood was carried to the wagon, and the parade pushed on, bees swarming to either side. The beekeeper was certainly aware of his audience, but no one paid the least heed as Shontande gestured to Thad to follow.

By the time they reached a village, Thad was fighting yawn after yawn, for he had been rising well before dawn each day in order to have his notecase dealt with before breakfasting with the king at first light. Also, in his years working as a delivery courier for the family of his friend Nalisse, Thad had crossed the kingdom so much that little was new. But all was new to the king, so he kept silence as, at last, they followed the beekeeper and wood guild agents into a small town built along a winding river.

Shontande and Thad waited as the beekeeper and the agents bowed in the peace to one another, and the apprentices were directed to take the pruned wood off, presumably to be catalogued and stored under the eye of the guild agents. The beekeeper then turned, hands propped on his hips, as he faced the young men on horseback who had followed him through the day.

"Peace, young honors," he said. "What may I do for you? I ought perhaps, in all politeness, to point out that business is all done through my office, nothing underhand, and my prices not lowered a jot."

Shontande and Thad slipped from their horses, and while Thad held the reins, Shontande approached the beekeeper and made a peace. "My intention is merely to learn as I travel about," he said.

"And who might you be?"

"Shontande," Shontande said, safe in the awareness of how common his name was. "I understand the taxes in this county are quite high."

"Quite high," the man responded, his considerable body shaking with his internal laughter. "You might say quite, though it would be as true to say the highest in the kingdom. If you are thinking of moving to Ariath, keep that in mind. However," he added as he turned toward an inn whose windows filled with golden light one by one, a welcome beacon in the purples of twilight, "I will say this for our count, there are no limits on what we may charge. None! We pay our taxes, and anything above is ours."

"And so," Shontande said, "this agreeable arrangement does not suffer from those who charge less?"

"We do very well indeed," the man said as he led the way inside the inn, where waiting servants bowed and led the way to a fine table as if this was habit. "Because not only is my honey pure linden, it comes from elder trees."

"Elder trees?" Shontande repeated. "If you are not too fatigued, I would be honored to learn about elder trees."

The beekeeper had run his eyes over the two, noting details of deference and decision. The one with the beautiful face had offered no guild or land title, and he was dressed as plainly as his companion, but the subtleties of his manner indicated that his was the deciding will. Indeed, the other, unspoken, led the animals off to be cared for as Young Beauty, as the beekeeper privately called Shontande, followed him to the table.

By this time, Shontande had also observed his host. He had been talking to people all over Colend, most of whom needed little coaxing. Here was someone who enjoyed his own importance. Shontande gestured to the innkeeper that the evening meal would be his to pay for, and with a courteous gesture, invited his companion to order whatever he wished.

It was the right move. The beekeeper expanded accordingly, and over three bottles of Gyrnian blue (which he drank most of) Shontande not only heard, in exhaustive detail, exactly why the local bees — after a disquisition on their many varieties — were better than anywhere else, and his house's methods of handling the honey equally superlative, but as the meal wound down and the five-generation distilled malt came forth (sweetened with a dollop of local honey, after the fashion in those parts), the beekeeper leaned forward and said confidingly, "I told you that we've elder trees, and that is true. But few know how old they are."

"Ah?" Shontande encouraged, lips parted.

"Trees so old," the beekeeper said, then paused to sip, eyes closed in pure enjoyment of a beverage he didn't often allow himself, which tasted (he felt certain) the better for someone else paying, "that they were here before Colend existed."

"Oh?" Shontande opened his hand, three fingers spread in the lily gesture, indicating pleasure in confidence. "So old, then? Back to Sartor's empire days?"

"Empire days!" the beekeeper repeated, shaking all over then wiping his eyes. "I believe the grandfathers of these trees were here before then, before the Fall even, when the Chwahir lived here." His voice lowered to a hoarse whisper. "Did you know that the first linden honey was traded by the Chwahir?"

"I did not know that."

"Fact! Though many do not like to hear it," he said with the comfortable assurance of one whose prestige has always guaranteed an appreciative audience.

Shontande murmured provocatively, "It is said in some place that we took a great deal more from the Chwahir than they did from us, trade-wise."

"Certainly the silk secrets," the beekeeper said, finger beside his chin. "For all the parade of the silk guild. But our trees I believe were planted, and tended, by Chwahir hands, for all they can't grow anything over the mountains anymore. Our oldest records, kept beyond time in a vault that the guild has preserved for millennia, contains fragile records in a handwriting that no scholar can parse." He whispered, as though disclosing something thoroughly discreditable, "We believe it is Chwahir in origin."

He sat back, sipped the last of his liquor, and blinked rapidly, as if he had lost the train of his thoughts. He glanced up, forehead puckered, and Shontande said, "Thank you for an enlightening conversation. It is quite late. Perhaps it is time to retire."

"Quite right, quite right," the beekeeper muttered, wondering how he had come to venture into all those old secrets, only told to the most trusted of his apprentices. But the young man's manner had been so sympathetic, so encouraging, so willing to be impressed . . .

He went off to bed on a swimming tide of fine wine and liquor that would guarantee little memory of the evening before, except in the vaguest terms as Shontande looked for Thad, who had arranged to take the only two bedrooms the inn offered.

After Shontande reported what he'd learned, Thad reflected on how deft the king was at eliciting confidences. There was no trick to it—no magic or mind-powers, though he had both to a formidable degree—it was his air of interest that brought out even the most inarticulate person. That air that convinced you that you were the most interesting person in the world. And it worked because, at that moment, you were.

Shontande finished, "I think I now understand how the count manages to dress, entertain, and most of all bribe on a duchas level, though her lands afford a fraction of that supplying Altan, Gaszin, and the rest of the big duchies."

"Highest taxes in Colend," Thad said, gesturing shadow-warding. "And no threshold on prices."

"Except of course what people are willing to pay."

Shontande reflected on how Ariath had come to be a county of luxury items. Ordinary people (other than servants) had been driven out, debt in Colend being a heinous crime. In social terms, debt was a betrayal of the social contract, which was both simple and fundamental: I provide you with this, and you in turn provide me with that, both of us agreeing with what constitutes fairness or parity.

Colend was also a country in which custom promised a safety net for unfortunates. Houses for the poor were run by guilds, but there were none in Ariath. The needy, sickly, the elderly with no family and unable to work must go elsewhere. With this sober realization in the forefront of their minds, he and Thad parted for the night, and next morning early, followed the river that fed into the much broader Klarenth marking the southwest border.

Shontande turned to Thad. "Today's news? Nothing was posted on the board there in Linden Village."

"Still nothing from the royal heralds," Thad confirmed.

Linden Village might have been too small for a royal herald, though every village and town was supposed to have at least a scribe receiving news from the heralds that could be written and posted in all city and town squares at the Hour of the Bird.

No official news was both good and bad. Good? No false proclamations in the name of the king. Shontande had gambled on the rivalries within the regency council not only keeping any of them from claiming the throne, but also from trusting the others far enough to forge his name on new edicts. He was still king.

Did he want to be king? Some days, as he traveled wherever he wanted, he had entertained the notion that he could walk away and be . . . anything.

Except that he couldn't be anything. Though he had been wandering where whim took him, he spent night after restless night reflecting on everything he'd heard, everything he'd been reading for years, and formulating and discarding plans for how to reform the kingdom. He couldn't step into one of these simple, charming houses along rivers and canals, fields and forests, and become an expert weaver, or saddle-maker, or dancer, or sved-stringer, without beginning with the most basic lessons.

Kings' most basic lessons were to think all the way to the border, and beyond. That much Shontande's father had impressed on him before he was assassinated. Shontande had done his best to read records teaching him that thinking, in spite of the council's efforts to prevent it: many was the night when they thought him carousing drunkenly while he lay on the floor in the crane chamber reading ancient records. While others his age had spent their years training to blow glass, or paint porcelain, or to spin and weave silk, he had trained to be a king. The only vital element he had missed was the chance to see his kingdom himself. Now he had done so.

It was time to think like a king.

"As for unofficial news . . ." Thad took out the note that his brother Bee had dictated to a trusted scribe student, and passed it to Shontande, whose expression shuttered as he read:

Thad, Count Ariath is spearheading an investigation. Under the pretense that S. had been spirited away by some unnamed evil—or has run away, driven by incipient madness inherited from his father—Duchas Altan is pressuring Honor Donais Alton to order the herald-guards to search and secure the king for his own safety. Led by Ariath, the regents are dropping hints, and using all their followers to spread rumor, about S. having inherited his father's madness. Two of the chirps have repeated these rumors, but the three most popular chirps are all reporting that the regency council is the source of said rumors.

The roses worn by those who believe the council is spreading false rumor have blossomed beyond the city into market towns, our scribe relay reports. Those who wear the regents' cyan lilies (blue for purity of intent, but cyan respecting the Lirendi blue) are mostly courtiers and their supporters, and some prominent tradespeople who deal with courtiers. There were others, but we are hearing that they are leaving off their lilies, some in question, others because they do not seem to feel the comfort of peer unity . . .

"Roses and lilies." Shontande folded the note and handed it back to Thad. Twice in market towns they'd seen people sporting fresh roses in their hats, at their waists, and painted on summer fans. And once they had seen lilies. "What else?"

"The rest," Thad was glad to say, for he'd seen the wince of pain in Shontande's face before it smoothed away. He hated the divisiveness in the kingdom, but the lilies he took personally. "The rest," Thad said, "is progressing excellently. Those I hired are all arrived in Bais Harbor, and practicing at their roles until we arrive."

"Then we are done. I've seen enough. We'll transfer to Bais Harbor."

Thad loathed transfer magic, which always made him feel like he'd taken a very bad fall from a horse. But he said nothing as Shontande went on, "Whatever else Donais Altan is thinking, he knows I would never strike a Colendi. Therefore we must prevent any awkward meetings. And we must not keep Sartor waiting," Shontande finished, his smile grim.

"Instead," Thad murmured, "the council will be left waiting as each day brings them closer to the opening of the Music Festival. And no king to pay for it."

They made the peace to one another and parted for the night, as, below those open windows, a silhouette retreated into the shadows.

Curtas had found them after several days' search. He had followed Shontande from region to region, sometimes creating obstacles that would keep the herald-guards from finding their king.

He would spend another week or say laying false trails to protect Shontande's retreat, and then, perhaps, he would go to Alsais.

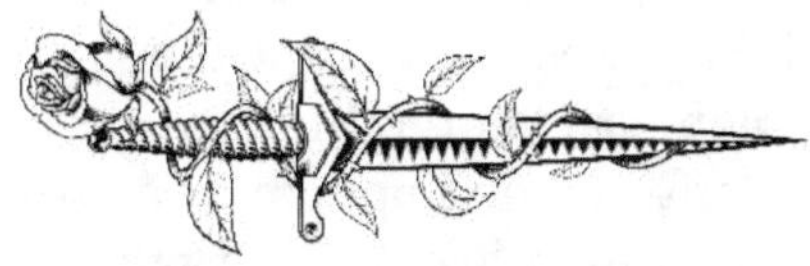

EIGHTEEN

Shiovhan, capital of Enaeran

Lyren-Sartora was certain that if she kept running around meeting the palace youths, she'd find the ones who'd lead the way to secret conferences, or something vital and interesting. Maybe the pages were the ones to follow. To make it fun, she insisted on a different illusory disguise each day, which Liere was happy to provide.

Liere went down into the city to explore. Without Lyren-Sartora's impatience, she could be as systematic as she needed. As a result, though she gained little truth from the third, fourth, and fifth-hand gossip about the political situation (and absolutely nothing about possible Norsundrian interference) she did discover a situation she found appalling: people in the poorer areas away from the river put out barrels and pots in hopes of rain because the fountains had long since been left to run dry — and of course they couldn't afford even the pittance the water carriers charged. In fact, a lot of them were water carriers, lugging buckets back at the end of a grueling day.

When she and Lyren-Sartora met at their room at Genda's on the third day, Lyren-Sartora chattered about everyone she'd observed, who was nice, who wasn't, and how confusing the palace was, with some areas closed off entirely due to fire and other damage.

She spoke steadily until they were ready for bed, then finally said contritely, "I didn't even ask how you spent your day?"

"I need to find out why the fountains have run dry," Liere said.

Lyren-Sartora was already bored. "I really doubt it's because of Norsunder."

"Still. It's a hardship for those already living hard lives," Liere said. "As it happens, I know the magic to fix it. I worked on a similar problem last year. I think I will. This might be just the gift I want to offer when I appear as envoy."

Lyren-Sartora agreed, wondering which would be more fun: to come as the envoy's scribe, or to sign up as a teenage page. As she flopped back on her bed, she decided that she'd pick the one that gave her the best chance of nosing outside important rooms, once she discovered where they were. Either way, let Liere *dare* to say she was lazy and didn't work at anything!

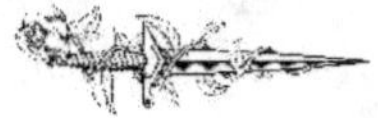

Next morning, Liere returned to the area she had explored the day before, on the city's lower level. She approached a young water carrier, a boy of about sixteen, whose skinny frame bent double as he dragged his cart.

"Pardon me, but could I put to you a question?" she asked.

"Just don't get in my way," the boy replied, his face hardening when he saw that she had no jug in her hands.

"Why don't the fountains work?"

The boy gave her a derisive scowl. "Are you stupid?" He cast his eyes down her clothes, then grunted. "Outsider. I don't know. Ask the king. Oh, right, we don't have a king, because the nobles are too busy fighting each other, as well as the Adranis."

"Would you do another kind of work if the fountains ran?"

He grunted, clearly finding her questions more risible with each breath. "Better than the mines," he finally said, deciding not to waste any more breath, as he had a hill to climb.

"Thank you," she said, pressed a coin into his hand, and moved away from his puzzled frown.

Perhaps that was the wrong approach. She turned down another street, and began to note the signs of hardship that increased with every street farther from the river. She had come to the conclusion that fixing the fountains would benefit more people than she would put out of work, when she remembered to scan on the mental plane. And caught a glimpse of herself from behind, the identity Elies. Liere bent down to fix her sandal, and glimpsed Elies's familiar form from the side as she examined light summer scarves hanging on a pole carried by one of the street vendors. Liere turned a corner, slid behind a stack of barrels, and waited.

When Elies appeared, walking rapidly and looking anxiously around, Liere stepped out to join her. Elies started, then flushed to the ears. Liere pretended not to notice. "I thought I saw you. What a lovely chance! Do you live in these parts?"

"Not far," Elies said brightly, her mind wide open.

With long practice Liere sifted the superficial flutter of emotion-charged images of chagrin and anxiety to avoid closer questions, then raised her mind-shield. It seemed that Elies had been directed to shadow Liere, without a reason stated.

Liere asked Elies to point out a good place for the midday meal, and when Elies pointed randomly and gave out a fast answer, Liere accepted that and took her leave.

She strolled along from dry fountain to dry fountain, trying on hats and gloves and examining woven mats, as she mentally mapped out the twists and offshoots of a very old underground river feeding into the great river. The magic to pull the water up to the fountains and purify it had long since faded. It was as simple as that.

Perhaps not as simple might be the ramifications.

As the light began to fade, she started the long trudge up the switchback road toward the upper level, and she sensed Elies turning away in relief, content that Liere was done being mysterious for the day.

When she got back to Genda's, she found Lyren-Sartora impatiently awaiting her in their room. "I got dinner." Lyren-Sartora flipped the cover off a basket. "Now we can talk."

"Thank you," Liere said. "That was thoughtful."

Lyren-Sartora rolled her eyes, and Liere wondered if she sounded patronizing. Lyren-Sartora was so quick—and so different from the girls her age among the Ones on Geth-deles, who had appreciated praise for good work as much as she had. People liked their efforts acknowledged, didn't they?

Maybe not if you've always been the center of attention.

". . . learning my way around the palace," Lyren-Sartora said. "One more day, and I'll have it all. I listened by mind as people get messages. No one here has heard of mind-shields!" Lyren-Sartora hesitated, then said, "I only listen that far, and no farther. It's just for mentions of Norsunder. I haven't told anyone what I heard."

Liere bit into her cheese and green stuffed bread. "This is delicious."

"I know!" Lyren-Sartora finished a bite, and grinned. "Before I get to my gossip, what about you?"

"I've definitely decided on my envoy gift, but the form will have to be magical artifacts that I can say were sent from Sartor. I don't want anyone knowing I am a mage."

"Good idea." Lyren-Sartora nodded soberly. "Julian told me they didn't trust mages. I definitely got a sense of that."

"Me, too. And so, your gossip? Anything about the jail rescue, or Prince Andri the Assassin?"

"You heard that, too?" Lyren-Sartora asked. "I did, but it was old stuff. No one knew any details." She launched into a detailed description of the staff members, who said what, and what they reported third-hand about Adon-Marsael n'Elsarion, and his nobles.

When she had talked herself out, they got ready for bed.

As soon as Lyren-Sartora dropped into slumber, Liere rose and noiselessly changed, used after five years of dormitory living to dressing without light. She slipped out of the room, and used illusion to blur her features; anyone looking at her in light would see someone neither young nor old, features bland, hair an unmemorable shade. She wore a dagger in a sturdy sheath under a panel of her summer robe.

She moved from shadow to shadow, scanning in both the physical and the mental realm as she slipped down the zigzagged streets cut into the ridge. The curfew bell tolled a warning. Revelers poured out of the taverns, inns, eateries and wine shops. Liere inserted herself into the stream as she worked her way down one of the paths toward the lower city, until the stream dwindled to a trickle, then ones and twos.

When she reached the ground above what had to be an underground river, judging by the geography, she slipped to the shadows, her concentration mostly on the subtle signs of moisture underground. And so she missed Marten, who was not only very good at shadowing, he had a natural advantage of which he was unaware: he had early in his life established a mind-shield, a consequence of his struggle to differentiate between the living and the ghosts.

He had little trouble following her until the storm that had been building all day broke with a spectacular flash of lightning, followed by thunder that shook dust from the stone walls. The sudden cataract of warm water left him barely able to make out his own hands in front of his face, and he lost her just as she turned down an alley to reach another street.

She nearly walked into three tall, heavy-limbed guards walking down the street in such a way that no one could pass. Raucous laughter and cursing echoed off the walls as the rain lifted just as abruptly, leaving a world of musical drips and plonks.

"What have we here?"

"I'm lost," she said in a quavering voice.

"You're found now," the tallest of them said mockingly, causing another crow of laughter.

"After curfew," the middle one explained, her lips twisting in a sour grin. "You're ours now."

The one on the left, burly and bored, added, "The mines don't care of the hands digging in 'em are male or female."

Liere did a quick scan. Two faces watching from behind shutters above, but no one else. Good. She just needed to concentrate—and the three became obstacles in a well-drilled pattern. She tottered toward them, hands clutching at her hair in a poor-me gesture that brought more laughter. She could read their intent easily: a little slapping around to relieve boredom, then back to the guardhouse and a mark on the scoreboard for all three.

She stepped between two, and in a series of moves they were never able to reconstruct, she hit the nerve in one's elbow, the side of the knee in the second, and the third was yanked off balance by a sudden tug on his ponytail, giving him a sharp neck crick.

Then thunder struck and the sky opened with a roaring fall of sharp hail that bounded and rattled everywhere. Their feet slid out from under them as painful joints refused to cooperate, and when they had righted themselves, skin stinging, joints throbbing, their victim was two blocks away, laying down a round stone that she muttered over.

Working fast, she mapped out the flow of the underground river as well as the ancient conduits that used the force of the flow to narrow to fountains. All that needed doing was shifting some slabs that had cut off the flow in two crucial places, no doubt as a result of a quake-mage who had eased a tremor somewhere farther upriver. It could have easily been repaired—should have been—except apparently the former king had not trusted mages. Or maybe it was his forebears.

Liere bespelled her stones, laid them down at the connecting points, and then clambered up onto a roof, and while rain fell all around her, she reveled in her ability to sense, master, and execute these complex spells. She had wrestled with magic studies for years before discovering that her own abilities were her worst enemies: centuries of carefully constructed magic learning had been put together on the assumption that Dena Yeresbeth did not exist. The Ones, coming at magic from a different angle, had enabled her to use her abilities instead of to fight against them.

When she was done, she was exhausted, but she had prepared hers and Lyren-Sartora's room as a magic transfer Destination. She transferred back to Genda's, recovered from the wrenching inner jolt, changed out of her wet clothes, draped them in the open window, and went to bed.

Spying covertly was not furnishing anything of use. Tomorrow, the envoy would arrive.

Marten arrived back at general HQ, to find Andri and Gared there, both awake.

"I lost her," he said. "Shortly before someone took out three of the night patrol."

"Dead?" Andri asked.

"No."

Gared replied, "Was it her?"

Marten turned up his palms.

Gared leaned forward, callused, scarred hands dangling between his knees. "Was she armed?"

"Not that I saw."

Andri sat back, pupils huge and black in the light of the

single candle, dark circles under them, a bad sign. As usual, he said nothing, just picked up his sword and hoisted himself through a window. They heard him go up onto the roof and his diminishing footsteps.

Marten dried off, changed his clothes, and retired to his long overdue sleep.

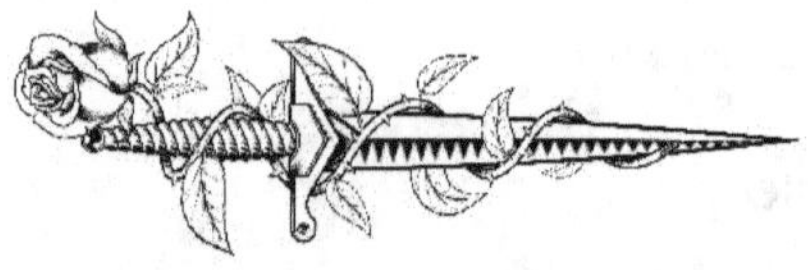

NINETEEN

Part of being a steward, Thad Keperi had learned, was not only knowing how to balance logistics with scheduling, but finding the right persons for a task.

How do you find the right people for a revolution?

When Shontande first wrote to him alluding to something important, he saved the letter, now safely locked away; Thad, whose mothers were both scribes and archivists, had been trained to see the world's communication system as the lifelines of history, and suspected that one day it might be a treasure:

There are two choices before me, become king in truth, or go away and do something else with my life. Bee will explain.

Bee had brought the sealed letter when he came home to Wilderfeld for New Year's Week the year previous. Thad often thought about that remarkable conversation.

In spite of the cracking cold air under a scoured blue sky, the brothers had walked along the frozen river under bare trees, where they could not be overheard, and here Thad discovered how close his younger brother Bee had gradually come to wary, private Shontande, whose first friend, Curtas, had turned out to be one of Detlev's gang, sent to infiltrate the Young Allies. For a long time after that he had shut himself behind an impervious wall of politeness, letting no one see his private self.

Bee's fingers tightened on Thad's arm. "I know he's been writing to you using the notecase King Senrid of the Marlovens gave him on his single visit. What has he said to you?"

"It's always been things he sees and hears. The rose garden, the seasons. He writes most when the Music Festival happens."

"Internal affairs?"

"Never."

"So I thought," Bee said, and Thad marveled to himself how odd it is when a sibling you always regarded as a child, needing your guidance and protection, is suddenly a man, and your equal. Bee said, "I've been instructed to talk to you about internal affairs, away from other ears. But only if you wish to be drawn into what might face Thorn Gate." Centuries ago, traitors had gone through that gate, never to return; the gate itself had vanished long ago, but its shadow lay in language and gesture.

Thad said, "I've always wanted to help him. I'm listening."

"I knew you would." Bee's voice lightened. "Here it is: no more, no less, than a revolution."

"Ah-ye," Thad breathed. "Thorn Gate indeed."

"But it will be Colendi-style, as established by our first king, Martande the Great."

"Ah-h-h," in a very different voice.

"The king has always been aware that the regency council strives to control what information reaches him. Also, to control him, always on the grounds of safety. He could not get near ordinary people to find out what they thought. Until he came to trust me. It took a very long time. He doesn't even trust the word *trust*." Bee sighed frost into the air.

Thad uttered a thought that he'd kept to himself ever since the memorial for the king. "Shontande was so much closer to Curtas than to me."

Bee nodded slowly. "I can hear in the king's voice, and sometimes even in his thoughts, though he lets little escape his shield, how much that betrayal hurts still." He tapped his forehead. "He's still angry over it, I think . . . I think the more because he misses Curtas. But could never trust him again."

Thad stared morosely at the blue ice over the river. He'd really liked Curtas. That was the problem. How could you trust yourself, even, in discovering that someone you thought your faithful friend was a spy, a plant, an enemy? It's true that Curtas had never done anything wrong, unlike some of the others of Detlev's notorious gang, but why couldn't he have told them who he was? *Trusted* them?

"The king relies on me to tell him the truth," Bee said, his stick cracking the icy crust over the snow as they walked. "Everyone talks before me, as if lack of sight equals lack of hearing what is said around one. Lack of mind as well."

"Bee—" Thad began, defensive on his brother's behalf.

"Peace. I worked, at his desire, to maintain that freedom. That, ah-ye, I believe you might call it invisibility." Bee raised his gloved free hand as he breathed a laugh that clouded in the air, froze, and fell in uncounted tiny crystals. "By never reacting, I hear the truth that the powerful would hide, and that the powerless dare not speak before the powerful."

"And so?" Thad's head had rung, not only because of the cold air burning fiercely down into his lungs. He'd sensed that he and his brother were being drawn into great events—as Thad had been when he was a part of the Young Allies. But that had ended with violence, their sister one of the first to die.

"It is not yet *and so*, but *and though*. And though the regency council speaks—and some might even believe—of their dedication to Colend, the truth is, they are gaining wealth at the kingdom's expense. And yes, I know your concern." Bee lowered his voice; Thad remembered his mind-shield then, after the fact, as Bee shifted to formal mode. "The king's first stipulation is that this revolution not be violent. At the first sign of Colendi lifting weapon against Colendi, he will remove himself for good, instead of for a time."

"For a time? He has a plan?" Thad asked.

Bee was back to informality, without the gilding of metaphor and allusion—and he had never learned the tricks of hand, eye, fan, to blur one's words. "Yes. And it concerns you. . ."

Thad reflected on that memory as he looked over the inn balcony at the entourage forming up under the warm morning sun. *And so, here we are.*

Shontande stepped out beside him, unseen by those below. "I never would have thought of theater players," he said softly, hands together as he bowed over them. "A garland for your crown, Thad, and rose petals before your feet."

Thad smiled down at the impressive array. They all looked splendid, and the gear and weapons were real, though

Thad had ascertained that the players were only trained in stage combat. Shontande did not want violence.

One of the actors—always aware of a possible audience—glanced up, and seeing Thad and Shontande looking down, flashed her sword up in salute. In a ringing voice, she cried, "Hail the king!"

A mighty shout went up, "Hail the king!"

Hard on that, their leader, an older man who was traveling as a scribe, declaimed in a mild voice that still carried throughout the sizable courtyard, "On stage."

At once the company formed into lines, everyone settling into their role. On a hidden signal, they bowed and made the peace, then moved to the bridles of their horses, awaiting the signal to mount.

When Thad and Shontande came down together, that signal was given, a melodic chord blown on three silver horns, and the company formed up. Thad looked back at them, every nerve thrilling: a year of careful work, beginning with traveling southward to see the players his friend Nalisse Aliad—who traveled widely for the wine guild—had recommended, and then, one by one, recruiting all the others.

The gate to the inn, which had been closed to all other custom for two weeks, was thrown open, and the curious all up and down the narrow street paused to watch as the cavalcade rode out in column, decorated horses prancing with tails high, riders erect and impressive.

They'd reached the end of the street when Shontande looked up at the sky, biting his lip. Thad, riding next to him, caught the movement. Shontande's profile had stilled. "Eh?" he asked, barely a breath.

Shontande glanced at Thad, the narrowing of his eyes giving away the laughter he was trying to suppress. "They think I'm another actor," he murmured, barely audible above the clop of hooves on cobblestones, and the rattle of gear.

Dismayed, Thad was about to explain that he'd had to tell them very little to make certain no word of the plan escaped.

But Shontande said softly, "It's true." And laughing silently, he glanced to the side as the street ended, giving a grand view of the narrow bay below, sea birds wheeling and diving, and the sun-splashed Sartoran Sea beyond.

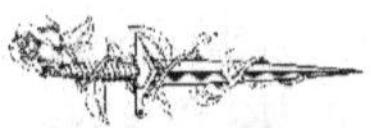

Atan: I believe I've discovered as much as I can by listening and talking to people. I think it's time to present myself to the court, which is presided over by a relation of the old king, near as I can tell.

I learned while studying diplomacy on Geth-deles that it's always a good idea to bring gifts, but since this is not an official embassy, I thought the gift did not have to be the usual caravan of precious things. I believe I have the perfect gift. I discovered that the fountains in the lower city had gone dry, creating difficulties for those in the poorer sections, much worsened by the ongoing drought. I figured I could fix these for them, which should lend my mission some credence?

But this is all new enough that I thought I ought to check with you first, as after all I am presenting myself as your representative.

Liere looked that over and sent it, proud of herself for having accomplished everything on her own. She hoped Atan would be pleased — would laud her idea, and her work.

She used her day to create tokens, laying spells on each. As she painstakingly labored over the tedious, exacting magic — it was never a good idea to be sloppy when dealing with running water — she let herself imagine completing the spell from the ridge above the lower city, and watching the fountains leap up to meet the light. The happy cries of the people at having water again.

That evening, late, she checked her notecase for the twentieth time, and found a note.

Liere: I am taking a moment away from a series of "emergency" interviews (what that means is, a someone from each of the twelve duchas all demanding that I listen to their ideas) because Shontande Lirendi is nearly here, complete with an entourage.

I don't know what his motive for this visit is, but everywhere around me I'm being pressured about regaining the Sartoran Music Festival. So preparing for his visit is going to be shaped by that.

Just now, another reminder. And tomorrow's schedule is worse, so I must be short. I commend your intent and ideas. But generosity in intent, I have learned the hard way, isn't necessarily accepted generously. I think we spoke briefly about the fact that mages are not trusted in Enaeran, which means if you are known to be a mage, you might, at best, be pressured politically, and at worst, outright endangered.

Do you feel is necessary to remain there at all? If you do, I encourage you to take the time to determine why the current authority (I forget his name, and haven't the time to look for my map with notes) has been content to leave more than half the capital city without water. Is there a way to—

All right, it's nearly midnight, and I am so tired I can't keep two thoughts in my head. If you would like to discuss it further, tomorrow?

In haste, Atan

Liere crumpled the note in her hand, feeling stupid.

She knew that just because one meant well, that didn't mean whoever one meant well toward was going to mean equally well, much less appreciate one's efforts. She'd learned that lesson in various ways at various times all through her life, but it seemed she had to learn it yet again.

She pulled out a fresh sheet of paper, dipped a pen, then sat there as a drip formed slowly on the nib. First of all, why *was* she still here? So far, no hint of Norsunder—at least, nothing obvious. But there were questions that she wanted to answer, beginning with the one about water. Then there was Prince Andri the Assassin.

Go or stay? When she began arguing with herself, she knew she was staying. Then she had better consider the method of presenting her gift.

She paced around the room. If Adon Marsael-Elsarion was suspicious of mages, it stood to reason he'd be ignorant about how magic worked.

There was an easy solution: Atan would be the giver of

the gift. Liere was merely the messenger.

Yes. That was the solution.

Sartor's prestige should guarantee no one would question how its queen would know that the fountains needed magic renewal. It might even be Sartoran mages had provided this service in the past, in which case there would be records, so presumably the mage guild would know the magic was overdue.

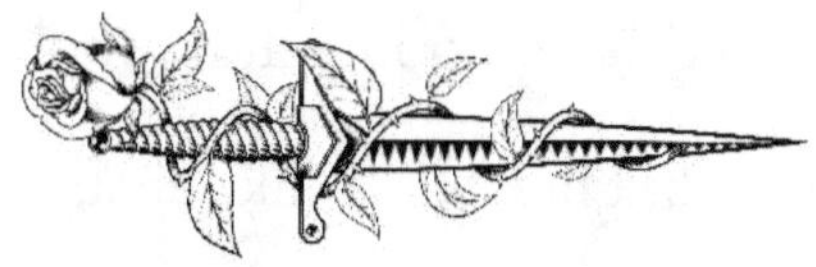

TWENTY

Lyren-Sartora loved the idea of presenting them-selves as official envoys—until Liere explained that they would do it with just the two of them, without a lot of pomp and display.

"Display goes with official invitations," Liere reminded her. "We wouldn't be here at all if Atan had relations with this country. Envoys are nothing more than diplomatic messengers."

"Got it, got it," Lyren-Sartora said with a sigh. "But I'm going to wear my pretty robe."

The next court day dawned bright and warm, promising to be another scorcher.

"Do you know what to say?" Lyren-Sartora asked.

"Atan wrote to me last night with suggestions for what to say in an envoy speech. Want to see?"

"Is it boring?"

"Frightfully so. Stiff, boring, lengthy, and as full of air as a pastry."

Lyren-Sartora snickered. "Never mind. Just remember, I don't want to have to be a scribe, stuck in a room. If I have to do that, I may as well go home."

"Lyren, scribes see *everything*—"

"Lyren-*Sartora*. And I'm your sister, or your cousin. Not your daughter. It makes me sound like a two-year-old. Or should I get a disguise, so we don't look at all related?"

"My pardon, Lyren-Sartora. Old habit. As the envoy's scribe, you can still be my relative—everyone expects relatives to be part of one's party—but you won't be an ordinary one. Perhaps they'll see it as a gesture of amity if you are an aide, not a scribe." Liere thought it was far more likely they'd see Lyren-Sartora as a spy, but then that was inevitable no matter what they did. Lyren-Sartora's age would be her best protection. No matter how suspicious Adon-Marsael might be, he would have no idea how well trained Lyren-Sartora was.

Lyren-Sartora brightened. "I like that. An aide—like a herald?"

"Yes! You will hold our letter in a very nice carved box with one hand, and the Sartoran pennon—*not* a banner, as we are not official—which we can borrow from Arthur, and I will hand off to you whatever tokens or passes we're offered, if any. You stand by me for the speeches, then you'll be free until there is some official function."

Lyren-Sartora was thrilled enough to swallow complaints about transferring to Bereth Ferian and back before they'd even breakfasted.

She couldn't remember ever seeing Liere dressed up. She wore the heel length over-robe she'd made herself, with a fine-woven linen summer blouse under it, and loose front-pleated linen trousers, but with expert illusion these had been transformed into sky blue, gold, and white, the gold in fine, interlocked crowns of three, reflecting the interlocked three crowns on the deep violet of the Sartoran flag.

Liere braided her hair in the diamond pattern made with four parts, weaving in sky blue ribbon. This braid went to her waist, below which the rest of her golden hair swung free halfway to her knees, simple but elegant. Perfect for an envoy. Lyren-Sartora stared in gratified amazement that Liere could look so impressive. Oh, Liere had turned pretty in her five years away, but Lyren-Sartora hadn't believed her dear, fumbling Liere could ever have that much *presence*.

Lyren-Sartora's own garments were a copy of the courtly tabards Atan's highest-ranking stewards wore when attending the throne room called Star Chamber. In one hand she carried a purple and gold Sartoran pennant that Arthur had had in storage, held at the proper angle, and in the other a box that Liere had let her pick on her own. Lyren-Sartora still beamed inside at the sincerity in Liere's voice when she'd said, "You have a better sense for style than I do."

Since they had no coaches or entourage, Liere had set a Destination at the foot of the long road along the ridge leading to the royal palace. The two appeared there, stood until they recovered, and in the bright summer sunlight began their long walk along up the middle of the paved road.

At first no one noticed them, but that Sartoran pennon caught eyes, and sure enough, runners went ahead to alert the palace that they were coming.

Lyren-Sartora reveled in the swelling attention as people backed out of their way, staring. She sent a thought to Liere: *What if that Adon-Marsael's finds out we were staying at Genda's?*

: Oh, I expect he's hearing that right about now. Not that it matters. Being at the very bottom of the diplomatic hierarchy gives us a lot more freedom, if no power except the prestige of being connected with Sartor; he will have expected us to do our due diligence in learning what we could.

Liere felt Lyren-Sartora's alarm subside, along with a somewhat sulky thought that she didn't need a reminder of the reading she should be doing, before Lyren-Sartora shuttered her mind.

Liere let the subject rest, and presently they entered the palace, which was scarcely cooler than being out under the sun, thanks to the crowds now pressing to either side. Lyren-Sartora stayed two paces behind Liere, making certain that the banner never came near Liere's golden head, and halted when Liere did, facing where a throne would be in there had been one. Liere bowed, and Lyren-Sartora dipped the pennon, feeling very much as if she were in a play. Only it was *real*. Eh, sort of real.

Liere then turned crisply to face Adon-Marsael in his chair. "I bring to Enaeran," Liere said in a clear voice that carried through the entire room without shrilling, "greetings from Her Majesty Yustnesveas Landis, Queen of Sartor."

Liere breathed out her loathing at being the center of attention. She looked neither right nor left as Adon-Marsael greeted her in passable Sartoran. Liere reeled out the carefully constructed periods that Atan had suggested, thrilling when Adon-Marsael responded in like language. This diplomatic ritual actually worked!

As the talk went back and forth, Liere watched the subtleties of his body, and listened to the assurance of his tone. She'd learned on Geth that customs and attitudes might differ, but humans were a lot alike in the main. It was exhilarating to see proved before her one of the Ones' diplomatic maxims: that if you treat an uncertain government as legitimate, its spokespeople are more likely to do the same to you.

So it was. The old pennon was surrendered to a pair of tall, tabarded servants to be carried out to the front and placed with Adon-Marsael's own banner. Here it would be placed ahead of those of the nobles sworn to him, he said and then added a string of fulsome compliments meant to be carried back to the ruler of the oldest kingdom in the world. He spoke in an equally carrying voice, so that every down-at-heel petitioner and secret revolutionary could hear him comment on how appropriate it was that Sartor be the first to welcome Enaeran back into the fellowship of civilized kingdoms in its new peace, and so on, so on.

Liere listened to the tone, not the words. The man spoke with an assurance surprising from someone who barely held grip on a war-torn, restless kingdom. His focus was on her, a tight focus that was nearly an instinctive mind-shield: she would have to break her own rule to delve past it, something she would not attempt unless convinced he had truck with Norsunder. There was absolutely no such sign.

At a gesture from Liere, Lyren-Sartora stepped forward and opened the box, disclosing the ribbon-tied and sealed envoy letter, with the tokens Liere had prepared—having chosen two of the newest and finest of the six-sided coins Atan had given her.

Liere lifted her voice and delivered her speech about gifts from throne to throne as the watchers whispered to one another. She caught the word "magic" breezing around the vast chamber.

Adon-Marsael was also listening to the crowd, and watching their reactions, while trying to keep his gaze on this admittedly stunning young person. How old was she? She looked no more than sixteen, and yet she didn't behave the way sixteen-year-olds did: she had not once touched that river of shining gold hair, or flipped it, or giggled, or bridled. She did not look at the boys, though Adon-Marsael could see his nobles' sons' gazes riveted on her, a few jaws dropped in unlovely faces, and skinny neck-knuckles working.

Here, it seemed, was a thoroughly unexpected felicity, and he meant to make the most of her decorative presence while she remained. A pulse of uncertainty caused him to study her more closely as he accepted the coins, on which he could feel the distinctive not-quite-buzz of magic. "How did your queen know that our fair city is in need of this magic?"

The envoy replied, "Oh, you must put that question to the Sartoran Mage Guild. I expect they have records about that sort of thing."

With a considerable sense of relief, Adon-Marsael pictured a dusty archive, and some old, shuffling mage pointing out in querulous voice that payment for mages visiting the Shiovhan fountains was long overdue. Though hiring mages for such things was very low on his list of urgent requirements, he appreciated how clever it was for some flunky or other to contrive a gift that put no one out. He didn't have to pay out a copperpiece, but he would be an idiot not to make certain the credit was his.

He raised his voice as he closed his hand over the tokens: "It shall be my great pleasure to see to it personally, after which we shall welcome Sartor's envoy and celebrate at the same time!" And, raising his hands, "I declare a city festival day, one week from now!" He gave a quick nod to the captain of the day guard, who rallied his lackeys and began ushering people from the throne room, the words "festival" and "celebrate" spreading ahead of them.

Adon-Marsael permitted himself a private gloat. In a single gesture, at the expense of these Sartorans, he'd heighten his authority, as well as his prestige, for he would be the one seen using these magic objects. True, he'd have to dig up the funds for the "festival" (which meant all consumables at designated sites from daybreak to sundown would be reimbursed by the crown), but that would not cost nearly as much as training and equipping an army—or for that matter, repairing those accursed fountains.

He decided that this was enough morning court for the day. Let word get out and do its work! Making the private hand signal, he relinquished the morning session to the scribe chief, whose team would write down the petitions, as he indicated one of the tall side doors.

Liere noted the brawny servitors in livery springing to open it as Adon-Marsael said, "Envoy Feriadar, is there anyone else in your party?"

Or, where are your underlings and spies? she read in his tone, but responded with even politesse, "It's just myself and my aide, for now. I really am an exploratory envoy, the lowest of the low, since we were not invited, and there is no diplomatic connection between our two kingdoms. If I'm sent back with favorable report, the queen will be delighted to establish communications, and send a full staff."

"Excellent," Adon-Marsael exclaimed, thinking that things couldn't be better. That would give him plenty of time to get control before Sartor sent a pack of spies. "Excellent! As a gesture of good will, then, I shall grant you ambassadorial status, *Honor* Feriadar, which will carry over when the treaty is signed. Anywhere you stay will of course be considered sovereign territory." He had not been sitting on his hands as Liere and Lyren-Sartora made their stately way up the broad street to the palace; he gestured and a silent steward brought an intricately carved and gilded token on a tray. "With this you may move about as you like. Our guard, and anywhere you choose to visit, will be honored to serve you."

Thus keeping track of my movements, Liere thought as she accepted the carved blue stone in its elaborate golden setting.

He went on, "But for now, please accept my invitation to take up temporary quarters in the guest wing."

Where he could surround her with his own eyes and spies, of course. She smiled and bowed. "I would be honored," she said.

"Needless to say, our festival will end with a grand ball in your honor, while the city enjoys its more, ah, rustic festival."

Liere once again bowed acquiescence, and the interview was over. Adon-Marsael turned her over to another waiting steward in blue livery, who began leading them to their new quarters as Adon-Marsael walked into the antechamber alone, rapidly considering how to stretch an already overstretched staff. Guards, of course; Talipin would have to find runners to report what he wanted reported.

Adon-Marsael would in his turn have to find a way to weave this young Envoy Feriadar into the court he was trying to build—but her looks and her youth should actually aid him there. He suspected those young noble youths would be falling all over themselves wanting to get a closer look, and if the smarter of them were not already sending their personal servants home to cadge their parents or guardians into being the first to issue invitations, he'd be quite surprised.

No, the social aspect would very likely take care of itself, once he got it going. Why did he feel that the conversation was unfinished? He paused before a window to look out at that new pennon hanging limply in the humid air as he reviewed that conversation. Diplomatic palaver, all of it, many actual turns of phrase familiar from a youth spent at court. Except . . . and then he had it:

That fresh-faced young envoy had spoken so eloquently to "Enaeran" and "Sartor's neighbors" and had used the formal verb forms addressing the people of Enaeran at large, but of course she had, quite properly, never actually referred to him as king.

Which brought him back to the motivations for sending an envoy right now, this summer, even this week. He considered what he knew of the Sartoran queen. She was younger than he was, and like him had lived through war, but she'd emerged at a much younger age into the shambles of war with Norsunder. And she held the oldest kingdom in the world.

This envoy was far younger still, but it would be an error to assume she was naive. *He* had been naive in assuming that other kingdoms were oblivious to events in Enaeran. Or that Sartor, with no military, wasn't capable of considerable influence in other ways.

He considered those coins with the magic on them, so generously given, helpfully offered. In his experience, nobody was helpfully generous for no reason. Scouting, was it?

"Oh yes," he said, snapping his fingers at his last remaining aide. "Genda's. I think it's time to shut that down, don't you think?"

The aide bowed, and effaced himself.

Adon-Marsael continued on his way. He could make this surprising encounter into a little test. If it worked for him — as he believed it would, with a little exertion well flowered with compliments — he should set about planning his coronation. Having representatives from Sartor was about as convincing a claim to legitimacy as anything, these days. But first he had to clear the obstacles from his path, such as Andri Malcolin Elsarion.

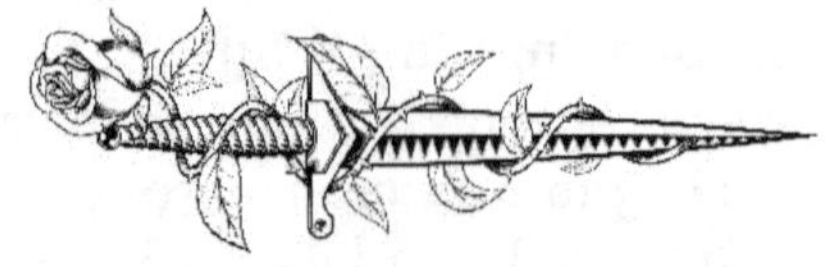

TWENTY-ONE

As Adon-Marsael had predicted, word propagated outward through the city with the speed of a stone dropped into still water.

"She's what?" Andri Elsarion said, stopping so fast that the hat he'd been clapping onto his head hit him in the forehead.

"Envoy," Elies stated.

"With ambassadorial status. The small one is an attendant, or a scribe," Marten added.

"Where are they now?"

"Assigned to the guest wing," Elies stated.

"Surrounded by snouts three rings deep," Andri commented—it wasn't even a question.

Marten said, "The new perimeter was being assembled when we left."

"And a festival at the end of the week, crowned with a grand ball?" someone gloated. "Hah! I think we ought to issue our own welcome at said grand ball, don't you?"

"Yeah," Bran drawled. "Seeing as how Marsael will probably forget to send an invitation to his cousin here." With a thumb toward Andri.

Andri grinned wryly. "Oh, I think the invitation's already been issued."

Marten was the first to catch on to what he meant. He said soberly, "To be accepted?"

Andri smacked Gared on the back. "Let's go see."

Liere's sharp ears caught a rustle in the still, hot night air.

Widening her awareness, she listened on the mental plane, catching a sense of intrigue to match her own. Laughter, dare. Two living beings approaching, one with a mind-shield.

"I think . . . we're about to meet Adon-Marsael's rival, or one of them," Liere said, glancing toward the long glass doors to the balcony, which they had left wide open in hopes of a breath of cooler air.

Lyren-Sartora danced onto the balcony, peering upward as Liere appreciated the excellence of the pair's sneakery. No silhouette created above the ridgepole. Steps quiet. They were swathed in dark colors, blending with the roof.

She saw nothing until they dropped lightly onto the broad balcony outside the salon midway between Liere's and Lyren-Sartora's rooms. The blonde with the long, tangled hair cast a fast glance around as the other one advanced on Liere, grinning, muscular arms flattered by a very fine linen shirt, deep blue as a midnight sky, and worked with embroidery in black vines. The shirt was further embellished by a sash of black silk, fringed at the ends. This festival garb accorded oddly with scuffed and shapeless dark brown riding trousers and down-at-heel riding boots, and his brown hair pulled up into a warrior's knot. In contrast, the yellow-haired one wore a shapeless tunic made for someone much heftier in size, dyed a rusty black, over dark brown riding trousers the same fabric as his companion's.

"Bagged yourselves one of the few furnished suites," he commented in a friendly manner.

Lyren-Sartora's hackles rose at the way both paid more attention to Liere than to her, so she rectified that in a voice full of challenge, "We were *invited* to have these rooms."

Liere watched the uninvited guests assess for threats, and lines of retreat, before the blond one said, "Welcome to Brydon," his voice low and husky.

"You are?" Liere asked.

"Andri." He leaned against the little table by the door, where he could see the entire room as well as make a fast exit, but he couldn't be seen from either door or window. He was lighter in build than his companion, long-waisted.

"And I'm Gared," said the brown-haired one in the fancy shirt. He was well-made, even handsome, with an open, friendly expression. "Elies told us the foreign visitor was an envoy."

Lyren-Sartora thought, Liere was right about that girl Elies! How did she do that? But they still weren't looking at her, so she stepped forward, hands on hips. "You're Andri the ousted prince? This was your family's palace?"

"There isn't much in the way of family left," he replied, and to Lyren-Sartora's frowning stare, he joked, "Do I look like an impostor?"

No, Lyren-Sartora thought, looking at the fine scars on his hands, the wary stance and muscular contours shaping his old clothes. Except for that diamond in your ear, you look like a poopsie. Of course she couldn't say that, because then they'd want to know who the poopsies were, and Liere seemed to want to be merely a Sartoran envoy. Talking about Detlev and his gang might ruin that impression.

However, Lyren-Sartora could treat them like poopsies: when in doubt, use an insult. "Yep," she said cheerily.

But he wasn't listening. His attention had gone right back to Liere.

Who forced herself to meet his gaze. It was more difficult than she'd thought, for he did not look away, or even smile, and for a few moments her vision tingled around the edges.

"Adon gave you a general pass?" he asked.

"Yes." Speaking steadied her.

"Don't trust him."

"What will you wager," she retorted pleasantly, "that in my next conversation with him, he will say the same about you?"

"I wouldn't take that wager," Andri said promptly. "Of course he will."

"Very well, then. Why shouldn't I trust him?"

"First, if you leave, expect to be tailed."

"Haven't I been already?" She turned her thumb between Andri and Gared.

"Yes, to see who was moving through our territory. Cousin Adon knows who you are now, right? You'll be tailed with intent."

"You've no intent?"

"Question only. That's why we're here."

Lyren-Sartora watched avidly. The exchange was fast, almost as fast as a mental contact. And they both looked so — so serious, as serious as duelists testing the other. And Gared watched, his friendly smile widening to a grin that deepened the dimples on either side of his mouth. Not hearing anything particularly funny, Lyren-Sartora sensed that meaning was evading her, and she *loathed* that!

Then Gared turned her way. "Tell us about your-selves," he invited, flicking the chair around as if its weight were no more than a thatching of reeds. He sat backwards on it, crossed his arms over the back and rested his chin on them. "Beginning with your names?"

Liere noticed in a brief glance that the friendliness of his blue gaze matched his smile. In contrast, hazel-eyed, blond Andri was bony, with a hawk nose, broad cheek-bones that gave his face a triangular shape, and a rangy build. Meeting his gaze was like staring at the sun, only it didn't burn, but intensified that sense that her veins ran with the spangles of sunlight on water.

"Liere Feriadar."

"Lyren-Sartora."

"Half the girls in our generation in Shiovhan are named either Liara or Sartora," Gared commented.

Lyren-Sartora's lips parted. Liere said swiftly, "Well, here are two more."

"You're related?" he asked.

"Cousins." Lyren-Sartora sent a challenging look Liere's way. "The Queen of Sartor sent us," she went on, twirling fingers in the air. To her, these two who moved so much like poopsies definitely had to be treated like them. That meant no respect, and outright hostility if they got bossy.

"What about us caught the interest of the world-renowned Queen of Sartor?" Andri asked.

Lyren-Sartora turned to Liere, who had been reflecting that to mention Norsunder to anyone who might be connected with Norsunder would not only be likely to get lies as an answer, but to warn them. "She is working on diplomatic connections. Enaeran is part of those she wishes to communicate with." And she deflect-ed pacifically, "This is a handsome palace, in spite of the damage we can see is still being repaired. Do you live here?"

"Nope. Our welcome would be—" Gared drew a finger across his neck. "If they nabbed us." He grinned, as if it all was a very great joke.

Then Andri shifted away from the wall and fingered the curtain. "Gared." He tipped his head toward the door to the balcony, then, with an apologetic glance toward Liere, he blew out the lamp on the little table.

The room plunged into darkness. As Liere's eyes adjusted, she made out the two ghosting onto the balcony. She moved to the door, looking down into the courtyard in time to see a tall figure pelting along the building on the other side of the court, the torchlight in a sconce catching on loose yellow hair: it looked like Andri's hair, but that was not his long torso. Whoever he was vanished as a squad of guards in blue sprinted around the corner after him.

Then Andri and Gared reappeared on a distant balcony, leaped to the rail and then to the roof, and flowed over it as silent as cats, vanishing in opposite direction.

"Well, that was stupid," Lyren-Sartora said as she picked up the sparker to relight the lamp wick. "That other idiot didn't even make it here. A friend of theirs?"

"A decoy, I should think," Liere said.

"Oh, so Gared and Poopsie Face could escape?"

"That, and to lead Adon-Marsael to assume that the two didn't make it to our wing."

Lyren-Sartora grinned. "Are you going to tell him? I would."

Liere said, "I thought we'd agreed to get more information than we give."

Lyren-Sartora shrugged sharply.

"I take it you were not impressed with them," Liere said, sitting down.

"Gared seemed friendly enough," Lyren-Sartora stated. "But I didn't like the looks of that Andri up close. He reminds me too much of MV in the bad old days."

MV, co-leader of Detlev's boys! It would be difficult to find two people more un-alike, Liere thought, picturing MV's lean, taut saunter, and the fact that he never seemed to go anywhere without at least six weapons on him. Andri was far more easy-going, and he had come unarmed.

It was Liere's turn to shrug. The spangles of attraction had abated some, leaving the room too close, and oddly empty. She knew what had happened, of course. She'd listened to the older Ones on Geth discussing their adventures into relationships, with plenty of cautionary tales about how desire distorted perception. She had even experimented a little with her old friend Dak, who had been forthright about his attraction to her, and she had found him sweet and appealing. But nothing had prepared her for the intensity of hot desire going both ways.

Lyren-Sartora eyed her, alert to a subtle change in the atmosphere that she couldn't define. But it definitely had to do with Liere and that poopsie-faced Andri. She pushed on. "Of course, Gared is nicer, and better looking, and probably smarter."

Her testing tone wrested Liere's attention to her, making her reach for the drift of Lyren-Sartora's thought. "You found Gared appealing, then?"

"Well, didn't you?" And at Liere's exasperating lack of reaction, Lyren-Sartora added, "Andri's too skinny. And bony, with that hawk nose. Isn't that always the way! The wrong one gets born to a title."

"You think that looks is the most important criterion for rulership?"

Lyren-Sartora crossed her arms. "I'm not that stupid. All I'm saying is, if one has to be born to rank, which we all know is a random thing, why not the pretty ones? Makes for better stories." She tossed her head back exactly the way Liere's sister Marga used to, which gave Liere an unexpected pang. "Let's go to sleep. Maybe we can finish our spying before the ball. I want to go back to Eidervaen."

They extinguished the lights and parted each to her room, the salon doors open between them in hopes of any movement of air. Liere lay back, composing herself for sleep, but her mind seemed unable to get past two things:

One, I can't permit attraction to distort my perceptions.
And two, he's hiding something.

She woke with a gasp, unaware of having fallen asleep, terror receding like sticky webbing as Lyren-Sartora shook her harder. "Liere! Open your eyes!"

Liere gulped in air and sat up. Lyren-Sartora fell back, heaving a sigh of relief. The room was dark, the air hot and close.

Lyren-Sartora's eyes were huge, starlight reflecting like tiny pinpoints in either pupil. "It was about Detlev. Wasn't it?"

"It?"

Then she recovered the nightmare that she'd slipped into.

Lyren-Sartora had heard it on the mental plane. Liere flinched, wishing she was better at shielding when deeply asleep. She felt sticky and headachy as she got up and stood in the open doorway, wishing for cooler air. "Yes. But he was the symbol, not the cause."

"He *was* the cause. I heard you," Lyren-Sartora whispered in a ragged, fierce voice. "You were at the Base, a prisoner, and he was gloating—"

"That was when I was eleven years old. Don't you see? My emotions were real to me, but the circumstances weren't."

"I don't get it." Lyren-Sartora scowled. "You're going to make excuses for Detlev's villainy, aren't you."

"Lyren-Sartora. I'm only talking about my specific circumstances, when I was a prisoner that time, at the Norsunder Base. Which I still dream about, I don't know why. Whenever Detlev came around he barked and snarled threats like a villain in a bad play, never carried any of them out, and I succeeded in scaring myself far worse than he did. Even that time in Geth, it was all noise on the surface of the mental plane, as usual with avid watchers ready to spread the word far and wide about how evil he was."

"You think that was fair?" Lyren-Sartora's voice trembled.

"No. But it was a lesson," Liere said. "The only way he could give me one. All my weaknesses were of my own manufacture, because I wouldn't listen to anyone else, and insisted on that impossible—stupid—goal of attaining omniscience by rejecting all human emotion."

Lyren-Sartora gulped.

"Don't get angry. You have to admit it was true," Liere went on.

Lyren-Sartora thought back, and nodded reluctantly. "One time—when you left—after we argued, and you got mad at yourself for being emotional, Erai-Yanya told me that you listened to her, and nodded respectfully, and went right on doing the same thing."

"Once I almost told her to mind her own business— humbly, of course," Liere said reminiscently. Then the smile left her voice, and she added, "Detlev's lesson was not out of place. Not when you consider that Siamis was your age when the Host took him. Only the things they threatened, they really did, and Detlev could do nothing but watch until he surrendered. That's what happened to Siamis and Detlev, all those years ago."

Lyren-Sartora stated, "All I want to know is that he has nightmares for all the rotten things he's done. And I hope he has them forever."

"I expect he does. Gloat quietly—I want to get some sleep."

"I will! Gloat, I mean." Lyren-Sartora flounced through the door, then halted, and sat down on the floor in the salon, her back to the wall, in case Liere cried out again, and eventually slipped into dreams.

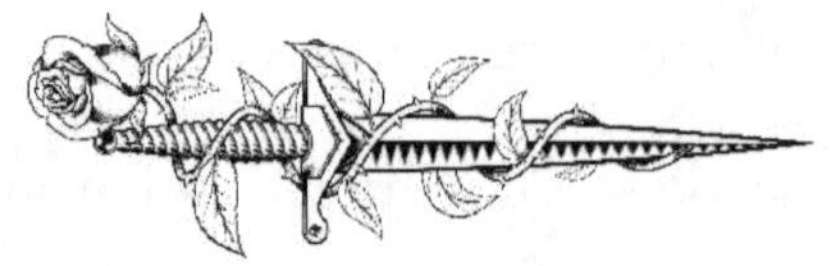

TWENTY-TWO

ext morning, Liere considered the nightmare as she finished braiding the upper half of her hair. The distortion made it fairly clear that the cause was not related to Detlev at all; he and that unrealistic cell with the ceiling so high it was lost in the darkness were generic nightmare setting, and that was not even Detlev's voice. In the light of day it was almost comical in its deformation. But instigating it was a whiff on the mental plane both elusive and foul. She had to know if that was here. And if so, was it connected to Andri Malcolin Elsarion?

She tied the three braids with a ribbon, and let the rest hang loose down her back. The cleaning frame had restored her linen outfit to freshness. Without the magic overlay, no one would recognize it as her presentation garb. Lyren-Sartora had already left; Liere stared down at herself, twitching her robe straight in hopes she looked like a proper envoy.

When did a person feel like a true adult, and not like a student undergoing yet another test? But there was no Sister Orchid waiting to be promoted to the next level here. Mistakes did not gain demerits anymore. This was real life, for everyone, including little Jaydi. She scolded herself for her timidity. You've had all the training. Make it work.

She reached for the door, then paused to glance around, wondering if their things would be searched while they were gone. Of course they would. All that remained visible in either bedroom were their few clothes—no papers, secret or otherwise. She carried her golden notecase in her inner pocket. She set a couple of tiny traps in her own room so she would know. Everything was information, no matter how small the detail.

Her explorations had given her a general idea of the layout of the central palace. She blended in with the steady stream of guests, or courtiers, or whoever they were, who walked at a leisurely pace toward the dining room for the last breakfast, making it easier for the liveried servant she sensed following her.

Liere paused in an archway, surveying the company. Three older women passed, followed by two men of military bearing talking in low voices, then a straight-backed, nose-lifted old man, his blond beard graying. He wore a low brimmed hat, though no one else did inside the building. Was she right not to have a hat?

After he stalked by, his indifferent gaze resting on her then moving away as if she were furniture, two well-dressed people her own age approached, their sturdy round faces turned toward her with obvious interest. Her return smile brightened her entire countenance — mostly relief as the short, round girl towed the taller boy, clearly her brother, Liere's way. "Honor Feriadar?"

"Liere will do."

"Ennis Laish, at your service." The girl smiled as she bowed, and Liere took her for one of those eager people who collect others for social purposes. Very well, here was a test of her training. "He's Halvor," Ennis went on, pointing at her brother, and once again Liere bowed as Halvor bowed. Liere noted that neither wore a hat indoors. "We overslept, and everyone else seems to have already gone on the chase," Ennis went on as they settled around the nearest table

"Lake breakfast," Halvor Laish put in, as a silent servant came around, offering various dishes on a tray.

"You're right, for I see old Baras Parael Otobris," Ennis whispered, tipping her head slightly toward the haughty old man sitting alone. "Now the Minister of Trade. No chase begins without him." A quick look at Liere. "Or his horrid daughter, but at least Thadara's not here. She must be hosting the boat breakfast."

She then went on to ask a few questions about Sartor, all of which Liere fielded or finessed. Nothing intrusive, just the sorts of questions one might ask of visitor, and then said, "I did not mean to interrogate you! Do you have any questions for me? Fair is fair!"

"Thank you! This Baras Otobris you pointed out wears a hat," Liere said. "Will you pardon my ignorance if I ask why he does, and you do not? I do not wish to trespass on a custom inadvertently."

"Means he's about to go out," Halvor offered.

Ennis rolled her eyes, and leaned toward Liere, eager to share knowledge. "It means no one dares approach, is what it really means, unless a social superior."

"Ah," said Liere, perceiving the distinction: a hat indoors indicated a personage too busy to be bothered. "Thank you. My next question, if I am not tiresome, is how would everyone know that a person is hosting an event, do you send pages, or speak in person? Or does everyone employ scribes?" *Like in olden times.* Liere had begun to realize that the people of Enaeran, whatever degree, did not use golden notecases. Magic, of course, she reflected as she was offered savory-smelling shirred eggs, and crisped bread with strawberry compote.

Ennis smiled. "Oh, no, she invites everyone by voice or by note, for then she gets the credit for generosity. Chases could be held in the wood at the north side of the preserve, which belonged to the kings, but the Otobrises prefer to host at one of her father's more remote holdings. Vastly beautiful and all that, but only first circle will see it."

Liere recognized that term, at least. "First circle, as in Sartor: the duchases and head mage?"

Ennis twirled her tiny three-tined fork. "It might have meant that once, but when *we* say it, it means your own social circle. Here's how my tutor explained it to me. Those she really wants, her first circle, they merely need say they will come, and she contrives it. Second circle are obligations. Third circle — the rest of us — oh, we are invited, but given no means to get there. And unless you are wealthy enough to travel easily, or desperate to consider yourself included in her set, you are unlikely to put yourself to the trouble of going."

Halvor glanced up briefly, his voice wry as he said, "Though with her, it's also Sartoran first circle. No one with rank below baras would ever be welcome. Our nearest relation to a title is our great-uncle, so we are not good enough for her."

Ennis lifted a shoulder, as if shrugging off this Thadara Otobris, then leaned forward. "In Sartor people are also named for the Great Sartora?"

Liere suppressed the desire to laugh. Or maybe groan. Both. Aware of Adon-Marsael's entry from the far archway, she said, "Others might be. I was named for my grandmother, a cranky old person completely unfamous." Hoping to skip past the Great Sartora quagmire, she said, "What will those not at the boat breakfast do this morning?"

Halvor shrugged. "Oh, there's gaming, for those who don't like hot weather. Otherwise people are mainly seeking shade." He twirled his fan.

Ennis barely waited for her brother to finish, before saying eagerly, "Aliara Riand already went down to the lake, or I'd have her recite her List."

"List?"

Ennis preened, and Liere had to reassess once again. Ennis's few questions had not once gone down the expected path—what famous people do you know, do you have titles in your family, and she had clearly been happy to answer. Liere understood that Ennis did not collect people for their social rank, she collected people because she liked people. "Her mother is something of a scholar, and for her birthday once gave her a list of all the ways 'Liere' is pronounced that she could find."

"I did that once—" Liere began, then stopped.

"Did you get more than twelve?" Ennis asked.

Thirty-two, Liere remembered. She opened her hand. "A bit more."

"Her mother didn't count the ones with the Sartoran *llyah* at the beginning," Ennis said. "She said that's a separate name, a much older one, *Llya-Rheya*, or something like that."

Liere smiled again. "Speaking of the lake, how long have you been here in Shiovhan?"

"Six weeks. I love court! Last night, I don't think I sat down once, I danced so much."

"Was there a party last night?" Liere asked, and at their nods, "I thought I heard music through the windows in the guest suite. How was it?"

"Fun!" Ennis fluted.

"Fine." Halvor stated, and with a little more enthusiasm, "At least it wasn't all formal court dances."

"You'd do better if you practiced," Ennis stated.

"I'd rather be riding while the weather is fine."

Ennis ignored him. "Colored lamps in all the trees—it was outside—excellent musicians. Played lots and lots of haltas, which is just the dance for the dark, twirling and whirling endlessly." She tapped her fingers lightly together in triplets.

Halvor sat back, and pushed away his plate. "Speaking of riding, maybe there's someone who wants to ride for wind, and not sweat through a day to see how many deer you can garland."

"I should think it's too hot even for the deer," Ennis said, smothering a yawn.

"They do give a better run when it's cold," Halvor acknowledged, his tone, like his sister's, the easygoing complacency of the person in the know who likes to share. "Though The Elsarion trained 'em himself, and says they do well in all weather. Which is why he had them brought to the capital."

Keeping the restless nobles busy? Liere wondered.

Ennis said, "Is there anyone you'd like to meet? I don't pretend to be on intimate terms with everyone, but we know who they are."

"What can you tell me about Andri Elsarion?" Liere asked.

"Prince Andri Malcolin, do you mean?" Ennis asked, after a blank moment.

"Never met him," Halvor said, shaking his head. "Bad rep. Very bad," he added under his breath.

"They say he comes around scouting money," Ennis whispered, glancing to either side to make sure they weren't overheard. "But that's rumor, nothing I know for certain."

"And yet it was his father who was king. The throne in this country is not passed through the family?"

"If he can take it," Halvor said, shrugging again. "The Elsarions themselves took it from the main branch of their family a few generations back, according to my tutor. Ah, Rossl is there, looking for me. Thank you for joining us." He bowed hastily to Liere, and went to join a friend at the other end of the great marble room.

Ennis chattered on, occasionally returning greetings, and performed introductions with an amusing air of pride. Liere followed her lead, rising when she did, and making slight bows at each introduction, until the approach of a young man in beautifully made livery of gray with a hint of blue and white piped with a thin line of silver down sleeves and the outside of trousers. This one was different from her shadow, who still stood behind a column . . . yes, over there.

The servant in gray bowed deeply. "His grace bade me extend his greetings, and ask if you honor him with a moment's conversation?"

Ennis cast a startled look up into Liere's face, then bowed. "I shall see you anon," she said. One last glance at the wooden-faced young footman, and she retreated circumspectly.

Liere had seen Adon-Marsael enter but she had not seen him leave. She got up to follow the footman with the once-broken nose and the purple sabre-cut scar on his jaw. He was obviously no recent hireling, and despite the light gray civilian livery with its badge over the heart, he moved like a person with long military training. He wore Adon-Marsael's own livery, she suspected, remembering the uncertain movements of those in ill-fitting royal blue. These in the gray would be his personal servants.

The fellow escorted Liere toward the great hall and the rooms back of the gallery. At the stairway Liere said, "Oh, just a moment." And she veered, crossing to an indoor pond that she and Lyren-Sartora had seen the day before. She paused to look down at the gold and silver fish swimming about inside. Her guide stood impassively, waiting.

Interesting. Then at least the semblance of being a guest—however uninvited—was to be maintained, though she had two shadows, the obvious guard in livery and the less-obvious shadow.

Liere turned away, smiled brightly, and said, "I just love goldfish!"

The liveried guard merely bowed, extended a hand toward the stairs, and up they trod.

He led her around the horrible library with all the stains, and down the marble hall to one of the formal salons—and through to a library, though its size indicated an inner cabinet, for private interviews. Would those be kings' own archives?

The guard opened the door, and Liere sensed the shadow peeling off to vanish down a back stair. In the room, Adon-Marsael sat between the two tall windows, papers on his lap and a pen and inkwell on a little table at his side. He rose, set aside the papers, and bowed. He was quite tall, ivory lace and pale peach over-robe setting off his bronze skin. His lazy-lidded dark eyes crinkled in amusement as he bowed. "Good morning, Honor Feriadar."

"Good morning, your grace." Liere bowed back.

He indicated two fine wing-backed chairs adjacent, and they seated themselves. "I hope you are com-fortable? Or as comfortable as can be expected. As Brydon, I'm certain you've seen, is undergoing extensive repairs," he added with a sardonic quirk to his smile.

"Very comfortable, thank you."

Adon-Marsael said, "I trust I will not sound impolitic if I ask why you in particular were sent to us? We're more accustomed to grim-faced graybeards. Might this be your first mission?"

Liere said, "I'm interested in your history, and in language. I did say that the Queen of Sartor hopes to send an embassy."

And here they were, back at the Eidervaen Accord. Liere smiled, keeping her voice light, and thrust before he could: "One of the questions puzzling the queen was the fact that Sles Adran to the east is a signatory, with an embassy, yet Enaeran is not."

"Sles Adran's capital exists from the days we were Enaeran-Adrani. A great deal of diplomatic under-standing is inherited, I am told. When we separated, we no longer shared those benefits—and have been in a defensive position ever since. As to the specifics of why the Elsarions did not become signatories, I cannot tell you, alas. I am still going through what private royal records remain," he said in a confiding tone. "A necessarily slow process as peace must be my first concern."

Liere sensed in his calculated drop in tone that in spite of his affability and apparent openness, he trusted little, while Adon-Marsael reflected that she had not really answered his question. Young she might be, but not stupid. What was the Queen of Sartor's true purpose? Clearly an impression of openness would be the best venture. "Feel free, Honor Feriadar, to continue your explorations. There is nothing to hide as we rebuild. Or is there a loftier title I should use when introducing you formally to what remains of our court?"

"Honor will suffice," she said, glad that no one here

looked for "Sartora" or "Queen in Bereth Ferian"—lofty indeed, so lofty those titles were nothing but empty air.

He leaned forward. "You mentioned Sles Adran, which most certainly hosts fine embassies from many lands, including Sartor. The Adranis are proud of their ancient civilities, and yet our semblance of peace is ephemeral as they continue, under one pretext or another, to hold land that is ours. You will meet Bartal Na Shagal's envoy and her partner among the guests. I am trying to woo them with pleasures rather than attempt to carve them up with steel. By all means woo them, too. Talk to them of Sartoran peace and plenty. I invite you. I exhort you!" Another openhanded gesture. "Truth is, I imposed upon you for this interview in discuss the ball I wish to host in your honor. Have you any musical preferences? I thought we might present a Sartoran theme, though we'd have to trouble you for instructions in current Sartoran fashion."

Liere was not going to admit that she had no idea what happened at Sartoran balls. Or any balls in this world—her first such gathering had taken place during her mission on Geth-deles. "I am flattered," she said with another slight bow. "Perhaps that is an honor a bit above my reach. It might be best saved for the ambassador to come."

"Very well. Have you any more questions while we have the luxury of this time away from listening ears?"

Ah, the trust ploy. "If I might trouble your grace to explain to me why King Bartal of Sles Adran will not make peace?"

Adon-Marsael glanced out the window. Liere felt the urge to look at what caught his eye, and suppressed it. He said with a sigh of weariness in his voice, "He would like to restore the two kingdoms as one great one, as we were centuries ago. Ruled by the Shagals. It could be said that the Adranis got the better land as well as a greater amount of it. But we got our freedom." He said it with the ease of a lifetime of repetitions, finishing with a complacent smile.

"One more question, if I may. Is there any truth in that vocal young man's assertions about a duchy or province called Geral, and triple taxes?"

"My father did indeed raise the taxes, preparing for the war Alored was talking against Sles Adran, probably as a last resort effort to bind together the court factions. It costs money to equip and train warriors, as you no doubt are aware, but Alored made it plain that anyone not meeting his requirements was foresworn, the price being their holdings. My father died along with most of the older generation in the first uprising. The taxes," he added, "haven't been paid since the troubles began."

"You're running the government on . . .?"

"My own fortune. Rapidly diminishing." His smile turned ironic. "Making me quite popular among all those who'd gone unpaid for several years. Regular pay and the slow resumption of trade excuse my ignorance about matters of state, I assure you."

Ignorance? "One last question, your grace."

Adon-Marsael smiled. "Please."

"Do you think there is anyone from Norsunder involved with any of these various contenders?"

Adon-Marsael laughed. "Norsunder? Are you imagining some sinister figure slinking through the night, offering an army of soul-bund warriors in exchange for my own soul? Though I have to admit, if such things did exist outside of the tall tales, the prospect of an army of obedient warriors sounds so very restful. And quiet. I mentioned obedient? So very *un*like my fellow countrymen, all of whom have an opinion, and insist upon sharing it."

She laughed with him because he expected it, as a bell bonged in the distance. He sat back; the little show of openness and trust had ended, and she realized she had almost fallen for that "ignorance" claim in spite of her recognition of it as a ploy.

She took the hint and rose. "I should not take up more of your time," she said.

"Come to me with any questions. I will make time to answer them, Honor Liere Feriadar, Queen's Envoy of Sartor."

Unlike our conversation just now, she thought as she went to fetch her hat. Ah, well, she hadn't given him anything either.

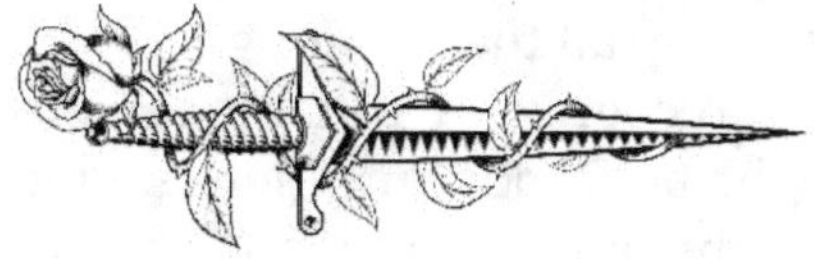

TWENTY-THREE

Lyren-Sartora sat on a rickety railing, eating the simple breakfast she'd just bought. Then she kicked off her slippers and wiggled her toes in the warm sunshine. As she fanned herself with her hat, she drew in a deep, happy breath.

She'd soon detected the page who had been assigned to follow her. But Lyren-Sartora had been trained by the best. It was not difficult to be ambling along a narrow street of wool merchants one moment, turn a corner, and then apparently vanish in any of four directions. The page never thought to peer up at the roofs before he sloped back up the hill in defeat.

That freed Lyren-Sartora to enjoy herself. Her nose had led her to a bakery, where she bought a small round of fresh bread; a passing vendor had sold her a cup of fresh milk still warm from the cow.

That finished, she examined her last coin, and felt the edging. What was its relative worth? It was thinner than Sartoran silvers, struck round instead of six-sided. She scrutinized the symbols along the edge, and in the center the profile of a bearded man with a winged cap. Who was he? How much history she didn't know! She frowned through the dusty air at the morning market-traffic filling the circle around a dry fountain. Six roads led off the circle.

One coin to spend. She scanned the roads, wondering why Liere was so stingy. One coin, when she could transfer Lyren-Sartora back to Bereth Ferian to get more. That had to be the result of Liere's life in that horrid little town in Imar.

Liere had talked very little about her early child-hood, at least to Lyren-Sartora. Senrid knew more, but get him to tell a person anything? Hah! "Ask her," he'd say. Not that Lyren-Sartora really wanted to know what it had been like living in a dreary little house in equally dreary South End, ordered around by a bullying father and made to clean house and drudge in a dull shop all the day long.

But she did recognize a difference between Liere and herself that might be important: Liere seemed to think that anything nice might vanish tomorrow, and anyway she didn't deserve it.

Who *deserves* beauty? It just . . . was. And it made life better!

Lyren-Sartora sat there on the fence outside a stable yard, reflecting for the first time about what effect worrying about money and not having to worry about money would have on children. She frowned down at the coin. No use in fretting now. She had a job to do: hunt for Norsundrians. And the sooner she either found them or else knew there was no sign of them, the sooner they could leave. A spurt of impatience zapped through her when she remembered the way Liere had been staring at that Andri fellow the night before. As if Lyren-Sartora wasn't even in the room!

Definitely time to get this mission over with. She had only herself to blame for insisting on coming, but who would have guessed it would be boring? She slid off, jammed her hat back on and her feet back into her sandals, and caught a glimpse of a brown-haired boy looking away quickly. But not quick enough. He was the same boy Lyren-Sartora and Liere had seen their first day in this city, riding that same horse.

She smothered a laugh, and walked down the middle of the street, veering only to avoid wagons and the occasional carriage. None of the carriages moved any faster than the rest of the traffic, Lyren-Sartora noted as she watched one go by, its four matched horses prancing and flicking their tails, the window-curtains pulled, the drivers in plain dress, and no livery. No horn-blowing outriders scattering traffic. Interesting.

Also interesting: as the crowd flowed back into the street behind the carriage, Lyren-Sartora turned away, looked in a store window, and saw the boy again, now walking, one hand on the rope rein of the horse. She was tempted to play hide-and-seek with her shadow, except if she lost him, how would she find out why he was following her? She contented herself with a straight trail to the horse fair, whose location she discovered first from passing minds.

She reached the fair, but hadn't progressed very far before she sensed both presence and intent at her elbow, and turned around. She smiled down into the boy's face as he glowered at her through messy, long-uncombed hair.

"Wanna ride?" The boy was so small, but his voice was deep and rusty-sounding.

"First, tell me why you're following me. Since I haven't done anything the least bit followable."

"It ain't what ya done," the boy croaked, "it's how ya looked."

"How I looked?" Lyren-Sartora repeated.

Wide gesture from dirty-nailed stubby hands. "Foreign." He added, eyeing her uneasily, "Howja know I was followin' ya?"

"Spotted you."

"Need help getting' up?"

Lyren-Sartora sustained a memory: Siamis on his first visit. Liere is sitting up alone in her room, studying something arcane. Siamis says, *Lyren, will you put on your riding clothes? It's time you got some training in self-defense.* Lyren's own voice piping back: *You're not making ME into any poopsie!* And Mac commenting, *Only a dolt turns down training when it's offered.*

Lyren-Sartora took a step back, and vaulted onto the bare back of the horse. To Jaydi's round gaze, she stated, "I believe I can manage."

Up in the palace grounds, the kingdom shimmered under the noon heat.

At the same moment that Lyren-Sartora — after a morning of steadily less covert trading of dares thoroughly trounced Jaydi by cart-wheeling down the length of a wooden railing — two young gentlemen drifted toward one another under the spreading beech trees in Brydon's royal garden.

Somewhat remarkable that no one ever really noticed Marten Eldias, for he was tall, slim, well made, with pleasant features, especially his dark eyes. But so it was. Those idly looking for trouble ignored the elegant young fellow with the self-effacing manners, his dress sword the lightest type of dueling rapier made, his hands those of a scholar and not a brawler.

Marten strolled under the trees as he tracked Liere's movements through the palace grounds. He watched a group of people at the lakeside load into a barge, its fringed cover hanging limp in the hot, still air.

A step at Marten's side, and there was Kizka, now dressed as a footman, in the duchas's livery, his wild hair strictly smoothed back and bound. He was bareheaded like a servant. He too came from one of the old, landed families, though like Marten's, his family and lands had been overrun by opportunists taking advantage of the troubles. As a footman Kizka had the run of the palace. Yet the livery made him invisible to most.

"Was she really in alone with Marsael?" Marten murmured, watching the slim golden-haired Liere just then entering the barge behind a laughing trio of young courtiers.

"She was."

"And?"

"Lanred listened at the door. Said she came from the queen of Sartor."

"Did Andri come up?"

"No. She asked about Sles Adran, and taxes. Envoy subjects," Kizka added. "I'd say she is what she says she is."

Marten sighed softly, watching Liere bend to hear something a gallant was saying, her hat hiding her face.

"Can you hear anything?" Kizka asked, glancing with meaning at Marten's high, smooth forehead.

Marten shook his head slowly. "Nothing. She's better than Andri at not letting emotions escape."

Kizka whistled below his breath, then said, "Well, he'll do whatever he's going to do. No help for it. I'd better get along before I'm spotted dawdling." He moved on down the grassy knoll, staying as much as he could beneath the canopy of bright green leaves.

Marten sat down in the shade, leaned back on his elbows, and watched as Liere worked her way through all the guests on the barge, and then, when the low craft touched the far end of the crescent-shaped lake (all that was left of the old moat) started drifting her way through those who had just finished the garland chase. When at last she joined a group making their way back inside the palace, he got to his feet and wandered after.

It was fairly late at night when Lyren-Sartora flung open the door of their room in the palace. Liere, who had just arrived herself, sat on the bed.

Lyren-Sartora dashed to the cleaning frame and leaped through. Magic sparkled down her length, semi-visible in the gathering gloom, and then she tossed her hat to the peg and collapsed onto the floor. "Ugh," she moaned. "It takes off the dust, but doesn't cool you any."

"No."

"It's never this hot in the north," Lyren-Sartora said.

Liere grinned at the ceiling. "So I noticed. I thought you were eager to become a page."

Lyren-Sartora sighed. "Not after I found out that all they do is polish and clean and mend until summoned, and then they are kept strictly *out* of listening range. *So* unlike in all the adventure stories and plays, in which pages always get to overhear the secret conversations! What did you discover?"

"Interview with Adon-Marsael, but it was all courtly talk, and he doesn't seem to believe that Norsunder exists. Or rather is any real threat. I introduced myself to those my age in court, but it was all more court talk. You?"

"I met up with one of Andri's followers, the same one we saw the other day. That's the boy Julian met. But he didn't bring up Norsunder, and he was still kind of suspicious, and his surface thoughts are really murky. Even trying mind touch made me feel like I was in a rocking boat in the middle of a mud storm. I figured, better to wait."

"Good idea."

"We rode around, and he explained the city to me. I tried to scan people we saw, but all I got was more seasickness from too many thoughts scrambling, and all of it boring." Lyren-Sartora turned on her side. "Is our visit here a waste of time? About halfway through the afternoon, I thought, what would Norsunder be *doing* here anyway? Why Jaydi and not one of the older ones? Maybe he's mixing stories with how real life is, the way I did about pages. In a story, a Norsundrian would be lurking around looking sinister and sending out evil thoughts. But is that real?"

"You probably won't sense them, but you could sense someone who is frightened by them," Liere said. "Something specific, threats. Once Jaydi trusts you, he'll probably be more forthcoming. *Something* disturbed Julian." Though as she spoke, Liere wondered if that terrible wound Julian had taken had distorted her emotions on the subject.

"Oh. Right. Did *you* find anything?"

"Not yet." Liere considered that mild-faced, dark-haired fellow who'd trailed her most of the day. His surface thoughts had merely reflected what he was seeing. "Anyway, Adon-Marsael is giving that grand ball for us at the end of the week," she reminded Lyren-Sartora. And when Lyren-Sartora clapped her hands, "What is it you expect at a grand ball? Romance?"

"Yuk, no!" Lyren-Sartora heaved a dramatic sigh. "Well, I wouldn't mind *seeing* romance. I would like that, I think, if the people are handsome and it's all . . . you know . . . elegant."

"Do they have to be handsome? Don't ordinary folk deserve romance as much as the comely do?"

Lyren-Sartora bridled at what she expected to be yet another lecture on her frivolity—earnest speeches on which she had heard plenty from serious, dedicated Oalthoreh, the head of the mage school, for Lyren-Sartora's own good. (The only discernible result being Lyren-Sartora's disinterest in learning magic.) But then she perceived that Liere's question was genuine. She really wanted to know.

"Of course everyone who wants romance deserves it." Lyren-Sartora sighed, struggling to express herself. "I just love the idea of music, and lovely clothes, and being admired, and dancing and dancing and dancing. Doesn't it sound wonderful to you?"

"No. But then you know I'm not much one for crowds."

"You have no romance in your spirit," Lyren-Sartora muttered.

"Perhaps not," Liere responded absently, for a new problem had presented itself. This would be Liere's first grand ball, and she had no idea what to wear—how to convey the right social signals for a Sartoran envoy. Though she usually ignored the question of clothing, during the past five years, she'd learned how they communicated before one so much as spoke. "I don't think I can make a ball gown, or at least, not in time."

Lyren-Sartora — who had many fine things — said knowledgeably, "The local fashionable dressmakers will be taken up with their usual clients. I think it's time to go back to Bereth Ferian. I know the tailors, and who among them would love to make you something pretty."

Liere said, "Should I wear Sartoran fashions or local? Is there a difference? Sartoran," she muttered. "If there is." She looked over at Lyren-Sartora. "All right, first thing tomorrow, we'll make a quick visit back to Bereth Ferian. You're in charge."

Lyren-Sartora clapped in glee. In a happy swirl of thoughts, she sprinted to her room, and threw off her clothes before stretching out on top of the bed, for it was too hot even for sheets. A visit home to snow and cold weather, with *her* choosing the tailor and the fashions, and in a few days, a grand ball! And if they conveniently found out about Norsunder that night (because at least in stories, everything dramatic happened at balls) then, after that, they could go back to their real lives.

TWENTY-FOUR

Eidervaen, capital of Sartor

Honor Vardathe Gaszin had enjoyed his post as Colendi ambassador to Sartor for many years, ever since Sartor had returned from its century of enchantment.

"The rose is fine, but for this occasion, I think the most formal robe?" he said to his chief valet, who bowed.

Implied in the presentation of the rose and cream robes was the weather, and Gaszin knew it was going to be both humid and miserable out in the sun, but needs must.

He sank into a cool bath as his servants scurried to replace all the summer court robes with his most formal wear, with all accoutrements. He leaned back, breathing in the soothing scent of orange blossom and loethe, permitting his mind to range back and back. Really, no one else in Colend's present court could possibly have been as successful as he — sent by the present king's father during one of his rare periods of sanity.

Vardathe suppressed an inward laugh. His and King Carlael's antipathy had been mutual from boyhood, but he also knew that Carlael (when he was sane) had been obliged to respect Vardathe slippery tongue.

He thought back to when everyone everywhere had exclaimed how glorious it was to have Sartor back in the world, but behind closed doors, they had wondered how much it would hurt Colend. Alsais, the world's finest capital city (so thought Vardathe Gaszin modestly) had come to depend upon hosting the yearly Alsais Music Festival — no longer *Sartoran* — moreover, the rest of the world seemed to

want it to remain that way, judging by how few petitions
there had been to King Carlael (outside of the Sartorans', of
course) to return the festival to Sartor. No petition had been
renewed a second year, and best of all, he himself had
finessed the Sartorans into a five year wait, which he'd
successfully gotten extended.

His greatest triumph. Vardathe Gaszin chuckled again as
he left the bath, refreshed and cool. He merely blotted the
water from his skin, and before he dressed, a touch of pepper
to his inner arm, and nutmeg to his breast. No floral scents,
not in summer. There would be enough of that in the heavy
air.

He pulled on a long shirt over loose trousers, then the
thinnest under robe, stored in astringent herbs. At last, the
heavily embroidered over-robe with its silver lilies, its weight
disagreeable in this weather. Still, he thought complacently as
he shook out the sleeves and admired the twined silver
embroidery of lilies and acanthus, to look at him was to see
Colend embodied.

People *liked* going to Colend. They liked it better than
toiling over the mountains and down into Sartor, unless they
were the archival sort, who enjoyed burrowing in dusty,
mildewed archives.

"All to their own," he murmured, giving a tug to one cuff,
and brushing back a lock of his hair as he considered
variations on his welcoming speech to the young king. No
remonstrance—not in front of Sartor's avid ears. So awkward
and irregular! Now Carlael's son, who had already strictly
speaking come of age, was unaccountably on his way to
Sartor, without having informed the regency council of his
plans. Even worse, word had begun to whisper through
Colend's court that Shontande might be flattered, threatened,
even seduced by the Sartorans (he was young, after all) into
giving the Music Festival back to Sartor. He had to be as mad
as his father. That was the only explanation that made sense
for this wild venture of his.

Over the days since the headstrong young idiot's
disappearance, a constant stream of letters had zapped by
magic back and forth from the embassy in Eidervaen to the
regency council, who wanted Shontande shepherded gently
but firmly home to their governance.

Vardathe Gaszin waited as two valets carefully put his

headdress on last. A satisfied glance in the mirror, and he dismissed his servants, then he trod to his desk, keeping his arms away from his body to prevent as much heat building as he could, and unlocked his desk.

There, in the most secret drawer, lay a transfer token worked into a trinket. This he slipped into an inner pocket of his sleeve, and returned to ruminating various possible words. The regency council had charged him to persuade their king to return to Colend, but if there was the least sign of any disaster, he was to transfer the king summarily to a Destination within the palace, whence he would be safely restored to order.

Ambassador Gaszin smiled as he ventured out to his second-floor balcony, which was draped with a huge blue and silver banner identifying the house as Colend's embassy. The great banner had been tastefully framed by purple and gold pennons in acknowledgment of their host kingdom.

He surveyed the scene in approval: streets clean as dinner plates, statues dusted and some laden with flowers, blue and white bunting—Colendi colors—suspended from the embassy on the Apsos Grand, the most exclusive row of buildings between the east end of the royal palace Rive Dien and the Grand Chandos Way. The expected entourage would be riding up the river road and turning onto the Grand Chandos, to assemble in the great parade ground along the southern face of the palace, which was so old it had several formal entrances, each from different centuries. Three from different millennia.

Gaszin had of course dispatched minions to the border to report on what they saw as soon as the pending disaster had been confirmed, but he distrusted the subsequent report. An army accompanying the young king? Pah! He knew Donais Altan, who kept a tight grip on the Colendi herald-guards. He would never have sent an army of them to Sartor without going first through him.

As the cavalcade reached the ancient Apsos City Gate (which hadn't been a gate for centuries), the waiting Sartorans blew the brassy ancient fanfare for a visiting monarch, and in answer the silver horns of home played the cascades announcing the advent of a Lirendi—and then swept into a salute to Sartor by echoing the even more ancient Sartoran triplets in four shifting keys. By the time that was done, the ambassador could see the foremost riders, bearing the silver lily of Colend on a celestial blue banner.

Behind them rode the boy himself. The ambassador had entertained the faint hope that this would be an imposter, revealing some sinister plot—so very much easier to deal with—but no, that was Carlael Lirendi's son. No one could mistake the auburn hair framing a striking face, or the long, exquisite body in its sky-blue riding clothes with the lily of Colend embroidered in silver. He was no longer a boy. Even more daunting, behind the young king, rank on rank, rode armed guards in Colendi blue tabards.

Vardathe Gaszin stood on the balcony, forcing a smile in case the boy, ah, that is, the young king might look up. Oh yes, his head swung to the side, the sharp-cut chin lifted: Shontande had seen the blue banner. He touched a long, slim hand to his breast in salute, his wrist at a neutral angle. The ambassador bowed low, hands together in the peace, as his entire staff ranged behind him took the cue and also bowed.

The moment the king turned right toward the parade ground, the singing began—ignored by Gaszin, who straightened up, dashed inside heedless of his expensive fabrics, dropped onto his cushion in his office, impatiently waving away the ward and unlocking his desk. He had to move fast. He shook his hands fiercely so that they would not tremble as he wrote the barest report to his nephew:

He has his <u>own army</u>. How could you permit <u>that</u> to happen?

He twisted the note, closed it in the case, sent it, and hurried downstairs, for he should have been on his way to the royal palace now. Relieved to hear the caterwauling still going on, he rushed down the inner stair and out the private door. He had to get to Star Chamber before the queen did.

Vardathe Gaszin well knew the importance of the Alsais Music Festival, but in fact he hadn't attended it in years, nor did he miss it. Music was like scents, something you used, and maybe enjoyed when nothing more important occupied your mind. The festival's importance was entirely political.

To Atan, however, the music had a far different meaning.

Historically, the Sartoran Music Festival had always begun with a parade around the Twelve Stations. In planning this royal welcome, she had laid out the route deliberately, an unspoken reminder.

Once the fanfares died away, the singing began at Apsos

Gate, the First Station. As the newcomers passed each station, a new verse was sung by a waiting group, first children, then adding deeper voices, with children still singing the chorus in descant. When they reached the grand parade ground, six hundred voices sur-rounded them with sound in threefold harmony, striking triplets in counterpoint.

The sound echoed off the stone walls, so beautiful it made Atan's throat hurt—an exaltation that caused Shontande to tighten his grip on the decorated reins so hard that the leddas cord cut into his palms, in order to ground him.

No one had told him how sound magnified by stone would thrum through bones and blood. Alsais did not have a building over three stories tall, and those of two stories were masked by trees. This ancient city of five-story stone canyons intensified the soaring voices, making him wonder if they had built deliberately to try to emulate the legendary cavern echoes of the morvende.

A heartbeat before they halted before a long palace entry, through the euphoric haze darted a grace note in another key: he understood that the volume of sound was the opening strike in a duel. Yustnesveas Landis VI wanted the Music Festival back, and this was her first move to get it.

He looked around, fighting the effect by focusing on sensory details. The smell of horse and stone, the watchful Sartoran guard, captained by a formidably heroic figure with deep-set, watchful eyes. The gathered courtiers parted ceremoniously, opening a path that led to the vast palace doors, which framed a tall young woman.

Gaze met gaze across the expanse, and the hazy mental image of a feminine silhouette to be easily court-ed and convinced to back him resolved into a woman as tall as he was, and if her shoulders weren't as broad, they were very near. An impressive bosom, made the most of by the deceptively simple lines of her robes, and an equally superb swell of hip above long legs indicated a generous build. The famed goggle eyes of the Landises stared recognizably across the expanse: most people, at this distance, had only pits for eyes, but hers could be made out staring with an intelligent, assessing gaze.

The threnody rose and fell in counterpoint all around as he brought his horse to a halt. He dismounted. The moment his foot touched the ground, the singers shifted key yet again, and chorus by chorus began dropping out as he walked up that long path alone, until the last to be heard was a child's high voice, pure as the ting of silver on crystal.

When he was five paces from the Queen of Sartor, that single voice ceased, leaving the two monarchs face to face.

Once Atan had a clear view of Shontande Lirendi, time suspended. The music that had stirred her so profoundly diminished to the back of her mind as she drew in a long, slow breath. Atan had heard that the Colendi king was gorgeous, but then there were those who said *she* was gorgeous until they learned better how she felt about base flattery. She also heard him likened to that colorful, problematical family, the Deis.

Her first glimpse was of his bare head. Brown hair — well, ruddy brown, with golden highlights: auburn. Shontande Lirendi might not be a Golden Dei, but the way he carried himself, his dramatic features, called to mind one of the most famous of all the Dei family, Taumad Darian, whose beauty had coined the term.

One long and exceptionally dreary winter she had gone through all records of the Deis, in part to discover how much of the legend was the usual hyperbole of individuals' accounts. She'd seen mage-captured images of the most famous Deis, all the way back to the brief one left of the first, the spectacularly beautiful Alian Dei, who had married Connar Landis. Alian's most famous children had been fathered by one of the king's captains. To these children she had given her own name, before she married into the royal Landis family.

From them, over the centuries, emerged the ones known as Golden Deis. Not that all those termed "Golden Deis" were direct descendants of either branch of the Deis. There were those like Liere, whose families had married away. But the defining characteristics still occasionally turned up: light brown eyes that looked gold in most light, golden hair, and vivid coloring in complementary hues. These were the fair "Golden Deis." But the term wasn't confined to fair-haired people. There were the ones with dark hair, often with vivid blue eyes, their complexions equally vivid, but all of them had dramatic coloring and natural grace.

As it happened, the mother of that same Taumad Dei had married into the nobility of the same kingdom Liere had gone off to investigate. The single moving image of Taumad had been captured by a mage when Taumad was about sixty, living on a pirate island. Even at sixty his sudden, slightly rueful laugh, the humor in his golden gaze, had caught Atan behind the knees. Shontande Lirendi moved with the same grace, and had that same quick, slightly rueful smile, the inward laugh that quirked the eyes, and—she heard as he dismounted, and thanked the child who had been chosen (after vigorous competition) to take the reins of his horse—the softly husky tenor that was somehow more attractive than the most stringently trained singer pouring out ancient song.

Once again eyes met. His, she was surprised to note, were almost as dark and dense a blue as her own.

His smile was pleasant, warm, even, without being a grin, or a smirk, but the subtle quirk of his eyelid, the twitch of one of his extravagantly arched brows, made it clear that he was watching her as closely as she watched him—and he was as fast, if not faster.

Getting the *Sartoran* Music Festival back was not going to be easy.

She lifted her hand, palm up, in the manner she had tearfully practiced so many times when she was fifteen years old and a new queen of a bankrupt kingdom a century out of date. Her silken sleeves soughed softly as she gestured invitation. He fell in step beside her, and as they passed between the great doors carved with stylized sunbeams, the shuffle of soft slippers and whispers behind indicated those permitted entry into Star Chamber falling in step behind them, two by two, in strict rank order.

Shontande Lirendi was close enough for her to hear the light sound of his breathing, and to catch a whiff of his scent. She knew he had been riding. She did not know how long, only that he somehow managed not to smell of horse.

Then he spoke. His Sartoran was charmingly accented, otherwise perfect. "Does it also strike you," he said so softly she barely heard him, "how absurd it is for hundreds of people to stand around in a crowd just to stare at two people?"

She had expected almost anything else, from formal rhetoric to flirtation, as she had heard plenty about his sumptuous life and strings of lovers. She slanted a quick glance his way, to find him waiting for an answer.

"We are not people," she retorted in the same undertone. "We're silk-and-gilt-wrapped symbols."

"Puppets?" His rueful amusement made her breath catch. She had fought hard against becoming a puppet in her early days; the fact that he said the word now revealed a great deal.

But here they were at Star Chamber. Whatever else happened, she thought as they entered the domed chamber, it promised to be interesting.

Star Chamber circled the great throne tree. Precedence was strict, ringing out in invisible orbits.

Today, Vardathe Gaszin took precedence of all the other ambassadors, as the visitor was his king. That put him directly behind the twelfth duchas, Korendemar. The duchas was a stiff Sartor-above-all snob, which meant he would not lower himself to speaking to a mere Colendi.

Good. Ambassador Gaszin did not have time or attention for the twelfth duchas, whose land had long since been lost—whose family had once been princes—and whose rank was entirely in name. The only duchas with less land was poor old Chandos, whose land had been empty for all the centuries since Norsunder Base was established not far beyond what used to be Chandos's border. The eleventh and twelfth duchas were supposedly acknowledged due to the merit accrued by their ancestors, but Gaszin was convinced they kept their titles merely because the tradition-bound Sartorans would not relinquish the number twelve.

He smoothed the sleeves of his blue robe embroidered with lilies and acanthus, and took up his place, he and the Duchas of Korendemar ignoring one another. After seeing that army himself, Gaszin had decided that it was best to act at once, when the young fool could not get at that army.

Gaszin had on the walk to Star Chamber rehearsed a suitably regretful speech about the boy's vagaries, sadly well known in Colend. Plenty of flattery and an (empty) promise or two thrown in the general direction of the Alsais Music Festival would smooth out the irregularity. But it had to be fast.

He readied himself as the young queen conducted Shontande around the circle. He must move before she took Shontande to the seat of honor next to that massive tree-throne, so very, lamentably Sartoran, and utterly out of his reach.

Trusting to the indifference of the two duchases, Gaszin took a single step out of place, readied the token between two fingers, and braced himself, as the royal pair paced closer and closer—Shontande taking in at a glance his posture, poised with intent.

Atan paused long enough to politely nod to the Colendi ambassador, as Shontande sidestepped. In that same moment the ambassador also moved, grasping a finger's breath from the edge of Shontande's sleeve. The man's gaze dropped to Shontande's hand, then his eyelids flashed upward in shock before he vanished.

It was done so coolly and smoothly that it looked planned, except that Atan recognized a mirror transfer when she saw one: in the space between one heartbeat and the next she realized that the ambassador had tried to force Shontande Lirendi into a transfer, to be foiled, for Ambassador Gaszin was no mage. That, the Sartoran Mage Council had ascertained years ago, when he was first accredited: they would never have tolerated a foreign mage at court.

Shontande Lirendi then extended a hand toward the young man at his right shoulder as he said smoothly, "May I present the new Ambassador to Sartor, Thad Keperi?"

Atan pretended she did not see Thad Keperi's eyes wide with shock. In her public voice, from which she suppressed any hint of surprise, she invited him to take his place at the head of the ambassadorial row, while in Colend, the former ambassador to Colend staggered from the Destination that had been prepared for the king, and shouted for servants— his brother—his nephew—the heralds.

The regency council gathered in haste, and once the furious "What?" and "How?" had died down, it struck them one by one that unless Shontande Lirendi overlooked Gaszin's carefully trained staff, they now had no ears whatsoever planted on the young king.

"He won't overlook your spies in your staff," the Duchas of Gaszin said bitterly, eyeing the ex-ambassador—who would now fall to him to house, as nearest relation. "They'll all be on their way home by tomorrow. You'll see."

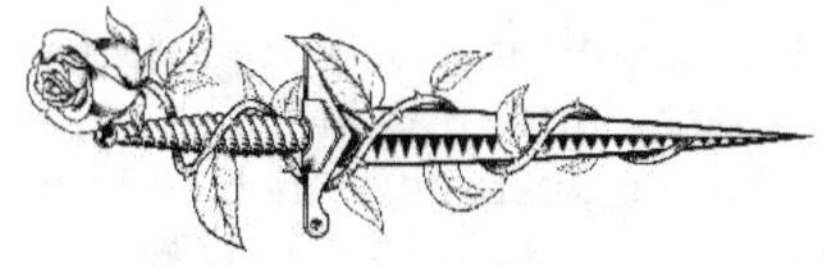

TWENTY-FIVE

Thad had learned enough about courts to expect that little would be required of Shontande the day of his arrival beyond listening to speech after speech of welcome, followed by a formal meal and more speeches of welcome, and then a concert or a play. All carefully calculated over the generations, and carried out meticulously by the ranks of heralds and pages whose livelihoods depended on everything progressing smoothly for courtiers trained over lifetimes to the rhythms of ritual.

Thad had expected to make his escape with the rest of the servants, but now he had been thrust onto the public stage. He and Shontande could not speak, though he was longing to. He set himself the goal of waiting for the long day to end, so that he and Shontande could get back to the royal guest suite and he could find out what exactly had happened before he found himself catapulted to ambassadorial status.

The long day ended with a concert in a grotto under the stars. Though he was sure the music was excellent, he was so tired and confused he only heard it as noise, his entire body one big ache. He'd forgotten how much endurance one needed to sit still and quiet hour after hour, like these pages.

At last it ended, and the melodic strains were gradually replaced by the unmelodic hum of voices as the Sartoran court began to emerge in strict rank order, the queen and Shontande in the lead, Thad directly behind them.

At the doors the long train halted as the queen turned to Shontande. "Tomorrow the invitations will no doubt begin to shower down, but I insisted that your day of arrival end early so that you may rest."

This was early? Thad would never survive.

The queen and her visitor wished one another a good night before parting.

Neither Shontande nor Thad spoke as the waiting page led them to the royal guest wing. Once they arrived, Shontande cast a fast glance around. The suite had been hung with exquisitely kept tapestries, which did not quite mask the fact that this wing of the building was built from gray stone blocks. Old, heavy, furniture filled the vast chambers, gleaming with fine carving and gilding. Shontande dropped onto a trunk, elbows on knees, and began to knead his temples with his thumbs.

"Headache?" Thad asked.

Shontande looked up then to either side in a way that jolted Thad. It was a warning that they could be overheard. They didn't know what hideys and nooks existed in this ancient pile.

Of course Shontande would think of that. Thad remembered that conversation with Bee as they crunched through the snow along the riverside. Bee had said, *You have to remember that he doesn't trust easily.*

But Curtas never actually did anything, except turn out to be one of Detlev's boys, Thad had said.

Ah-ye, Thad, this distrust reaches far beyond Curtas. You have not considered the effect of growing up watched from waking to sleeping, every bite observed, every breath, every utterance considered. Privacy for our prince was only possible inside his skull.

I should have known, Thad had said remorsefully. *I glimpsed a little of it the day he walked in the former king's memorial. But surely he gets some privacy in private moments, now that he is of the age for such?*

When he is in the chamber of cranes, yes — but even then, there were those hired to appeal to the prince, and report on —

Thad had raised his hand, stopping Bee there. He could imagine the rest--which might explain the lack of favorites, and the constant stream of partners that contributed to Shontande's reputation for amorous extravagance.

Of course he would expect spies now, until he could ascertain on his own whether or not they existed. Thad turned away to order some willow steep, and kept his steps noiseless.

Shontande sat motionless, head bent, until the arrival of the bitter brew, which roused him from reverie. Listening on the mental plane was never simple, especially among strangers, and most especially in a group. But the speculative glances, the angles of head, the tones of voices, had shocked him into considering the Sartorans' own motivations and intentions. Something he ought to have been doing from the start of this adventure.

He forced himself to swallow the hot steep, then set down a bowl-shaped cup, so different from the tiny lily flutes of home. As the headache—not very bad—began to recede, he again listened on the mental plane, this time to his environment. Unless he had a spy with a very fine mind-shield, no one was in the immediate vicinity. "Thad, let me begin by apologizing for springing that surprise on you."

Thad turned around, hands open at the angle of question. "Ambassador Gaszin vanished. What happened?"

"Vardathe Gaszin, no doubt at the council's insistence, tried to force a transfer on me. No doubt there was a Destination prepared in a room surrounded by guards, all for my own safety," he added with a bitter twist to his mouth. "That's why you are now ambassador. The queen accepted you so fast I suspect she disliked Vardathe Gaszin as much as I did at that first glance. So even if he turns up here again with another transfer token, he won't be accepted."

"I am ambassador for how long?" Thad asked faintly.

"As long as you like," and seeing Thad's utter dismay, Shontande smiled and said with sympathy, "We'll find someone else if you really want out. But the first step is to take over the embassy. Send all the servants home, with pay—as officially recognized ambassador, you have that power. Then search it from top to toe for spy eyes. I'll give you a token that will warn of magic hidden anywhere."

Thad sighed with relief. "That is more my sort of task. The thought of giving speeches harrows me to the soul."

"I'll see to the speeches. I can reel off that sort of thing in my sleep. But Thad, the more I think about it, the sooner I want to move out of this palace and into that building. Which is sovereign Colendi territory."

Thad looked around with a bewildered air. "I thought we were safe here."

"Oh, we're safe enough. But I hadn't known I would be quite so on display here. All through the day there were at least four . . . no, five, assessing my, ah-ye, market value? Political value? Somewhere between the two."

"Ah."

"I acquit our royal host, as yet; no one knows better than I how much a court will maneuver behind the ruler's back. But I think I'll have a stronger position, yes, if I withdraw to our own territory. Bringing me to my third order, one that will suit you, I believe . . ."

While he laid out his plan to Thad, at the other end of the palace, Atan had also retired to avoid the inevitable crush of questions she couldn't answer, and opinions she didn't want to hear.

Rel was waiting. Atan lifted the protection-warded coronet from her head and tossed it onto a side table as she said, "Yes, he's handsome, yes, his manners are perfect, all the phrases properly poetic, meaning he was no doubt rehearsing them at the same time I was practicing my welcome words these past few days. Only I don't have that charming Colendi accent. *Why* is it charming? What dictates charm? Don't tell me 'current fads'—records three centuries old talk of charming Colendi accents."

Aware of the sound of her own voice, and that she was talking too fast, she shut up.

Rel put his arms around her. "I expect we're raised to hear it as charm. It certainly doesn't grate on the ear." He gave her a last squeeze, and seeing the tension still in her face, he stood behind her and began removing the hairpins from her braided hair. She sighed, shut her eyes, and relaxed into his ministrations.

She knew that Rel's Colendi friends—Thad Keperi being one of them—were not courtiers, and he'd never met the king-in-name-only. She didn't bother asking if there was a difference in accent between layers of society, as there was in Sartor, and had been for ages—so entrenched it was like different languages that happened to have a lot of cognates.

"Most important, he's a mage." As she spoke, he dropped the last of her jewelry onto the side table, and began to knead her temples with his thumbs. "Oh, thank you, thank you. Nobody saw him mirror the transfer spell on that token but me. And the now-departed Colendi ambassador. He was that fast, and that subtle. Which makes me wonder what he's really here for." She said suddenly, "I wish he'd never come."

The violence of this statement caused Rel to bend down so that he could see her face. "Because?"

"Please don't stop. I hadn't realized how much my head ached."

He began to massage her scalp and the back of her neck.

She sighed, and presently said, "Because the Council watched him like a circle of starving predators. They will be harassing us both for a state marriage."

Rel lifted his hands, and came around to hunker down in front of her. "But that's nothing new."

"I know." She closed her eyes, pressing her hands against her temples. "But there is a difference, I just discovered, between hypothetical marriage talk with a hypothetical prince and having a live one turn up. A very . . . *presentable* one, probably the most eligible one on the continent. One look at him, and I could see Leathan already combining the two kingdoms—to Sartor's benefit, of course—and horrible Peranda Yostavos considering how much power might be wrung for herself, and there was Irza looking him over as her future pet."

The acid in Atan's tone surprised Rel. Irza's selfishness was nothing new, so why the vehemence? "He might have something to say to that," Rel responded reasonably. He wished, suddenly, that he'd been able to see what had happened at that much-rehearsed, very public meeting before so many eyes. He waited, and when Atan said nothing, he moved behind her and returned to massaging the rigid muscles of her shoulders.

As for Shontande, when at last he was alone in the sumptuous bedchamber reserved for visitors of state—scrupulously cleaned and polished, but smelling faintly of mildew that he suspected had seeped into these ancient stones behind all the tapestries and carvings—he sat cross-legged on the enormous bed, took out his golden notecase from his inner robe, opened it, and with the little chalk he kept inside, wrote:

Senrid: I am here.

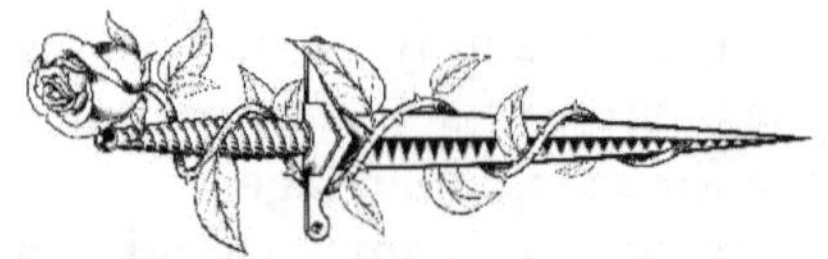

TWENTY-SIX

Shiovhan, capital of Enaeran

Liere opened her eyes to breeze-tossed shadows dappling the cornice in the early morning light, for she'd left the windows and curtains open. The hot wind was intermittent, bringing through open doors the scents of dust and crushed grass, and sending scatterings of white puffs of cloud across the sky.

They were ready at last, after an interval that had turned out to be unexpectedly complicated. "What is your desire?" the dressmaker had asked.

"Something Sartoran—velvet and lace, I guess," Liere had said, remembering Atan's light-hearted comment about donning velvet and making four bows.

"Not velvet in summer. You'd die from the heat," the dressmaker said. "Even if the mages bring cold air from the heights."

Confused, Liere relayed Atan's words, to hear a laugh. "That's an expression, 'pull on your velvet.' It simply means to dress formally. Velvet is for winter, but I assure you, no one in Sartor's court wears lace now. Not since the conflict rose over the Alsais Music Festival. In protest. For you know, all the best lace is made in Colend."

"I had not known," Liere said contritely, aware that she had thus avoided a pitfall she hadn't known was there. "What do you suggest?"

"Fashions vary," the dressmaker said in the confident voice of a master of one's particular realm. "Formal dress could be said to swing between two extremes: lines that emphasize gender differences, and lines that diminish gender differences. In Sartor presently, as in Colend, the differences are all but eradicated—everyone wears robes in flowing panels. It's important that the fabric move well. Colend's summer fashions drip with lace, the snow look, but Sartor favors trims of embroidery, braid, and the like."

"Sartoran sounds simplest," Liere said, wishing she could dress to be invisible—still not accustomed to the fact that no matter what she wore, her days of being invisible were over.

Between their daily visits by magic transfer to Bereth Ferian for fittings, Lyren-Sartora had drifted in and out all week, ignored as The Envoy's Aide. She watched avidly as the palace staff prepared for the Envoy's Ball.

An army of people cleaned, and then brought in fine furnishings and decorations that had been kept elsewhere. In a beautiful rose marble ballroom, servants with very tall ladders restored crystal lusters to chandeliers from crates where they had been packed in old cloth wadding.

The day of the city festival and ball, the servants carrying newly-polished silver trays and bowls from the kitchen area toward the rose ballroom glanced upward as wind whipped down the main hall, bolstering the sense that a storm was on the way.

Adon-Marsael had made the most of this opportunity to demonstrate magic—under his control. Servants had set up a canopy in blue and gold midway along the ridge. As courtiers gathered in a half-circle, and the steep roads leading to the ridge were packed with city folk, Adon-Marsael stood with Liere, the guest of honor, and he made a speech about peace and prosperity. Liere remained motionless beside him. He was the focus of attention as he finished his speech, his people in the crowd yelled and clapped, then trumpeters tooted a fall of notes as he brandished the coins that Liere had worked the magic on.

She had included precise instructions with the coins, and it seemed Adon-Marsael had practiced. He repeated the phrases like an expert as he tossed the coins into the air. The gold spun, releasing the tangle of spells, then vanished (back to Liere's room, had anyone known it), as in the city below, the ground rumbled briefly.

People murmured, looking startled, then cried out in surprise and pleasure as brown water shot skyward from some forty fountains in the city below. The fountains swiftly lowered to a more normal height, running pure and clear.

For a time the courtiers watched the city folk below rush to the filling pools below the fountains, dipping gourds, pitchers, and buckets, carrying them away to fill rain barrels just in case. Then, as the excitement below began to wane and the merciless sun beat down, most of the courtiers closed around Adon-Marsael, congratulating and flattering him as they retreated to the palace and shade.

Liere walked with a few of the young people she'd become acquainted with. Ahead a man turned to his companions. "At least that rabble won't be sneaking up here to raid our river water, now."

"The fountains won't last," predicted a woman with the comfort of one who will not be discommoded. "Magic is notoriously unreliable."

"Keep your estate guards vigilant. The rats will swarm again. More for the mines," someone else stated.

Liere endured a pulse of guilt, wondering about the water carriers. But they'd had a full week of warning. She hoped they'd found other work.

When people began dividing off to ready themselves for the ball, Liere slipped away from the crowd, and took one of the paths down toward the river. Pausing beneath a spreading tree, she threw illusion around herself, and spent the remainder of the day walking along, listening to people celebrating having access to water again. If there were disgruntled water carriers, she saw none of them. That was cheering, far more fulfilling than her fruitless scanning for any hint of Norsundrian interest.

She returned at sunset. Lyren-Sartora was there already, having bathed and dressed. Liere stepped through their cleaning frame, considering that enough of a nod toward personal preparation, and shifted to her new ball outfit.

"All right," she said. "I'm ready."

Lyren-Sartora paused in the midst of braiding tiny sprigs of fragrant blossoms through her hair, and gazed at Liere in mock horror. "No, you are not!"

"No? I'm clean, clothed, and tidy. What else is there?"

Lyren-Sartora jumped up, her braid half-undone. "Liere, have you ever looked in a mirror?"

"We didn't have mirrors on the island, so I got out of the

habit. I'm not tidy?"

"Liere, you can't tie your sash at the side, not with this gauze—see, it creates a bump, ruining the line. Tie it at the back. A bow, no knot. And don't let the under-blouse bunch up like that." She tugged the offending fabric free, then began rearranging it as she spoke. "Work it together with tiny pleats here and here, see, it lies flat!"

Liere gave up, and held out her arms so that Lyren-Sartora's quick, clever fingers could twitch and press the fabric into hanging in graceful folds.

Liere wondered where Lyren-Sartora could have learned to dress with such flair and taste. Surely not from Siamis, though Liere had seen him dress elegantly when he wished, just as he once looked sinister. She was convinced that his was the mind behind Detlev's super-lative house. She couldn't imagine Detlev ever noticing such things as styles in buildings or clothing.

When Lyren-Sartora resumed fixing her hair, Liere looked at her fondly. As an aide, Lyren-Sartora had chosen an outfit of tunic, loose trousers and overrobe, made after the fashion of Atan's inner palace staff. That and the blossoms woven by ribbon through her braid were charming, and Liere sighed at how effortless Lyren-Sartora was at achieving such grace with so little.

Lyren-Sartora's brows twitched. "What's wrong?"

"Nothing's wrong. I was just admiring your hair."

"What? It's *brown*. *Everyone* has brown hair. Yours is that shade of ripe wheat, of golden coins. That is what I call pretty."

"But it's common enough in some places," Liere said.

"It's still beautiful. Mine is ordinary." Lyren-Sartora gave her an acute glance. "Maybe when I turn fifteen, I'll go to a colorist and have them make it . . . emerald green. That would be very pretty, worn with complementary colors." As Liere sighed, Lyren-Sartora added airily, "At least you didn't say *you're too young*. Then I'd have to throw up on your nice new dancing slippers. Anyway, we are on an adventure, and it doesn't seem that colorists are popular here. I wonder why that is."

"Could it be the general distrust of mages has kept hair-coloring to cinnabar and bark dyes and lemon for those who want it lighter?" Liere suggested. "Hair colorists are mages, after all."

Lyren-Sartora gave an airy shrug. "Anyway, everything is fine. I'd much rather be a hero than beautiful. *Don't* say anything about heroes. I *know* how terrible it was to be Sartora, the Girl Who Saved The World. Come! It's time for the envoy to make her bow."

Liere followed, silenced not by Lyren-Sartora's words, but by the hurt they revealed, so carefully hidden until now. Who had been saying what to her about her non-heroic qualities while Liere was gone?

When they reached the main state wing of the enormous palace, Liere watched people converging on the golden glow reaching out so invitingly from the great doors. Their emotions were so clear: expectation, excitement, ambition, greed, anticipation, hope, longing, and ardor. By now Lyren-Sartora knew her way unerringly along the bewildering byways of the palace, and successfully brought them to the right doors as the bell rang.

The doors stood open, golden light from the chandeliers pouring out. The door steward in fancy blue and gold livery rammed his rod on the marble floor with a *crack!* "Honor Liere Feriadar, Personal Envoy of Queen Yustnesveas of Sartor," he bawled portentously.

Lyren-Sartora knew that she, as a mere aide, would be ignored, but someday, she promised herself, it would be her name sonorously pronounced, and everybody would turn to see her, and she would bring everybody together with grace and style and harmony.

Liere looked around with appreciation at a vaulted chamber built mostly in rose marble, with gilt arabesques up along the walls. The ceiling was painted like a summer sky, with stars scattered over it, some fitted with crystal so they glittered, reflecting the light from the three great crystal chandeliers suspended below.

Around the floor: white lyre-backed chairs with curved gilt legs. Above them, on the far wall: a gallery on which a full orchestra had gathered, though as the arrivals poured in yet only four or five musicians were playing.

Liere and Lyren-Sartora turned to the right as Adon-Marsael approached. He and Liere bowed, then he conducted her to the grand carved chair in the place of honor—next to his chair. Very like a throne. Lyren-Sartora, remembering that she was an attendant, faded back. She glanced toward the far corner, where half a dozen young nobles of her own age stood about, looking self-conscious in their finery.

Lyren-Sartora drifted toward them, but glanced once more at the crowd gathering around Liere and The Elsarion. Decidedly Liere looked the best of the group, Lyren-Sartora thought critically, though her over-robe, layers of cream-colored gauze trimmed with gold-edged ribbon embroidered with berries and leaves along the edges, was simple, even severe compared to the lace, ribbons, and tassels around them. Beneath the robe she wore loose, floaty trousers and a long tunic of a deep wine color that contrasted with the gold of her hair.

Lyren-Sartora turned her attention outward. Struggling financially Enaeran's courtiers might be, but everyone had put up a brave front. The fashions here definitely emphasized gender differences. Many women wore tight-waisted, low-cut gowns with sweeping skirts. The men's tunics fitted to the body above the wide sashes, then flared into skirts cut up the sides. The sashes were silk, with long dancing fringes, wider sleeves over very fine lawn shirts. The trousers below the tunic hems were loose, stuffed into high, glossy boots, kind of like in Senrid's country, but with folded tops and decorative elements, though a few men preferred skirted robes and embroidered slippers. Some of the guests—mostly men, only two women—wore dress swords in baldrics.

No one wore weapons to a ball in Sartor, Lyren-Sartora knew from having watched from the gallery a couple times, at Atan's invitation. Would everyone wear weapons to a ball in Marloven Hess? Lyren-Sartora couldn't imagine Senrid giving a ball. For the first time she wondered what the grownups there did for fun. When she visited Senrid, she usually just played with Crystal Ingrid.

Horns peeled out the fanfare announcing the promenade. She'd heard the same fanfare in Eidervaen, only from a distance. *Oh, it's so old a custom I can't tell you when it began,* Atan had told her once. *And like old customs, I imagine it comes and goes over the centuries. What I do know is that it dates back to the rebuilding after the Fall, when we first began the four bows. We promenade the room in a square, saluting east, west, north, south, for each of the Old Cities.*

Adon-Marsael crossed to Liere, the guest of honor. They

bowed to each other, and Lyren-Sartora held her breath as he made an inviting gesture to lead the way. The breath escaped in a relieved sigh when Liere turned and put her hand on his arm as if she had done it a thousand times. She must have learned that on Geth-deles, Lyren-Sartora thought proudly.

The company looked as grand as a tapestry parading around the room, making a bow at each corner. Who were they watching the most? Adon-Marsael, of course, but other than him, an arrogant-looking gray-haired man, and a thin young woman whose sallow skin was not served well by the deep violet of the panels of her overdress. That was easily the most expensive dress in the room: a robe divided into two narrow panels in front that formed arrow points, embroidered with gold, over a pure white gown of some gossamer fabric that seemed to float. The sleeves belled slightly, also edged with gold, ruffling just above her elbows.

After the promenade the dancing began, every bit as intricate as the ones in Eidervaen, a complicated geometry of figures with stylized gestures and steps. Lyren-Sartora watched, delighted, until it occurred to her that Liere could not possibly know the dances.

Sure enough, Liere stood off to the side, chatting with a short, round young woman. Lyren-Sartora caught the name "Ennis," before the latter went off to dance, and Liere remained behind, watching with that concentrated expression she got. She wasn't even going to try to dance?

Lyren-Sartora sighed, and turned her attention to the others. Ennis, whose cheeks already glowed bright red and sweat beaded her brow, twirled with a beak-nosed partner whose loose trousers and shiny boots couldn't hide chicken legs. They weren't at all what Lyren-Sartora had pictured, but she remembered what Liere had said about ordinary people and romance.

Her perspective shifted; she saw Ennis laughing, and the little grin her partner gave her as he spoke, too low to hear. Ordinary people, dressed in their best. A sense of joy suffused Lyren-Sartora as she turned from them to the room. They were all beautiful, dressed in their finest as they moved to the rhythms against a gorgeous background. Seen like this, they approached her still-hazy ideal of living art. *How* she wished to live among people for whom grace was as natural as breathing, every moment one of beauty!

Lyren-Sartora suppressed another sigh, studying the individuals again, as if Norsundrian influence might somehow reveal itself. Her critical gaze flashed first to their host. Adon-Marsael was handsome enough, and he danced very well, but his smile was the polite, bland smile of the bored noble, and his current partner was a stout man with silver-streaked hair and a long, supercilious nose. Diamonds flashed every time the man moved.

Lyren-Sartora glowered at those diamonds. They were very fine diamonds, but . . . gemstones were merely rocks, though they were rocks that gathered light. But summer was the time of fierce light, and who needed more? If *she* were giving a ball in summer heat, she'd declare that everyone must wear flowers, and leave the gems for winter, when you need the brilliant points of light.

And then laughed at herself. When would she ever give a ball, living as she did as a guest in Bereth Ferian, Land of Libraries? She studied the dancers as two couples traded partners, then combined and separated from the figure behind them. In the center or the room, Adon-Marsael twirled with that sallow young woman in purple. Purple wore a definite sneer on her face, her nose lifted as if she was aware of being watched. No, as if she expected to be watched, as if it were her due.

Lyren-Sartora turned her back and made her way toward the refreshment salon through the double archway, where all the underage guests seemed to have gathered. A clot of boys and girls were busy piling little plates high with the best delicacies. Two girls were retying one another's sashes. Lyren-Sartora winced at the shrill giggles coming from a cluster over by the statue of some old king in the corner. Those giggles were the extra loud kind, not coming from humor, but from nerves, with a strong sense of 'Look at me! Look at me!'

Lyren-Sartora sneaked another look Liere's way just as Liere took the hand of a tall woman with long black hair for her first dance, not counting the promenade. Was this partner someone important? Lyren-Sartora was observant, but not omniscient; she did not comprehend that after five years of living strictly among her own gender, Liere felt most comfortable dancing with other women while she was mastering complicated patterns.

Liere moved like she'd trained hard in martial arts, with

a flair and precision that amazed Lyren-Sartora. Maybe those obnoxious poopsies were right about training not just to fight, but to move well. Though she would never admit that in any of their hearing, ever, ever, *ever*.

Lyren-Sartora laughed to herself and turned away to hunt for her favorite pastries, after which she might go out onto the balcony and dance by herself.

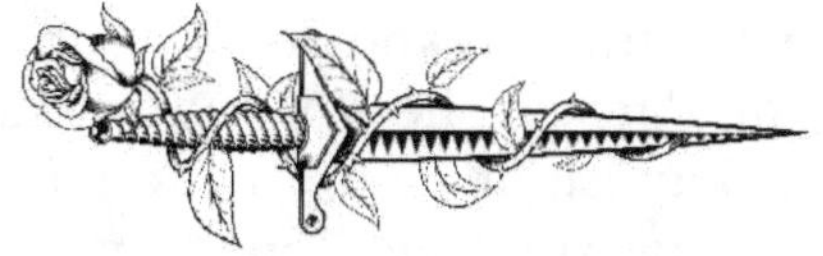

TWENTY-SEVEN

From the other side of the ballroom, another covertly watching Liere was that same tallish, thin figure in violet. Honor Thadara Otobris had once overheard Prince Andri Elsarion admitting to one of his tiresome, low-born flirts that he loved seeing blondes in violet. Though she excoriated Andri's rude and uncouth behavior—which she attributed to the low company he insisted on keeping—he had royal blood in his veins. He needed someone to take him in hand, and through him, the kingdom. Restore it to its proper order.

She was that someone.

Thadara had no illusions about her looks, but she made use of what she had. She wore only violet to any function at which the prince might possibly appear. That was her concession to his tastes, otherwise she dressed to befit the rank she intended to grace.

She made the rounds of the ballroom, as she always did, greeting those whose rank required it, those she might ally with one day, and those she considered to be trouble. Her eye caught several times on the new envoy, whose grace seemed innate, though she was ridiculously young. Really, what was that queen in Sartor thinking? Or, was sending this mere girl a deliberate insult? Unless she was a actually a princess, doing her year of service. She might be useful in future, if that were true.

When the latest dance ended, and the envoy moved to get something to drink, Thadara drifted over to intercept, and made her bow, saying with nicely calculated condescension appropriate to someone who couldn't be any older than sixteen or seventeen, "I am Thadara Otobris, heir to the Baras of Otobris. How does Enaeran compare with the glories of Sartor?"

A question certainly filled with hidden barbs! Liere answered diplomatically—and as soon as Thadara recognized the diplomacy, she stopped listening in order to fashion her inquisition from another direction: "Circumstances have prevented me from visiting Sartor, though the Otobris family attended the Music Festival for centuries." And to demonstrate her knowledge of the Sartoran language as well as its custom, she switched to that tongue to drawl, "I suppose you are from a back-ground of exalted birth, doing your year of service?" Her voice was somewhat high, a little nasal, and despite the outdated accent, sharp with condescension.

Caught by surprise, Liere glanced into the face of someone her own height, dressed in a shade of violet that did nothing for her complexion. Her light brown hair, burnished to a golden sheen under the candlelight, towered in a complicated arrangement strung with gemstones, and held together by a gold band that looked like a royal coronet.

Liere tried to breathe past the effect of that con-descension. There is always a reason why, she reminded herself. But she was unsettled enough for words to escape her—in pure Sartoran—"I'm a shopkeeper's daughter."

"Really?" Thadara actually took a step back, as if Liere could sully her by proximity. "I suppose the Queen of Sartor knows what she's doing," she murmured and moved away without another word, leaving Liere gazing after in astonishment.

Then the meaning struck her. Thadara saw a deli-berate insult in Atan sending someone of such low degree.

Regret pulsed through Liere, settling in her gut. A diplomat was supposed to finesse, asking more questions than she answered. Gatherings like this, shaped by music—so stirring, but so dangerous in its freeing of mood—were for the diplomat primarily political events, whether personal or societal or governmental. Senrid had told her that, long before Liere went to the Ones for training. She knew it, and yet she'd managed in four words to blunder on the personal as well as the societal front. Now to discover if she'd also failed on the political.

Liere glided to the side, and then through the open door

to the terrace beyond the ballroom. She wandered to the pool and dabbled her fingers in the cool water as she strove to regain her equilibrium. To steady herself, she lifted her head and did a perimeter sweep. Light winked briefly on the jointure of a crossbow there at the roof, and at the other end, she saw an armed silhouette by the garden gate.

Another reminder of Senrid. What was he doing in Marloven Hess, on the other side of the mountains? Did he even knew she was back in the world? She glanced westward, but she halted the impulse to reach on the mental plane. Not here, not now.

But the moment's urge thinned her mind-shield enough for her to become aware of someone's focus: Gared! There was a brief glimpse of herself from his vantage, lit by the golden light streaming from the open doors; she shut it out before it could make her dizzy. It was there long enough to give her an idea of location. Gared was over that way, hidden somewhere in the shadowy trees.

Once more she dipped her hands into the cool water, and patted her cheeks. Then she made a quick mental scan to locate unseen guards. None of them had mind-shields; they were largely bored. Only one watched her, his interest idle as he wondered what life was like in Sartor; the other watched the swarm of starflies, their colors winking in and out, a reflection of the stars overhead.

She made a visual sweep. In the ballroom, a lively taltan played, and couples crossed the double doorway, her eye catching on two young men dancing together, performing elaborate kicks and leaps in addition to the complicated steps.

Near Liere, a group of four wandered near the flowers, and high laughter echoed from around the corner: children, Lyren-Sartora among them, trying to catch starflies with cupped hands and then release them to the air. It seemed Lyren-Sartora had managed to make some friends, or at least fit herself among the youngsters whose guardians had brought them to get social seasoning.

Liere wandered around the fountain, near to the garden, and drifted close to the great ferns. Another quick scan. No one was watching her at all. She slipped past the ferns and groped a little way along a path, gliding between the moon-pale outlines of beech. She smelled cedar.

A soft voice exclaimed, "Liere! You couldn't have seen

me."

She almost said *I heard you*, but didn't. Ordinary envoys did not have Dena Yeresbeth — or if they did, they didn't blurt it out! "I came to find cool air."

"Came right to me, eh?" Gared said, chuckling. "I've been sitting here watching you, so I suppose it's only fair if you've been watching me. Though Andri will put my ass in the wringer for being clumsy. You look like you're having fun," he added.

"I am," she said. "Why are you watching me?"

"You're much better to look at than Adon-Marsael, or the rest of 'em. Andri put me here," he added, unnecessarily.

"Why?"

"To watch."

"From the shrubbery? Is it the company or the locale you object to?"

"I wasn't invited." He laughed softly. Then added in his friendly manner, "Brydon's my home. Father was Master of Horse for the Elsarions before they were duffed, mother was a queen's guard. Died protecting the queen."

"I'm sorry," Liere said.

"It was long ago," Gared said easily. "At least I had my father for many years. Others lost everyone." He shifted position, the leaves rustling slightly. "Just that, sitting in the bushes all night is hot work. It's going to rain before too long, at least."

In surprise Liere glanced up, and this time she saw what she'd failed to notice before: a vast gray blotch moving steadily across the sky from the northwest.

"Is Andri here, too?"

"He's busy. But he'll be back later on."

Leaves whispered overhead, and a cool breeze ruffled over Liere's skin.

"Mmmm," Gared said. "Here's the cold air. There'll be thunder."

Liere had been listening on the mental plane; when she sensed curiosity from one of the guards, she turned and began strolling back.

"Have fun," Gared called in a soft voice.

Wind swept the terrace, bringing the first splatters of rain. Liere batted down the panels of her over-robe as she fell in step behind a couple who had been trysting on the grass a little farther along the garden.

As soon as she stepped back inside the ballroom, Adon-Marsael appeared out of the crowd. "Ah. There you are, Honor Feriadar?"

She turned, forcing her bland diplomat smile. Adon-Marsael's hand opened in a gesture of invitation as the orchestra played the opening strains of the step-and twirl, whirling haltas. That baras-heir Thadara had been antagonistic enough to have chattered about Liere's lowly status by now to any who wanted to hear. Time to repair what she could. She joined Adon-Marsael.

Haltas was a two-person dance. His hand slid around her waist, a light, almost imperceptible touch. It felt so strange to be standing to close to somebody she did not really know. How odd it was that just when she was feeling like a grownup—that she was doing quite well—first a memory, and then a touch, would jolt her right back into the old awkward Liere.

It did not help how aware she was of being watched from all sides as they began to twirl at a sedate pace to the center of the room. Thadara Otobris danced by in the arms of an extremely handsome boy with black hair and dark eyes framed by the longest eyelashes Liere had ever seen. Thadara's profile was scornful as she glanced Liere's way, her mouth busy. No, that glance was Adon-Marsael's way, but included Liere in a raking gaze from hair to heels.

If Adon-Marsael noticed, he gave no sign. "How does Enaeran appear to you, O Sartoran Envoy?"

"I've met a number of very agreeable people," she said—falling back on the safety of mindlessly bland, but very, very diplomatic words.

"Speaking of agreeable, is my once-royal cousin Andri Malcolin lurking somewhere around tonight?"

She looked up into his face, not hiding her surprise. "I have no idea."

"I don't know whether to be disappointed or relieved."

"Disappointed?" she asked, recognizing a cue.

"It would be somewhat of a relief to get him safely under lock and key, but on the other hand, a pleasant evening unmarked by excitement has its advantages."

Liere imagined Senrid's affable scorn: *You really think people are unaware that you've got this grand ball locked* down by at least two perimeters of guards? "It's a rather warm night for extra duty," she observed.

Adon steered them between a laboring young couple and a pair of stout, stalwart noblemen stepping around and around with the inexorable force of great bells set to clanging. "They get paid extra," he said, confirming her guess. "And they know they're fortunate to get paid at all."

"I take it I was the lure, then, your grace?"

"An irresistible one, I'd thought," he said, and at her expression of surprise, he added with a slightly raised brow, "You don't want the customary gallant personal remark, do you? Surely you know by now that Andri always manages to meet pretty young women."

Liere appreciated how, in the midst of a compliment, Adon-Marsael managed to disparage Andri and obliquely insult her by implying that she was one of numberless droves. She smothered a laugh, saying, "Tell me instead what you expected your once-royal cousin Andri to do."

"Come to impress you by discommoding as many people as possible. There are actual wagers at certain establishments about said disruptions."

"I see! How often have these disruptions happened?"

"Enough. It's the timing, rather than the frequency, you see." Adon-Marsael laughed again, then said reminiscently as they started back down the center of the room, everyone dancing around them, moons and stars rounding the sun, "The first one was just after I'd secured the palace here, and was trying to reward my supporters and woo the old king's people, who were sadly at a loss. I thought giving a ball would be a signal that normal life is going to be reestablished. I didn't have but a part of my household here then, and we were a trifle overreached, shall we say, in security." He paused.

"Go on, your grace."

"I rousted out musicians, and cooks, and all the rest, and the evening was just approaching what I'd call social success when his rabble showed up at all the doors and windows—" He nodded at the far wall.

Liere glanced.

"Yes, right here. The brats had my people at knifepoint, and Andri and the rest moved in, fanning out. All quite orderly, and very well practiced. Not everyone was armed that night—and a lot of them who were wouldn't be much use in rough work, especially after drinking down wine punch half the evening."

"Did anyone get hurt?" Liere asked.

"Not that time. They all froze, just as if some mage had come in and laid a spell on them, like in the Gardens of Shame of the old days. I've always been skeptical. Can mages lay spells that freeze people, then let them live again?"

Liere was about to say *Yes, in fact I know that spell*, but stopped the impulse, and said, "That question ought to be put to the Sartoran Mage Guild."

"Anyway," he continued, "Andri sauntered in, cool as you please, with this crack-toothed ancient he'd managed to dredge out of retirement. Some old Elsarion family retainer from the days of our mutual Uncle Thunder — that would be Trevor Elsarion, Grand Prince and Commander of the Army. Andri led this dodderer around to all the guests. When the old geezer thought he recognized some item looted from the Elsarion family vaults, one of the brats removed it while Andri waved about this ridiculous sword that's been in the family for generations."

Liere laughed at the rueful expression on Adon-Marsael's face.

"My party, of course, was a disaster. Though provenance could be questioned, and some of the jewels might have been genuine, if recent, gifts — loot has changed hands several times since the original trouble — they were all insulted. After the guests had been thoroughly dejeweled, Andri and his urchins vanished again, and I had to spend weeks smoothing out the repercussions of that."

"I should think it would have harmed Andri's cause more than yours."

"You'd think so, wouldn't you? Except this is Enaeran. Style and dash earn approval whatever one's side, and I'd been left standing there looking like a fool."

"I'm not certain I comprehend."

"Kill someone you don't like in a duel that both sides agree to, and the families ignore one another for a year or two after, as is traditional, but humiliate someone, and you can torch off a feud that will last for generations, because no one heeds trivial details like law — which changes with every upheaval — if they have lost honor. Not that that quite describes the situation that night, for all he got was jewels, and I managed to hold onto everything else, despite a few days of snickering behind my back."

"Ah, I see."

"His subsequent appearances have been well timed. So, yes, I confess I set this one up as a lure. Do you object very much to being the bait, Honor Feriadar?"

"I would have refused had I been asked, your grace," she said, trying to match his easy style. "It does not seem the proper behavior of an envoy, who is expected to remain strictly neutral. But since we are all here, and people seem to be having a good time, and there has been no disruption, why, I am very much at your service."

He laughed. "Thank you. Very gracefully done, I salute you."

"From what I understand," Liere said, "he is a son of the former king. What of his claims?"

"Cousin Andri hasn't any claim, except that of blood. I'm certain that in Sartor mere mention of the name Landis quells thousands, but I assure you that the same does not hold for Elsarion here, at least not his branch, though the older branch still retains some of its luster—probably because they've been wise enough to remain up in their mountain vastness during all the trouble."

"A complicated family, then?"

"You might say that. Though I admit that I've put forward my family connection, but that only as a sop to the very old traditionalists, you might say." He swept them away from two couples who nearly collided, moving so fast that Liere danced on her toes, her over-robe fluttering behind her. "As for Andri, I told the boy two and a half years ago that if he could take Enaeran, and hold it, I'd retire to Geral and raise racehorses."

"And so?"

"And so he turned brigand. Or maybe that was just his band of cutthroats, but he gathered them, and leads them, and so he gets the rep. Then—" Another sudden twirl. "There is the little matter of the murders."

"Murders?"

"Rumor grants him the relatively grand title of assassin, but these were just murders. At least ten, perhaps as many as twenty. That we know of. Another claimant for the throne, and three of the Liberty party might well have vanished in this way. He was seen, repeatedly, in the area either before or after. The one time I did manage to get hold of him, however briefly, he admitted that he had been present at some, and he wouldn't answer when I asked if they were done by his hand or at his command."

Sickness pooled in Liere's middle. "And then?"

"And then we caught and hanged one of his thieving followers, and that by outright coincidence. They're all far too adept at evading my people, Bartal's, and even the agents of the freedom movement. Benefit," Adon-Marsael added, "from his years as a disinherited prince, evading his father's own guard. Whatever his explanation, one thing appears to be clear: he stands outside the law, by inclination as well as by decree."

He made another fast glance out the window, tension tightening his face briefly as lightning flared in the distance.

Liere said, "It seems very expensive to throw a ball to lure one person, even a former prince."

"Little else I can do." He glanced under heavy-lidded eyes toward the door. "Oh, they all have orders to seize him—big rewards, promotions—but it's a waste of breath."

She wasn't quite certain how much of his wryness was irony, but shrugged inwardly, aware that she didn't care what he thought of her.

The music ended, and Liere found herself back where she'd begun. Adon-Marsael smiled, bowed, and turned away, to be engulfed by his own people; when he emerged from the crowd, he was dancing again, with the sallow person in purple, whose nose was in the air again as she spoke very, very intensely.

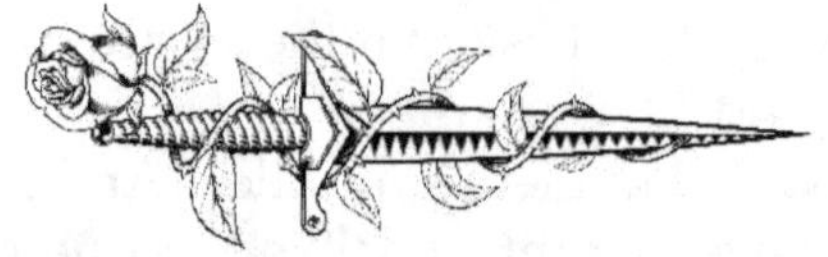

TWENTY-EIGHT

It had taken Shontande Lirendi weeks of thought to choose an appropriate gift, and then a couple more weeks for Bee and Thad to organize smuggling the gift from the palace and conveying it safely across the kingdom to be added to the baggage going south to Sartor. So much could have gone wrong, but Shontande refused to risk magic transfer. Everyone knew the larger or heavier the object, the more likely it would burn up, or vanish in that mysterious *between*-space. He could not risk something so precious as well as priceless.

It had arrived safely with the king and the new ambassador, and was now ensconced in the guest wing of the Sartoran royal palace, where Shontande did not intend to remain long. A sleepless night spent at the windows overlooking a beautifully patterned garden had given him the semblance of a plan. It was time to bring out his gift from the secure wrappings in the cedar trunk. Shontande held his breath until the tapestry had been carefully lifted and set on the well-scrubbed floor within the inner salon of the royal guest suite.

At a gesture from Shon, Thad and his valet cautiously unrolled the ancient tapestry. Then they stood back, staring down silently at the art, which was roughly five paces across and three deep. At the center two men stood together, wearing pointed beards, doublets and tight pants, their long hair streaming down their backs. At their right the same grand entrance Shontande had been welcomed at the day previous, recognizable in essentials, but differing in details —

such as (at far right) a vast garden with mountains as a backdrop, and above, a blue sky shading to gray.

Shontande's gaze strayed to the central figures, from their positions obviously friends. Thence to his ancestor's face, and his wistful expression; Shontande had been studying this tapestry since he was small, contemplating that expression and what it signified. It hurt worse than he'd expected, the idea of never seeing this tapestry again, except maybe as a visitor sometime in an unknown future.

Thad dropped to his knees, bending over a corner of the tapestry until his nose was almost touching the weave. "Every thread is different," he murmured. "I mean, not just a different color, but the texture varies in the way they're woven."

"Brocade and damask. Embroidery as well, in the elements on the kings' clothes. Here and here, the front row of flowers." Shontande stooped, pointing. "It took ten years, so the records say. As many as twenty expert hands before it was finished—made by so secret a method that even the real name of the process is secret." Shontande opened his hand in the fan gesture for *perfect blossom.*

Thad did not pretend to any mind powers, but he could see Shontande's regret by the way his gaze lingered on the tapestry. "One thing I saw yesterday, this place is packed with old stuff," he said doubtfully. "I hope they'll appreciate this one."

Shontande let out a slow breath.

It was time to get ready for his first day in Sartor. According to the schedule the Sartoran scribe assigned to them had furnished, this would be a formal court day—with a tour planned afterward to the mage guild and the scribe guild, the two most important of the guilds. Tomorrow the archives, more guilds, and so on through the week, with plays and musicales each evening, ending in a grand ball at the end of the first week.

Thad dispatched two of their trusted servants to Apsos Grand in order to make an initial survey of the embassy, with a letter of credit in hand. Shontande knew that the regency council might be—no, were—busy plotting against him with fresh vigor after his expulsion of the former ambassador, but they would never wish to lose melende before the world by denying that credit. The Lirendi private fortune was

Shontande's, and however much they might have dipped into it for their own purposes, he knew there was plenty of reserves.

He dressed in Lirendi blue and white before descending to the interview chamber exclusive to the reception of royal guests. The Sartoran queen did not leave him waiting long; he could not help but reflect that the Colendi would contrive to have them arrive at the same time—unless they wished to convey an insult. After the exchange of pleasant nothings, Shontande had Thad and two of the actors present the tapestry. Giving his few words of gratitude for the visit and his hopes that she would like this small gift, he turned to this young queen who Senrid had promised would be on his side, and . . .

She stared at the gift that cost him so much thought and heartache, her face a blank shield.

He was surprised at how sharply Atan's disappointment hurt. She tried to hide it—one might say her demeanor was expertly polite and pleasant, for she was too experienced not to have that much control—but she had no idea how sensitive he was on the mental plane, and so had not troubled over a mind-shield. He had to exert himself to shut her emotional reactions out; a blast of emotion could take him by surprise, but any reach on his part would be trespass.

Atan lifted her gaze from the tapestry to its giver, and wondered for the first time why he was really here—that is, what he expected. Ah, no doubt that would come out. She signed to her servants to carry it to her own interview chamber, where it would be on display for the rest of his visit, in case she had occasion to invite him there, and after he left it would be carefully wrapped up and added to the countless other ancient tapestries stuffed away in various underground chambers honeycombing this palace.

She delivered her most gracious speech inviting him to accompany her to court. Where, she decided, she would get a little revenge.

Thad was then able to make good his escape.

From time to time over the long morning she glanced at Shontande, a little irritated that her eye wanted to linger. He really was an artist's delight—everything, she reflected ruefully, that the Landises as a family were not. But beyond that, he was actually listening, or else he was far better than she was at pretending an interest. No yawns, no suppressed sighs. His gaze flicked from speaker to speaker without going blank from boredom.

The same could be said for the two guild tours, Shontande's first foray into the central district. He looked at everything with interest, he listened to each speaker, he said the right thing afterward in that maddeningly charming accent. No fault could be found, and yet by the time they parted to ready for the evening's entertainment, she was fuming with frustration.

She found Rel in her interview chamber, studying that tapestry.

"Why are you looking at that thing? It's fine, and it's old, but a moment's thought might have suggested that Sartor has no dearth of old things. Did he think we are barbarians?" she said, coming to stand next to him, bumping comfortably against him.

Rel shook his head slowly. "There's something about it that's different."

"There is nothing whatsoever about the Music Festival in it," she stated, annoyance back again as she scrutinized what she'd barely glanced at before. "What do you find different from any other old, moldering thing from centuries ago?"

"Who are they? The handsome one looks familiar."

"The beanpole with the gopher face is my greats-grandfather Eniad Landis, king of Sartor at the time. The handsome one is Martande Lirendi, first king of Colend. I imagine there must be a million statues of his pretty face all over Colend, ordered by his admiring populace, if not by him." Rel's brow lifted at her sarcasm, and she relented. "He and Eniad were close, and this must depict the day Martande was granted Colend, so to speak. Look at those beards, and those stuffed jackets! Those pants—could they even sit down in them?"

"Doublets," Rel murmured. "Armoring was frequently fitted into all that decorative stitchwork."

"It's beautifully done—a very faithful representation of this palace at that time, I can tell, having seen many pictures of that garden, and the outer gate of the time. But Martande is not exactly important to us. Nor is Eniad one of our most famous kings. Though admittedly he had an excellent reputation. A rarity, a good king and a good person. Is that

Shontande Lirendi's hint? I need to know what is in his mind; I was a fool to assume he was coming here to give the Music Festival back."

Rel slid an arm around her, his gaze resting on the tapestry. To him, this was a perfect diplomatic gift: ancient, precious, beautiful, depicting an agreeable moment, a salute to respected figures of history who were allies.

But he was not a king.

"That reminds me. A message came in earlier." He tapped her personal golden notecase, which no one but Rel was permitted to touch without permission. Rel could read anything in it, but he was not to take it out of the room because he had never managed to hold onto one longer than a week or two. "Senrid wants another meeting."

"Already? Did he hear something?" Her voice sharpened with alarm.

"Not that he said."

"Have you even had time to try the patrol drills?"

"Those can still happen, to be reported on later. Atan, Senrid and Shontande Lirendi need to meet now that he's free of that regency council. Colend is pretty much indefensible, even I saw that when riding back and forth across it. According to Thad and Bee both, Shontande has never been permitted by the council to discuss the subject, and they seem to believe they can prevail by sheer will. If Norsunder comes, they won't last a day."

"That council has prevailed by sheer force of will so far," Atan commented. "But in sending Ambassador Gaszin home Shontande dealt them a very smart blow."

Rel dipped his chin in a short nod, his quick smile one of approval. "And your acceptance of Thad helped it strike home."

"Yes, because I loathed that Vardathe Gaszin. I don't want to be a part of Shontande's long-distance duel with his regency council. And I must say, though he's given no hint about the Music Festival, which annoyed me more than I expected, at least he's given no sign that he expects me to take part in that duel. Perhaps my cooperation in other matters thus far might gain us the Music Festival back? Eh. Let's cooperate once more; I'll write to Vidanric of Remalna tonight."

Rel had gone back to studying the tapestry, his head

tipped consideringly. "This art here really commands the eye. I'm trying to figure out how it does that. I think there's more going on here than you might assume." He slid his arm around her shoulders. "I'm getting the impression the day went badly."

"*He* was a perfect guest. What you'd expect from a Colendi. *I* was vindictive," she admitted. "In Star Chamber, he sat there well within the range of my privacy wards, and I could have explained what was going on behind the self-serving speeches. I didn't. But I will admit he paid attention. It was the same with the tour afterward. He gave each pompous speechifier all his attention, as if they two were alone, and when he spoke, there was that pretty accent. I could see every one of those crusty duffs falling for him, like a row of pins in the children's game."

Rel thumbed his jawline, then turned to her. "He has to be aware of expectations. Did any of your court bring up the Music Festival?"

"No. I did not expect them to. The ones with the most ambition will no doubt try to get him alone, because they'll want the credit of eliciting his promise. If he can be flattered or beguiled into giving it. The blunt instrument of court-wide moral force will come later. I was thinking about whether I ought to lead it," she further admitted, and when his response was a grunt, she added, "Nothing to say to that?"

"I see it as a Sartoran governmental affair. I'll do some listening around if you like."

"Please do. And what do you suggest I do, since you didn't hail my hint about throwing the entire court at him as a brilliant idea?"

"The schedule has him in public pretty much for days, am I correct?"

"You are. Tours, a poetry reading, concerts — lots of those, with intent — the ball at week's end. The day of the ball is the first open time. Traditionally everyone stays home to recruit themselves for dancing all night."

Rel lifted a shoulder; Atan and he had agreed when she began attending purely social affairs that he would stay away, rather than serve as a target. Her court still expected her to marry to benefit the kingdom.

Rel said, "Before the ball, send a personal invitation. Take him somewhere. Just the two of you. Let him talk. A ride around the city walls, maybe? Somewhere he doesn't have to be the focus of all eyes and ears."

Her unsettled emotions resolved into challenge. "It would be splendid if I were the one to convince him to return the Music Festival. But I know, I *know*, best not to harass him about it. I've learned the hard lessons about demands I can't enforce."

Rel gave a short nod. "I'd never met him, as I said. No one had. He's been effectively a prisoner, with ribbons for chains." And though Atan knew it, he decided a reminder might be a good idea now. "Thad, Adam, and Curtas used to tell us how lonely he was, before it turned out Adam and Curtas were Detlev's spies. From what I gather it never got better, outside of a single cousin he rarely got to see. Give him a chance to talk."

"I know. I remember." Atan tried to shake herself free of the disappointment about the Music Festival. She had been foolish—it had been too easy, to unrealistic to expect so grand a gesture. "Tsauderei told me when I was a child that you get to know people in three ways: by reputation, by pen, and face to face. Time for me to try the last one."

The next few days were a repeat of the first. Shontande Lirendi was the perfect guest, impeccably clothed, polite, well-spoken, attentive. It occurred to Atan that he had been performing that part since the sudden death of his father when he was small. Of course he'd know exactly what to say at every formal occasion: a whole lot of airy nothing, elegantly spoken.

The night before the ball, she had dictated to her personal scribe the changes she wanted in the following day's schedule (for she did not have the luxury of a day spent lying about); by the time the ball ended, a beautifully written invitation, on gold-embossed paper, would be slipped under his door.

Thad, who had spent a week renovating the embassy, was waiting for Shontande when he returned from a concert. The seal invitation sat on the low table before him.

Shontande had intended to write a letter, but he recognized the Sartoran royal seal on the folded paper, and dropped down beside Thad. He picked up the heavy paper, but instead of reading it, leaned back on the low couch, his formal robe spilling in shimmering folds around him. "All evening as I listened to Austere Era polyphonies, I was trying to word a letter to Senrid. How does one say, 'Friend, how could you be so wrong?'"

"You think it was a mistake to come to Sartor?" Thad was aghast. This had been the most exhausting week yet: he'd labored hard at refurbishing the entire embassy, and then there was overseeing the secondary task he'd been assigned, not even a third complete.

"Ah-ye, forgive me for being unclear, Thad." Shontande made the peace, bowing as if Thad were the master and he the servant, for he knew quite well how hard Thad had been working. "I complain merely because my gift was a disaster," Shontande said. "I should have foreseen it. Nor am I blaming Senrid, because he has never been to Colend during the Music Festival. For all I know, Marlovens don't even have music. He can't know how important it is to us — and, I'm beginning to perceive, to the Sartorans. That, I ought to have anticipated. I think that my welcome, surrounded by music, was in hopes that I was here to give it back. As if I could! Probably as well they don't understand that I don't have anything to give outside of my personal belongings, and even those, I had to smuggle out lest I be interrogated."

Thad agreed with an unhappy bow. "I am also at fault. I've known Senrid longer, but somehow I expected he knew."

"We can share the fault, for whatever that will bring us," Shontande said with a wry smile. "Secondly, Senrid could not have known just how assiduously the court here would be weighing me up as a prospective consort. The first day I attributed to curiosity, but it has become more, ah, intent."

"How is your being a consort even possible? Colend is so far away."

"They ruled us once. I'm certain they'd find a way to do it again."

"Did someone say something to you?" Thad asked. "Or did you . . ." He tapped his forehead.

"Trespass that way would be an ill-return for my welcome," Shontande said gently — being Colendi, he could not bring himself to say 'No!' even to Thad. "Even if I could hide it. Which would be difficult, even impossible. Every day, though I've only attended the most formal functions, and tonight I confined myself to the stiffest and oldest dances, I've encountered little clues, and recognized others in retrospect. I am not certain the queen knows," he added unexpectedly. "There has been no sense of courtship from her so far, but then I am unfamiliar with Sartoran courtship custom."

His gaze fell to the invitation. He slid his finger under the seal, then read the contents. "Ah. Perhaps it is to begin after all. She is inviting me to a ride around the city. The two of us." He laid the invitation down.

Thad raised his hands in Rue as he said, "One thing I am very certain of: the guild chiefs will be pressing the council by now."

They thought of the warehouses and storerooms full of decorations waiting to be put up, the wagonloads of food ordered from all over the kingdom in preparation for the visitors who were even now embarking on their journey — those from farthest away already on route — all waiting for the king's seal that would release the funds for pay for it all. And no king.

They both glanced toward the innocuous trunk behind the finer trunks full of clothing and accessories. The plain trunk had cloaks and embroidered shoes, but at the bottom, another, very plain locked box, which held the royal seal and the celestial blue ink, made with melted silver, with which it was used.

Both wondered who would break into the chamber where it was kept — and what would happen when they discovered it missing.

"Bee will let us know," Shontande said, as if Thad had spoken aloud.

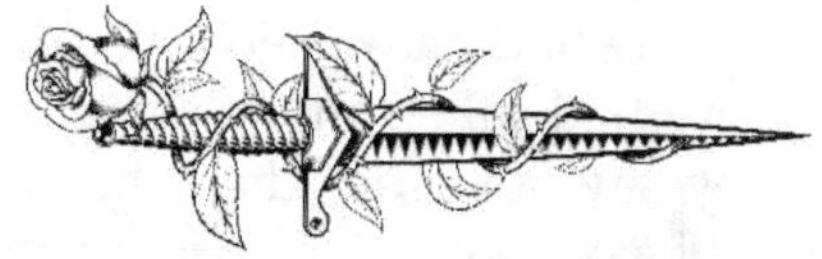

TWENTY-NINE

Shiovhan, capital of Enaeran

Liere woke gasping, her heart beating in her throat: another nightmare. Third this week. Fourth.

The mental reek of danger tangled with dream shards. Real threat or merely the same old stupid nightmare from childhood? Dawn blued the east windows, thunder muttering in the west. That would account for the rumble of iron-shod boots on stone in the dream. The parody villain's ludicrously ranted threats — the figure was so distorted it was barely recognizable as Detlev anymore — died away. Caused by a whiff of Norsunder or not?

Liere rolled out of bed and dashed through the cleaning frame moments before Lyren-Sartora's door opened, and though Liere was now fresh, in the midst of brushing out her tangled hair, Lyren-Sartora said accusingly, "You had another nightmare. Didn't you?"

"I did —"

"I *told* you, it's that poopsie-faced Andri," Lyren-Sartora said triumphantly.

"How could that be? I haven't seen him since the night he and his friend showed up. These nightmares are the same silly stuff I saw in nightmares when I was ten."

"I think we should just leave." Lyren-Sartora sulked, arms tightly crossed over her chest.

"I thought you were enjoying the rides and boats and picnics."

"I have been." Lyren-Sartora tossed her head. "Especially since that horrid Thadara Otobris person was kicked out of the palace right after that ball last week. And no, I was *not* listening to her mind. She was blasting her nasty thoughts right *at* everyone at that ball. So yes, it's been great fun."

Lyren-Sartora's gaze shifted. It was true, she'd had fun all week, but what she had truly enjoyed most was at night, when she and Liere had fallen into the habit of comparing notes on what they saw and did, then they'd talk about all manner of things. Last night Liere had wanted to hear all about Lyren-Sartora's first year after Liere left for Geth. Lyren-Sartora had then gleefully complained about what a bully Siamis was, forcing her and Mac to do housework and garden work for no real reason, and Liere hadn't even tried to argue when Lyren-Sartora insisted how unfair it was.

That was because Liere had easily translated her complaints into the unpalatable truth that Mac and Lyren-Sartora had discovered that bratty behavior had consequences. Siamis had put them to work, mostly doing useful things, such as washing windows and floors, and weeding the vegetable garden. Siamis had worked right alongside them, "spying, to make sure we did it," Lyren-Sartora had said in disgust. "Though he seemed to *like* it. He said it cleared his mind. And Mac, being a boy — which means an idiot — claimed all the windows and floors after Siamis told him that it would make his arms stronger. I was happy to let him have the indoor chores. I didn't mind weeding so much, because a garden looks so lovely after all the toil, whereas dusting and polishing just leaves everything looking much the same . . ."

Lyren-Sartora rambled on until late, Liere making sympathetic noises and never interrupting. As far as Lyren-Sartora was concerned, these days could go on forever, just like this. Except every so often she'd see Liere stiffening into alertness, or her gaze would go diffuse, and Lyren-Sartora was sure Liere was thinking about *him*.

She understood about crushes. She'd had one on Silvanus ever since she was nine. But that just meant she loved to sneak over to the stable and watch him training the horses. A crush was fun, especially when he smiled at you, but Lyren-Sartora didn't want to *do* anything. That was a door behind which adults went, about which Lyren-Sartora had learned when she wanted to know why, with fifty-three rooms in the residence wing alone in the Bereth Ferian palace (she and Mac had once counted them *all*), Arthur and Roy still shared a bedroom. Arthur had sent her to his mother to explain, and three sentences in Lyren-Sartora had raised a hand. The entire subject made her squirmy. The important point was, Liere was *not* going to go behind that door, especially with poopsie-faced Andri, and leave Lyren-Sartora behind *again!*

Liere said, "We can leave, if you like. I'm still not completely convinced that somebody from Norsunder hasn't been lurking around, though I can't imagine why. Nor can I find proof either way. We can return to Atan and report that we did our best."

"Fine with me," Lyren-Sartora said recklessly—though she would miss Jaydi, who was fun, and she'd miss the picnics, and the pretty flower lanterns with little candle stubs that the young people made and floated out on the lake at night.

On the other hand, if Liere was willing to leave, then maybe Poopsie Face was no threat after all? "Or we can stay a few days more," she said airily. "You're the envoy. You decide. Hey!"

Lyren-Sartora glanced into the salon, and noticed that a paper had been slid under the door. "It's that pompous paper, the kind the Almost-King uses." She pounced on it. "Another grand ball, I hope? I want a costume one, so I can go as . . . oh. It's for you only. Looks like Almost-King wants to blab at you."

Liere took the invitation: Adon-Marsael requested the honor of a private interview.

Liere lowered the paper, considering. All that week, she had continued to play the part of Sartoran Envoy. She'd attended every event she was invited to, which at least enabled her to become more familiar with the enormous, rambling palace.

Some ministers and their families lived in the undamaged portions of the palace, some did not. The rest lived in the fine houses along the ridge overlooking the city, lined along the palace's garden on the south side. The north side was wilder, a royal preserve, eventually bumping up against the winding river that drained via a spectacular waterfall into the great river. That area was too rocky for building, but was popular for summer picnics.

During all these pleasant social events, Liere had tried to sniff out signs of Norsunder, while aware of being watched.

She glimpsed Elies and Gared but never saw Andri Elsarion, though she sensed he was around. She also caught sight of Adan-Marsael's considering gaze a little too often for it to be accidental, and wondered if she was still a lure, the way she'd inadvertently been the night of the welcome ball.

She laid the invitation aside. "Why don't we pack up, just in case I find out that we're done here? Your job will be to fetch the banner from the protocol herald, if I give you the signal." She tapped her head.

"Do we have to bother with that old flag? Arthur had a closet full of banners. We can just use our transfer tokens." Lyren-Sartora touched the butterfly hair clasp that Liere had bespelled with a transfer spell, in case Lyren-Sartora felt danger and they were not together.

"We're representing Atan," Liere reminded her. "This is a kingdom in which mages are distrusted. It would not just be rude to transfer away in front of people, it would have repercussions that might harm relations between Atan and the people here. We'll depart properly and carry the banner down into the city, and then we can transfer. Or we can send the banner back to Bereth Ferian, and just be us, if you want to find Jaydi and tender your goodbye. We'll no longer be envoys, so we'll be able to transfer away whenever we want, as long as we find a secluded spot to do it from."

"I'm already packed," Lyren-Sartora stated. "And we don't have to go. I'll stay if there's a grand masquerade planned," she added, for she'd discovered that now that they might actually have to leave, she was ambivalent. Maybe she'd misjudged the situation with Poopsie Face after all.

With that thought in mind, she put on a pretty summer robe and ran out to find something fun to do; if she had to leave, she was going to enjoy the friends she'd made among the palace children as long as she could.

Liere crossed more slowly to the state wing under a mackerel sky, the air breathlessly still. Every plant in the garden seemed to be wilting.

A waiting page accompanied her up to the royal interview chamber. She entered with her noiseless tread, catching Adon-Marsael massaging his temple with a thumb. Then he looked up, and she wondered if that little moment of weariness had been for her benefit. She bowed, saying, "A headache, your grace?"

"Doesn't this weather give everyone a headache?" he asked with a smile that was more of a wince. "Come, sit down, Honor Feriadar. You've had a week among us, and no questions? Is there any way we can serve you?"

No governmental leader would set aside what surely was an arduous schedule, on a blistering day, to ask so idle a question. It had to mean he wanted something from her. When she demurred politely, he went on, "You are sure to be promoted after your successful visit to our humble kingdom; you are well spoken of everywhere, much preferred to the Adrani ambassador, if truth be told. No surprise, that."

He smiled in a way that invited her to share the mild joke. She smiled back, then he went on with the compliments. When she returned another polite answer, he seemed a little astray, as if he had expected more enthusiasm on her part. At least more reaction to the flattery.

He definitely wanted something. Were they going to sit here all day before he got to it? He thumbed the skin under his eyebrows again, then said, "You might be aware that Andri Elsarion has been poking around more this week than he has since winter." Implication: here at last was the cause of his headache. "He certainly isn't lurking around to speak to me, or he'd easily find me. I think the lure is our very young and, if I may be pardoned for observing, comely Sartoran envoy who has drawn his interest."

Her confusion solidified into conviction: all these invitations had not been for her sake alone. They had probably had Adon-Marsael behind them. She'd continued to be his lure, but it hadn't worked. He was giving up, or?

". . . so easy to speak to. Everyone says so. I'd hoped that, were you to encounter my troubled cousin, you might even discover what it is he wants. Or what he assumes might be his, ah —"

"Claim?"

"Demands, I was thinking. There are so very many claims on that throne downstairs. Including Bartal na Shagal's. For you know we were once one kingdom; that land between the two great rivers has been in dispute ever since. There is also Andri's own cousin, Trevor Macael Elsarion, but at least he has the wisdom, or perhaps merely the lack of ambition, to remain far from Shiovhan. It would be so very helpful if Andri would do the same."

Chill gripped Liere. She understood now: Adon-Marsael had permitted her to move about freely, while he had his people lying in wait to pounce on Andri Elsarion, if he showed up uninvited. That was a matter between them. She had merely gone about her day as envoy, enjoying the events. But now he wanted her to deliberately participate in luring Andri into a trap. Her stomach lurched, causing her to send a questing tendril—

To encounter a solid mind-shield.

Mind-shields early became second nature to those with Dena Yeresbeth; it was akin to shutting out noise. People without Dena Yeresbeth had to be taught to make mind-shields. It was easy enough, but it took a conscious effort. Adon-Marsael had to know Andri had Dena Yeresbeth—the question was, he'd learned that from whom?

It no longer mattered, she reminded herself, and she sent the mental signal to Lyren-Sartora. Time to go back to Sartor. She summoned her most diplomatic tone. "It is such a shame that we were not to meet, but alas, you are very right about my prospective promotion. Since I have delivered the queen's message and gift, I have become increasingly aware that I might have overstayed, due entirely to your generous welcome and to the excellent company I've discovered here."

She added more praise and moved smoothly to her regret that she must depart, until Lyren-Sartora's distinctive internal voice came: *Got it, made my bows.*

Liere rose amid a morass of mutual compliments. Liere sensed the sharpness of Adan-Marsael's disappointment. Then he seemed to accept the inevitable. No doubt his trap would still happen, but she would not serve as bait.

When she got back to their rooms, she sat down to write a quick note to Atan, reporting their imminent departure, and asked if she ought to do anything before they left.

Lyren-Sartora showed up then, her arms full of blossoms. "I don't know why people gave me flowers. That is, what am I to do with them when I'm supposed to be leaving?"

Liere said absently, "The flowers are meant to smell good inside a stuffy, hot coach. Remember, most people do not use transfer unless they can help it. And in these kingdoms, even when they need it, they usually don't have it."

"Right. Ah, I don't want to waste them. I'm going to set them in these decorative vases, put the rest of the basin water in them, then we can go. Surely the servants will like them."

"Good idea."

The golden notecase flicked its magic signal against Liere's hand. She took out a small strip of paper with a strong, unfamiliar hand: *She is out riding. I'll convey the message. Rel.*

Liere tucked the strip of paper back into the notecase, and picked up her carryall. Lyren-Sartora stood back, admiring the flower arrangement. Which was beautiful. Was that skill really entirely natural?

"I'll take the banner," Lyren-Sartora said, dusting her hands as she turned away. "My last task as an official envoy aide. Can I use my being an envoy's aide in the future, if someone asks what I am able to do?"

"You can, and you even may."

"Oh, Liere, it's too hot for that."

Liere only laughed as she took one last glance around, her gaze snagging on the balcony where that quick conversation, so much like the opening feints in a duel, had taken place. Lyren-Sartora noted that diffuse gaze and swept out, breaking Liere's reverie.

They left.

Lyren-Sartora chattered blithely as they descended the stairs. "Of course I couldn't tell them who I really was," she said in Sartoran. "And the ones who wanted to know where I lived in Eidervaen, I had to lie and say we had scribe dormitories, because I could tell at least two wanted invitations to stay with me. Not really *friend* friends . . ."

The cloud cover had thickened, occasional mutters of thunder in the north. Liere widened her senses in an effort to descry whether that sense of tension poised before action was her imagination, or the weather.

". . . and for fun I sometimes mentioned Bereth Ferian, and more than half of them looked at me as if I was saying la-la-la. They have tutors! Imagine not knowing where Bereth Ferian is! Siamis made us learn all the major kingdoms on the map before we were allowed to go ice skating that very first winter, and I was *eight!* . . ."

They reached the end of the long walk, and turned down the main path to the lower city.

"Everyone is staring at the banner," Lyren-Sartora commented, breaking off her complaints about Siamis. "Do we want that?"

"All the way to the inner city below," Liere said. "We've got four watchers behind and parallel to us."

That was soon three; when they reached the lower level, and made their way through the crowd toward the great stable alongside the river where wealthier merchants hired transportation, they were down to one watcher, whose thoughts were as plain as a shout: his orders were to see them actually get into a coach and leave.

They joined the crowd waiting in line, Liere standing with her eyes shut to avoid vertigo as she spread her awareness wide. When she caught their overheated, impatient watcher looking northward toward the gathering clouds, she quickly threw illusion over herself and Lyren-Sartora, dulling their clothes and making her hair dark.

The spy looked back. His gaze passed them. He glanced around in alarm—Liere spotted two people about to get into a coach, and threw a shimmer over them, no more than sunlight glinting off the hair of the taller one. That was enough to catch the watcher's eye before the woman vanished into the coach.

Relieved, the spy turned away, and began the long toil back toward the palace to report them as properly departed.

Liere said softly, "Gone. Let's go around that corner. We'll send the banner, and plan our next move."

Lyren-Sartora obeyed, and away went the banner. The sidestep put them in the full glare of the sun; most people were trying to stand in what shade they could find. "Would you like to say goodbye to Jaydi?"

Lyren-Sartora looked up at her. "Is he close?"

"Very," was all the time Liere had to say before they were surrounded by several of Andri's gang.

"There you are!" Jaydi squawked in his hoarse voice, bouncing up to Lyren-Sartora without any apparent reaction to the oppressive heat.

Andri emerged from behind a stack of barrels and sauntered toward Liere, low hat brim shading his face. "Ready for a ride?'

Lyren-Sartora turned away from Jaydi to glare at Andri. "What is this? Some kind of trap? Do we get a chance to say what *we* want to do?"

Jaydi's eyes rounded. "Don't you wanna visit us?"

Andri spread his hands. "Go or stay." And to Liere, "We

wanted to offer you a chance to see *our* Enaeran."

"Please," she answered, as Lyren-Sartora heaved a hissing sigh.

"It'll be fun," Jaydi said, tugging on Lyren-Sartora's arm, his eyes pleading.

"Oh, all right," Lyren-Sartora said to him, and to Liere a sharp thought: *We'll say goodbye and then go. Today!*

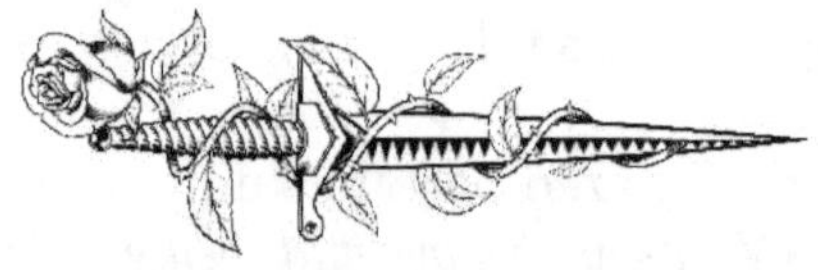

THIRTY

Rel and Atan had risen before dawn that morning, for she wanted to breakfast together before she walked the Napurdiav and he took off to Tansaree to stay with the old duchas while running Senrid's latest assigned exercise.

Alas, the rest of the world seemed to be united in blasting their plans, for one interruption after another ruined the breakfast.

"Most of these polite inquiries," Atan said, rolling another strip of paper into a, inky ball, "are barely concealed demands for schedule changes. They all want Shontande Lirendi to grace this or grace that. It appears he is referring them to me." She looked up. "You've stayed in Colend. Is that their idea of diplomacy?"

Rel eyed the little mound of paper pills, which would eventually be taken away, soaked, and pressed into new notepapers. Atan only rolled them like that when she was bothered. It reminded him of the way a cat would flick the end of its tail. "I suspect it's a Colendi way of saying no. Perhaps he expects that if one or another event is important, you'll let him know."

Atan sighed as she wiped her fingers off. "The latest one is Lirza's bid to host a masquerade."

Lirza. There was the probable cause of the irritation. "Where would she hold it?" Rel asked, knowing that the obnoxious beauty had recently ended her marriage, a bitter enough parting that her former husband's entire family had united in ensuring she left with not a tinket more than what she had first arrived with. With no fortune, she had moved back to her parental home. "Ah. Of course her mother will want to host it."

"Correct. I very much believe it's Lirza whose spies found out—or made up—the rumor that Shontande Lirendi's clothes, from the skin out, are not made with buttons."

Rel had always known that about Colendi styles. "So?"

"Any buttons." Atan drawled the word *any*.

Rel just looked puzzled.

Atan then remembered that Rel had spent most of his life traveling, usually with one change of clothes, which he bought whenever his old outfit fell apart. He'd seen the world's variety of fashions, and paid no attention to any of it.

"Implication," she said, "that Colendi in effect dress in nightwear all the time."

"Lirza and her sort find *that* suggestive of the bedroom? Or as the Colendi say, the Crane Chamber?" Rel asked.

Atan laughed. To a man who preferred, when possible, to wear nothing at all to bed (as she very well knew) it probably wasn't suggestive of anything except extra laundry.

"They appear to," Atan said. "What galls me is that Lirza seems to think that she has only to crook her finger and whoever she wants will come running. No, what galls me is that men do come running."

"Some," Rel replied. "The rest of us run the other way."

Atan eyed him. "She crooked her finger at you?" That was new. "Recently?"

"No, not recently. Numerous times. After she was first married," Rel said. "I expect she thought that her being married would prevent common Rel the Traveler from expectations of anything more than serving as her toy. But as I found those crooked fingers very easy to resist, I forgot all about it."

His deep voice was even, a rumble in his chest, but Atan knew him better than anyone. Had there been the slightest wry inflection on the word common? Reminding her that he had yet to tell her what else he had discovered about his background. His father, the mage Mondros, he'd disclosed: disinherited from a family that had held a military governorship. But there was still a very blank space where his mother was concerned, and Atan knew better than to assume indifference on his part.

He would speak when he was ready. She said, "I was

sorry when Lirza inveigled that poor man into marriage. I hope he learned something. I'm surprised she didn't beggar him. She certainly tried. Ah, listen to me. I'm turning into as nasty a gossip as she is. And I'm missing my labyrinth time. I almost wish I hadn't invited Shontande Lirendi to ride. For one thing, it's going to be a blistering day."

"Talk to him." Rel leaned down to kiss her. "I've got to get my things together."

She glanced at the sandglass and let out a yelp. It was already later than she'd thought. She dashed into her room to change, promising herself an extra-long walk on the morrow.

The city bells began their clang when Atan left by her back door, avoiding the prospect of lurking courtiers, or the servants of courtiers. Shontande Lirendi was in the stable yard, waiting.

She apologized for her lateness. He protested that she was not late—as both very well knew—but when relative strangers relying heavily on politesse meet, the second one to arrive always must apologize; falling into this timeworn pattern gave them each something to say. Unfortunately, those well-worn groves in the conversational path also postponed actual conversation.

The early part of the ride remained like that.

Shontande had had a week to consider her flash of disappointment about his gift, that he knew she had not meant him to see. Until he understood how to maneuver, he would make no reference to the Music Festival—all while waiting for news from home.

Home? Or not home? Was he a king or pretending to be a king?

Gradually the polite exchange gave way to longer and longer pauses, each sunk in thought. He only realized how long the silence had stretched when Atan pulled up atop a cliff overlooking the city, and she made another effort. "This is our most famous vista. You'll find countless paintings, drawings, embroidery, mosaics, and so on all over the city, some hundreds of years old, from this vantage. I'm told there's a drinking game formed around identifying by the details the year a work was made."

Alsais had no nearby mountains. It was always painted from the rivers. Alsais. Home or not home? "What do you think, your majesty, when you look upon what I've read is the oldest city in the world, and you know that it is indisputably yours?"

"Please call me Atan," she said, "when we're not in public."

He bowed over his horse's withers, wondering if this was the commencement of courtship.

She gazed over the steep tile roofs of her city, grouped around its central white tower. "The title is indisputably mine. That was never a problem. These frog eyes of mine dissuaded even the most skeptical from disbelieving my ancestry. All during those early years, my chief fear was that Detlev would come to finish off eradicating my family, beginning with me. 'Your majesty!'" She shook her head. "It was a very long time before I ceased to hear that as mockery, a reminder of my total inability to rule."

He knew exactly what she was talking about. Only for him, the mockery had come in reverse. As a small boy, stunned by the violent death of his father, the royal honorifics had been his father's. He'd heard them as the last connection to his father; it was only in recent years that he flinched from the emptiness each repetition implied.

But these things he was not ready to say. "One might observe, it is a customary expression, like the bow toward a gate that was destroyed centuries before. Or, perhaps, the wearing of a velvet cloak that is never meant to actually sustain the elements." He won the laugh he'd expected, then he adroitly turned the subject. "From the windows of my suite, I see a very fine garden. Not so much of it, for the trees, but it seems there is a labyrinth? You in Sartor call it the Napurdiav. Yes?"

"Correct."

"Ah-ye," he said softly, two separate notes. She found the expression curiously compelling—not pronounced at all the way players on stage brayed it. "I did not know it is still observed, this very ancient tradition."

"Very ancient," she agreed. "Walking the Purrad has gone in and out of fashion. I walk it each day, as I find it clears the mind wonderfully."

"Do you know," he said with a glance slanted her way, "our first king, Martande Lirendi, when he had the city of Alsais rebuilt, he laid it out on those lines?"

"I did not know that," she replied. "But surely it's not still there? I mean, no one has ever told me."

"Oh, it outgrew those outlines within a few generations," he said. "But the arc of those lines are still to be found, if one knows how to look. Especially in the gardens, how they are planted."

They were actually talking! Rel was right. "Tell me about those gardens, please," she asked as they turned the horses and began to ride back down the mountain.

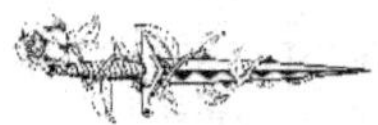

Shiovhan, capital of Enaeran

While they returned to the palace, on the other side of the Sartoran Sea and a little to the west, Marten Eldias stepped out of one of the many back doors of the Morvende Cave inn, and strolled into the alley behind a cart laden with straw that was making its way to the inn yard next to the stables.

He looked around at the rain-washed old buildings, none of which were the least prepossessing, especially here at their backs. People began appearing at windows, pulling airing bedding inside after uncertain glances skyward, and sweeping tiny courtyards, and carrying market-goods in and out. Cooking smells mingled, enticing promise mixing with the smell of hot brick. Everyone longed for the storm to break the heat.

Marten reflected that it's not just discerning the living from the dead that forces one to see what one ordinarily might pass without seeing. There was also the prospect of being watched. Did the ghosts feel that way? He passed one that was thinner than gossamer, mere blurs of light. What could such a ghost think? Or did it think? Was that blur of color the fading attachment to a place? Or was it possible that this was another sort of being, and not a ghost as humans understand ghosts?

In this, the old part of the city, before a succession of rulers began laying out streets in lines, there were numerous circles built around fountains, with narrow, winding streets connecting them, streets that were once paths and now were scarcely wider than those ancient pathways had been. Carriages did not negotiate these streets, and big parties of riders were forced to go in double lines, if they broached them at all.

Of late, Adon-Marsael's growing force of peace-keepers did broach the streets. On regular patrol, no surprise to anyone. It largely reinforced the illusion of peace; anyone who didn't want to be seen found business elsewhere through the morning hours.

Spies, of course, also wandered through, and no one could be absolutely sure who those were. Except in certain areas, where the poor lived in ancient houses jumbled together, and each person was known to his or her neighbors. Marten thought about how the poor in such areas banded together, facing outward, as it were; was the closeness of houses a reflection of physical proximity?

Only in the sense that those in power have betrayed them with constant wars, Marten decided.

That he was noticed from time to time he knew because just a couple months before, someone on the ridge had twitted him on his taste for low places. To which he'd replied in the absent way he'd assumed ever since setting this pattern, *I go for the food, you know. It's so much better there than anyplace along Elida Way.* And sure enough, it had been accepted, because somewhere someone in Adon-Marsael's informational chain knew that some of the best cooks from former noble houses had been hired to the eateries along this way. He and his reason were also sufficiently dull that—so far, at least—no one had bothered to put together the fact that his departures and reappearances at court were often at least a night apart, and occasionally longer.

He made his way slowly along the arc described by the alleyway outside the buildings on these circles, occasionally glancing up. The Morvende Cave was a long, rambling building that had once been half-a-dozen separate shops, but over the past several generations, steady success (and neighbors' lack) had caused the inn to expand. The final step was the joining of the pleasure house at the south end with the inn-buildings all along the west.

It was into this building that Marten drifted once or twice a week, emerging onto this tiny back alley, and making his way through the tangle of morning traffic a little way along this torturous route until he vanished into the back of a very tumbledown old house on a row of houses that had mostly been burned, and all were abandoned.

But one house had managed to keep its roof intact. The back portion had been turned into a stable. "Hullo, Skinner," he said to the scrawny boy in the midst of currying a horse.

Skinner waved the brush in greeting.

Marten passed by and entered what used to be a shop-room, then stopped in surprise. The dusty, grimy old room with its abandoned furnishings had been transformed. Gared was energetically sweeping the last of an impressive pile of dirt and mold out the front door.

"Ah," he said. "I believe I comprehend."

Gared's head turned. He grinned at Marten. Nodded at a wad of cloth and a bucket of water. "You can do them shutters." He jerked his thumb at the spider-webby window shutters, which hadn't been closed for half a year.

"Very well," Marten said, rolling back his sleeves with care. "I take it, then, Andri has decided to attempt to bring Liere to us? Word has gone through the palace that the envoy departed this morning."

"Andri said to clean the storeroom."

"He is so sure she'll consent to come here?"

"He thinks she will."

Marten was not going to point out that Liere was an anomaly, but then he reflected that they all knew that—had known it since the day they first spotted her walking down the middle of Weavers' Street, moving like a rope-dancer and scanning like a captain on surprise inspection. Only Thadara Otobris assumed she was a fool, but then, to Thadara, most people were fools, an attitude that had gotten her booted out of court for the second time in two years.

"Perhaps," he said finally, as he moved to the second window. "Though I do suspect that she's hiding as many secrets as he is."

Gared laughed. "Life around here's gonna be fun, right enough."

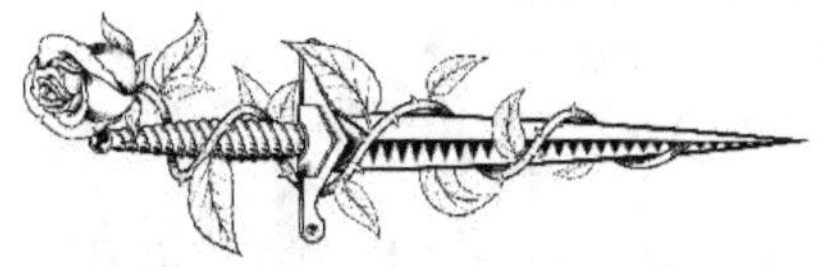

THIRTY-ONE

"**T**his way," Andri said to Liere. "They'll be all right. Jaydi knows every dog door in the city. Right now there are four patrols looking for me. We'll take a detour. Avoid Cousin Adon's roamers."

Liere held out her hand, indicating for him to lead the way.

When she was small, her only defense had been her formidable mental gifts, which included the ability to gauge — how she did it, she still didn't know — how people heard and reacted to voice, tone, emotional color-ation. Sometimes — if you really perceived a person's range, if he or she wasn't on mental guard against you — you could pitch your voice in a few words and cause immediate, instinctive reaction. It only worked for moments, and not with everyone, and not all the time.

She had seen Siamis use it once or twice as a form of command, and she knew that Detlev could use it that way as well. There was no chance she could command Andri to do anything, assuming she'd gauged him at all, but she didn't want that. What she wanted —

"You are a murderer?"

— was reaction.

And she got it.

Not much physical reaction, for he'd already begun to turn at the sound of her step, but for a moment — so brief — his mindshield dropped, and there was that same powerful and uncontrolled contact, so strong it was almost a physical pain to endure it, but beneath it a flash of anguish, alarm . . . and guilt. Then it was gone into a sensory murk so intense it was painful, the most immediate reactions anger, exhaustion, question.

She shut the inner door and fought to steady her breath, to maintain outward calm.

He frowned, but not in anger. It was more of a wince, the sort that came from severe headache. "No—" He drew in a breath. "No."

She pretended she hadn't heard that first hesitation. She had her answer—or enough of one for her to take the next step: though she had sensed guilt, that could be for anything. A stolen purse, an unkind word. There had been no image to match murders, which suggested he either murdered so regularly it had no more effect than changing his socks, or he had not done it. "Thank you for not spoiling last night's lake party."

"Unfair! Out of all the court affairs Cousin Adon's held since he grabbed the kingdom, we've only rousted four."

"As his grace himself pointed out, it's the timing that counts."

"True." Andri grinned unrepentantly.

"Then you did have a reason? Besides whatever it was you took away?"

"Since we've got the rep as thieves and criminals anyway, why not let it work for us? One of those was a diversion while we freed a prisoner, the son of a noble he wanted to force into compliance. Another was to break up a meeting to prove his control isn't as tight as he wants his followers to believe. So on. Another, we were just being rowdy—a deflections—ah, it seemed a good idea at the time. Though I don't know if he's fooled. Despite the speeches about lawlessness and the like."

Andri paused a pace from a narrow opening in a dilapidated fence. He tipped his head. "I think he'd like to believe it, or he wouldn't be chasing me quite so hard. I do know that that's why he doesn't want me talking to the ministers, the would-be ministers, and those who maybe ought to be ministers, but whose name, or holdings, or connections are not quite high enough."

"Of course he doesn't want you gathering support."

"You might not believe it, but I'd like to work this without another bloodbath if I can. I take it you knew you were bait all through the week?"

"He admitted it himself. I think he was about to ask me

to be part of a specific trap, but I chose to depart, as my mission is complete."

Andri betrayed no surprise at her word about a trap. "What else did he say?"

"Comments about your lawlessness and lovers."

"Not the murders? Surely he brought those up."

"He did."

Liere had also been scanning on the mental level, and knew that there were two separate sets of patrols searching, their intent a blare on the mental plane, but as yet no one had seen them.

They reached a secluded little alley behind a jumble of dockside storehouses. A horse was tied under the shade of a makeshift awning patched with old sailcloth. Andri indicated the blanket-saddle, and she used the stirrup to mount, nice and neat and not the least bit flashy.

He vaulted up behind her. Oh. Her nerves, unsheathed, her senses sharpened by that same golden fire sent her thoughts reeling. The shifting of the horse, Andri's breath on the top of her head, the arm that brushed against hers as he reached to take the reins, each sensation was distinct, alive with shivery heat, with wordless promise.

It was the smell of smoke that enabled her to get past proximate glory. Smoke meant danger. It rose in a thin trace, brown against the clean-washed southern sky, but then her ear encountered his chest, the loosened laces of his shirt.

She—just—had enough presence of mind to sit up straight again.

"Ho." Andri's voice resonated through her bones. "Ratface and Kizka must have gotten a little too enthusiastic."

"What?"

"I asked 'em for a diversion. From the noise and stink they set fire to half the outbuildings beyond the old rental stable back there. Eh, it was all tumble-down anyhow."

Clanging bells brought all the patrols to form a bucket brigade. Andri rode the horse up a steep path along the waterfall. Cool mist bathed their faces, and caused the horse to snort and toss its head in approval.

They came out at the top of the path, where the courtiers had been picnicking not two days before.

Directly into the wilder portion of the gardens he rode, well beyond the ordered cedars and beech. They glimpsed a ruin in what once might have been an ordered garden. "That's where stubborn princes were mewed up, a couple generations back," he commented.

Beyond that, the northern end of Brydon's perimeter lay hard against rough country, jumbled by old rivers. They rode in silence until the horse nickered softly and tossed its head, and Andri guided it to one of the streams. He slid off. Liere did as well, standing on a long patch of emerald-colored grass while the horse drank. With the absence of old habit Andri slapped his sword aside, then dropped down onto a rock. Liere stood where she as he squinted up at the sky.

"We still have time," he observed. "Are you really from Sartor?"

Get more than you give. "I came from there to here," Liere replied.

"Why?" He bent, picked up a granite pebble, and tossed it on one hand.

"The queen was concerned about the troubles here."

"We've had trouble off and on all my life," Andri replied, as the stone glittered in the air, then smacked down on his palm. "Why now?"

"I believe the present ruler when she says she is concerned."

"Concerned enough to send someone through to find the dried up fountains," he commented. "I wonder if that causes Cousin Adon sleepless nights. He might be worried about Sartoran interference, but the lower city hailed that gift with relief. It was well done. Much better than some statue, or a set of golden goblets, or whatever else rulers usually send to other rulers. Or would-be rulers. Want to sit down? It's so hot." Andri's flat rock lay under a shady oak.

She could see him better standing at a distance; she waved a negation. His smile was singularly attractive, dimpled at either side. She forced her gaze away. "I understand that you have used your lawless reputation to cover your investigation, or communication, or faction gathering. But if you wish to reestablish peace, why *do* you exist outside the law? It can't really be just for style, as his grace intimated."

"What law would that be? Or whose?" He tossed a stone into the stream. It skipped over the water, sending liquid shards of sunlight into the air.

"The last government, for starters?"

"My father's? Did you know under my father, you could be arrested for wearing a weapon on the streets after dark? If you were common-born. Nobles could carry weapons. And use them at whim. Trade with Sles Adran meant double export tax, based not on the selling price of the merchandise, but who was selling it?" Andri's husky voice roughened. "Or would that be, say, the laws of fifty years ago, before that particular civil war, when nobles could kill anyone on their lands deemed able-bodied, who refused to serve the unpaid five years in their guard?"

The wavering reflection of sun on water highlighted the sharp bones of his face, but when he moved, the brim of his hat shaded his eyes.

"Or would that be the unspoken laws that bind kin? Most of my family has died at the hands of kin," he added, as thunder rumbled louder in the north. "How about military law? You could get yourself stood up against a wall for asking the questions you've asked. Social law? Guild law?"

"Moral law?" she countered.

"The most adaptable," he retorted, "of them all." He got to his feet and dusted off his trousers. "Hungry?" And at her nod, he dug his hand in his pockets, patted the old black woolen vest, then added with a winsome smile, "Got any money?"

"Yes," she said.

"Then we can eat without having to steal it. What a luxurious thought!"

Liere's emotions veered on the periphery of vertigo. It was a relief to move — as if physical location would sever her from unanswered questions, or from the intensity of Andri's presence.

The ride back was somehow easier, east and then south as a wind began to kick up. Dust swirled around them as they rode into the city not through the gates but winding among a jumble of garden plots and kilns and smithies. Overhead, tens and tens of scavenger birds flew in upward and downward spirals, dizzying if your eye attempted to follow a specific bird, but exhilarating in the whole.

The silence had grown protracted. Liere glanced up behind her, and caught his eye. There it was again, the scattering of stars across the mental realm, the visceral wring—both pleasure and a kind of exquisite not-pain—when their gazes met. The sun caught the diamond in his ear, flaring with light, then cooling to cobalt blue.

She faced forward, scarcely noting several urchins chasing through the crowded street like darting starlings. "Do you not mind the risk, riding barefaced thus?"

A soft laugh. "I don't think false whiskers would convince anyone. What else is there? Wig? Eye patch? No, I don't think any disguise is going to work."

I could disguise you, she thought. The concept, she had learned from the Ones, could be as simple as a state of mind. Except I'll always know you. Such a conversation would shift her onto dangerous ground, so she said, "Do you always steal food?"

A child darted out to take the horse to the young woman in charge of the stable. "We're here for a meal," Andri said to the stable chief. "Post only."

The young woman ducked her head and led the horse to a rail built alongside a water trough, and Liere followed Andri inside a broad room partially divided off by low walls with colorful decorations. The tables were all carved of the same mellow golden wood, though they were different sizes; on each were pretty ceramic bowls full of dried herbs and blossoms; the shallow bowls reminded Liere a little of the shallow cups with decorative handles that she'd seen all over Marloven Hess. But those cups were used for drinking. The smells above the potpourri were enticing: wine-braised fish, slow-baked turkey, and fruit pastry.

"We usually eat somewhere else," Andri said. "Work for meals."

"You trade labor for food?" Liere repeated as they wedged into a small wooden table tucked into a corner between a long table at which a huge crowd of people were celebrating some guild member recently promoted, and a round table at which five women were piecing together something with wood as they chattered and ate. From the flushed faces and frequent toasts and heady aroma of beer, the celebrants had been at it for some time. "But you do steal."

"Not here. Only from places that can well afford it."

"No one can afford it in their own view," she said.

He lifted a shoulder. "We steal meals—and what-ever else we can lift—most often from the turncoat who took

Marten's house and lands and fortune. Kiska's. But that's a long ride, especially in the heat."

Liere was surprised that Andri would consent to be stuffed into this corner with no exit except past all those people, until she turned her head, and discovered that there was some kind of door in the wall, partially obscured by an embroidered coat in an old, gaudy Sartoran style, hung up as a decoration. Elsewhere the walls sported three old hats, one showy with spangles, and behind the women hung an old, scarf pieced out of tiny diamonds of silk dyed bright colors.

She returned her gaze to Andri, to discover him watching her with a grin that brought out those long dimples. Her entire body flashed with inner light and heat.

Then he frowned. "Ho. I hate it when someone leaves right after I get through the door."

Liere turned, half-rising, but it was too late; whoever had left was already gone. She listened on the mental plane, but all she got was the jumble of emotion-driven voices around them. Impossible to sort for someone she didn't know and hadn't seen.

"There are dirty dishes over there. Maybe whoever left was finished?" She pointed at a table on the other side of the room. "What do you want to do?" she asked. "Not this moment. As goal."

"Regain my kingdom."

"'My,'" she repeated. "The assumption of birthright, the most common reason in history, often a law. Many consider it the worst reason."

"Do you?"

"Yes. If there is no better."

"That's somewhat surprising, coming from a Sartoran, with thousands of years of Landis kings behind them. Including the can could be just as bloody when everyone has different ideas of merit," he retorted.

"No argument from me. Do you have a reason besides birthright?"

"I want to fix those laws, for starters." He spread his hands. "Cousin Adon's not going to do it."

"And yet he says he is."

"For the nobles. A lot of forced miners and warriors at the front would agree with me on that." Andri leaned an elbow on the table, and his cheek on his hand, his gaze flicking around the room again, then returning to her face. His eyes were greenish, the color people called hazel, with flecks of other color; she'd seen that color in countless people before, but gazing at his eyes felt like sticking her hand in a fire. Except she relished the burn. "What did you come here for?" he asked.

"I told you, at the behest of the Queen of Sartor. You invited questions. I'm asking questions."

He turned the other hand up, an open gesture that called Senrid to mind again. "Nobody ever asks about legal reform. What they want to hear from a prince is, 'What's in it for me?' Even from a deposed one wearing stolen clothes and boots he repaired himself." He grinned briefly. "First I need to get rid of Cousin Adon, who is in the process of consolidating power for all his friends in the name of building a defense against Sles Adran."

She couldn't resist the fire again, scarcely aware as someone came to the table bearing two plates of wine-braised fish, rice mixed with greens, and thin slices of peach. The woman held out her hand as she set the plates down, and Liere fished out two of her six-sided Sartoran coins.

The woman glanced at them, eyes narrow, but shrugged, and they were left to eat. "Sartoran coins are unknown?" she asked.

"More unusual," Andri said. "But I imagine every-one in the world takes six-siders."

A few bites in, Liere said, "You have Dena Yeresbeth."

Andri put down his fork. The planes of his face shifted as he gritted his teeth, then she rocked back as he made contact, not questing or furtive, but deliberate. His control was rough — it was like someone screaming in one's ear — but his ability was considerable. As strong as hers.

The attraction echoed back, burning far hotter than mere fire; she shut her eyes. Control was very old habit, but this new kind of intensity made her breath short.

Andri watched her with interest. She was so . . . beautiful wasn't the right word. Too often heard, about so many people. It had almost ceased to have meaning. And everybody was beautiful at times, everyone. But this Sartoran Envoy with the common name, her slender body muscled like a dancer, her entrancing mouth, which could go from severe to sweet within a heartbeat, her calm, steady gaze below a high, intelligent brow with its faint question, she was like liquid sun. Except that sounded as insipid as "beautiful."

Her brow puckered subtly, and that sweet mouth, which always seemed on the verge of smiling, softened downward at the corners. Andri shifted his gaze away from her face to discover that he'd missed what he should have been listening for: the rhythmic tramp of feet emerging from the rumble of distant thunder as shadows moved across the front windows.

Regretting the meal he'd only half-eaten, he glanced at Liere—and saw her stretch a hand toward the ceramic bowl of rose petals he'd been ignoring.

She was thinking, *what would Senrid do, what would Senrid do*. Senrid would use whatever's at hand, distract and run.

The front door opened, and in came a huge, grizzled guard captain in gray, a chin-lifted older woman next to him. She looked around, and pointed in Andri's direction. "There," she said loudly.

A squad of determined guards split up and streamed around the tables.

Andri's and Liere's eyes met.

She said, "You won't—" at the same moment he said, "Avoid killing—" He flashed a grin, muttered, "Get the horse. Meet at Woof Well."

Liere spun the ceramic bowl expertly through the air. It sailed low over the heads of the celebrating workers, showering them with petals before the bowl smashed into shards against the wall. The workers leaped up shrieking drunkenly, getting in the guards' way as they tried to thread between the tables. Andri vaulted over a table in one direction, and Liere dove beneath a table in the other. She shoved a chair ahead of her to clear through the tangle of legs; someone yelled orders, three people crashed over the chair, and she was through like a minnow, up and around the back tables as the guards tried to bull their way through the drunken customers and the furniture after Andri.

Liere slid out the back, threw a subtle illusion over her clothes, altering the colors to dull green. She slouched into the stable yard. A guard stood near the girl in charge of the rail horses. He was barely seventeen from the look of him, clenching a cudgel determinedly in one hand, his other hand tight on the hilt of his sword, as he shifted his anxious gaze between the door and the alley access.

Too anxious. Liere needed to be too uninteresting to look hard at. She whispered again, blurring her features into age, her hair to gray. Then she hunched further, and hobbled up to the stable chief. The guard glanced at her and back to the door.

Liere pressed a hefty coin into the hand of the stable chief; of course at the touch the illusion vanished. The young woman blinked, then looked down at the coin, and a positively stupid look blanked her face as she turned to another customer.

Liere laughed to herself as she led Andri's horse away, giving it a reassuring mind touch. She walked the horse until she was out of sight of the guards, then snapped away the illusion spell. She walked the horse around the side of a brewery, then mounted and rode away. Presently, she asked a girl her own age where Woof Well was.

"You don't know Woof Well?" The girl clutched her basked tight.

"I'm new to the city," Liere said.

The girl shrugged, and gave Liere directions to an otherwise undistinguished municipal well around which the local dogs congregated, as the missing stones had probably once contained dusty runoff, forming shallow pools. A pack played about, tails wagging, tongues lolling, as children played with them, splashing in and out of the now-brimming fountain.

The well was central to a small roundabout that once had probably been a trade center, for three major roads met there, the stones uneven, the buildings low, made of granite, built to last, and not with an eye to artistry. Over the centuries they'd been added to in different styles, the balconies flagged with fresh washing. This was in the southeast part of the city, farthest from the palace in the northwest, with its river access.

Liere dismounted and walked the horse in a slow circle so it wouldn't look like she was waiting, pretending an interest in the small bakery, the scribe-and-messenger storefront, and the ironmonger, who had the biggest place.

She was being alert—so she thought—but jumped when a shadow flickered on her right, and Andri step-ped up next to her. "Sartor trains its envoys very well," he commented, the image of her expertly tossing that bowl of petals and then vanishing through the door in three whirling sidesteps still vivid. "Want to see the hideout? Jaydi has probably taken Lyren-Sartora there by now."

Up one of the winding side streets they headed. The part of the city they had entered was old and run-down, with very narrow streets. The houses were built in rows, which was obviously a danger when fire broke out, as not one would burn, but several. Here and there the noise of hammer and saw indicated some rebuilding. The horse dodged around a parade of wheelbarrows full of bricks, and around unrepaired holes in the streets.

They rode under an archway between two sets of joined houses. Someone had built a room over that archway; a hand thrust a mop out and shook it into the street.

Children had chalked drawings on either side of the rough plaster of the archway, with slogans; Liere glimpsed scrawls that made little sense, then they emerged into a busy courtyard next to yet another row of houses that turned out to be an inn that had joined several once free standing buildings. From an upper story window a slender young woman emerged, and leaned her arms on the sill, her ribbon-laced blouse loose. Her face was merry, her hair tousled.

"Andri!" The young woman, probably five years older than Andri, kissed her hand. Her gaze shifted to Liere, and she winked, giving Liere a knowing grin.

Liere smiled back as Andri kissed his hand then called, "Banisa!"

Banisa turned away, vanishing inside; the sound of women's voices laughing drifted out in the warm air as Andri pulled up.

"You're known here," Liere said.

Andri lifted a shoulder. "People here don't talk out-side the community."

"You're a part of this community? I thought your father was unpopular."

"It was difficult for a while. But we've made a place here."

They dismounted, and a gangling boy just starting to lengthen dashed out of a burned shop, blinked up at them behind a wild bush of hair, then ran to the horse, making odd noises in his throat. The animal welcomed him with head-tosses and whuffs of pleasure.

A short time later they entered a burned-out shop, one

with its roof intact. Beyond the ruined front, the rest of the shop was untouched; the fires must have burned at either end, for this was the middle of the row.

There was a narrow chamber that had probably once had goods stored in it, with a fireplace at one end. Someone small had decorated the bricks with handprints dipped in white paint.

On old furniture sat a few boys, including one she recognized: the slight, quiet, elegant one she'd seen at the palace.

Andri began naming them at one end and moved to the other, paying no attention to rank. Jaydi's older brother, the stable boy, had adopted the name Skinner—which (Lyren-Sartora explained later) nickname was earned by the way the boy had skinned in and out of places.

"Not all of us live here," said Marten, the dark-haired young man Liere remembered seeing at the palace. "Kizka is a page. Andri's cousin Bassl sneaks in from time to time, but sleeps at the palace—"

Blue-white light startled them all, followed by a roof-shaking volley of thunder.

Rain roared down, droplets splashing up again, as all up and down the street people shouted with glee through wide-open windows.

As the thunder died away, Marten offered to give Liere a tour, and when they vanished down the narrow hallway, Gared said, "Any trouble?"

"Nothing outside of a wasted meal. We got three bites before someone ratted us out to the snouts for the reward."

"Oh? The envoy doesn't seem flustered. Or did she expect you to . . ." Gared waved a finger like a sword.

"Me?" Andri grinned. "She was faster than I was."

Gared's brows shot up. "The Sartorans train their envoys for action? I thought they were supposed to be all talk and magic."

"They are—according to Porganal." Andri named the Adrani ambassador's aide, known since Andri was a boy.

Gared waved a hand. "Adranis," he said. "All liars. Who believes 'em?"

"Porganal was in Sartor's scribe guild before going back to Sles Adran. Porganal himself doesn't know one end of a sword from another, and he has to have been in whatever training they give a lot longer than she was — he's twice her age."

Gared's grin vanished. "You think Liere's from Her?"

"No. Hiding something, yes."

The grin was back. "Fun!"

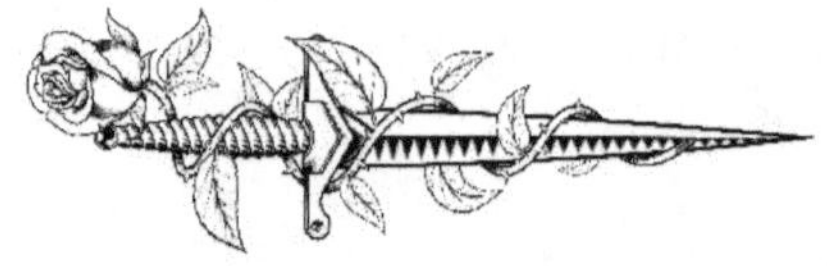

THIRTY-TWO

After that outing above the city, when Atan returned to the palace to change from her riding clothes, she avoided the private room where she and Rel usually spent time. The room felt so empty without him. She detoured through the interview room, where she paused, blinking at what she first took to be a new tapestry. Who had moved things without permission?

No one had. After a moment's scrutiny she recognized the two figures at the center: it was merely Shontande's gift. She hadn't remembered the light in the sky being the pewter of an oncoming storm. Odd, how it sobered all the colors, shifting attention upward.

She thought no more of it; she had three meetings and as many private interviews to get through before readying for the ball. And what was this note Rel had left behind? Liere? With relief Atan saw that Liere had not written back, which meant whatever was going on was not important enough for Atan to drop everything else and shove yet another item into an already crowded day.

By the time Atan got through it all, she had little time to dress for the grand ball. Once again she passed through her interview room, avoiding her private chamber—and that tapestry had not changed. The colors were just as bright as she remembered from the day she received it, glowing warmly in the candlelight. At least the sky no longer looked threatening; the eye was drawn to the garden in bloom, a cheerful sight.

She trod dutifully across to the Sky Hall where the ball was held and sank with relief into her chair at the head of the room, set to endure the fewest number of hours before slipping away. Shontande Lirendi turned up directly after her arrival, looking impossibly handsome in shades of white, yellow and gold, with crimson accents, all of which brought out the golden glints in his auburn hair.

Atan found herself amused as pretty much her entire court began circling around him like a storm vortex. She was entertained enough to forget how tired she was, just watching him whirl and step and hop, melody after melody, without ever sitting down. A handsome and predatory baras did his best to lure Shontande toward one of the side arches, to be intercepted by horrible Lirza, armed with glittering diamonds, used fan and languid fingers as she, too, attempted to get Shontande off alone. He included both, talking the while, and remaining gracefully elusive. Atan wished suddenly that she could hear how he was deflecting the two predators, and though she had not intended to do anything but sit there like a statue of one of her ancestors, she found herself rising when a line dance ended, and sailed toward them like a war ship riding the wind.

". . . show you where we entered, dodging Norsunder," Lirza was saying. "For you know, I was one of the Rescuers. I was a mere child, of course . . ."

"Perhaps another time?" he said. "My schedule, there are many events."

"I am completely free tomorrow," Lirza replied. "And for you, I can be free the rest of the week —"

"Unfortunately," Atan interrupted from behind, "I had already planned to conduct our royal guest over the castle and revisit that old story."

The baras bowed, Lirza deferred with a pretty pout, and Atan turned to Shontande as a haltas struck up. "Dance?" she asked.

He held out his hands in assent.

They began the step-turns, as Lirza made a commanding gesture to one of her admirers, and the baras to one of his.

"We don't have to dance long," Atan said. "I notice you haven't had a chance to sit all evening."

"Ah, but I am accustomed to such evenings," he replied. "I would not willingly forgo the pleasure, unless you desire it."

"Are your dances so much like ours? I'd heard they vary

greatly."

"Ah-ye, some the same, some different, but the patterns are much alike." His clasp was light, cool, utterly impersonal, but she was still aware of his breathing, and the rustle of fabric as he moved. It was . . . odd, not unpleasant. "I have missed a step, then?" he asked.

"No. What makes you say that?"

"Your attention." He furrowed his brow briefly, then flashed a smile. "Like so."

"It's just that I almost never dance," she said. "I usually sit as long as I must, and then steal away."

He glanced to the side, as if noting that Rel was not present, but he had too much delicacy to ask. He'd already seen that Rel did not attend any court affair, though he was twice spotted with the guard. "I love to dance," Shontande admitted ruefully, and then spent the rest of this one describing various Colendi dances, causing her to laugh at descriptions of his blunders when he was first learning, though she did not believe he ever could have been clumsy. He had not had the freedom to be clumsy.

The music ended sooner than she'd expected. They ended up very near her throne. She sat down again. He bowed and the courtiers closed in on him once again. He took the hand of a shy count's son who had barely reached the age of court appearance, and off they went to join one of the foursomes making up down the center of the room.

Atan watched, wondering who among her courtiers competing for his attention would eventually succeed in getting him alone. She found she hated the idea of it, which surprised her enough to examine the reaction more closely. It had to be due to Lirza. Anyone else, it was not her concern, but Lirza would manage to make what ought to be a private affair a court matter, and she'd relish every moment of the drama. Or that seventeen-year-old, whose heart was too obviously in his eyes.

When Atan finally got back to her suite, the bell clanged the first hour after midnight. The tapestry had silvered — now she had to look at it first thing — and what had looked earlier like sunlight reflecting off the upper walls of the stitched palace now seemed like fire.

She blinked tired eyes and turned away, her gaze lighting on her golden notecase. She laid a hand on it, and discovered that a note lay therein. She was tempted to let it wait till morning, which was not very far off, but she knew she would lie awake until she discovered who had written her.

The note was in Liere's tiny, neat hand:

> Atan: to let you know that I have officially withdrawn the Sartoran banner, but I am still here in Enaeran. I am still not entirely satisfied about the question I was to pursue. I am staying with some locals—your cousin will be pleased, L-S says to add. I hope all is going well with your royal visit.

Atan sat back, staring down at the paper. On an ordinary day she might have returned a single line, saying little more than *It's going well enough*, but she was alone, Rel very present by his absence, and tired as she was, her mind was wide awake.

This was Liere, the Girl Who Saved The World, now grown past that terrible stage wherein her gifts seemed to overwhelm her. Liere had returned poised, with formidable training, and she had always been discreet.

Atan dipped her pen and wrote in Old Sartoran:

> It is going interestingly, I believe I can say. I don't think I've ever heard of anyone claiming sovereignty by being acknowledged through another government, but then the Colendi are always going to do things their own way.
>
> Yes, interestingly, that's the word I want.
>
> We will discuss this in person on your return, should you so wish.
>
> Atan.

The sky was uncertain the next day, the river a broody, restless gray, not promising for the prospective regatta, but the younger courtiers, having put time and effort and gold into decorating their racing craft, ventured out anyway. Atan had offered Shontande Lirendi a place on her royal barge, which would afford a fine view of the faster single craft competing for a banner.

But halfway through the race the skies opened up, clearly settling in for one of those drenching summer storms that occurred in Sartor this time of year.

"I'm afraid the party is ruined," she shouted over the roar of rain.

"It won't go as fast as it comes?"

She lifted a hand toward the low gray sky, no vestige of blue in any direction. "We're probably in for two days of it." And, to be polite," Is there something I can do for you?"

"Why, yes," he replied. "That tour? Of your palace, along with the story about how you retook it from Norsunder? I would very much like to hear that."

Surprised, she agreed, and mentally reordered the following morning. That was easier with Rel away—and if she again forwent her labyrinth walk.

They met not long after sunrise. She'd decided not to make this tour long. Surely this sophisticated, subtle person would be bored with a blow by blow of what had mostly been a lot of blundering by ignorant teenagers. Rel had been the only heroic one, taking on the Norsundrian commander—though he'd lost that duel. But he'd won Atan the time she'd needed to rip through the last of the century-old magical bindings.

Shontande Lirendi was not bored. He looked and listened with that focused intent that she found characteristic, as if he listened for what was not said as well as what was said. At the end, she forced a shrug. "Not very gratifying altogether. If Detlev had turned up, for example, none of us would be alive today, I am convinced, whatever is claimed about his neutrality now."

"Do you believe that neutrality?" he asked, gazing down at the great square through the tall windows.

"I try to. At least publicly," she said, and he gave a soundless laugh. "Any further questions about the reemergence of Sartor into the world?" She thought of the Music Festival, of course, and tried to think of a natural way to shift to it.

But his mind raced in a different direction. "I find I cannot adapt your clever plans to recover my own kingdom," he admitted with a rueful flash of smile. "And it was clever. You and your companions could not know what was arrayed against you. I," he breathed, "know very well what is arrayed against me. To return to your adventures in recovering your kingdom: you survived. And no one ever disputed your right."

"I believe," she said slowly, "that the only one who disputed my right was me. I knew my lineage. Tsauderei and Gehlei each made sure of that. And yet I spent fifteen years living in a hermit's hut with two outfits to my name, both made by myself. This . . ." She flicked a look at the vaulted ceiling overhead, carved with interleaves acanthus. "Though it belonged to my family, it still doesn't really belong to *me*. In the way one's first home does."

She stopped there, but he said, "Go on."

"Nothing more than I feel like a caretaker."

"Are not all monarchs caretakers?" he retorted, without any heat. "I expect you know nearly as much of my situation as I do. Your ambassador surely writes to you as often as my chief scribe does to me."

I know that there are only three weeks left until Mid-Summer's Eve, when the Music Festival has always begun. She thought those words, but she could not say them; she understood now that until his sovereignty was accepted by the regency council still holding his palace as if they had the right, even if he wanted to give the Music Festival back, that was a gesture only a king could give. And he was right now only a king in name.

"Your majesty is an important figure at your end of our continent," she said, trying to be supportive, but as soon as the words were out, she winced, hearing how very false they sounded.

"My majesty," he repeated, the words a mocking drawl — the mockery self-directed, and not at her. "Whatever happens, that term will haunt me to my dying day, I expect. Or, if I prevail, do you think I could ban it?"

She laughed. "Tsauderei once lectured me on the subject. Your majesty — your grace — your honor — chief this and captain that. We all agree to it because it's an order we know, because if we don't have our traditional hierarchy, the alternative is to go at each other's throats the way my neighbors to the east in Sarendan did, trying to force a new hierarchy on one another, all in the name of equality." She gave him a quick look from her protuberant eyes, as rain ran down the glass an arm's length from them both. "If you would prefer to return to conventional speech, say the word, King Shontande of Colend. I confess I am being selfish. I rarely get to speak freely."

"Shontande will do, or even Shon, which is what Thad calls me. I've had a surfeit of grand titles while all decision-making was done by others in my name," he murmured.

She gave him a narrow, assessing look. "That's what I've been told, and yet you are here, and not leading a pack of heralds to lock down Alsais?"

He clasped his hands behind his back, his profile somber as he gazed at the streaming flagstones down below. "I would prefer not to have to lock anything against my own people, though against the likes of Norsunder? A very different matter." He straightened up. "That reminds me. Senrid has written to me—"

"Yes! I received a note this morning. Thank you for reminding me. With your permission, I've cleared tomorrow night."

"Please." He accepted with a graceful, open-handed gesture.

The bell clanged; as well, Atan decided. This was probably not the time to express worries about how often those meetings in Remalna were becoming.

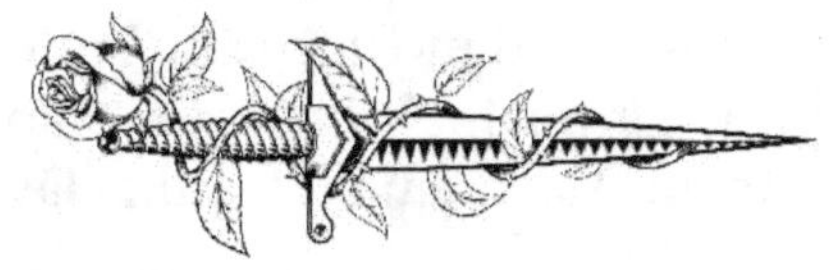

THIRTY-THREE

Atan and her royal Colendi guest met again the following evening in her interview chamber.

From here they could transfer from her rarely-used private Destination without scribes or court knowing that both were leaving the kingdom—something her first circle council had done its very best to forbid her to do, purely by moral suasion.

She could see the sense of it, but there had been far too many attempts at coercion by guilt or obligation, half the time for more personal reasons than state, in spite of lofty speeches. Atan did acknowledge the dire predictions about what would happen if she were killed or captured. She and Tsauderei had arranged some formidable wards, and she had a transfer token on her person that would whisk her straight to Tsauderei's protected valley at a word.

Once again they transferred to the tower room in Remalna, where Jilo slouched, looking like a pale-faced, molting crow next to Tereneth Larensar, King of Erdrael Danara. Atan had not seen Terry for two or three years; he had turned into a pleasant-faced young man, the scarring on his face fading. He still hid the missing fingers on one hand, but that appeared to be long habit.

His grin was genuine and friendly as Atan presented Shontande. "Finally," Terry exclaimed. "Did you know I tried to visit you once, after sending a lot of letters? I'm sure you never saw a one."

"Ah-ye, yet another correspondent, I see." Shontande bowed, gesturing Rue with his hands together, adding, "I must apologize for the, ah, let us say, the vigor of the regency council's attempt to cocoon me in safety."

"They certainly did that," Terry said. "I got the distinct impression they considered me uncouth, but this is the first I heard of my being a threat. No, no, don't apologize again, certainly not for them. *You* are not at fault. Have you met Jilo, King of—"

"Not a king," Jilo muttered to the ceiling.

"—not-a-king of Chwahirsland?"

Shontande could see how acutely uncomfortable Jilo was, but he also had learned through Senrid the cost Jilo had paid for years in trying to better life for the Chwahir. He rose, and made a full bow, with utmost respect. "It is an honor to meet you," he said. "It grieves me more than I can express that the evil Wan Edhe is back, fouling the Chwahir people and land with his presence, but I know what you tried to accomplish, and what you did accomplish."

Jilo had gone red, then paled at these words, his gaze dropping to his tightly gripped hands.

Shontande then turned to their host in a kind attempt to draw attention away from Jilo, whose gaze remained lowered, his eyes shuttered behind the dark lines of his lashes.

"I visited Colend directly after I left Senrid's academy," Vidanric said to Shontande. "It was a splendid stay. What a beautiful city Alsais is!" He glanced at the door, then back to at Terry; he saw that Jilo had recovered his composure, and addressed them both. "Speaking of Senrid, he called this meeting, and he's usually right on time, if not early. Do either of you know what might be keeping him?"

Jilo said, "I've been spending the summer in Erdrael Danara. Only heard from him yesterday by note. Said to come today—oh."

They heard voices echoing up the stairs: a piping child's, another shriller child's, then Senrid's clipped tones, "Thank you. No, I can send them back down."

Meliara's high, clear voice responded, "After Elestra raids the cakes I sent up for you? I'd better come too."

Quick steps pattered up the stone stairwell before two small girls burst into the room, one a weedy urchin with a heart-shaped faced framed by tousled brown braids, and a smaller girl with wispy blonde curls.

Shontande looked up with a polite air of interest as

Senrid entered behind them, as usual wearing a white shirt over black uniform trousers stuffed into riding boots. His face had lost all its boyish roundness to planed cheekbones and jawline. His hair was still blond waves squared at the back. "I'm sorry we're late, but somebody decided to step in a fresh horse plop and needed a bath." He turned a mock-solemn glare at the smaller child.

Crystal Ingrid looked away in the manner of a four-year-old who thinks that if she doesn't see trouble, it's not there. She hid behind Elestra, who began a shrill, "Can we play, can we, can we?" as Meliara appeared at the top of the stairs, arms crossed.

"Scat," Senrid said to his daughter.

Crystal Ingrid skipped out and down the stairs with Elestra. Their shrill squeaks of delight faded as Senrid said, "I probably ought to have left her behind, but I did promise Elestra I'd bring her."

Meliara said with a sigh, "Your girl is always so tidy. Unlike mine. It must have been an accident."

Senrid said, "Oh, it was deliberate. She figured out that all the local dogs would smell it and follow her. She loves dogs. Wants one."

Meliara's brow furrowed. "She can't have one?"

"I told her that she can have one when she's old enough to take care of it, and her response was that there were servants for that."

Senrid saw understanding in half the faces before him, and blankness in the rest.

"In her defense," Meliara said, not quite squaring up for battle, but on a note of question, "isn't that a natural response for someone who lives in a castle with a lot of servants?"

Senrid replied, "I see it as a thoughtless response. Our history makes it clear that assumed privilege like that is one of the paths to tyranny. I told her that we would revisit this conversation when she understood what it meant to be responsible for a life. She accepted that, but she tries to lure any dog she finds for playtime. Today's experiment netted some dozen dogs."

"I did the same with horses," Terry admitted. "Not the part about stepping in what they left behind, but I used to sneak down to the stables every chance I got."

"I see," Meliara said, and Vidanric was secretly relieved

when her brow cleared; he knew that his big-hearted wife was quite willing to use up this precious hour wrested from five demanding lives in order to go to battle, unasked, on behalf of Senrid's daughter. But here she gave a nod of agreement—or at least truce—and vanished down the stairs again.

Jilo's light brown eyes shifted from one to another at this evidence, yet again, how different everyone's life was from his own. He never would have dared to even think about a pet, lest Wan Edhe find out, and of course take great pleasure in killing it before his eyes.

Senrid was always sensitive to the quality of Jilo's silences, and said briskly, "I've wasted enough time." He had tucked a rolled paper under his arm, which he flicked out on the table. "Of you all, Terry has the best defensive territory, as his kingdom is mostly vertical, and his Mountain Guard knows every valley and stream. Norsunder might take it, depending on how many they field, but they'll have a very hard time holding it." He looked across at Vidanric. "You've lived in Colend. Want to sum up the problem there?"

Vidanric nodded politely to Shontande. "There really is no defending Colend once they cross the river on your western border. All your rivers are fordable. Alsais has no walls, and is full of glass."

"How long . . . ah-ye, you are saying that we will fall no matter how we try to defend? And yet, is not Marloven Hess the same sort of territory, mostly flat land with rivers through it?"

Senrid sat back. "This is not to slander your . . . you call them heralds, am I correct?"

"Herald-guards."

Senrid turned up his palm in a quick gesture. "Those I saw on my one visit looked alert, their patrols well-spaced. They'll give Norsunder a fight, if you tell them to, but there are not enough of them, moreover they are essentially foot warriors—trained to deal with civil problems, without escalating to violence, am I right?"

"You are."

"In other lands, there are brave individuals who volunteer for militias, or join defensive forces, who get a few years, or a few months, of training, and who might find in the heat of battle that running makes more sense. Or even surrender—to save what they can. What we Marlovens have is an army probably four, five times the size of yours, and they are horse warriors, trained for uncounted generations for plains warfare."

Shontande put his hands together in the peace, and Senrid went on. "That doesn't mean we'll win, if Norsunder sends enough against us. All we can confidently predict is that it will be bloody, because generations of tradition make surrender, unless directly ordered, unthinkable. But discussion of my kingdom is useless for our purposes here, which is to address the prospect of imminent attack. If we knew we had ten years, even five, our conversation would go differently."

Shontande made a graceful gesture of acceptance.

Senrid said, "Secondly, the ground, while similar, is not the same, beginning with the fact that all our cities are walled. Vidanric?"

Vidanric said to Shontande, "I recommend an organized retreat, once you know they're coming. The more you set up and practice in advance, the more effective it will be. And it will take not only effort but coordination. You're not the only one who would be employing this strategy," he added, extending a hand to include his royal palace, and thence his small kingdom.

Shontande stared down at the map of the east end of the continent, with Colend in the center, and Chwahirsland directly to the north. On the map, the terrain looked exactly like that of Marloven Hess. He stared at the neat lettering and the painstakingly drawn rivers, each with correct windings and islands.

Now he understood why Senrid had insisted they meet face to face. Shontande was sick at heart, aware that he'd come with a hope of hearing about some miracle strategy, some trick that would save his kingdom from being overrun. Not only would this miracle save his kingdom, but he could carry it back to use against the regency council . . .

Ah, there was no use in following that mental path. "I understand," he said slowly, his hands flexing once, "that we can't win. Though our herald-guards do train defensively."

Senrid said, "Whoever attacks is bound to know exactly how many you have. Depending on their intent, they will probably engage you along the western border, then once your heralds are fully committed there, send a secondary force over from the east. Or the south. Or Wan Edhe will send his bully boys over those mountain notches from the north, though my guess is he won't like being told what to do."

Senrid glanced Jilo's way, to receive a decisive nod. "Depends on the why of the attack," Jilo mumbled. "He'll cooperate if he's forced to. If there is a gain for him. For example, if he's promised Colend's throne."

Shontande managed to hide his recoil, but both Senrid and Jilo felt it in the realm of the spirit. And both understood the visceral flinch.

Shontande tried to shift the subject. "The why?" he repeated. "Aren't they fighting to be fighting? That is actually a good question . Why *is* Norsunder coming? Why now? How many?"

"Last first: we have no idea," Senrid said. "The only concrete fact we have is that the lighter mages have successfully kept Norsunder from opening rifts from Norsunder-Beyond to here."

Atan said, "Norsunder Base holds a finite number of enemy warriors, which number has been furnished, if intelligence from Detlev is to be believed. Norsunder-Beyond, which could presumably hold millions — we can't know — still has to transfer one person at a time, just as the rest of us do. Of course you understand that transfers anywhere but a very few places are dangerous."

"The air can catch fire, and whoever transfers vanishes in it. Or vanishes," Shontande said.

Atan gave a nod. "So we can come here, for example, but we cannot bring a host, even one by one, as the air, the space — whatever it is between that place and this place — becomes rapidly more volatile. The few Destinations that seem to be free of that limitation — "

"The few we know of," Senrid interrupted.

" — yes, the few we know of are guarded, warded, and will be destroyed if the attack comes," Atan said. "We in Sartor have Norsunder Base a few days' ride south of us. Whatever happens, we know they will come north, and we will be engaged first. What I've been trying to learn in these sessions is how to plan for that."

Shontande's expression was bleak. "Do you think this threat of war is due to Detlev putting another of his deceptions into practice?"

Senrid's fingers drummed absently on the edge of the table. "I believed so, once, but I've been convinced differently. And if you look at his present position, squatting in a house with no defensive walls over there off Sartor's border, with no army, when he could easily have stayed on as one of Norsunder's commanders — if not the commander in chief — it really begins to look as if, for some reason, he's removed himself from the prospective conflict."

"But he must know why the rest of them are attacking soon. If it is soon?"

"If he knows, he hasn't shared it . . ." Senrid began, then shook his head. "Maybe he can't say. We don't know what kind of wards were put on him during his centuries under the heel of the Host of Lords. What kind of damage he sustained. He might even be unable to fight. None of us know." He leaned forward, his right hand still drumming absently against the side of the table; Shontande's gaze was drawn to a lacing of old scars at his wrists. "This is what's important. Assuming that everything Norsunder does has Detlev at the center, and all the rest are faceless subordinates, is a mistake."

Shontande bowed slightly: point made.

Senrid went on, "I've been trying to find out what I can about other prospective commanders, and what they want, because that will shape their attacks."

"Don't they all want to conquer to make themselves kings?" Terry asked.

"Some," Senrid said.

Atan sketched a sign of repudiation in the air. "There's one called Bostian, who wants to be king of Sartor."

Senrid turned up his palm in agreement. "But that's actually a good thing, because he'll want to hold it to have something to be king of, rather than destroying everything. Remember Kessler Sonscarna's attack on Everon? That was a burn-and-destroy assault, cut short, actually, by Detlev, because in destroying so much of Everon he knew they couldn't hold it over winter. Mad Prince Kessler didn't seem to care. He burned his way across Everon merely to give the back of the hand to another, now dead, Norsundrian commander."

Shontande nodded soberly. "Thad told me. Prince Kessler retreated after he burned most of the capital. Left the people to starve."

"Kessler Sonscarna will not fight for Norsunder," Senrid said. "But we have to face the prospect of someone who uses a similar approach."

There followed a discussion of different types of ground, of logistics, and ended with an overview of the likeliest targets; Shontande had assumed that meant government, and was not wrong, but he had completely overlooked the scribe world, connected by scribe desks, and the complicated, centuries-old magic that had produced the golden notecases of the present day. Of course the enemy would want to either compromise those first, if they could, or take it all down entirely, keeping communication solely for themselves, and the world cut off from one another.

Shontande had been trained to use a rapier. He was actually quite good at it. He had assumed that defense would entail gathering all who had been similarly trained — strength in numbers — but that assumption had burned to ash halfway through a detailed discussion between Senrid, Vidanric, and Terry about the ratio of information to command style. He had never thought about communication in a military sense, or logistics. All his life, communication and plenty had all been there, a flow as inexorable as a river.

When a bell rang in the distance, Senrid looked with sympathy across the table to Shontande, who felt utterly overwhelmed. "Take a little time to think it through. As much as you can. We truly cannot plan for all contingencies. Nor can we train for them all, but we can talk through as much as we are able. War is an ever-changing and shifting process, each commander with a different goal, and a different style of command. There will be new tactics and goals at all times."

"So far," Shontande commented, "that much resembles everyday life."

"I'll grant that," Senrid said. "Here's where it differs. War means using force. Destruction. Which is easy to do, and tough to clean up. It means killing, which means someone has to die. Human nature itself is erratic. Battles have been won that looked impossible, and have been lost when it looked easy. The will of each side to make sacrifices can't be predicted until the moment someone chooses to strike their flag or lay it down."

"Strike . . . ?"

Senrid looked away, then back. "Fight to the death, the

last one alive cutting the flag in half so that the enemy wins nothing but bloody ground and pieces of cloth, and then falling on his sword."

The silence after this was brief, but potent: everyone there was aware that none of their lands had a name for such behavior. But the Marlovens clearly had been there before.

Senrid gestured violently, his hand flat, as if wiping his words from the air. "The important thing here is, I know you've got some, ah, matters in your command structure to be corrected. My suggestion is, since you're waiting anyway, take what time you have to think out your defense plan, always keeping in mind that especially in a war of resistance, from the hills, so to speak, to protect as much as you can your ability to maneuver. Once they pin you down, they've got you."

"Thank you." Shontande bowed in the peace, his voice soft, expression bleak.

Atan promised that Rel would be with them next time, and that broke up the gathering.

Shontande and Atan arrived separately back in Eidervaen's royal palace. She took one glance at his diffuse gaze and said, "Come have some Sartoran tea. If you have questions I might be able to answer, I am at your service."

Shontande thanked her, and soon they sat in one of her private dining chambers, where hot steep and freshly baked pastry was brought in.

Shontande sat motionless for a time, his long, clever fingers wrapped around a porcelain cup. Then he raised a bleak gaze, though there was a hint of humor in the twist of his mouth. "Senrid came armed to that meeting," he observed. "I saw when he went to the window overlooking the yard where the children played that he had knife hilts in his boot tops. Is Remalna under more threat than I was aware?"

"No, not at all. That, I am told, is Senrid's relaxed mode. Did you see that he had his sleeves rolled to his elbows?"

"I did. Is that not his customary uniform?"

"Yes, but my point is, if he suspects danger, he wears his sleeves long and knives hidden in them. I don't think I've ever seen him not armed. Ever."

"It would never occur to me to go armed," Shontande said. "It seems he never goes not armed. Perhaps that explains why he believes we Colendi cannot defend ourselves, given similar terrain."

Atan smiled wryly. "I thought so, too, before we began having these meetings. The difference is larger than that, I think. In Colend, Rel told me once, the average young person thinks about what sort of artisan to become, if all other things are equal. Would you say that is a fair assessment?"

"Given inherited work, perhaps, yes. Silk-makers tend to make silk, and glaziers glass, and so on, but they are not bound to it. Yes, fair enough."

"In Marloven Hess, Rel says, the average young person—mostly boys, off and on historically, but includes girls now, too—they think of the army." She gave him a sober look, then said in a low voice, "The Marlovens will fight to the death to hold their land, because for generations that has defined their honor, and because they obey orders or die. But we Sartorans?" She tapped her chest. "We think only of holding out long enough to evacuate as many as possible, and minimizing the damage. Honor is bound up in protecting lives, and that which defines us as Sartorans, which is our art and our history."

Shontande bowed, and soon rejoined Thad. After explaining the entire meeting, as Thad listened in growing horror, he finished, "And what does melende demand of us?"

Thad spread his hands helplessly. "Ah-ye, I cannot think how to answer! Melende is predicated on civilized behavior! Melende and warfare are like us and Geth-deles, circling the sun while never seeing the other."

"But it's coming. They all believe it is coming to crash into us and our melende, want it or not."

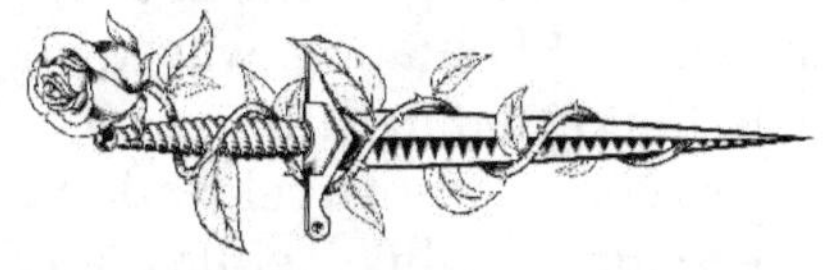

THIRTY-FOUR

Everyone in Colend knows that it takes two weeks to set up for the Alsais Music Festival, which officially begins Midsummer Eve.

During those two weeks (which have had many names, some facetious, and all typically Colendi, which is to say, made no reference to "work" or to "preparations") regular work has traditionally been given over to preparation for the festival—materials and labor paid for by the crown, first week the cleaning and decorating of the city, the second week the preparations for the onslaught of festival attendees.

The process had been refined over the past century, during the time Sartor had disappeared beyond its enchantment. From farms around Alsais, guarding ripening produce yet to be picked (by an army of locals ready to spring into action, with a promised feast at the end) to builders, painters, drapers, bakers, cooks, costumiers, florists, and all the rest, everyone counted down the days before those two weeks would begin, anticipation simmering in the summer heat.

But first the crown had to release the funds with a Letter of Permission to pay for it all. This Letter of Permission was an order, written in the distinctive blue ink only used by the monarch, and sealed with the royal seal.

Two guild chiefs, one noble-born, the other aspiring to rise, had secretly promised the regency council that they would abandon work and begin setup, king or no king, once the regency council gave the order on the king's behalf. Both these guilds catered primarily to nobles. The rest of the guild chiefs awaited the Letter of Permission.

This was their lawful prerogative.

They had the moral high ground, and they knew it.

During the weeks Shontande was away, the regency council had feasted and flattered the guild chiefs. They had hinted at largesse to come, grants, relaxation of taxes, and on finding that the chiefs, while polite and appreciative, remained obdurate—not a single turnip would be picked until the king's Letter of Permission was received—they had hinted at laws for public disorder. A crisis was imminent, debated behind closed doors, in gardens, in boats along the canals: who ruled the kingdom?

The banks, age-old establishments, were as immoveable as stone: according to the laws laid down when Colend seated its first king, tax moneys were only released from storage in a Beyond on receipt of an order sealed with the special, magic-infused silver-blue ink that was only held by the monarch. Whoever that monarch might be.

Shontande Lirendi was still in Sartor, and the Keeper of the Seal had vanished when the king had. No one knew for certain who had the seal, or even if it still resided in the royal suite. The very idea of the seal not being in Colend was unthinkable—so the regency council firmly asserted to one another. In secret, they dispatched this and that servant to search, to be warded off by Bee and his scribes, who vigilantly guarded the royal suite. The regency council still (against the king's stated orders) held the rest of the palace, but they had not been able to set foot in the king's rooms. And the herald-guards could not act without royal invitation, so insisted Donais Altan, in spite of pressure from his brother on the regency council.

The three-week mark came and went in a lengthy and loud summer storm. The regency council, aware of the inexorable passage of time, and with no eyes on their wayward king, had united once more to send to Donais Altan instructions to arrest the guild chiefs who refused to cooperate with their order to send for supplies to begin the Music Festival preparations.

The herald-guards dispersed to various points around the city—they said, in practice maneuvers for the festival, but the "points" all corresponded with the domiciles or offices of guild chiefs. This much, Donais Altan reasoned, the regency council could command. Public order was important. But arresting guild chiefs in their own homes, that was solely the king's prerogative.

The chiefs held firm.

The herald-guards remained poised.

The Duchas of Altan and his brother eyed each other, at a standoff.

Another long day passed, on the surface business as usual, but everywhere people stood in tight knots, talking in hushed voices, breaking up and moving away at the approach of anyone else.

The canals' barge polers continued to ply their trade for all who produced the proper coins, but the sweet scent of roses drifted heavily on the summer air. As yet no one had arrested a one of them in spite of some ridiculously fulsome rose garlands worn round hat brims, on clothes, and along the gunwales of boats; everyone from high to low knew that the barge polers, notoriously stubborn as well as strong, were in effect giving the back of the hand to the current holders of the palace. But there was no law against wearing roses.

That night, as another storm broke overhead, three people decided to act.

None would ever talk about it later.

Two of them had the same idea. When the Duchas of Altan bumped into the Count of Ariath outside the king's suite, his screech was as loud as hers. So loud that if thunder had not broken directly overhead, the entire palace would have been roused.

Her recoil caused her to trip over the curled foot of a side table. He tripped over her trailing robe. They hit the cool marble floor with painful thuds. He cursed as he felt for the candle he had brought for lighting once he was safely inside. His fingers encountered her candle first.

Lightning flared, blue and bright, revealing each to the other.

"I am only surprised," he said sourly, "you have not tried to declare yourself queen before tonight."

She would have, had she gained enough support. But she hadn't, because, "If you had not interfered, in search of your own crown," she retorted in a hissing whisper, "I might have taken the position that was always to be mine, had not our king gone mad."

Thunder died away, and a brief lull in the pounding of the rain overhead silenced them. "Where is that benighted Scribe Keperi?" he asked.

"We're rid of him for perhaps an hour, by a false note," she said shortly. "Saying the king summoned him to an inn outside the city."

The Duchas of Altan uttered a short laugh; he had had the night scribe summoned away on much the same futile errand. (It should be noted here that neither knew that Bee was in regular contact with his brother Thad, who had relayed Shontande's suggestion that he fall in with the supposed lure, and witness from a distance, since the crisis was upon them.)

The Duchas of Altan lit his candle, motioned ironically for her to precede him into Shontande's empty chambers, and they shut the door.

There is no need to report their subsequent conversation, which was, typically, full of innuendo beneath the flattery and the pretense of serving the Colendi cause: they agreed that if either of them found the royal seal, they would unite officially in a marriage of, ah, let us call is legal necessity, and as king and queen—the seal strictly shared—restore Colend to its proper order.

But no seal was to be found in those quiet chambers. The scribes had been guarding empty rooms. They were forced to retreat, both to discover their respective suites lit and their families and servants awake and alarmed as their absence — to which they attributed a sudden wish for amorous dalliance, which unlikelihood (for it was well known how much each loathed the other), soon spread mirth in a very witty poem, and turned up as the twist in a very witty play.

While they labored to lie their way out of their would-be attempt to take the throne, Shontande's first friend, Curtas, moved unnoticed through Alsais, reflecting on types of love.

Colend had so many verbs for love, but if they had one for the way he felt about Shontande Lirendi, he had not learned it. It certainly was not a simple matter of lust, as they had both been too young for those feelings the last time they had seen one another face to face. When they first met as boys, it was the fierce friend-love that comes of discovering someone who thinks a lot like you, and cares for the same things in a similar way.

As Curtas eased himself behind a string of pages in the

cloud blue of the palace scribes, dashing from dripping awning to dripping awning in the brief lull between cloudbursts, he thought about how much assumption plays a part in love: he had assumed their friendship transcended Shontande's royal rank, and Curtas's connection with Norsunder, nebulous as it had been. He was one of Detlev's boys, and Detlev was at that time part of Norsunder. Curtas's own life in Norsunder at that time had been one of endurance and avoidance, rather than conviction or ambition.

Shontande's rank was no secret, it was something they both ignored. But Curtas's life had been a secret until several assassinations occurred, two of those being Thad's sister and Shontande's father. Though Curtas had not been responsible for any of them, he was a part of the group that had compassed two of those deaths — which Shontande found out in the worst way possible.

As a new storm thundered overhead, and the only people out were those who had to be, Curtas spotted three relatively easy openings in the guard pattern. Thus he was able to move about to evaluate the situation.

When dawn blued in the east, Curtas paused outside the garden gate leading to the attached house belonging to Donais Altan, commander of the herald-guards. He offered his covered basket. The gate guard lifted the linen, expecting to see food, and glanced cursorily at the delicately decorated pastry swirls in shades of lily blue with sprays of green leaves in icing, without seeing that the pastries were hardened into staleness, the icing brittle. An alert guard would have been immediately suspicious, as no Colendi noble ever ate morning pastry, or any pastry, that was not fresh; Curtas had deliberately chosen the last dreary moments before the night guards were to go off duty, and his apron and basket identified him as a delivery person, of which there were many at this time of day. The guard saw what he expected to see.

The guard waved a tired hand and Curtas passed inside, pausing to bend as if to dislodge something from his sandal. A quick glance back; the gate guard did not bother to see that Curtas turned right to the kitchen path, rather than left to the steward's door where deliveries were customarily made.

Curtas had never met Donais Altan. He took his time moving up the path so that he could assess his surroundings. Donais Altan had a very high rank, and was brother to a duchas and a descendent of one of the oldest families in the kingdom, but he (unlike his brother) did not live in a large, impressive manor. The garden was austere, confined to shady pepper trees and cedar along the western façade, and herbs for kitchen and for scent.

Curtas was an accredited master builder. With an expert eye he approved the pure lines of the one-story house, each small wing looking into a pool or a garden. Near the kitchen, he ditched the stale pastries in a compost heap, and carried his empty basket on his arm as he bypassed the kitchen, which was lit, heads bobbing back and forth inside the windows: kitchen folk always began the day early.

He found an unlatched sliding door, and checked mentally: no one inside the room beyond. He slipped in, and proceeded slowly, fighting the threat of vertigo as he moved and sorted on the mental plane at the same time. He was not good at it—ah.

He found Donais Altan, who had just emerged from a cool, herb-scented bath. Always thoughtful, Curtas waited until the man had put on his pants and his under-tunic before he noiselessly slipped inside, and before Donais Altan could cross the room, flexed his hand. A dagger dropped from its wrist sheath. He tossed aside the basket.

Donais Altan tried to defend himself, but though he was well trained, Curtas was superlatively trained—as well as twenty-five years younger.

"Sit, please," Curtas murmured. "I am here to talk."

"Talk, then," Donais Altan said, sitting on his bench again as he—slowly—began to put on his stockings and the soft, low boots the herald-guards wore in summer.

"I saw that your heralds are poised to arrest the guild chiefs. I hoped to talk you out of that."

"I've received orders," Altan said, but in a tight, tired voice. His brief glance up at Curtas betrayed the dark-smudged eyes of someone who had slept little of late, if at all.

"Not from Shontande," Curtas said.

Donais Altan twitched at the lack of honorific, but he was fairly certain he knew who this was—though years had passed since Shontande had provided a minute description along with the regency council's orders for arrest on sight.

"From the highest authority present in the kingdom," Donais Altan said, even more bitterly.

"Is that their justification?" Curtas asked. "I'm certain they are pretending that they are acting in Colend's best interest, but do you believe that?"

"We're on the verge of riot," Donais Altan said. "If I move fast, it will remind people that we are here. And will act to protect public order, for their own safety."

"Rescind that order," Curtas said.

Donais Altan looked up sharply.

Curtas gestured with the knife. "I can hear your ambivalence. Let me make it simple, and I'll take my chances of getting out alive: either you rescind that order, or I offer you violence."

Donais Altan shook his head slowly. "I'll lay down my life in a heartbeat if it will protect the kingdom."

"But dying by my knife only gets you out of your dilemma. Surely your brother, and the rest of them, will simply replace you with a toady. They probably have one waiting."

Donais Altan's jaw tightened, and Curtas knew there was someone out there who saw a chance for advancement, whatever the cost. Furthermore, Donais Altan was aware of it. Probably had even received a threat from his elder brother.

Curtas said swiftly, to get Donais Altan's attention back where it belonged, "You know those barge polers are not going to give up their roses meekly. They are fiercely loyal to Shontande. Your king. So which is it to be?" Curtas gestured outwardly with the weapon, but made no move toward Donais Altan.

"If you're not going to gut me, put that dagger away," Donais Altan said irritably. "If I thought for a heartbeat that my life stood between an assassin and the king, I would already have made my try."

"But I am protecting his will," Curtas said inexorably. "His direct orders, as read in the streets weeks ago. And everybody your herald-guards are poised to arrest knows it."

Donais Altan shut his eyes. He knew just how much trouble there was going to be in the family if he did not obey the council's order. There was going to be trouble either way. It would have been easier to deal with trouble from the streets and canals.

Curtas said, "Can you not see? Those everyday people wearing red roses feel a sense of purpose. Even power, which is not always defined by steel." He waved his knife to catch the light, which limned the edge in a flash, then vanished as he slid the blade into its arm sheath with a snick. "They are *choosing* their king. The regents desire to strip away that sense of purpose, which they feel is reserved only to them—and whatever little they might see fit to dole out to the king. They are taking power entirely unto themselves, and they want you to take the first steps in using violence to preserve it so that their hands are clean, even though their motives are not."

"I won't use violence against our own people," Donais Altan said quickly, then halted, dropped his head into his hands, his voice tense. "No, don't say it."

"Then I will say this: the power of the roses is chosen. The power of the lilies denies that right to choose, forcing them back to the child's status of being chosen for."

Curtas had backed to the door as he spoke. On the last word, he snatched up the basket and slid through, shut the door, and wedged the sturdy basket handle under the latch.

He bolted down the hall. From behind came the rattle of the door as Donais Altan tried to open it—but no voice shouted the alarm from that far room.

Curtas slipped away, and found a place to hole up to catch a little sleep while he waited to see what would happen. When he woke abruptly after a brief sleep, he remembered where he was. A cat bounded away, having sniffed him and rejected him as not interesting.

He got up, thirsty, grimy, and tired, and moved from the alley to the side canal to assess the situation. No noise—that he could hear. Good sign or bad?

He turned, then stilled when he recognized Bee leaning against a wall, one foot propped behind him, his head bowed, eyes closed. Curtas knew that Bee was not only listening to the sounds around him, he was listening on the mental plane, his Dena Yeresbeth being far advanced beyond his own.

Therefore he had been waiting for Curtas to waken and emerge from his hidey-hole. Bee said, "Do you really think that we need you to resolve our affairs?"

"Yes."

Bee showed no reaction, but waited, his head still down.

"In general, of course, you don't," Curtas said. "But this was a specific need. Donais Altan is caught between two loyalties, on one side his oaths, the old order, and his family, and on the other the spirit of those oaths, which might be said to encompass the wishes of the populace. Most of the kingdom wears roses. I saw it in person as I shadowed Shontande on his tour. Did you know how widespread the roses are?"

"Yes," Bee said.

Curtas said, "Every Colendi who speaks to Commander Donais Altan falls on one side or the other. I, an outsider, thought I might be able to find a third path."

While Curtas spoke he sensed what Detlev's boys called a niff on the mental plane. He made no attempt to shield from it.

"You are on Shon's side," Bee said at last—neither approving nor disapproving.

"I had nothing to do with what happened to your sister. I am sorry."

Bee raised a hand, and Curtas fell silent. "It isn't just that. Shon's resentment goes back to Detlev's interference in his father's life, for what appears to have been mere experimentation. A whim, for he didn't even bother to try to take the kingdom. Shon can never forgive that, and you are associated with him. It might have been different if you'd told him before. Trusted him."

Sick to the soul, Curtas accepted these evenly spoken words—all of which were true, in a sense. In another sense, they involved a secret so deadly that of all Detlev's boys, only Adam and David knew the truth of it, and they had promised to suicide if ever they were caught.

"I couldn't," Curtas said, husky with regret.

Bee remained silent, and Curtas walked around the corner before transferring to Detlev's house. Bee slid his hand around his walking stick and made his way back to the palace by a circuitous route, pondering what to say about his encounter with Curtas. The last time Curtas's name came up was five years ago, after the surprising rumors about Detlev leaving Norsunder. When it became clear that no one was going to seek retribution—deserved a thousand times over— Shontande had told Bee, and Thad, never to mention Detlev or his followers again in his presence.

Bee knew that Shontande was going to want to know what had happened, but he decided that a message was the wrong way to go about telling him: once Shontande was back in Colend, where Bee could hear his voice, his breathing, he'd know how much to say.

When Bee returned to his chamber among the royal scribes, his chief page awaited him. "Runners to the herald-guard patrols went out with orders to face out, not in."

"Face out, not in," Bee echoed, his understanding of the words "out" and "in" being tactile, as in, you put a thing in a box or chest. You took it out. "What is the king to understand by that when I report it?"

"Facing outward means protecting against anyone who might interfere with the guild chiefs," she said very carefully—very carefully indeed, for she knew that at this point every word, every action would be written down by the scribes. Her voice trembled a little as she said, "Facing inward would have been the signal to contain the chiefs and not let them leave. Maybe preparatory to conducting them to the Hall of Reflection."

"He is awaiting the king's command, then." Elation burned through Bee, though it was far too early to claim victory. He controlled his reaction, saying only, "Tell Herald-Scribe Jais that it is time to release the King's Request."

"The King's Request," she repeated carefully, for she knew that there had been two proclamations prepared, the other being the King's Thanks, which would have been his abdication decree, exhorting the Colendi as his last order to comply with whoever had seized the throne.

Before the sun reached the midday high point, a little over two weeks from the zenith of midsummer, the chirps were busy crossing back and forth: Donais Altan's heralds were back patrolling, except for those who had offered, in polite language, full of thanks for their service and praise for their accomplishments, to aid the regents in vacating the palace. That was the first order of the King's Request.

Thad, far away in Sartor, looked down at a little strip of paper beginning, *King's Request*. There was another line, but he didn't see it as his eyes had blurred with tears.

"Thad?" Shontande said, startled and instantly concern-ed.

"Get the seal out, and I'll ready your king's ink," Thad said, laughing for joy. "Bee's scribes are readying to receive and copy your Letter of Permission: the roses prevailed."

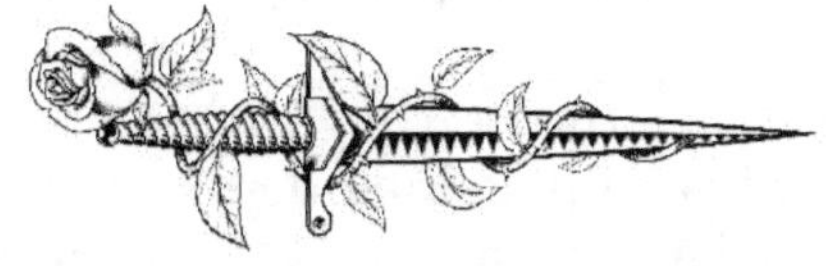

THIRTY-FIVE

Life with Adri and Gared's gang was noisy but surprisingly merry. If Liere overlooked the entire gang running off twice to cheer at two separate duels, and if she discounted the fact that Andri vanished every night. And if she overlooked the fact that her twelve-year-old daughter was studiously ignoring her.

The duels did not end in death, at least. As for Andri, he might be one of those night persons, and his disappearances were likely nothing more than visits to his lady friends; that first night, he went off with Devea. Liere assumed she would see neither till morning, but Devea was back within a turn of the sandglass, her arms full of jars of honey, which she set on an upended barrel with a grunt.

"Can I give you a hand?" Liere asked. "Everyone seems to have a task except me."

"You're a guest, aren't you?" Devea smiled up into Liere's face. "But if you'd like to help, can you reach that shelf up there? The honey — when we have some — goes there."

Liere's long arms easily reached.

"Just ask, if there's anything you want to know," Devea asked, with an avid glance that revealed to Liere a lot about the silent questions going on behind her back. They had adopted all kinds of people, it seemed, but she was the first envoy.

"I wonder why Andri doesn't at least try to disguise himself," Liere said.

Devea leaned against the prep table, blinking dark brown eyes in surprise. "Why should he? The snouts would know him even in false whiskers or a limp, and the rest of the city is behind him."

"They are?" Liere asked, pausing with a honey jar in each hand.

"Why does that surprise you? Oh, you heard a lot of lies from the King of Liars up on the ridge, of course."

Liere put the jars down, saying, "I heard a little, mostly to Andri's detriment, but . . ." She quickly outlined the interrupted meal and the chase.

Devea's puckered brow cleared. "Oh, there's always someone greedy for the reward. Or a relative to a snout, or the like. You can wager she got a brick through her windows for her pains."

"On Andri's orders?"

"No! Any of the boys did that, he'd thrash them, or worse, Gared would. He has a heavy hand, that one. Our orders are, hands off the locals. But her neighbors would see to it."

Liere continued stocking the honey as Devea went on about how they'd managed to get it through a complicated trade, and the subject dropped.

The next morning, Liere asked Marten, as she helped chop onions, if winters were more difficult, or does the Wood Guild still deliver Firesticks? (In other words, did they steal the one in the stove, cooking those onions?)

"Oh, yes. I see why you ask—our distrust of mages in general," Marten said, as he stirred the onions in his big iron pot. "Which must seem strange to you Sartorans, throwing magic about every day."

"Not every day. Life is mostly the same as life here. More amenities, perhaps."

"I'd like to witness that one day." He smiled. "Somehow the firesticks are not considered magic in the untrustworthy sense. Some think the firestick delivery every autumn is too old to meddle with—trying to change that would be like trying to change a mountain into a river. Others don't think of firesticks as magic, in that they don't change shape, or do anything but catch fire and give off warmth."

"Then no one interferes with the firestick distribution?"

"Oh, now, that's different," skinny, vivid Ratface said from where he was shredding potatoes and other root vegetables. "There's always someone trying to take them, especially during the bad years. I remember we learned to go in a pack. Gared and Andri out front with steel ready. No one harassed us *then*. Now it's just the snouts finding some way to accuse you of a crime so they can confiscate them and sell them on the side." Wham-wham-wham-wham! His knife slammed hard into the chopping block. "Done!"

"Those who need warmth usually find a way to it," Marten said, as the smell of browning onions drew people from all over the house. "We who serve in the palace are found most often there. Some labor at eateries. And some sneak into attics of warm houses to sleep."

"Ah, we're hardy," Gared said, waving a hand.

"Except Andri always gets a cold," Kizka cracked. "You could use his red nose for a beacon."

"All true," Andri said, leaning in the doorway, "except now I have to thump you for disrespect in front of—oof!"

Ratface hit him in a body tackle, and that turned into a general wrestling match.

"Not in the kitchen," Marten said above the clatter and bang of buckets and boxes and a small table tumbling into a wall. "Unless you want to pick your food off the floor. The unwashed floor."

The wrestling shifted to the next room, as brisk betting went on at the side. Not that anyone had anything to spend. They mostly wagered hated chores.

That went on until Marten called, "Food!"

Abruptly the fighting ended as everyone got a big dollop on a plate or bowl. Lyren-Sartora retired with the younger ones to sit on the roof with their food, where it was marginally cooler with the sun going down.

Liere wondered if those who ate with at least one utensil had been raised in the upper levels of society; the others ate with their fingers, or scooping the hot fried potatoes, onions, and root vegetables bound with egg into their mouths with bits of bread. They sat anywhere—in chairs, on tables, on the floor. Ratface perched on a stool, his knees under his chin, the plate on them, his bare toes clutching the edge of the seat. One hand held his bowl, and the other pushed food into his mouth as fast as he could chew it. Next to him handsome, elegant Bassl, dark of skin, eyes, and hair, sat straight-backed, his dish on one knee.

"What's the news about the throne?" Gared asked Kizka.

"Carpenters coming to repair it. The official word is to check for woodworm, but word is, gilders and upholsters are being consulted. For an undisclosed future. But the orders for refurnishing the royal wing aim for Harvest Festival."

Ratface's (empty) wooden plate crashed to the floor, clattering as it spun. "You're gonna let Marsael make himself king!" he yelled at Andri. "Why aren't we taking *action!* We been ready for *years!*"

Liere held her breath; she liked these people, but felt sick at the prospect of Andri loosing his skilled brawlers on the nobles up on the ridge, most of whom she also liked.

"Nobody's letting him do anything," Andri soothed. "I still have to try to reach the freedom movement people."

"They're idiots," Ratface exclaimed. "They split up over that voting thing."

"Dockside still likes 'em."

"They like us better," Ratface declared, and several echoed in agreement.

Gared lifted a shoulder. "Can't believe Vec about much, but you can believe him about the river."

"Which is why," Andri said, "I want to give them both."

"I don't see why," Ratface muttered, rocking back and forth on his stool, his fingers working restlessly at a splinter at the side of the seat. "Idiots. Idiots! Can't even make up their minds about their own stupid way to make a kingdom run without a king."

"That's what voting is," Andri said. "A choice. You pick the one you think best."

"But what was so good about that brute Navalin? He beat and threatened the wheelwrights and the drivers into voting for him."

"Yet some people still wanted him," Fronsa muttered in disgust. "They wouldn't vote for Parion because she's old."

"And she has no roaming bullies," Bassl added before sampling the tangy berry juice someone had brought. He set it down with an elegant shrug, the cup immediately pounced on by Gil, the biggest and huskiest of the boys, and the quietest, Liere had discovered, except for Skinner.

"I have to find out where Parion's gone to ground," Andri said. "Talk to her in neutral territory. I've told you, if she and I agree, we'll convince 'em."

"Still think it's a waste of time," Ratface muttered.

Bassl looked up. "We are cutting it very close," he said to Andri with an air of question.

A couple of the bigger boys muttered that there was nothing wrong with a big fight—as long as Talipin and his snouts got their heads busted. Andri sent them all out on a run, followed by sword drill, adding to Gared, "Make 'em sweat."

Then he turned to Liere. "Seems you've something to say?"

Liere wondered what he'd seen in her face. Then she realized that he'd been watching her, and there was the heat again. She clasped her hands around a knee and said slowly, "I was just remembering, oh, a conversation. Between an envoy and a ruler, which took place when another ruler was making a state visit."

Andri sat down across from her, as Ratface lingered in the doorway, listening. Once that focused attention would have made her bite her nails down to the quick. She drew a breath, firmed her resolve, and said, "The lesson was that the visiting monarch—he was young, and new to his throne—had a demanding regent at home. He could have started a battle, but instead he made this state visit to the other kingdom, whose ruler acknowledged his sovereignty."

Ratface pointed at Liere and snarled, "Didn't you just do that for Marsael?"

Gared yanked Ratface out of the room, Andri following. Voices rose in the hallway, then halted abruptly. They returned almost immediately, and Ratface came to Liere, avoiding her eyes as he mumbled, "I know you were just doing what you were told."

She said softly, "I would like to make amends if I can."

He jerked his head in a nod, then Banisa poked her head in the open window, saying, "Duel! Over by Sheepshank Canal."

"Anyone good?"

"Someone's challenged Jipael the Scar."

"Ooh! Ought to be good!"

Liere heard Lyren-Sartora's voice fluting above the general stampede. The children had come down from the roof and pelted up the street. Lyren-Sartora rather pointedly seemed to be pretending to be an orphan, as most of those children really were, and ran with their pack, largely uncontrolled except very loosely by Andri and Gared.

Liere closed her worry and guilt away in her heart, and helped collect the dishes as the room mostly emptied. She did not have to look to know that Andri was gone; she could feel his attention otherwhere. So odd, this new sense. In a way it felt like the first time she leaped into the air and flew, that summer in Delfina Valley where Tsauderei the Mage lived. Frightening and exhilarating at the same time.

Later that night, Lyren-Sartora reappeared in the room set aside for them. There was a single trunk, and bedding on the bare (but swept) floor, but that was nicer than many of the other rooms, and they had it to themselves.

"It's fun here," Lyren-Sartora said as she fluffed her thin blanket over her. "As long as nothing stupid happens."

Liere prudently did not tug that dangling string. "Sleep well," she said.

Liere remembered Ratface sitting on the balcony edge above a horrible drop to the marble floor as he baited Adon-Marsael. It would be too easy to dismiss him as merely a brawler for the sake of brawling. Which made her wonder what Andri was doing, if he didn't intend to challenge Adon-Marsael with steel.

In short, his answers that day when they rode out-side the city might have been true—she had sensed that they were—but were not, after all, complete? After exposure to Siamis and Detlev's way of telling exactly as much truth as they wanted to reveal, but not everything, she ought to have seen that. For that matter, had she not done the same, hiding her own origins, and the fact that she was a mage?

The following day, Liere discovered that the few cleaning frames in that part of the city had all been lifted from the houses of nobles after the overthrow of the king. When the magic wore out from regular use by a crowd of people—an entire street or even two sharing a single cleaning frame— they'd shrugged and gone back to dipping in the river during summer, and basin washing from lugged pails in winter.

The fountains had definitely improved life. As for the former water carriers, it was Lyren-Sartora who discovered that they now operated the newly-opened public baths. "They say it was Poopsie Face's idea," she admitted truculently. "Got it out of some history book, and called the water carriers together the night of our Envoy Ball. Jaydi says that when the fountains dried ages ago, the wool guild took over the baths. Anyway, all last week, the water carriers kicked the sheep out, and now everybody wants to go to the baths. Poopsie Face insists that everyone should go free in the water straight from the stream, and only pay for the warm baths, and extras like soap and towels, for now. I hate cold water when my hair gets wet, no matter how hot it is outside. I get chilled."

Liere responded to this hint with a few small copper bits. "No more," she warned. "Until we figure out a way to earn it."

"You still don't want to tell them who we are?" Lyren-Sartora asked.

"We won't learn anything if we do," Liere said.

"What's there to learn? Poopsie Face is an idiot, but Jaydi and the others are fun." With a miffed shrug, Lyren-Sartora ran off.

Liere went to the baths with Elies and Devea. As soon as she walked in, she smelled the dankness of water impurities, but when she asked, Devea said breezily, "Oh, that's bound to go away once the water flows enough. Everyone says so. Underground ways are still cleaning out all the old dust."

Liere was not so sure; the grime from so many users had to go somewhere, usually either floating in the water or sinking to the bath floor unless magic sent it underground. Putting a magical filter around the perimeter was a relatively simple matter—a similar project had been one of the tests for the end of her first year among the Ones. It was merely a matter of repetition.

That night was another hot one. Andri had vanished on one of his night prowls, and the remainder of the group had staggered in after Gared had run them to the river and back, and then set them to sparring. Liere slipped away and ran back to the baths, which were less crowded, so late. She covertly took care of the purification, laying down interlocked spells that would last at least ten years.

The following day, everyone was commenting on how fresh the water at the baths smelled—you could even feel your teeth clean, just like those cleaning frames the rich had!

"All it needed was to clean out the old pipes, just as we said!"

Liere smiled to herself, relishing her ability to help without anyone knowing, therefore no unforeseen consequences. Too bad there wasn't a way for the cleaning frames to suddenly begin working again. That would definitely draw attention, and suspicion.

She laughed to herself when Lyren-Sartora bounced her way that evening, saying privately, "At least the baths don't stink anymore!" She then sniffed in Liere's direction and ran off, the center of Jaydi's pack of orphans.

Lyren-Sartora was enjoying herself enough not to want to leave, so Liere was free to take each day as it came, as she tried to tease out the sense of danger that had sparked those nightmares, and to answer the questions that kept rising to mind.

The fifth day she tripped herself up. She was helping in the kitchen when she noticed a slight greenish tinge to the rain barrel, and when she put the dipper to it to sniff, Marten, who was chopping turnips, called, "If you're thirsty, go to the fountain, or drink from the hot water pan on the stove. Don't drink from the rain barrel until we boil it."

Liere worked the purification spell over the barrel as Marten was busy cracking eggs into a big mixing bowl. Then she backed off, dismayed at her thoughtlessness. This was worse than the cleaning frames magically fixing themselves!

Then she remembered her fountain ruse, and dug the lowest denominator coin out of her inner pocket. She'd just tossed it into the water, and watched the greenish flash of magic remove the invisible fingerprints and grime from the coin, when a shrill voice startled her, "What have you done?" Fronsa stalked in, elbows aggressively bent, fists on her skinny hips.

"I had a purification spell left over from my envoy mission, so I used it in this water that everyone shares."

Fronsa scowled. "We could have sold it!"

"I'm sorry," Liere said contritely.

"Why?" Devea the tailor said from behind Fronsa. "That was a generous thought." And to Fronsa, "As for you, you sell something like that, and everybody lands on you, wanting to know where it was from."

"Oh."

"So scat."

Red to the ears, Fronsa sashayed away, hips swing-ing.

"Don't mind her," Devea said to Liere. "Has green ears."

"Green ears?"

"Jealous. Wants a piece of Andri. He brought you in."

Liere blinked. "I don't mean to . . ."

Devea waved her off. "He won't dally with her because she's the jealous type. Won't share. Too much trouble for the fun, that kind."

"Ah," Liere said, heady with a conviction that at last she had a glimpse inside the tangled vines of adult relationships. "Is that what the rest of you do?"

Devea was broad, her top low-cut, her grin lascivi-ous. "I don't speak for all the girls here. Some of the boys aren't interested in us. Me and the candlemaker sisters up the street, a couple others here and there, we share Gared and Andri around. Sometimes Bassl." She heaved a dramatic sigh. "*Everybody* wants Bassl, but he mostly likes the boys. As for Gillor, we might all be bricks for the attention he pays us, and anyone else except his wagon-driver, when she's in town, Ratface is too much trouble—he never healed right—and Kizka isn't awake yet. But Andri and Gared, they like the girls, we like them, and everybody is happy." She had a deep laugh that invited one to share the mirth, then she stepped closer. "Just don't expect Andri to stay the night. Come and go, that's him, if you know what I mean . . ."

Liere choked on a laugh of surprise—she did know! Now she felt very sophisticated that Devea, who was older and experienced, treated her like an equal.

". . . been that way ever since the troubles. Kizka says he spends most nights over at the palace library."

"The library?" The word slipped out. Liere remem-bered sensing that Andri was around, but she had assumed he would be stalking, or being stalked by, Adon-Marsael.

"Library. Looking in the oldest, moldiest stuff, too, Kizka says—"

"No! Let me through!"

Voices rose in argument outside the door. Liere and Devea left the kitchen and ran out, as did everyone in the alley, to find Fronsa valiantly trying to keep a huge young man from storming in.

Over Fronsa's head, the young man exclaimed, "Devea."

"What is it, Vec? You know we're supposed to meet us in

neutral territory."

Vec pushed back against Fronsa as he said impatiently, "This is no challenge. I know I owe Andri for busting my brother free."

"Fronsa, let him by," Devea said.

Fronsa let go, a grasshopper contending against a bullfrog, and gave a sniff as the young man swaggered toward them. He paused to take in Liere, giving her a slow up and down. She remembered that she was among grownups, and gave him a slow up and down right back — smothering a laugh as Vec blushed to the ears. "Never saw you before," he said with a silly grin.

"Never mind that," Devea said briskly. "You can flirt with Liere later, if she wants the trouble of a big lunk whose best love is his beer —"

"Piss, Devea! You know that's not true!"

" —what's brought you over our way?"

"House to house search," Vec said succinctly, seri-ous again. "Tonight. Not just the snouts. I mean, them, too. It's Marsael's blues."

Everyone in the room turned to Andri, who'd appeared from somewhere. His eyes were smudged dark beneath, his hair tousled more than ever. Liere wondered if he'd been asleep.

"Thanks, Vecalin," Andri said. "I'll remember that."

Vec vanished, and Ratface burst out, "You gotta get out of the city, Andri. Those soulsuckers would be happy for any excuse to kill you. We should go and scrag 'em first."

"Hold hard," Gared protested. "I know a lot of the snouts from the old days. Blues, too. They're not that bad. Most of 'em. But they take orders, because that's their life."

"And Talipin?"

Marten said, "He is desperate to become a noble. He thinks what he does will gain him a title. He doesn't see that the more dirty work he's willing to do, the worse he's despised. I feel sorry for him. Though that doesn't make him less dangerous."

"Cousin, ride out tonight. Now," Bassl urged.

"Not arguing," Andri said to him. "You'll have to stay on the ridge. No sneaking over here. Marten can get any messages you have. I need you listening in court, you and Kizka both."

"I'm on my way," Bassl said. "As soon as I see you out the door."

Kizka lifted a hand in agreement, as Andri said to Liere. "You were talking about sovereignty. I might be able to use that. But I need some diplomatic talk. Want to take a ride?"

Liere thought immediately of Lyren-Sartora. She was ready to say *I can't*, but how would she explain her relationship with Lyren-Sartora — who was still ignoring her? And why should she hover over her? Lyren-Sartora would be the first to snap "You left me for five years!" — to which there was either five years' worth of answer, or none. She was safe enough here, despite the political unrest. She did know the illusion spell, so she could blur her face if Adon-Marsael's people even scrutinized children. And she had her butterfly hairpin for transfer, which Liere had noted with silent approval that she wore every day.

Yes, it might be good for Lyren-Sartora if Liere left for a day or so, rather than hover here to be ignored. Liere could sort out her own questions on this ride, without an audience.

Except for Andri. Which would be a challenge in just about every way.

Didn't the Ones say she needed to be challenged?

"Let me fetch my carryall and my hat," she said.

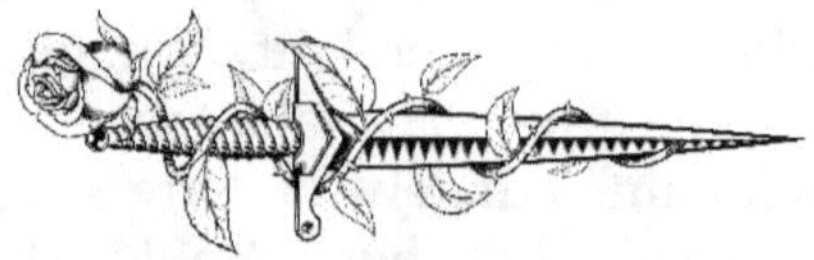

THIRTY-SIX

Gared said to Andri, "Up above the falls?"

"Meet you there," Andri said, and turned to Liere with an air of question. "We'll have to run for it until we get outside the city. They'll stop every rider."

"Very well," she said calmly — so calmly that most there wondered if she understood what he meant by making a run for it. Ah, she'd soon find out.

She went upstairs to fetch her things, which sat as usual next to her neatly rolled bedding; she had said nothing to Lyren-Sartora about leaving her own bedding in a tangle each morning, though usually she had tidy habits. Liere knew a silent protest when she saw one.

Liere picked up her carryall and her hat, turned — and there was Lyren-Sartora standing in the doorway, arms crossed. "Where are you going?"

"For a ride."

"For how long?"

"I don't know. That is a good question. Maybe I ought to take this blanket. Yes, I will." She folded the blanket and began to roll it up tight. Since she had only one change of clothes, it would fit right into her carryall.

Lyren-Sartora burst out, "You can't just leave!"

"Why not?"

Lyren-Sartora's indignant gaze flashed from Liere to the window, then to the ceiling, and back. "I thought we were going to be together."

"Lyren-Sartora, you've been avoiding me ever since we left the palace. You now have the opportunity to have me completely out of your way for a short time." Then, overriding what was sure to be more complaints about Andri, she said, "There is a search to commence this very night. Though I know we are not the target, I feel very certain that our presence would be reported to Adon-Marsael."

"Yours," Lyren-Sartora stated. "He never so much as looked at me."

"My point remains."

"You can do illusion . . ."

"I can, though you know how flimsy those are. If the searchers are earnest, and examine every face, then they will have two things to report: my presence, and my having done magic."

"Illusion isn't *real* magic. Even I can do it!"

Liere was silent.

Lyren-Sartora sighed, knowing she had lost an argument that she wasn't even certain had a point. Except her resentment against Andri Malcolin Elsarion. About whom she had no real complaint; try as she might to discover something unsavory about him other than those nebulous rumors about murders, she'd learned only that he and Gared looked out for the orphans, Devea and Banisa saw that they were clothed, Marten saw that they were fed. The worst she heard of Andri was that during winter, when they were all holed up, he made them practice reading and writing before he'd do sword drills with them.

All she was left with after five days of trying was that she didn't like the way he looked at Liere. And even worse was the way Liere looked back.

She spun about and flounced away. "Do what you want."

"Be safe," Liere's voice floating after her. "Contact me if you need to."

A brief, intense mental touch, very like a huff, was the answer, and Liere smothered a sigh.

A short time later, Liere and Andri ghosted up a narrow alley and vaulted a fence, silent as cats. The city of course was dark, save golden lights in windows here and there, and the starlight overhead, with a thin crescent moon sitting above the river. Andri took a very circuitous route, to be expected if there was a hunt on.

It felt good to run hard again. She hadn't had any real exercise since Lael stabbed her; at least he no longer whispered in dreams. That shoulder sometimes ached dully, most often at night, but otherwise she was back to normal, and had been longing for real exercise this past few days — really, ever since the grand ball and its vigorous dancing.

Any time they heard footfalls, Andri did not wait to see if it was friend or foe. He turned abruptly and chose another way. He seemed to know every yard and barn and alley, no matter how rundown. She ran on her toes the way she'd been trained, leaped, pulled, swung and balanced, laughing inwardly even when, after an especially difficult climb from roof to rock to wall, as they ascended the ridge to the upper level, she found herself a little breathless.

She deepened her breathing, giving her body a silent command to heighten its use of air. This exertion would leave her hungry and thirsty, but water, at least, could be found as long as they paralleled the river. The only flaw was how sharply her shoulder ached if she demanded too much of it, so she shifted all pulls to her left hand.

They didn't speak. The air was so still that sound would carry. They had to get out of the city first.

Her fourth and fifth years among the Ones had included far tougher runs if not every day, at least a few times a week, so it never occurred to her that Andri was testing her limits, and finding none, in the sense that she kept pace with him; in a race he would outrun her only because his legs were much longer, but he had no doubt she could cover the same amount of ground without flagging. Except for a slight hitch on her right side, she was exactly as fast and as agile — with no extra effort.

The Adrani ambassador's aide, a friendly soul, had told Andri that Sartoran scribe training for the diplomatic field was mostly focused on translation, fast notetaking, memorization, and conducting oneself in every sort of circumstance, from the most formal to casual. "Sword fighting and the like?" old Porganal had repeated, laughing. "Scribes in the diplomatic service are supposed to use their wits! When the steel comes out, we go home. No, no, my boy, you're mistaken. Oh, your envoy might have taken private lessons — many do, you know — but that's entirely recreational."

This was not a recreational run, and yet Liere paced him while still taking in the moonlight on the river below.

Who was she? The others had accepted her, so quiet and self-effacing and helpful she was, but that was to be expected from an envoy. Even Gared, who had reason to be more cautious, had stopped worrying, saying only yesterday, "Anyone who can listen to Marten while chopping potatoes day after day can't be a threat."

They made it without being caught.

Gared himself was waiting uptrail from the waterfall, beyond a cluster of gnarled pine; in spite of the systematic search going on, an understanding had for years existed between Gared and the independents who hired out horses. They knew that he could be relied on to exercise the stock, and while he wasn't a fully trained and officially svedded farrier, he knew enough to identify and fix most problems. Gared, in turn, knew who favored Marsael, and those who distrusted or even roundly loathed Adon-Marsael's forming government. When he came through the great barns, he made sure only the latter saw him saddle up and add feedbags for two animals. In turn, it was understood without a word spoken that a certain amount of free labor would be his and Skinner's trade for this loss of vigilance.

Andri's favorite horse was waiting with Gared, the spotted one Liere had met before, named Battleax by Jaydi and friends. Battleax was sturdy if shaggy and unprepossessing in appearance, a middle-aged animal who still liked long distance with due care, and traveled well with the mostly black companion Liere was pointed to.

She started when she saw a short rapier in a saddle sheath. Gared ranged up, eyeing her expertly. "Guessed about right," he said. "Want to make a pass or two to test the length?"

Liere had not told anyone, she was sure, that she could use a sword. She had not gone to their practices because her shoulder, though healing well, still hurt. Avoiding the question, she said, "What will you do if it's too long or too short?"

"Try better next time," Gared said, laughing as he turned away. "The cloth bag behind the feed is from Marten—a few early apples, a hunk of cheese, and the rest of today's bread. Keep your eye sharp!"

Andri had already mounted. He lifted a hand, and they were soon off, the animals surefooted along the mostly flat path winding through a wooded patch along the ridge above the great river.

They kept to a brisk but not headlong pace, covering as

much ground as they could before the moon sank and darkness closed in enough to make it dangerous to push forward.

They stopped alongside a stream, and set up camp on a grassy bank. Marten had also included a firestick—the household only needed the one for cooking—which meant they could toast the hard, stale bread, and melt a bit of cheese over it. Andri tended to this, deft from long habit, as Liere rubbed down the horses, each noting the other's expertise.

When she sat on the other side of the fire, Andri smiled across from her, the shadows deepening the long dimples on either side of his mouth. "Sovereignty," he said, firelight limning his long hair, and outlining the sharp angle of one shoulder. "What did the Sartorans teach you about that? Specifically the king with the grabby regent, who used another king to establish his sovereignty?"

Liere had just crunched into her toasted bread and melted cheese. She used the time it took to ingest the bite to mentally weave her way among the potential pitfalls his questions opened. She did not want to lie. Aside from the moral quandary lies put one in, they were so very hard to remember.

"I think," she said presently, "it might be more useful to talk of specifics. One new king's experience might not make any sense to another new king, even though they share the problem of an acquisitive regent."

"Does the sovereignty-granting kingdom need to be a large one?" Andri asked. "Of course it does. It was surely Sartor, or you wouldn't be learning about it, yes?"

"Not necessarily. Don't you study world history? Or at least events on this continent?"

"True. Started to, anyway. Eh, here's what I'm thinking. Since I need to be out of the city for a time, we'll ride to Otobris. Then on to Martan north of us. It's a small kingdom, probably unknown to pretty much everyone outside its borders."

"Root of the name Martande," she murmured. "Itself a Sartoran name."

"Right. Sartor's centuries of authority appropriated clear up at the north end of the continent, by a place your queen has probably never heard of."

Liere shut her eyes, picturing that elegantly drawn map

on Atan's table. "You would be wrong."

"Heh! I've strayed from my point. Martan was a duchy until it broke away from what used to be Ideygo. It's about the size of my own family's holdings, mainly famed for its excellent beer. And wool."

She dipped her head in a nod, with an air of courteous listening.

"My sister Alismira married the crown prince years ago. They recently inherited the throne. I guess they sit on thrones. If they didn't have thrones, my sister would make sure they were built." He tipped his head. "I doubt their influence would amount to a mouse's squeak with Cousin Adon. Some kind of official acknowledgment might be gratifying to receive, but my motivation here is the knowledge that Alismira is also rich. I could really use a trunk of gold." He pointed at Liere with his half-eaten bread. "Help me dream up some diplomatic language to convince her."

"Is there any family loyalty?" she asked. "Do you exchange—" She brushed her forearm against her inner pocket, which held her golden notecase, remembering that those were virtually unknown in Enaeran. And Andri's way of life would make letter delivery difficult.

"Not a whit of it," he said cheerfully. "She hated me from the moment I was born because my father wanted to leave the kingdom to a son. She flattered herself into thinking that she'd inherit if there was no me, but I suspect my father would have repaired the rift with the main branch of the family, and put my as-yet-unmet cousin Trevor Macael in as heir, sooner than let her inherit. We haven't had a lot of success with queens."

Or kings, Liere thought, remembering references to civil uprisings so frequent it sounded as if they were generational—or nearly.

"At any rate, Alismira said she would only marry a crown prince. She got the only one available at this end of the continent, whereas our parents lost their throne as well as their lives, and I definitely lost the first and almost the second. Think pity is the approach to use? I can grovel, if you think it would help. She's used to my groveling. My earliest memories are of her mashing my face into the mud until I yelped that I was a worthless worm over and over." There was no resentment in his voice whatsoever, only a sort of wry, rueful laughter.

He seemed to intuit her reaction for he said, "Between my father's howling about my learning the old ways, my mother's howling at him as well as the rest of the world, and my sister's bullying, I ended up spending all the time I could with Gared. After my father imprisoned me and took away the heirship, I ran away to live with them. Gared was thirteen. I was halfway to eleven when I first took up living with them."

Liere shivered, her mind filling with images of her own father, but worse. Louder. Her father had never beat her or Marga. He had flayed verbally — emotionally — not physically. She retained a distinct memory of King Alored from her flying visits when she broke Siamis's enchantment. He had frightened her. Both the king and queen had.

"Best thing that ever could have happened to me. It was Gared's father, Master of Horse Inmael, who taught us the most, before he was assassinated." Andri's soft, slightly husky voice hardened briefly. "I'm pretty sure Cousin Adon was behind that. Eh, very sure. Backtrack a little, Alismira married north when I was six. She might have mellowed since then. They haven't tossed her out, last I heard."

Liere had finished her bread by this time, and bit into a small apple. It was very sour, making her mouth pucker.

"What are you thinking?" he asked.

"Why would Gared's father be assassinated? He had no political importance. Ah. Because he was known to harbor you?"

"We think he knew what was coming. The last thing he did was to send us over the wall on a spurious errand. We came back to find the horses gone and the house burning. We dunked ourselves in the horse trough and ran in anyway. Found him dead. A dozen stab wounds. But he'd taken several of them with him over the ghost falls."

"How old were you?"

"Fourteen."

She intuited from his even tone that exclamations of pity would be out of place; that had clearly been the beginning of a long stretch of living on the run amid the chaos of Enaeran in the grip of revolution. But the two boys had made lives for themselves, and for a number of others orphaned by the problems.

She took a last bite, then tossed the apple core into a

clearing, where the seeds had a chance if they took root. Then she drew her knees up and rested her chin on them. "I'm wondering why you want to endure what I can see, from my outsider's perspective, is an enormous amount of exertion as well as risk. You have a free and merry life now. Will it truly be so much worse if Adon-Marsael makes himself king? If you do oust him, you'll be starting with nothing, from what he said. The treasury is empty."

"It is, but I know who's sitting on most of it. Besides him. Don't believe his story about using his own inheritance. It's a lot more complicated, and it's also bound up with Sles Adran in ways I don't quite understand yet. Thadara Otobris—did you meet her?—found some very suspicious papers when we broke in not long after the second wave of troubles, right before Adon-Marsael took Shiovhan."

"I met her briefly."

Andri looked away, then back. "She was rude, I suspect. She has a genius for instant understanding of numbers that I have to sit over and study—but she also seems to think the world is peopled by fools, and it would be a lot better with her in charge."

"Would it?"

"Depends on your view. She's even more rank-dazzled than her father. Thadara is excellent when she talks about taxes and exchequer, but get her on the subject of blood and rank . . ." He shook his head. "She has this theory that your Sartoran Dei family—one of whom happened to turn up in my own family tree some eight or ten centuries ago, and in her own a century later—is meant to be the kings of the world, and if everyone would just heed this wisdom and take their proper place, we would all have peace and plenty."

He gestured largely with his half-eaten apple. "But we all have some quirk that makes us a mockery to our enemies, and our friends sigh. I certainly do. As for your first question . . ." He leaned back on his elbows, head tipped back, reading the vast scattering of stars. "As for why I endure it, I think about that. Often. Debate it. But I know when I started. From the beginning, when Master of Horse Inmael took me in, and every time there was a problem he'd turn to me and ask what Prince Andri would do."

"Not Gared?"

"Gared is as clear as water and as strong as a tree, but he

won't lead. Gets tied up in the last thing said or done. He hates choices. Even though he's older. He was always my shield arm, not my leader. So I'd pipe up, brat that I was, and invariably Master of Horse Inmael would tell me how and why I was wrong. Never angry, never cruel, like my father, or belittling, like my mother. Not long before Master of Horse Inmael was killed — I really believe he saw it coming — we had a talk about what to do when there were too many choices. How to decide which was most important, balanced against what was fastest, or cost the least."

Strategy, she wanted to say. She was certain he knew the word, but it might not have been in the everyday vocabulary of a boy whose education stopped around age ten and of a master of horse, even if the latter instinctively grasped strategy. And somebody must have recognized that by watching Andri's actions from a distance? "What did he say about choices that were all bad?"

"When the choices were all bad, he said, always try to protect as many people as you can. After we were on our own …" Andri shrugged. "When something happens, they all turn to me and say, what next? Ever since I was ten, I've always been trying to plan for what next."

He fell silent, and she sensed that he was going to come at her with a personal question. It would be fair, too. He'd shared his personal history. But she was not ready to share hers. It was so very *freeing* to be with people who had no idea she had once been that miserable mess, Sartora, The Girl Who Saved the World. These Enaeraneth took her as she was, and she reveled in it.

She fought a sudden yawn. "How far is Otobris? Ought we to get some rest?"

"Sure. We're still too close to the city, and ought to ride with first light." He killed the firestick's flame with a swipe of his hand.

Too close to the city; though she did not expect to have to use the sword, she made sure it was within reach of the grassy spot she chose for rest. She folded her blanket into a roll the way she'd learned among the Ones. Though when she slept outside, and lay looking up at the stars, it was always those nights in the forest of Drael when she was ten that she remembered most. She and Senrid and little Devon had been on the run, but the fear had faded from those memories, leaving only the fun and challenge of those long conversations she'd had with Senrid while Devon slept— conversations and arguments, though never rancorous.

Once she was in her blanket roll, she wriggled out of her robe, and laid it on the grass to air, sleeping in her singlet and the soft cotton-linen drawers she'd become accustomed to among the Ones, very like swimming shorts, except undyed. She stretched out, her body comfortable, but her mind raced with questions. And minute sensory awareness: the softest of summer breezes brushing her hot cheeks; the scent of wild lemon balm and lavender; the thud of a somnolent horse setting down a hoof, and, closer, the rustle of fabric as Andri took off his baldric and the rattle of his sword in its sheath as he laid it down.

She turned on her side, her eyes now adjusted to the darkness. She looked toward him, making out his silhouette, and the soft glow of starlight on his long hair. Though he'd said "sure" to the idea of rest, he sat against a tree, gazing off over the stream toward the river.

Her eyes slowly closed. She had just enough strength to send a quick tendril to Lyren-Sartora, and caught an image of running along a fence and laughter before Lyren-Sartora grumpily shut her mind-shield. Liere accepted the *so there!* knowing it was not serious, and gratefully sank below waves of exhaustion. She did not waken until the insistent prick of something cold, and pointed, on the point of her chin.

She opened her eyes—to the sharp end of a sword blade two fingers from her nose.

And Andri grinning mercilessly from the other end.

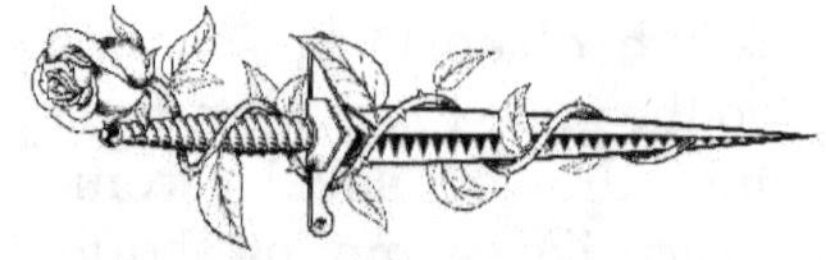

THIRTY-SEVEN

Shock propelled her up, sword in hand, blade whirling. Memory smote her beneath the shock: the ice-burn alongside her shoulder blade. Lael's whisper.

Sharp pain blasted away the memories with the first hard block of steel on steel. She had reached with her right hand from habit—she had trained first with her right to blend with the others—but swapped hands between one movement and the next.

Within six fast moves she knew that she wasn't going to win this bout. Though she had speed to counter size and strength in most situations, here the difference between five years of hard training and a lifetime of it was against her. But she was annoyed enough to make him work for it.

Her ire was difficult to hang onto when he crowed with appreciation at every near hit. As for Andri, never before had this game been quite so dazzling. He liked girls of all types, but a girl who could fight—especially a beautiful one—made him feel sixteen again.

When at last his point tapped between her collarbones she swept an ironic salute, then tossed the blade so that it stood in the soil, vibrating. "What," she snapped, "was that all about?"

"We all do it," he said. "Keeps us alert."

She opened her mouth to express her opinion of this "game", then the sense of his words hit her: she had been included in the *all*.

Did she want to be included?

Ah, there it was, a truth she had managed to miss for five days. This sudden fight underscored the difference between her being here out of curiosity, and him being here because this was his home, his life.

She was curious. He was committed.

When people dedicate their lives to a cause, you get things like waking up to the point of a sword. The last of her ire vanished.

Leaving her aware that she stood there in her underclothes. He looked away quickly, reddening to the ears. She stared back, intensely aware of him barefoot, his shirt unlaced. She ripped her eyes away from that gap that revealed the entrancing curve of his collarbones, the open shirt plunging midway down his chest. She turned to her tumbled blanket. Blinking away the image that would not go away, she picked up her summer robe, and headed down to the stream to wash her hands and face.

She had her back to him now, but she was still acutely aware of the sound of his footfalls in the grass, and the rustle and thump of gear; when she straightened up from the deliciously cool water, blinking droplets from her eyelashes, she found him right behind her.

Once again heat flared, so intense she took a step backward, looking up in question. His expression was difficult to interpret as he held something out. Her gaze fell to the object on his palm—a little pot with a latched lid.

"It's salve," he said. "Good stuff. I could see you favoring one arm but I didn't know you took a recent stab wound."

Liere had entirely forgotten that her shoulders were bare, her summer singlet having only finger-wide strips. "Oh," she said. "It's nearly healed."

"No, it isn't. And someone knew precisely where to hit you to take your arm out of commission. I wish you'd said something. I never would have given you the Wake-Up."

"Is that what you call it," she said with a praise-worthy attempt at sounding casual. "I would think it ought to be called the Heart Failure."

"You didn't even blink," he countered. "I had no idea envoys saw action. What happened?"

She took the salve pot, and walked away to perch on a rock, which gave her something to do with her hands, and her eyes, as she reined hard on too many sensations. Feelings. She fingered bit of salve. It was slightly gritty, and smelled bitter—willow bark was certainly a component, and hemp—but not unpleasant. As she reached over her shoulder to rub salve along the dully throbbing new skin, she said, "It was a mission that ended badly."

"Are there so few envoys in Sartor that they'd send you on another so soon?"

"I volunteered," Liere said, and at the question she glimpsed in his face, "and Atan didn't know about this stab wound."

"Atan?"

"The Queen of—"

"Sartor?"

Too late she realized she'd let Atan's heart name slip out. Would a lowly envoy know that? Maybe. Use it? "We all call her that," Liere said, a little desperately as she pulled on her summer robe and began doing up the ties.

His back was turned. He rammed the blade back in its sheath, dropped that next to the horse tack, and then loped down to the stream and submerged himself, clothes and all.

The fraught moment dissipated, leaving Liere scolding herself for witlessness. All very well to enjoy the fire, but not if she was going to let her wits burn up. She cast a troubled glance down at Andri, who straightened up, his yellow hair smacking against his back, splashing water everywhere. His shirt plastered to his skin, translucent enough for her to admire the play of muscle, and even to make out the puckers of scars here and there. Yes, he would know all about the state of healing cuts—and how to place them.

Time to get her mind in order. She turned away to see to the horses, while he submerged himself again in the runoff from the mountains, the chill shocking his focus from saddle-wood to his wooden brain. Worst time to have his mind in a fog of lust! Though it was true that he and Gared continually tested their followers by catching them by surprise (or asleep) with the roundly hated Wake-Up, this was the first time he'd done so without warning.

It was a test, but it was also a tease—and he was the one who got burned. He was never going to stop seeing how her golden eyes had flicked open, then in two tight parabolas— the center point her hips in those soft cotton-linen under-things that both revealed and concealed, the straight line of her long golden braid a counterpoint—she struck back.

Where to go from here? Usually he knew perfectly well, and it would be fun for both parties, but he was as uncertain as a boy again. There was not just a mystery here, but a quality he had never before encountered. Though he had learnt its opposite.

It's just that the timing was so very wrong. Or possibly right. But he could not take a wish, which got stronger every day, for real.

He surged up from the water again, to find her seated neatly on a rock, both horses saddled, and munching a breakfast of oats.

"Ready when you are," she said, settling her hat on her head.

He sloshed out of the stream, knowing that he'd be dry by the time the sun topped the trees on the other side of the river. "We can gnaw the last of the bread, or wait until we reach Zivhan, probably by mid-morning. It's nothing more than a trade town, but being at a crossroads, it's got a very good inn."

She agreed, he pulled on his waiting socks and boots, slung on his baldric, clapped on his hat, and they were soon riding.

"We've got a long day's ride ahead, and I'm curious about your last mission," he asked. "I recognize that state details probably can't be shared. And I probably wouldn't know the names even if you said 'em."

She was going to demur, but then she thought, why not? Geth-deles was a world away, and here was a chance to get a new perspective on her actions—leaving out the magery. It might be interesting, and enlightening, and it would put off the chance for any more personal questions.

"I'll make up names, to protect the innocent and the not-so-innocent," she said, which would explain kingdom names he'd never heard of. She only altered Daumnek-Pol Leteur's sea guild into the local scribe guild, avoiding possible questions about why sailors would get involved in government disputes: she did not want any questions that would lead toward Geth-deles being a two-mooned world made up of island archipelagos.

She also tried to edit herself out of it as much as possible, in an effort to sound more neutral, but he had been reading and making and listening to reports his entire life, and successfully fitted her right back inside the elided bits.

Sometimes they got sidetracked, the longest when Andri

described the similarities and the differences between that corrupt government and what Andri knew of Adon-Marsael's. Talking that over carried them into the trade town, where they got a meal, and continued while moving dishes about on the table to illustrate their points.

But when Liere reached the end at last, she fell silent for a time, then said, "The wound happened when I tried to rescue a friend's brother from an assassin. Who could have killed me, but said he did not have orders, and so he put me out of commission, as you said."

Her even, detached tone did not quite mask her deep regret. Andri sensed it, but made no direct reference to that, or to his sudden, fierce desire to find said assassin and gut him. Instead, he turned the talk back toward the scribe guild and their quest for an honest government, which led them onto the subject of opinions of ordinary people.

Liere had been finger-combing and rebraiding her hair, her hat tucked under her thigh, as they rode. He looked from that hat to the curve of her thigh and away as she dropped the braid behind her, then asked, "I notice you don't favor the freedom movement's idea of voting, but in all other regards you seem to want the views of the water carriers and dock workers, am I right?"

"You are. I don't think voting is ever going to work," he said, doing a sweep of the countryside: no rising dust of a posse, no sudden upward flights of birds disturbed by someone lurking in the underbrush. "I should not say ever. It won't work now, because too many people don't understand what it means, that it isn't a choice for the moment, like what to eat, or who your next flirt might be. It's choosing for life. Ideally. I really thought that Honor Parion would be the only true choice for her own faction, but a lot of them, it turned out, just liked the idea of airing their opinions, or following the lead of their friends."

"How was the vote accomplished?"

"How else? You go stand before your candidate—all lined in a square—and be counted."

Liere nodded, and said slowly, "There is such a thing as crowd moods. Haven't you seen that? Why not use the guild method? Surely your own guilds do the same. Vote with colored sticks put into a box, and then counted?"

"But guilds know their own numbers, so it's harder to get

away with adding extra sticks. We talked about that. Paper, too. Many cannot read, but don't want to be left out. The candidates facing everyone, and voters standing before them, seemed fairest. Open. Everything seen. But, yes, I know crowd moods. People clumped with friends to clamor for the youngest, the handsomest, the one who promised free beer, or other impossible things."

"Like?"

"Like taking over Sles Adran, and moving the capital here. He made a rousing speech, all about loyalty and togetherness and the great future of Enaeran. Oh, the cheering at that! It sounded very fine, but no one listened when we asked, how, how, how, sounding like a hooting of owls."

He gentled the horse, who had spotted a grass snake and sidled worriedly. "People—our people—it seems, mostly follow a leader. If there has to be a leader, why not me? Living the life I have, I believe I'd look out for the water carriers and the messengers and the miners. I mean to. I don't believe Cousin Adon will."

Liere said, "Was it Gared and his father who caused you to begin listening the voices of the common people?"

"In a sense."

"How is that an answer, in a sense?"

"You really want to hear it?"

"I do."

"All right, here goes. Around that time . . . things . . . happened, keeping most of us, ah, me, in hiding for a time. When I rejoined the rest, it was to discover that harvest time was on us, and we were facing winter with nothing stored, and scarcely a coin between us. Bassl pointed out that there were nobles looking for hires to pick crops. I said I'd do it, somewhere I wasn't likely to be recognized, and asked for volunteers. We figured it would be a lark."

Liere remembered laboring in the Ones' garden. "That must not have lasted long," she commented.

"Ah, the work wasn't hard, no harder than obstacle runs and drills all day. Tedious, more like. But as I worked alongside commoners from all over, I listened to them talk about what was going on in the capital. Most didn't care whose ass farts on the throne. That was cold water in the face! The people are so weary of troubles in the capital, they don't care who rules, they just want whoever it is to leave them be."

"I am not surprised," she said.

"One old geezer was quite bitter when he said that whoever an army is led by, they still trample fields, sometimes steal — it's called foraging — setting the farm folk back so they suffer another tough winter."

"True," she said soberly.

"So, 'in a sense means 'going to pick crops and then talking to them, not something noble-born people think of doing. I already knew what Gared's father had said about all people having a right to be protected. Listening during the harvest work brought words to life, I guess I'm saying."

"I see that."

"It's the real reason I've been trying to win over the factions. Find out what they want. Figure out a way to get it to them. Isn't that what Master of Horse Inmael meant? Nobody else is doing it. Certainly not Adon Marsael. He's too busy entertaining the nobles, and pushing all his conscripts to cross the border into Sles Adran, so we can 'forage' there. And those who refuse get shoved in the mines, which haven't been repaired in generations."

Close the mines, she wanted to say, do you really need more steel? But she remembered saying that to Senrid, a long time ago. *Tell that to Norsunder*, he'd retorted. *Oh, yes, and Perideth. Oh, and our frisky neighbors to the north, who used to be part of us.*

Few things are more unwelcome than an outsider giving helpful advice on how to fix generations of conflict. Her part, she decided, was to listen. And to learn, and besides, she knew from the burn along her eyelids that she had had fewer than four hours of rest, and he had had none at all. Nobody thinks well when tired, no matter how determined. How passionate.

She paid for the meal, bought some extra to be eaten later, then they departed. The horses were slower after half a day on the road, but neither of them noticed. They were both too tired for much conversation, both thinking ahead, and arriving at no conclusions except that he didn't want her to leave, and she didn't want to leave. But who was she? And who was she to be?

Riverland, forest, a hilly region outlined by low, mossy border walls, all passed with scant notice. When the sun dropped at last beyond the western mountains and the long summer twilight began to blue, Andri said, "Tomorrow we'll reach Otobris. We may as well camp now. Spare the animals."

She agreed with some relief; travel on Geth was more often by boat than horse. She had been doing small exercises to relieve aching muscles, but that added to little sleep was beginning to tell.

This time it was she who unpacked their provisions while he saw to the animals. Her hand checked when it encountered a dusty bottle of wine. She had not added that. He must have got them to add it when she was finishing her meal.

Why not?

She was grown now, and no longer in training. She could drink wine if she wanted to. Who was to stop her? Though as she pried off the waxy seal, she still felt a little as if she were still playing the role of a grownup, pretending she knew what she was doing.

"We don't have cups," she observed when Andri had washed his hands in the nearby spring-fed pool, then sat down.

"Cups?" he repeated as if he'd never heard the word, and shifted over to be in arm's reach before taking a swig. Then he held out the bottle to her.

This was a first! Perhaps, she thought as she took a swallow, feeling adult is encountering one new thing at a time, things that adults do. Then the taste hit her—sweet and tangy and mellow. It burned pleasantly going down; two more sips and she was already breathing against an agreeable headiness. Definitely time to eat!

The rice with bits of grilled fish wrapped in cabbage rolls warmed nicely over the firestick. She discovered she was ravenous. They ate all that, mutually agreeing to save the round of nutbread and the boiled eggs for the morrow.

They talked about the Wake-Up—Andri described the time Gillor reached for a broom instead of his sword and began swinging that twig side out—and another incident in which Fronsa catapulted up and decked Gared, then dropped straight back to sleep, without remembering any of it. Then he tried to get Liere to talk about her own training.

She gave him a general description, with lots of detail about specific assignments, but nothing about how much training Sartoran envoys got, or what she had been trained for. It was so, so, so, *wonderful* to be just another Liere, or

Liara, as they pronounced it here, to be accepted for herself.

They laughed and drank, wine and that heady sense sharpening her focus so that she shut out all else but him, the starlight molding his strong bones, the casual strength in his arms, the generous curve of his lips. The taut lines and promising curves of a masculine body, *his* body. The older girls among the Ones had told the younger girls that getting the first time out of the way with a good friend was the easiest—and many had offered to be that friend to those who sparked to girls.

Liere had liked her fellow Ones, some a lot, but no spark happened. It really wasn't all that much of a spark when Dak made his endearingly fumbling speech, but she'd taken the opportunity just the same, because friend he certainly was. And though it was a little awkward, sometimes hilarious, it had proved to be satisfactory to both.

But that pleasant sense was nothing to the river of fire coursing through her blood now.

She watched as he set the bottle on a rock with meticulous care; someone would surely come along and appropriate a good bottle.

"Tomorrow," he said. "My errand should take no more than an hour. Though it'll be faster if you go with me."

"Oh?"

"What I'm trying to say is, you can wait beyond Otobris's border wall if you like. Gared would. He won't go there."

"First tell me," she said, then bit mildly numb lips. "Why your errand would be shorter if I am there?"

"Thadara might spare the usual lecture," Andri said with a grin. "Oh yes. Against that, I should mention there's always the danger of her father seeing me, in which case we'll be on the run. He hates me. Eh, he hates everybody, though he'll bow to Adon-Marsael if he can gain promotion to duchas. But me, he hates, because he knows he'd never control me."

"Ah," she said. "Why would I sit out, if there might be a chase?"

This was so in line with his own sentiment that he laughed and leaned over to kiss her. She tasted the wine on his warm lips, and then returned his kiss with wine-fueled fervor. Her head floated pleasantly somewhere between her shoulders and the stars as they spread her blanket on the grass.

And then, for them both, the sun exploded.

Pleasure was ephemeral, a delight to get and to give, and if laughter lingered, he accepted the gift. He had never before met and matched with one whose passion, wide open to the flood in the realm of the spirit, drenched the senses, making every breath a caress. At first she was slow, exploratory, thoughtful, and he reined himself, very like holding the breath at the bottom of a lake until he nearly couldn't bear it— but then came a cataract of pleasure so intense it nearly obliterated him.

For Liere it was the same, heightened by wonder; she, unlike him, was experienced with the way Dena Yeresbeth intensified sensation, but never before in sharing, in pairing. When at last she spiraled down from the heights, there was that delicious sense that she had truly stormed the door that had been closed, and in discovering an entirely new wing, had left behind the last, cramping bindings of childhood.

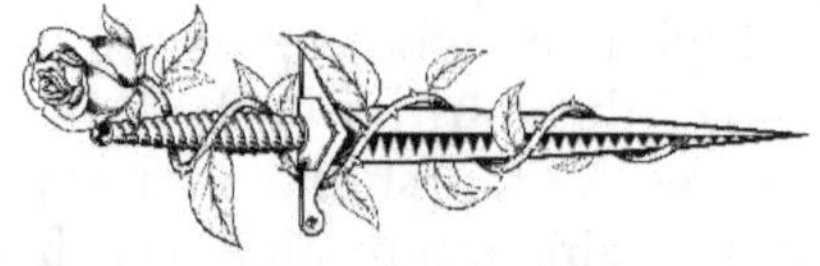

THIRTY-EIGHT

iere woke to the exhilarating sense that all the world had been made new.

Early as it was, Andri already had the horses saddled, finishing their breakfast. She wondered if he had slept at all.

After she splashed herself clean in the stream, he offered to rub salve into her cut. She pulled her braid over her other shoulder, sensitive to his touch, which was gentle, the salve numbing.

They gobbled down the boiled eggs and then broke the stale bread, each keeping a piece to gnaw as they rode into the bright morning.

Andri, it turned out, had friends in Otobris — unknown to the baras, of course. "The blacksmith here is married to the sister of Bassl's favorite tutor. They'll hide the horses for us, but we'll have to hoof it from there."

"I could use a good run," she said.

He laughed. "So could I."

The morning was cool, for once, even cold in the shadows, the first promise of the winter to come. Liere had learned to relish a good run once she settled into the rhythm, though she disliked running in hot, muggy weather. Which was the case a good deal of the year on the island where she had lived for over four years. She had become inured to it; a run, like this, through bracing air, was exhilarating, making her feel that it was good to be alive.

They ran side by side, keeping a rhythm — his steps a little shorter, hers a little longer — neither speaking until the forestland gave way to a vast garden that appeared to be generations old: smooth lawns marked by picturesque or aromatic trees, and gardens planted with an eye to seasonal blooms.

Now and then they caught side of the baras's vast palace. People in Enaeran, it seemed, had been going in for great houses for the past several generations. The sight of this highly decorated palace that housed two people and the servants who tended them threw Liere back to her father's utter disgust at the arrogant waste of nobles' vast manor houses in Imar—some very old indeed, including one that apparently the Fer Eiders were in some way descended from. Her father had been very bitter about that, but no one had dared to ask what story lay behind it.

The closer she and Andri got, the more the Otobris palace reminded her of Imaran palaces, even with scaffolding along one side, where artisans and workers were busy adding more statuary to the roof line.

They slowed to a trot, then a walk, as Andri led them along dips in the landscape, until they reached the back garden where foodstuffs were grown, the whole masked by walls of trumpet lily vines to spare the eyes of the noble pair should they go walking.

It also kept unwanted visitors from being discovered.

"There are exceptions," Andri said low-voiced as they approached the house, "but mostly her servants like me, and her father's hate me on his orders. Anyone who has stayed with him this long is committed."

They entered through a window someone had left open, and then began a long journey through what appeared to be an endless set of hallways set at right angles around courts.

She thought Andri knew where he was going until he paused at an intersection, turning his head from side to side, his eyes closed. Scanning on the mental plane. Ordinarily he kept a tight mind-shield, but it was gone now. He could not move and scan, nor could he send out what she thought of as tendrils, that is, scan very carefully from behind a mind-shield.

: *I thought you were familiar with this place?*

: *Been here twice. It's their house on the ridge I know.*

His shield closed, and he turned to the right.

One more turn and he paused before elaborately carved double doors, then opened one. Liere entered at his shoulder, with a clear view of the young woman reclined on a divan on the other side of the room, a scattering of books, a lap desk, pen and ink set aside. Because she was behind Andri, who blocked all of her below the eyes, she could see without being seen for a heartbeat or two. Thus she saw Thadara Otobris's expression brighten to surprise and lip-parted delight—and then immediately shutter when Liere came into view.

Did Andri see that? No, for he was talking as he looked down at the scattering of books. "What are you reading?"

"Nothing earlier than last century," Thadara drawled, wishing she'd worn her pale violent morning robe with the long ribbons. Far superior to the dull, unfashionable thing the shopkeeper's daughter was wearing. The gorgeous shopkeeper's daughter. Andri was so predictable in his low taste. "Yes, I know you keep mining the old archives, though I cannot imagine why. Especially the foreign ones." Thadara gave a fair approximation of a shrug, though Liere could see a vein beating fast in her neck. "But you're always going to do everything least likely to help your cause, are you not?"

Andri grinned. "Bracing as ever, I see. If ever you say anything kind, I'll be worried that you are ill."

"I *am* ill," she retorted. "Of boredom. But officially, I'm retired to recover from an unstated illness. Isn't that absurd, when the entire court saw Dear Adon send me away? But in court, we are 'sick' if we are exiled. What do people do when they truly are sick? Claim to be exiled?"

"Recuperating, probably," Andri said, perching uninvited on the low oval table carved with running foxes around the edge. "You met Liere, did you not?"

Thadara had been ignoring Liere until then, though patches of dull red on her cheeks betrayed her irritation. "I thought you returned to Sartor," Thadara said to Liere. "What made you throw in your lot with Prince Pirate here? No, I can guess," she drawled, her tone ripe with innuendo.

As a cutting remark it failed, and not because a part of Liere's reason for staying *was* her interest in Andri. Thadara Otobris had no mind-shield, and her emotions blasted like discordant trumpets on the mental plane. Beneath the frustrated longing and lively irritation was hurt, and at the top driving ambition.

Liere felt sorry for her, but gone were the days when she would bow to those who were nastiest to her, as if she deserved their opprobrium. "I might be able to help," she said.

"How?" Thadara shot back.

"That we shall see."

"She's going with me to my sister's for starters," Andri said.

"Your sister's! Why ever would you do that? Especially now?"

"Especially now because Cousin Adon had put out the entire guard to drag Shiovhan to find me."

"He'll wring it out of your . . . followers." Liere, and Andri, heard the word "rabble" that she barely suppressed.

"Oh, they dispersed as soon as I left. He won't find any of them. My guess is, once he fails to by today, he'll use a couple days more to search the surrounding countryside."

"But Martan is so far away!"

Andri lifted a shoulder, and Liere understood that, though Thadara was a part of his plans, she did not know the whole. Did anyone, besides Gared?

"I'm going to beg her for diplomatic support, though I doubt it'll be much good. But if she listens, I'll try to turn that into gold, which will help very much."

"Diplomatic support is a terrific idea," Thadara exclaimed. "Though you're going in the wrong direction. Martan can't do anything for you, even if they want to. But Sartor can. Why aren't you there? I presume she could even get you past the lowest layers." Thadara indicated Liere with a dismissive hand.

"Because I'm here," Andri said patiently. "In hopes of getting Parion's address from you. I want to plead my case in person."

"Oh, her," Thadara said irritably. "I tried. Believe me, I tried. She's a lost cause."

"Even so."

Thadara rattled off the name of a street in a village, a quick mental image with her words conveying to Liere a sense that the woman lived near the great river, close to the city. "But you don't need her, Andri. You really don't. What are you waiting for? Everyone in court, except for Dear Adon's particular followers—my respected parent included—is on your side, or at least neutral. But how long will that last if you don't do something?"

"A lifetime," he replied gently. "Or it's not really loyalty, is it? Prudence, at best? I know, I know. I have a few things to settle, as I've said. And then I will."

Thadara's response to this not-quite-snub was to launch into a knowledgeable description of whom he could rely on among the nobles, and those not to be trusted. Surely Andri already knew all that. Liere understood that she was being shut out, and waited patiently, her mind running back to the beginning of the exchange—specifically Thadara's demand that Andri act soon.

Devea's casual words a few days ago lit up in Liere's mind, like the sun coming up over a shadowy landscape, revealing the details hitherto shrouded. Unlike Sles Adran, which had several large cities besides its age-old capital, Nente, Enaeran had one city of size: the capital. There were numerous trade towns, and countless villages, but Enaeran did not have the population Sles Adran did, according to Atan.

What that meant in political terms was, whoever held the capital effectively held the kingdom. So, if a good part of the courtiers living on the ridge were in favor of Andri's reclaiming his father's kingdom, and if the city below was behind him, then what *was* holding him back?

Did all these nights spent in the royal archives have anything to do with this question? Liere had gained the sense that he was aware that his education, at least in state matters, had ended when he ran away to live with Gared and his father, but one would think if he was trying to catch up, it would be modern works he'd seek out, not long-outdated scrolls and the like—

". . . had better go," Andri said, rising.

"Help yourself to my father's gold. In that chest, right there. He'd hate knowing he was contributing to your welfare."

Andri flashed a grin.

"I don't suppose you'd use some of it and get something to wear that is suitable to your rank?"

"When the time comes," he said cheerfully.

Thadara hissed a sigh. "Take a couple of my horses as well. They're fast."

"Battleax is fast enough," Andri replied, still cheerful, and turned to Liere. "Ready?"

She extended her hand, then gave Thadara a polite bow.

"I suppose the diplomatic visit was your idea?" Thadara addressed her directly, and when Liere hesitated, she added, "At least you're not stupid. I've been trying to get him to go to Sartor for years. Or even his ancient relations over the mountain, though the Marloven reputation is terrible. But that might actually help through intimidation. Anyone," she stated, "but Bartal na Shagal of Sles Adran. He's a snake."

Thadara picked up her lap desk and dipped her pen with a jab.

Andri led the way out, and they retreated along the same labyrinthine path they had arrived in.

As soon as they reached the cover of the trees beyond the garden, Andri said, "Thank you for accompanying me."

"You used me as a shield," Liere observed.

"For that I apologize. Hoped you wouldn't notice."

Liere considered the matter; it seemed her presence had prevented a far more unpleasant confrontation. "She did raise a very good question."

But Andri did not ask for the question. He bent his head, and for a short time the only sound was the crunch of their footsteps in the duff. Then he said, "What do you know of magic?"

Magic? A pang of surprise so sharp it was almost painful. "Why do you ask?"

He looked at her, surprised. "We always hear about Sartor and its ancient magic. There's even a guild for mages there. A school."

"All true." She modulated her tone.

"Enaeran has had a difficult relation with magic in this kingdom," Andri said. "Our history makes some of it clear. I was very surprised when you turned up, from Sartor because of that history."

"Oh?"

"There used to be a number of mages, doing all the things that we have to hire them in to do now. One reason why only the wealthy can afford cleaning frames, though I've heard that ordinary people have them in Sartor."

"True."

"They even send letters by magic."

"True again," she said, aware of the slim golden notecase in the inner pocket of her robe.

"Did you know that one of my ancestors issued an

invitation to all the mages, to host a convention to share knowledge. He gave them a magnificent chamber, set with comestibles and comfortable chairs, made a great speech of welcome and led the toast with spiced wine. All their cups were dosed with enough white kinthus to kill them. No mage would come to Enaeran after that."

"Was there a reason for something so terrible?"

"Politics." He sighed. "We . . . ah, there's the smithy."

They found the horses rubbed down, saddled, and waiting; they didn't linger, and began to withdraw along a different route than they'd come.

Once they were well away from any domiciles, as the horses picked down a steep, mossy bank to a stream, Liere said, "Why did you ask about magic?"

"What," he called over his shoulder," are the limitations of magic? Are you taught that? You must know something about it, having brought those magical items that restored the fountains, and the one that made our rain barrel drinkable."

"Limitations in what sense?"

They splashed through the stream, then her horse stumbled on a slippery pebble in the reeds. Liere jolted, as Andri reached over and grabbed her horse's bridle. "Duck."

The word had scarcely left his lips when an arrow hissed by Liere's ear, and thunked into a tree.

Andri ripped his sword free, wheeling his horse. A second arrow shot toward them—this time Liere heard the creak of the bow that she'd missed before—and he struck it out of the air.

"Ride," he said, smacking her horse's rump.

She bent over its neck as the frightened animal surged up the opposite bank and bolted between the close-growing trees. Hoofbeats thudded behind her, Andri at her horse's tail.

A short distance on, the crashing of branches and trees heralded two riders coming at them from the right. Liere brought her sword out, guiding the horse right-handed as Andri pulled Battleax back and bolted up on her right.

The attackers split, one to each. Liere had not trained long at fighting on horseback, but at least she was seated, so she did not have to keep track of her own physical movements while scanning for the attacker's intended moves. Fueled by fright, she whipped her sword in a bind, and jabbed her tip into the attacker's upper arm.

Just as his hand flexed in reaction she yanked, and his sword flew off into the underbrush. She glanced. Andri was turned her way, his assailant having fallen off her horse, cursing as she clapped a hand to her thigh, her horse running off.

One last glance the other way. Liere's attacker had circled to help his partner, then they were obscured by trees as the main pursuit caught up with them. Liere and Andri raced neck and neck as soon as they cleared the forest. When they reached one of the low boundaries, and both horses sailed over it, the baras's pursuers were forced to hedge off.

They rode on for a time, halting when they crossed a trickle of a stream. They let the horses water quickly, then urged them on at a much slower pace. "Are Thadara's horses faster?" she asked presently. "These two seemed splendid racers to me."

"No, she likes to think so. She rides hard," he said, with a slight head shake. "Like her father. I wouldn't let her near Battleax."

Liere winced, and a silence fell. They stopped once again to water the horses, and then set out at a walk, Liere's mind running through that strange conversation, and then moving toward the prospective journey. They were a long way still from Martan, even before they reached its mountains, and hadn't there been a sizable lake up there as well? That would have to be ridden around. Did he know how long it would take? Should he be gone that long?

Why . . .

Oh, so many questions. She looked over to ask the first, to discover that Andri had fallen into reverie. No, he had fallen asleep sitting up. His head bobbed with each step Battleax took, his face slack, the marks under his eyes pronounced. He hadn't slept the previous night, either, as far as she could tell; she remembered hearing him splashing in the stream but she'd been too drowsy to wonder long at it.

How many days had it been since he'd slept?

She couldn't answer any of those questions, but there was one thing she could do: cut the length of this journey. She dropped a little back, and retrieved a couple of silver coins, which she held on the side away from him. Trusting to the noise of the animals' hooves, she turned these into transfer tokens, then repocketed them.

Presently, as the sky clouded up, Andri woke with a snort. "We'd better find shelter. We'll have to abandon the north trail, and backtrack slightly, in the direction of the river. There's a good-sized trade town." He hefted the wallet of coins he'd liberated from Thadara's money chest.

"Does Baras Otobris have authority there?"

"It's part of Enash, and the Count is on my side. Partly, I think, because he really hates Otobris." Andri flashed a grin. "He might try to send a party. It's an easy guess we'd hole up there, unless they think we're heading back to Shiovhan. But if so they won't get far." He sighed. "I hope the blacksmith will be all right. He's the only one in Otobris, so that's something. Someone must have seen two extra horses and blabbed."

The sun rimmed the far mountains, and lightning blued the twilight, when they rode into the town. They chose the inn closest to the city center. Andri asked her to go order food while he arranged the stabling and accommodations.

She entered the common room, which was decorated with battered old shields on the walls. She chose a corner table with a clear field of vision, and two lines of retreat, one through a wide window and the other through the kitchen. When a sturdy child came to her table, she said, "We'll have two of whatever the day's plate is."

The child scampered off shrilling, "Ma! Two plates!"

Andri sat down across from her. "I've been considering the problem of distance. I've actually never been farther than Ovaish, which is a couple days' hard ride north of here. Making a run for Martan seemed excellent at the outset. Less excellent even before Thadara offered her opinion."

Liere leaned forward. "She seemed to think that your diplomatic reinforcement implies coming back with a borrowed army."

"I know. She has been trying to get me to do that all along. I haven't read enough history — I need to catch up — but even I can think of several situations in which neighboring armies invited to help pacify the people hammered said people into a veneer of peace and then settled in themselves. As if she didn't have Bartal's try in living memory!"

"I got the impression she regards the King of Sles Adran as particularly untrustworthy in that regard. In any regard."

"And she's not wrong. But bringing in anyone's army

would be, to me, a sign I've already failed. I see that as the turn in the road toward becoming my father." He sat back. "Truth is, I think . . . I believe I wanted to test my status with my sister. And perhaps my persuasive abilities. Alismira being a tough case in any sense. Stupid idea. Let's give the horses a rest tonight, and set out as early as we can. Shiovhan ought to be finished with the searches by the time we return. Cousin Adon will have riots on his hands if he pushes it much longer."

"There is an alternative." Liere slid her hand into her inner pocket, and laid her silver coins on the table. "These are called transfer tokens," she said. "You could say they are for emergencies, but I can use them at my discretion. They will take us by magic to a Destination. And back."

He frowned down at the coins as if he was having trouble comprehending this sudden break. "These can get us straight to my sister? And back again?"

"Yes."

"Horses, too?"

"Nothing larger than humans, and it does not feel good. Nor can one bring things. Or, only small things, and the jolt will be much rougher. Though things can be sent, but it's dangerous. Sometimes the things just vanish. But we will be fine, using these coins." She looked at those dark circles under his eyes; that nap he'd taken hadn't done much to repair them. And it could not possibly have been comfortable. "I suggest we get some rest tonight, and go in the morning."

"Why do you have two—oh, of course, for your little scribe, the cousin."

"Correct."

"I wish I'd known about your transfer tokens before," he said, then he smiled. "No. Take that back. I wouldn't give up our ride for anything."

Liere blushed, and he laughed, and blushed too. "We'll go in the morning?" he said, raising his eyebrows.

They went into the hired bedchamber hand in hand, and this second time was even better than before. But when it was over, and she was ready to curl up beside him and sink into blissful rest, he rose, and kissed her softly, and said apologetically, "I have to go. It's . . . safer."

"Safer?" she asked drowsily.

But he was gone.

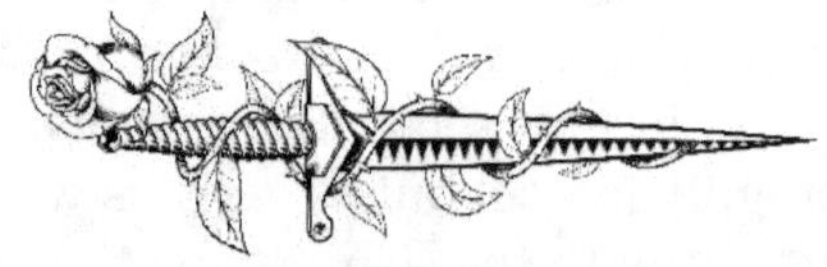

THIRTY-NINE

If sleeping apart wasn't related to the reason he hesitated about making his move against Adon Marsael—and for that matter, the mysterious murders—then she might as well go back and rejoin the first year girls on Geth.

She was fairly certain by now that these things were all related, but she knew better than to push. He did not trust easily. She sensed that he wanted to trust her. Something was keeping him back, and whatever it was cost him badly needed rest.

It was almost as if he was afraid to sleep. Which smacked of Norsunder if anything did. And yet she sensed nothing. And she checked every night before she composed herself to sleep.

Since she had this time to herself, though she craved her own rest, she forced herself to rise, send a tendril to check on Lyren-Sartora—whose non-verbal response made it clear she was playing a game in an attic room near the river, then she shuttered her mind-shield. Buoyed by Lyren-Sartora's well-being, Liere scrutinized the floorboards as a temporary Destination, and braced for long transfer.

When she recovered, she shivered in the still, cold air of her room in Bereth Ferian; here it was daylight. She dashed through her cleaning frame, grabbed more coinage and her nicest summer outfit of cloud blue edged with wheat-colored braided ribbon, then ran to the Destination chamber to look up Martan. If they had a scribe guild, they very likely had a Destination chamber. Even Enaeran had one, though it might have been built over. She would not attempt trying to locate it.

Rather than teach Andri about Destination patterns,

release spells, and all the rest of it, she worked Martan's Destination into the silver coins. Magic's complexities could come later.

That done, she braced, and transferred back to her inn room. Her head panged, and she fell gratefully onto the tumbled bed, dropping coins and clothing beside her.

As usual she woke as soon as the window began to blue with predawn light. She picked out the five distinctive Venn coins that she had chosen to form a better Destination, laid them on the floor, and worked that pattern into the coins for their return. Then it was time to dress. When she came downstairs, wearing the blue outfit and with her hair freshly combed, the innkeeper greeted Liere with the local honorific for young women.

Liere greeted her, asked that the room be kept as it was, and went into the common room, thinking about that honorific as she scanned for Andri. What turned a girl into a woman in the eyes of the world? In her own eyes? It didn't seem as simple a matter as age, though in more formal societies there were Flower Days and other coming of age ceremonies, then the wearing of different clothes. Hairstyles. Hats. Rings. All outer markers of status.

Perhaps assuming the outer trappings of adulthood was all it took. Look like an adult, you become an adult. Though she had had a visceral abhorrence of such old saws as "Turn a smile to the world and you'll smile inside" — those were too much like her father's annihilating *Smile when customers enter! They want to see you cheerful and ready to serve!* when Liere and Marga forgot humble faces. *The customer is always right*, he'd repeated, yelling at them until he was dark red in the face. *If the customer wants to kick you, then you did something kickable.*

She shook her head, willing away old memories. Why was that coming back? Thunder in the air, probably; her head panged briefly, and she was glad that they would be transferring soon. Only where was Andri?

As soon as she thought it, here he came. "I've paid up through tomorrow, so the horses will be fed and get some gentle exercise," he said. "I like the stable people here. It's clean, and both Battleax and Smoke seem content. What's for breakfast?"

Shirred eggs and elderberry jelly on pan bread filled them, then he said, "How do we do this?"

"It's considered rude to transfer in the sight of others, except in Destinations," she explained, and they left the inn.

He didn't speak until they found a narrow alleyway between two buildings, and stepped behind a stack of empty barrels. He said, "Destinations are . . ."

"Chambers where transfer magic will take you. Say 'Martan' three times while holding this coin, and the transfer will force you through a door in space to Martan's Destination. I'll go first so you can see what it looks like."

She held the coin on her palm, said Martan three times, and the magic seized her and flung her into Martan. She'd just taken the first shuddering breaths of recovery when Andri appeared, then staggered to the waiting bench, distinctly green in the face. 'Oh," he said. "I see why my ancestors hated it."

"It'll fade fast," she said, as a page came up to them with lister steep on a tray, and inquired who they were.

Liere said, "We request an interview with her majesty Queen Alismira."

Andri gulped down the steep, then grinned. "That actually worked! Tell Alismira that her brother is here."

The page vanished. Liere braced for anything from burly heralds or footmen stampeding to toss them out to a cold royal inspection; surprisingly quickly they were requested to follow a new page, who took them down a beautiful hall tiled in rose marble. Through double doors—"Look at me, going through the front door for the first time," Andri muttered under his breath—and they were presented to a tall, darkhaired woman whose resemblance to Andri was confined to the shape and color of her eyes.

She came forward, hands out. "Oh, Andri," she said, looking him up and down, taking in his long, half-laced shirt with the billowing sleeves, sashed low on his hips over saddle-worn loose trousers stuffed into equally worn boots. The battered hat he'd pulled off on entering the room. "You really are ragged, aren't you?" Her tone was not cruel. Her voice trembled a little. Then she set her hands on his shoulders, and pulled him into a hug.

He was stiff for a moment. Liere could feel his suspicion as she hastily pulled off her own hat, but Alismira Elsarion held onto him, murmuring, "I never thought I would see you again," then he relaxed enough to give her an awkward, tentative pat on the back.

She released him, then indicated cushions around a low table with a practiced, regal gesture. "Come. Sit. What brought you here? Are you on the run from Adon Marsael?" She pronounced the name as two distinct entities — clearly she did not think of him as Adon-Marsael n'Elsarion. "The rumors from the south have been disturbing. But not surprising. Of course he'd do his best to remove you from his ambitions."

"You know him?" Andri said, bewildered by this welcome.

"Indeed I do! He courted me assiduously when I was no older than your companion here. But at the same time he was maneuvering behind Father's back." She lifted a hand dismissively. "You must have come for something. It could not be to see me, for which I don't blame you. I was a wretch to you, I recall distinctly."

"You probably can't do much to help my claim to sovereignty, but I thought, ah, why not?" His tone was casual, but his eyes searched her face with silent question.

"Only the prospect of an army would do that," she said. "Which we don't have. You'd have to apply to our Marloven relations for that, to which I'd say, be careful what you ask for."

Andri raised a hand to wave off the idea. "I'm not that stupid."

Liere bit a protest back. Would a lowly envoy claim to have known the Marloven king for years?

"What I really need is money."

"For?"

"Nearly everything is ready," he said. "I want as bloodless a change as I can manage. Cousin Adon thinks he has the old guards, but he's been favoring his Marsael blue-tunics too obviously, and I know most of the captains, those who survived, from the old days. They will come back to us if they get regular pay."

"Look at you, little brother! You're ahead of where I was at your age."

"Same with the staff," he said, sweeping past her interruption. "Who can blame them for wanting a living in return for their labors? I'll also need to cover everyone until I can wrest the treasury back, but that's going to take some effort. Though I know where most of it is. Money would make things easier."

Alismira tapped a finger against her chin, then said, "When I married Edared, I brought a marriage portion through Grandmother. She left us each one, did you know that?"

"No," he said.

"Cousin Adon probably stole yours when he took the royal seal," Alismira said. "Father never trusted anyone but himself, so it was all kept in a vault beneath the palace."

"That much I know," Andri said. "I've been there. It's empty."

"I still have Grandmother's behest. I'd intended to save it for my children, but all things considered, I think it only fair that you get it. I don't need it. My children will inherit plenty from Edared's family."

Andri sat back, blinking. "That easy?"

"Easy?" Alismira gave him a crooked smile. "From what I hear, you probably don't know what easy is. Let's say that I think it just. Though rumors from Adon Marsael's court have you rampaging about murdering right and left—at the same time, chasing, or being chased by, every girl in the kingdom. Edared remarked that even the world's finest bedroom boytoy would scarcely find time for all that."

The joke might have brought out his husky laughter, but Andri's face shuttered at the mention of the murders; sensing that she had spoken amiss, Alismira turned to Liere. "And who are you, besides Andri's companion?"

"Liere," she said, bowing.

"She was the Sartoran envoy," Andri explained. "The idea about sovereignty was hers."

Alismira's good-humored smile Liere's way altered to interest. "Oh?"

"That, too," Andri said, answering the unspoken question.

"Let her speak for herself, Brother?" Alismira suggested.

Andri made a wry face. "Yes. Right. She's always so quiet . . . because I'm talking again." He looked up at the ceiling painted with stars, the marks of tiredness in his face very obvious, his cheekbones sharply shadowed. He was getting thinner, Liere realized.

Alismira lifted her voice. "Menrit?"

A side door opened, and a servant entered.

"Conduct my brother down to Secretary Fadin. He is to write a draft for the sum listed as 'dowry' and address it to Andri Malcolin Elsarion. Go with her," she said to Andri.

They went, and Alismira turned to Liere, and spoke in Sartoran—slightest dated, slightly stilted, but fluent. "He looks like a wreck. Why isn't he sleeping? Are you the bedroom girltoy in this duo?"

Liere shook her head. "He's been that way since I met him. His friends say he doesn't sleep. I saw that that was true, your majesty, but I do not know why. I don't know how he manages."

Alismira's eyes narrowed, making her look more like her brother. "What's going on down there in Shiovhan? The rumors are fairly wild, and the only aunt I trusted for the truth was killed in the recent troubles. Is Andri still close to his cousin Bassl?"

"He is, your majesty."

"Good. His mother was related on our father's side. The only one of the family worth anything, I sometimes thought. So, you taught Andri about sovereignty? Tell me about it."

"Not quite, your majesty," Liere said, trying to remain composed under Alismira's unblinking scrutiny. At least she was remembering her honorifics, and using the formal version of the verbs. "I only reminded him of a case in another time and place. Wherein a young king whose regency council was reluctant to lay aside their duties, though he was full of age, went abroad and was acknowledged formally by a neighboring ruler."

"That," Alismira said, "sounds rather like the sorry situation the young king of Colend is in. I hope he does something similar, though I suppose he'd have to wait as Midsummer is nearly on us, and the Colendi rulers always presides over the Alsais Music Festival."

Liere kept her face bland. It was not surprising that Alismira knew the situation in Colend, but it seemed she was not apprised of the latest news in Sartor.

Alismira leaned her elbows on her silk-covered knees, looking very much like Andri, as she said softly, sympathetically, "Who *are* you?"

Her gaze was steady, but the question there was almost suspicion.

There it was again, that question. Who *was* she?

Back was that earlier sense of absurdity at Liere's stated wish to be herself, while at the very same time she had been busy fashioning a persona. The truth was . . . the truth is, I am who I am, but I do not trust you not to just see the myth.

She was thinking that, but she was so tired, and still so bedazzled, the words slipped out, "Liere Fer Eider." Then she held her breath, furious with herself for the slip.

"I know that name," Alismira said slowly. "I remember reading that that remarkable hero had some spell that kept her in childhood. Yes? No? Your accent is not Sartoran," she added. "You speak it perfectly, but your accent is more like that heard on the other side of the Elgar Strait, more 'e' sounds than 'a's. You are her, aren't you! The girl who—"

Liere was too tired to lie, and she couldn't bear to hear those horrible words, *The Girl Who Saved the World.* "I am," she said hastily. She would be leaving soon, she reminded herself. The shackles of that old life would not attach to her again. "But Andri doesn't know. I don't want him to know," she said firmly. "I went away. Got some training. I'm trying to start a new life, without the expectations of that life."

Alismira sat back, taking in Liere's high, intelligent brow, the earnest golden gaze. She did not have Dena Yeresbeth, but she did have the sensitivity that was its first level. From the moment Liere walked in, Alismira had gained the impression that this beautiful young person was shielding her candle flame. Now she knew that the light was far brighter than one candle. "And you ended up in Enaeran, of all places?" She shook her head. "Life is so very strange, sometimes. I always thought you'd be replacing the queen of Sartor, or Chief Mage of the World. If there is such a thing."

Liere thought of Tsauderei, but she raised a hand in negation. "If there is such a thing, I've never heard of it. As for me, it was really only a matter of being in the right place at the right time."

"Oh, no. Oh, no, you won't get away with *that.* I remember you. I remember the horse of lightning. I wanted to *be* you. That power, which even intimidated my bully of a father, though he would never admit it. However, I do understand wanting a fresh start," she said in a different tone, her head to one side. "I got one when I came here to marry Edared. And I experienced a normal life for the first time. Has Andi told you anything about life among the royal Elsarion family?"

"Andri has not said much."

"I can assure you it was terrible. And if he didn't tell you that I helped make it terrible, he ought to." Alismira sighed. "There are all kinds of venoms in the world, but I learned that the most deadly is anger. It spreads one to another, and lingers, growing like an evil moss. And it's at its worst when kings and queens bare the fangs of anger, because their venom doesn't spread one to another, it spreads in the hundreds. More."

Liere nodded, not knowing what to say.

Alismira went on. "Here's what is even worse than that. I didn't know how angry I was."

Liere said with sympathy, "That must have been painful."

"Painful! Ho! I came here with court training. My mother had grown up in the court at Nente, spending days with the likes of the Duchas of Denwy, sister to King Bartal. Mother loathed coming to what she regarded as a backwater like Enaeran, but she saw to it that I left with perfect court manners. Style. Taste. Yet two years in, Edared said to me, this isn't working, and we must part, but he would give me this and that."

Liere shut her mind-shield hard against the battering of Alismira's residual emotions, the remorse and old grief.

"I said, why? He said, you're too angry. I said, I'm not angry! When have I lost my temper with you? I never have. For I had too much control for that! And you know what he said?"

Liere shook her head, her eyes enormous, steady, and compassionate.

"He said, Alismira, you *breathe* anger." Alismira sat back, her hazel eyes wide. "It took almost that long again to begin to see that he was right, and then it took even longer to begin to cure the venom. I looked at Andri when you came in, and I expected to see it. He has cause, and he looks terrible, but he doesn't whiff of anger. If anything it's fear. But not the fanged venom that I grew up with. And I am very, very sensitive to it."

"No," Liere whispered. "He's not."

"And that's why I'm giving him my marriage portion. He can do what he likes with it. But I hope he does get rid of

Cousin Adon, because *he* is very angry."

"Does he have cause?"

"Does he have cause?" Alismira looked toward the window, uttering a little laugh. "Of course he would say so. And believe it. Self-righteous venom is not like a recipe, seven apples, two spoons of honey, a pinch of cinnamon, a dash of flour, and bake into tarts that come out the same every time."

Liere said, "Yes, I see that. It was a foolish question."

"Not foolish, if you never encountered the like."

Liere thought of her father, angry, yes, but mostly frustrated that the world did not march according to his perception of proper order. She thought of her subsequent years frozen emotionally. As if she'd sleepwalked through most of it. Or rather lived a long nightmare, and so much of it self-imposed. "My experiences were . . . somewhat different," she said. "Your majesty," she added belatedly.

"Forget that. Not from you. If you don't have your own title, you should. No, I can see you're about to protest, and you did say you wished to begin anew. Ah, Enaeran is an excellent place for that! What with all the trouble, they know little of what happens outside their borders. Some don't know what happens outside their fine houses there on the ridge —"

Andri entered, waving a piece of heavy paper. "Talking about home?"

"Yes. And I was just telling her I trust that you will get rid of Cousin Adon." She had gone back to her home tongue.

"I intend to try," Andri said.

Alismira rose, and Liere did as well. "I would invite you to stay, but if you truly intend to circumvent his Midsummer announcement of his coronation come New Year's, then you had better get started." She held out her arms, pulled Andri to her, and murmured, "I don't deserve forgiveness, but I will try to earn it."

"Forgiven and forgotten," Andri said lightly.

Alismira then surprised Liere by holding out her arms to her, and she found herself clasped warmly in an apricot blossom-scented embrace. Then Alismira stepped back, her eyes bright with unshed tears. "Find out what ghost is riding him," she whispered. "You, I can trust."

Liere's throat hurt; she tried to think of what to say, but the servants were there, and Andri was thanking his sister, and promising that if he succeeded he would send word.

"I shall wait for it," Alismira promised.

Liere remembered her bow, and the page led them back to the Destination. Liere explained the pattern she'd made on the floor in her room, and they transferred back. Both fell onto the bed to recover, Andri chortling as he stared at the Letter of Credit, with its magical sved glittering at the bottom.

"Who would have guessed?" he said. "I had a bet going with myself whether she'd order me out again — back door for the likes of you — or sic the guards on me." His eyes were also bright as he stared at the paper in his hand. "She was such a surprise."

You don't know the half of it, Liere thought.

FORTY

"I can't believe we're going to miss the Music Festival," one musician whispered to another in Kifelian, Colend's language.

Her partner shook his head. "And miss the last of this adventure? We have next year, and the year after, and the one after that, and so on, to compete in the festival. But how many people get to pretend to be the heralds for a king? I plan on telling this story to my grandsons."

They passed below Thad, who ranged through the embassy, checking to see that all was ready for the dinner Shontande was hosting for Sartor's queen—just the two of them, his last gift before departure two days hence. Two days absolutely packed with grand events.

This last gift had begun as another grand event, a masquerade ball, and the big embassy ballroom was ready, but a few days before, Shontande had returned from another masquerade whose theme had been Famous Lovers. Shontande was dressed severely in black and white, his only decoration fine gold links at each wrist, with even finer chains looped gracefully to diamond rings at each longest finger. When Thad first saw Shontande appear dressed like that, he found the impression both compelling and intimidating: not many dared go as Prince Tivonais, who was reputed to have been beautiful, irresistible, and heartless.

Whatever message Shontande was trying to convey was apparently received by the Sartorans, though he danced all night, as always. "The masquerade is off," he'd said cheerily to Thad, as the first rays of sun blued the east windows. "I changed my mind. Invited Atan to a simple Colendi dinner, and she could not hide her relief."

Though Shontande had danced all night, he seemed to be impervious to exhaustion, for he knew he would soon be going home. He moved through his day, buoyed by a constant awareness of elation that did not diminish even when he thought of all the work awaiting him in Alsais. But it was work he wanted to do, longed to do—and dreamed of doing for years. He had been ruminating the order of the needs ever since Bee's private message that by the end of the second day of the three, the regents had vacated the royal palace in Alsais.

Bee had said, *They withdrew amid great parade, as if this had been the plan all along, though I suspect the scent of roses lingers in the air for a certain count and a certain duchas, even though the actual blossoms have been cleared away and everything scrubbed clean.*

An atmosphere of hilarity had overtaken the Colendi embassy—Thad's with a hefty dose of irony: he had finished renovating the embassy just in time for Shontande to be leaving it.

But then, Thad reasoned as he ran downstairs to check on the progress of the meal in the kitchens, living here for a while would be splendid recompense for him being stuck behind as interim ambassador, until Shon could get settled in Colend. And find someone trustworthy, who would also be acceptable to the queen.

Thad's old friend Nalisse had come at his urgent request to take over the embassy kitchen. She looked up at his entry, wiping her forearm over her brow. "It's all coming well," she said before he could ask. "All the molded delicacies are beautiful. We're readying the last stage—the foods that must go directly from preparation to service."

Thad wanted to take her hands—to kiss her—but she was still moving, and all the cooks were watching. "Thank you," he said, and raised his voice. "Thank you."

"It's not a simple meal," Nalisse could not help observing in a low voice. "It's authentic Colendi—in that everything is what we eat at home—but simple, it is not."

"Simple," Thad said, "for a queen."

Nalisse rolled her eyes. "Ah-ye, there is that. But I wonder . . ." She surveyed the beautiful dishes, many decorated with fresh flowers, or garnished with aromatic herbs. *What his purpose is?* She couldn't quite say it, because at home, most of these sweet and savory dishes, delights to all the senses, were the common language of the Chamber of Cranes. But it didn't do to say such things out loud when it came to kings and queens.

She shrugged her long braid behind her, and moved to examine a pail of eggs just brought in.

Thad took the hint, and ran back upstairs to inspect, for the fourth time, the inner chamber, in case its pristine state had suddenly and mysteriously transformed into a sty.

As he stood in the doorway reassuring himself, on the other side of the Grand Chandos Atan sat in a cool bath, reflecting on Shontande's invitation. "I can't promise you a grand spectacle such as this," he'd said, his diamonds flashing as he gestured round the brilliantly lit ballroom of black and gold marble, "but perhaps it will be a new experience? Everything will be Colendi — the food, the scents, the music."

The scents?

Atan didn't think anyone had ever mentioned scents when issuing an invitation. She found that intriguing, and even a little daunting; Sartorans were not ignorant about the communication of scent, and everyone appreciated spring flowers, or the first fresh breeze after a rain, and the like. But the Colendi, it seemed, had raised scents to an art, if not precisely a language, along with so many other things.

She'd meant in the few days since he issued his invitation to study up on what this or that scent meant (assuming she recognized it) but her tasks had overwhelmed her, right up to her recent, wearying interview with representatives from Mardgar Harbor. There was no time to — *play games* — she conscientiously amended that thought, even though she hadn't spoken it. There was no more time. If she got confused by some Colendi circumlocution, she would simply ask.

When the sandglass ran out, she emerged from the bath, flung a towel around herself, and padded to her private room, where she stood before the tapestry Shontande had given her. She had made a habit recently of looking at it each day — several times a day, as she passed to and fro, as always trying to discern the message below the surface.

"What you have to understand about Colend and their concept of melende," Rel had said before Shontande arrived, "is that it's not the same as honor. It's akin, in that integrity is bound in there, and trust, but in place of bravery or self-sacrifice in a military sense there is an emphasis on harmony. Melende means everyone leaves the room not just alive, but with their dignity intact."

Dignity intact. How did that translate with respect to this gift?

At first she'd regarded it as yet another ancient thing, but she sensed thought behind it. Maybe a message. What? The odd thing was, it never looked quite the same.

One morning she could have sworn that the roses were at the front of the garden, but somehow the roses appeared to be behind the starliss, and the sky, which she was very certain at one point had looked like pewter, was the pale eggshell blue of a spring morning just before the sun rises.

Her gaze turned toward the window, where the last of the sunlight slanted ochre rays, glowing in those rises and the many hues of the starliss, and then the obvious—Rel had noticed it right away—struck her: the tapestry changed with the light.

Ice flowed through her veins. She knew now what she was seeing. This tapestry was one of very few extant in the world, made by a secret process. Shontande Lirendi hadn't told her just how rare this was, and he could have justifiably bragged. But he'd left the discovery to her. Ancestors had written about the amazing tapestries whose colors changed with movement of light, not just through the day, but through the seasons.

Atan had spent her childhood caring for her own clothes. When she'd gotten old enough, she'd made them. Before then, she'd seen Gehlei at her loom, so she understood warp and weft. Ignoring her wet head, she bent close to examine the tapestry, and wonder bloomed within her as her eye traced along extremely fine threads of a multitude of colors and shades, brocade-weft, warp both visible and invisible, here lampas-woven, there embroidered in exquisite damask-stitch.

It was very nearly priceless, and depicting as it did Colend's first king—who possibly even modeled for it—made this gift more in the nature of a sacrifice.

No, it was more like an apology, one made from the very beginning.

Or was it?

She glowered at the depiction of her ancestor in the tapestry. "There wasn't even any Colend in your day," she said. "You couldn't have found him as confusing as I find his descendent. Could you?" Then she transferred her glower to Martande Lirendi. "Melende or no melende, we're going to have it in plain words tonight. Do we get our Music Festival back or not?"

A bell rang in the distance. Lay ready been laid out, but though it was another warm night, she discovered that she was tired of linen and lawn. She asked for her favorite outfit, a fine summer tunic and trousers of watered silk in her beloved sea green, the running patterns in the weave looking like shoreline ripples.

Her eyes met her chief maid's in the mirror. "See to it," she said, "that that tapestry is affixed to the wall, with the usual preserving spells layered over it. I don't think it's going to storage after all."

A short time later she left the palace and walked the short distance to the embassy, which was visible from the royal library windows. Her honor guard, wordlessly interpreting her desire to walk alone, paced in parallel at a respectful distance, turning away only when Shontande Lirendi came down to the front door to welcome her himself, instead of sending a steward.

He was not, she saw immediately, wearing diamonds and chains, or elaborate braids threaded with hard, glittering gemstones. His hair was mostly loose, except for the part bound up in a clasp that looked like a leaf or a feather. He wore flowing silk of complementary shades of very pale dusky rose.

"Welcome," he said, leading the way inside. "You have not been to Colend, so we thought we would bring it to you." She only had time to reflect that she had avoided this embassy under its previous incumbent, and then music gripped her attention. Women's voices rose, braiding three melodies into polyphony. The singers stood in the central garden, each holding light in their hands as twilight blued around them.

When Atan drew nigh, she saw that the lights were little candles set into lilies made of stiff paper. As she passed, each holder bowed, then turned to the pool along which they walked, and set the lilies floating. Servants holders on the other side of the pool opened their hands and paper globes rose into the air, so that the effect was a star field below and above them, the globes rising slowly toward the stars far overhead. Glowglobes set in crystal softly illuminated the courtyard around them, creating no shadows.

When they reached the other end of the garden, Thad was there waiting to greet them. "Everything ready?" Shontande asked.

"It is indeed," Thad said, bowing. "Welcome, your majesty."

Were Colendi really so informal? No, Atan thought. This was staged to create a casual atmosphere.

As if to corroborate, Shontande turned his head, giving a little nod to his singers, releasing them. "Come upstairs?" he said to Atan.

"Lead the way," she said, and then, catching the glint of gold at the top of his head, "That golden clasp. It's very elegant. What is that, a leaf or a feather?"

Shontande blinked, then said, "Ah-ye, the hairpin!" He reached up and pulled it out, as his hair unknotted and tumbled down his back. "Here, take it! It's made in the shape of a flame chestnut. I have a dozen similar ones. My cousin likes these, and invariably gives them to me for Name Day gifts." He laid it on her palm.

It was not a clasp at all, but a pin, still warm from his hair. She closed her fingers over it, very aware of how easy and graceful he was in pulling it out, and how intimate a gesture it was, in a curious way: she was hit with a sudden image of him in an intimate setting, how he'd elegantly shrug out of ornaments and clothes instead of wrestling with clasps, buttons, buckles . . .

She shook her head to rid herself of that image, and discovered that he'd already started up the stairs, as if the little gift were truly as ephemeral as a leaf on the wind.

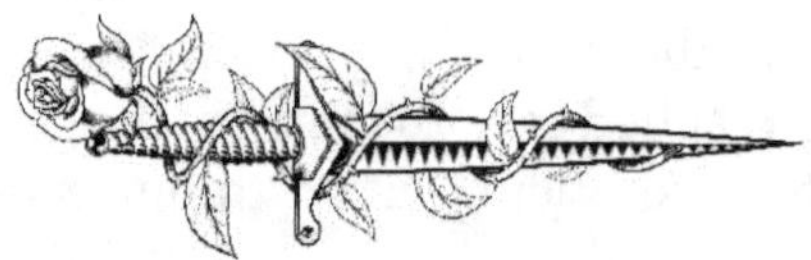

FORTY-ONE

Her instinct was to firmly place the golden hairpin back in his hand, then she remembered that Rel had said that Colendi gave gifts as a regular thing. Gifts on arriving, gifts on leaving, gifts to celebrate or commiserate gifts long-anticipated, gifts to surprise. Calculated and spontaneous. To refuse, would it deny melende? Or worse, would he guess where her thoughts had gone?

She spoke, trying for nonchalance, "I'm surprised you have any left. Surely others among the Sartoran court have admired them."

"I do have many, but—I know the fault is entirely mine—I do not find myself on a footing with your court, to share and to understand the sharing," he said over his shoulder. "Does that make sense? I know all the words in Sartoran. An excellent language, but very formal, or perhaps that is true only for those of us who grew up learning it in a formal atmosphere? One feels the weight of history in it, yes?"

"I certainly did when I puzzled over Ancient Sartoran," she said as she slipped the hairpin into her inner pocket.

"Times out of mind my tutor would take an hour to read a sentence, for each word, it seemed, would have meaning five centuries back, ten, even more. I recollect being six or seven and pitying Sartoran children younger than I was first encountering the term *morvende*, for the cave people I was never likely to meet, but being required to learn that 'fen' or 'ven' in Ancient Sartoran meant groups of people, and that those words might once have meant 'clan' but by the time the Venn adopted the word, the meaning had shifted to '*the* people,' connoting an elite group as distinct from 'tor' or the general rabble, and that morvende had adopted 'ven' before the Venn ever troubled the southern half of the world. Oh yes, and that they had added 'mor' which meant 'makers' but could also connote 'other'."

"You really had to memorize all that as a child?"

"I assure you, I did."

"I'm surprised you didn't loathe us from the outset," she exclaimed, relieved that the awkward moment had passed without notice. "I was taught by Tsauderei, and there were all the lessons in old meanings, but only when I asked. I thought of them as stories. There was little else to do, living in a cottage in a mountain valley."

"It sounds very peaceful," he said as they entered a room where a young woman waited. "Thank you, Nalisse. Is everything ready?"

She bowed to them both, and signaled to waiting servitors, all young, to bring in covered trays. The melody from below faded away, skillfully picked up by musicians plying strings and winds from behind a screen depicting a cloud of starlings caught in upward flight.

Food in Colend, Atan soon discovered, was light. Puffs, thin slices, layers, in small amounts, displayed like floral arrangements—often with actual sprays as decorative touches. "All the herbs can be eaten," Shontande said. "Some are quite acerb, but bracing after a complicated sauce. They clear the palate."

He kept up a flow of mild talk as she sampled the exquisite morsels on small dishes, the eating utensils really not much more than sticks with tiny tines on one end. They forced one to very small bites.

Scents there were, blends that made her heady even before she sipped the crisp, mellow golden wine. Shontande began by telling her amusing stories about the various dishes—where they came from, when he had first sampled this or that one—and then brought the talk around to gifts again. "We learn to make such things, human nature being in this, as in all things, unpredictable: the most fabulous and elaborate masterpiece made by a master can be valued less than a scribbled poem on a scrap of paper and slid beneath a pillow before departure, if the poem is fashioned for one person."

"Perhaps that sentiment is universal. Even if the poem is not very good?" Atan asked, picking up her wine, and then setting it down again when she realized her lips had begun to tingle.

"Even if the poets in fashion would unite in indifference. If it's from a beloved object, and the beloved sees self reflected in the words, it can become the world's greatest treasure."

"Is that not common to human nature, wherever we are born?" she exclaimed. "It certainly is not so very different from us Sartorans. Oh, I remember my first spring, when we were so very poor after a hundred years away, and war before that. Flower Day arrived that spring and all we had to give one another were flowers. Of course I was showered with garlands, each more elaborate than the last, but the one that I pressed between linen pages as a keepsake was the awkward one Rel made. His very first."

Shontande put his hands together. "That is exactly what I meant."

"Meaning," she said, biting her lips to restore feeling, "is not lessened for not being quantifiable."

"True," he said, leaning forward to pour more wine in that innocent-looking fluted glass, which she'd emptied how many times?

"No, I think I've had enough." She remembered belatedly that Colendi didn't say no, but he did not recoil, or even blink.

Instead he set the carafe down, and signaled with no more than a glance, then said, "My understanding is that in most lands that celebrate Flower Day at all, the meaning of gifts such as garlands is left to the adorers, whose codes of gallantry give narrative license." His hands flicked apart, a quick graceful gesture. "It is for them to appreciate the adored's manifold attractions. The adored in turn graces their efforts with reward, or with friendship."

"Such gifts," Atan said, thinking of that long-ago day, "I think are most successful when the meaning is understood between giver and the one gifted . . . ." She sidestepped the terms *adored* and *adorer*. Maybe the meaning was less intimate in Colend? ". . . not just understood. But the same meaning. Which is not always the case."

"Ah-ye, so it is, so very true. Meanings can be misunderstood, or rather intentions. Or missed altogether." He flashed a quick smile. "Like myself, who did not perceive immediately that lace is not worn in Sartor, and I must confess I took chill when I removed the lace from my formal robe. So carefully chosen, alas! My tailor will no doubt have to recruit himself with essence of hibiscus and steeped asterides."

So he had noticed that the absence of lace was an insult. Of course he had.

He laughed silently, and leaned over to touch his cup to hers. She caught a whiff of his scent, and stopped herself — barely — from breathing it in.

But she must have done something for he looked an inquiry.

"Your scent," she said, aware she was talking randomly. "It . . . is something only grown in Colend?"

"There are four scents," he replied. "Some wear more. I am more conservative."

"Four?" she repeated, intrigued.

"A drop of Endeavor to each wrist." He turned his palms out, the movement drawing her eyes down to his beautifully shaped hands. "A touch of Serenity below my right ear."

Her glance shifted; she stilled, caught by the soft sigh of his breathing.

"And Repose," he murmured, "at my left hip."

Her mouth had gone completely dry, and her heartbeat drummed in her ears, but below that she was aware of the rustle of her silk sliding over flush-fevered skin. She looked up to meet his steady gaze, and understood the gift he was offering: himself.

She understood now. Among the Colendi, gifts were simple: a golden hairpin, a night of pleasure. It meant little more.

And why not?

For a long moment, as the musicians played on, she remained poised between two choices: for the first time in her life, the vows she had made with Rel — so easily made — felt like constraints. Oh, how she had prided herself on the tranquility of her life, easily overlooking the attractions of anyone else.

She understood between one heartbeat and the next that until now, she had never been seriously tempted to break those vows. It would be so very easy to answer that unspoken question with a smile, even a look, and . . . She suspected that what happened after would be pleasurable, maybe even superlative. Young as he was, rumor was united about his mastery of the sensory arts.

She closed her eyes, trying to think past the intensity of sensory longing. The body's wants were direct, and simple. But she had read enough of her ancestors' writings to understand what happened when those longings rose to priority over duty, responsibility.

Vows.

The truth was, she was not Colendi, and to accept this gift would not be simple at all. For it would begin with the breaking of vows.

She opened her eyes. And though no word had been spoken, somehow it was possible to look away; he was no Prince Tivonais, collecting hearts the way his mother had collected diamonds. He turned to regard the person bringing fresh steep, who was dismissed with a nod, and he poured out the fresh brew into fine porcelain cups himself.

She sipped the steep. Its burn helped clear her head, and she sipped again, as he said, "I've twice now had occasion to walk the Napurdiav labyrinth, but I must confess, other than finding the morning air refreshing, and the ever-changing scene restful to the eye, I have, perhaps, not the wit or the knowledge to appreciate its further meaning? Yet further meaning I believe there is."

"Some," she said, relieved at so innocuous a subject, "merely think of four stations, but I think of four elements. The ground patterns, the stones, and the trees are not merely pretty patterns, though they are that, too. The Purrad represents a sense of safety for the dispossessed. There is harmony in the combination of water, ground, air, and also in the trees . . . Some regard woods as weird and frightening. They last beyond human spans. They extend past the boundaries of human culture. They intimidate us because they are great and imposing, but to those who look past that perceive the four elements that transcend and heal . . . Am I making any sense at all?"

"I think I understand. Sometimes we have to bring meaning to a thing before it can work, yes?"

Atan was thrown back suddenly to Peitar Selenna, who after his first walk of the Purrad had stood in the snow all day long, until night, unmoving. They still did not understand what had happened. Even Tsauderei was puzzled. But Peitar, whose friendship she still missed to this day, had been a person of still and deep waters.

Thinking about Peitar helped further clear her mind. "And sometimes it can strike someone with profound meaning that cannot be explained. One has to ask, did years of reading create the experience, or not?"

They went on like this until the steep was drunk, trading ideas about the ephemera of meaning, until she discovered the bell ringing midnight. Where had the time flown?

"I must return," she said. "I thank you for the lovely evening." He rose with her, and they began to walk downstairs.

Halfway there, she stopped him, and, remembering that he would be gone in two days, and he was not the sort to make dramatic public gestures, she said, a little sadly, "We are not going to get the Music Festival back, are we?"

He waited until they reached the bottom of the staircase, and it was only then that she remembered echoes. Clearly the wine fumes were not entirely gone from her head.

He drew her out into the soft summer air, not speaking until they reached the pool, where candled lilies still floated about, golden glows gleaming. In the reflected light his gaze was direct and so intense it caused a kind of glittering pain that Atan, sensitive this night in a way she had never before been, made her glad this young man was going home soon.

"Human beings," he said, "are absurd. You and I could put on the clothing of laborers and transfer to Goerael or Toar, and walk out, and people would ask if we were apple pickers, or something that requires tall people. Rel, of course, will be co-opted for the military wherever he goes, whether he likes it or not."

"That has already happened," Atan said. "As for me, when I was a child I lived in a one room hut, with two donated outfits, and a gown I made myself for the far-off day I might be a princess again. Our hierarchies are mirages."

"They are a game. A blood game, in some places." He glanced up at the stars, then back. "Have you looked at our Colendi history at the time Sartor vanished?"

"Of course—"

"Really looked," he asked gently. "Past the persiflage and pomposity? I know Sartor was beggared by war, but we were slowly eroding, and could do nothing about it. All along the west and south, the duchases promoted themselves to kingship in all but name. They mimicked our fashions, spoke our language, but flattered themselves into exalted states, and we either smiled and accepted—and imposed tariffs instead of taxes, as we could—to avoid wars we could never have won. So our baras, who insisted that that title was old and vulgar, coming as it did from leaders of war bands, were really doing the work of counts, a respectable title, and they consequently were elevated, and then the most ambitious counts could not possibly accept mere baras as peers, and so we ended up with nine duchas in a diminished kingdom. That was nine petty kings, all competing with one another. And then Sartor vanished after a devastating war, and two years of the Music Festival suspended."

Atan considered for the first time what that must have been like from the outside, two years of so important a festival let languish.

"It was actually the idea of my ancestor's ambitious younger sister. She had pretensions to musicality. And of course she presided. It also nearly bankrupted us, that first year. But by the second, she knew what not to do, what to do, and . . ." He held out his hands. "I would not be exaggerating to say that bringing the Music Festival to Colend saved Colend."

"So this long story," Atan said, endeavoring to keep her voice steady, "is a . . ." *Colendi* ". . . roundabout way of telling me that we will never get our Music Festival back."

"What I am telling you is that Sartor will always be Sartor. Its symbols and language are fundamental to our civilization, at least in the south, and I'm told the influence goes north most places as well. Whereas Colend is largely a state of mind we all agree on, exactly the same way we agree on duchases and counts and kings, though we are all born equally naked. And in the minds of the southern world, it has become the Alsais Music Festival. The city is now integral. That is part of its attraction now, for they don't come for just the music. It's the spontaneous concerts on the canals, the tasties sold by the roaming vendors, the theater of the streets as well as the stage, the parks and perfumed gardens."

He held up his hand, gesturing a graceful circle. "The entire city is a park. It, unlike most of our capitals, was never a fortress. As Senrid and Vidanric said, it is impossible to defend militarily. Likewise it will never be permitted to sprawl beyond the water boundaries, and so the competition to live there is ferocious. Any house—any shed—deemed to lack charm by its neighbors will likely result in exile from the city. So *everything* is art, wherever the eye falls. I wish you would come visit, and see for yourself."

"I know," Atan finally admitted. "People want to go to Alsais as much as they wish to attend the festival. This is what most of our visiting diplomats mean, but don't quite wish to say."

And saw the truth of it in his dropped gaze.

Not that she'd doubted, after noticing that the most passionate speeches in favor of returning the festival to Sartor were spoken by her own people. The other ambassadors (outside of that oily, unlamented Gaszin) had expressed sympathy that was more or less sincere, but she suspected that their instructions from home were just that, to sound sympathetic without promising support.

In short, though their ancestors might have liked traveling to Sartor every summer, their peers now preferred going to charming, perfumed, park-like Alsais.

He said, "To make certain, after my first night here, I had Thad pay an army of scribes hired from one of our neighboring kingdoms to go about asking people why they wanted the Music Festival. We had twenty of them here in Sartor, and twenty in Colend. I have a stack of results, if you would like to see it."

She raised a hand. "I suspect I know what's coming. Politics was a priority here, though everyone professes to like music."

"That was certainly a priority among the nobles, but many of your guilds expressed concern about where all the guests would be put: all the old houses belonging to the nobles in the old days have been filled since Sartor's return. The old stages are now shops. There are other logistical considerations."

"None of which they spoke to my face," she said grimly, but that was an old regret.

"At home, there are generations who have grown up around service for these weeks," he said. Those roaming vendors I mentioned? They are all singers or storytellers, and their tasties, as their snacks are called, have been refined again and again over the generations. Everything is art."

"Say no more." She raised her hand. "I understand. And

yes, though not this year. For various reasons, including a full schedule, but next year, I will come see what you Colendi have done with it. Thank you."

They bowed to one another, and the waiting guards took up their stances as she walked back.

Where she found Rel in her rooms. "You're back!" She walked straight into his arms.

"You're trembling," he exclaimed. "What happened?"

"Ask me in a couple days," she murmured into his chest, the edge of the golden hairpin poking into her rib; she knew it would always be a reminder. "But the short answer is, we lost the Music Festival."

"So why not start your own?" he asked, ever calm and practical. "It doesn't have to be Midsummer. Why not spring, or harvest, or even midwinter, when everyone needs diversion? Sartor, as you have said, does not have to be tied to its traditions. And somebody in your past started the first one."

It's not that simple, she was going to say, but then all the tension rushed out of her in a sigh. It could be simple. She had the power to make it simple, if nothing else.

"Hold me," she said, and he found that a satisfactory enough answer.

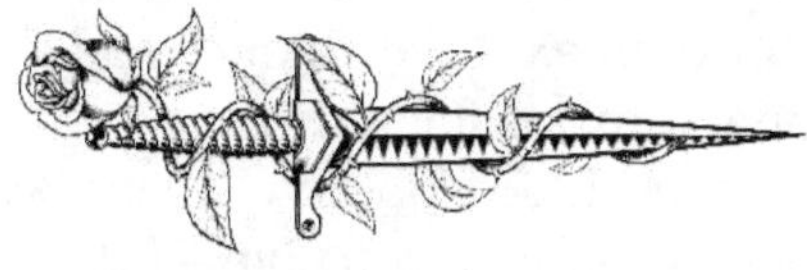

FORTY-TWO

Outside of Shiovhan, in Enaeran

When Andri turned to leave her that night, she caught his hand, saying as gently as she could, "Even if you are a kicker and a flailer when asleep, I don't mind."

He paused, his pupils huge and black in the light of the single candle. "I wish it was that easy," he said and reached for the door latch.

She tried once more. "If you think that there's danger because of Adon-Marsael or his followers, you've seen by now that I can handle myself. "She then remembered what Devea had said, and added quickly, "I'm not trying to be confining here. I'm perfectly happy sharing you with others you like, too, but while you are with me, I'd like more of your company. If you trust me enough by now to stay, or tell me why you can't?"

He stilled, and his voice was raw. "Valdon could handle himself, too. And Old Invor. And I trusted them both. But that didn't save them." Then he slipped away before she could say another word.

The next day, as they headed south, the subject remained unspoken, but very much present in her mind.

Andri often took out his Letter of Credit to admire anew, but glad as he was to have it, Alismira's change of heart seemed to be what he valued most. It became clear to Liere that possession of a small fortune meant little, except as a tool, a means to gain his end.

It was midday before he asked what she and Alismira had talked about while he was gone.

She had expected that question at the outset, and so had

had time to consider everything that was said. "She did not swear me to secrecy," she assured him. "I expect that what she said about your family would be nothing new to you. She did talk about her own experience once she left Enaeran . . ." And here she gave him a brief summary.

At the end he nodded soberly. "Once we're done with Adon-Marsael—assuming I survive—I'd like to see her again." A quick, rueful smile. "Nasty as that magical coin of yours felt, it was tremendously handy to go and to come in one morning. I'm surprised the world is not full of people popping in and out the same way."

Liere shook her head. "Two or three transfers like that in a day, and it takes a lot longer to recover. Too many and you might end up with nosebleed and a violent headache. Everything aches, right to the bone. And then it might be days before you can face it again."

"Ah."

"We're told our ancestors had a way around that, but it's been long lost, both the method and apparently the magic." She sensed that the questions very soon would shift from what she knew of magic's history to what magic she knew. Magic was not going to aid him in any way she could see, even if he knew she was a mage. Time for the subject that meant the most to him. "What can you tell me about your plan to remove Adon-Marsael?"

"Changing constantly," he said. "Probably change again as soon as I get a report on the past few days."

"Begin with the goal. To replace Adon-Marsael?"

"And limit the damage. Here's where it gets difficult."

"Let me guess," she said. "You can't let him know you want to avoid violence, because he feels no such constraint. Beginning with using hostages against you?"

"His favorite."

"And if you don't comply, you get the blame."

"He considers that elegantly neat." Andri cast her a speculative glance. "You got that in a week?"

"Well, it's not exactly a new tactic. Historically, I mean. But also, it's the way he talked about you," she said. "The robberies and the like, you've been masking your campaign to build support, yes?"

"True."

"That's why you're always seen around the palace, and

not just to pounce on people's valuables left lying about. Though that's what you want him to believe."

"That's what he wants to believe, too. But I'm not sure he does." Andri hesitated, and then she remembered those mysterious archive trips. She waited for him to explain, but he said, "Go on."

"That's all I have." She smiled through the road dust at him, and though it was hot enough to wither leaves, to him she looked as cool as a spring day.

He lifted his hat and wiped his arm over his forehead. Life was ridiculous; he faced possible annihilation in a few days, he was hungry and thirsty and sweating through his clothes and didn't remember the last time he had been able to sleep except in little snatches, and yet he could still get saddle wood at the mere sight of her. When they stopped at the next stream they found to water the horses he would throw himself in. It was either that or find some shady spot and dally with her for days . . . he very much wanted to do that . . .

With a snort he straightened his spine. Cousin Adon. Yes. "I know he makes promises of peace to the nobles, but he's said things before the guard captains that make it clear that his peace doesn't extend below the ridge."

He went on then to describe the captains, and other people Liere had never met. She could not contribute here, except by listening. When he got to various nobles, she offered her own observations, which often sidetracked into anecdotes. It wrung her heart, hearing how people who had all been friends as children, sharing games and learning, had been divided by the violence of their elders.

"The important thing—the crucial thing—is, if I can't convince him to give up, and I don't think I can, I've striven to insure that his command to torch the city in removing us is not obeyed. Everything comes down to that. If I can't persuade the captains to put down their swords, then I may as well give up."

She nodded soberly. "Though I don't truly know these people, or what motivates them. What they fear, and what they want. I do understand this much: if they put their faith in you, if they obey your commands rather than his, then he can rant and threaten but it won't happen."

Andri laughed. "He's not much of a ranter. He's more persuasive. But even if he were more like my father—now *there* was your ranter — if that was the worst of it, it would be easy. He's more likely to have primed people like Talipin, who have staked their lives on his cause, to smash their way through to get to me, no matter what, or who, they smash. I've tried to make contingencies for that."

Liere bit her lip. How she wanted to help! But what could she do? She was even more determined to hide her identity. She could see no advantage to it, only drawbacks. Beginning with the expectations that the Girl Who Saved the World would wave her hand and magic would somehow restore everything to rights. (Whose rights would be up for debate.) Those expectations had ground her down for so long, and she knew they would pop right up again like weeds. Alismira's reaction, though in every other respect wonderful, had made that clear. "Queen of Sartor." The thought sent a spurt of laughter through Liere. Rueful laughter, beneath it a flinch.

Also, there was the overriding worry that revealing who she was might make Lyren-Sartora a target. Since leaving Shiovhan, Liere had always found Lyren-Sartora either asleep or busy, her mind-shield stubbornly shut. It was normal for a twelve year old to want to be the center of family attention, Liere reminded herself. And she would be again, she promised herself, whenever this . . . this interlude ended.

Coming out of that reverie, she realized that the pause in conversation had become a silence, and once again Andri had fallen asleep in the saddle. She remained vigilant and let him slumber.

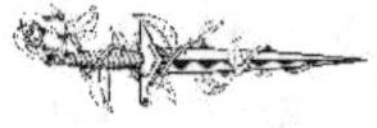

He'd arranged for food and fodder, enabling them to camp outside. Once again, in a dell scented with wildflowers, they shared bread, cheese, and wine, and themselves. Later on, when she was drowsing on the edge of sleep, she heard the chuff chuff chuff of him running off to vanishing in the woods.

She knew she could track him. From the sounds, he was not nearly as adept at woodcraft as she had become, though he was an expert at maneuvering in a city; from her second year on there had been regular stalks across the wild terrain of their island, in which the older girls had tracked the younger. Liere had spent a lot of time lying along a tree branch, or crouched in water up to her nose, as she watched the searchers move slowly, examining every leaf, every mark in the ground. Losers got the finders' laundry and garden chores on top of their own for an entire week, strong incentive.

She knew she could stalk him, but what then?

He probably knew she was capable of tracking him. But he wanted, or needed, to be solitary. It seemed to be more complicated than a matter of trust, but one thing she was sure of: right now, being trustworthy meant letting him be solitary.

Once again she checked on Lyren-Sartora (still no contact) and then closed her eyes.

The following day, late, they reached the tiny village where the freedom movement leader lived, to discover her cottage empty except for a couple of big pieces of furniture too massy to move.

Andri turned away, looking worried. "She might be with her daughter," he said, then peered skyward. "We've got thunder coming. Let's leave the horses at the northern post, and take the rest on foot, shall we?"

Gared had arranged with the stable people to have his friends on duty at that post. The young woman in charge of the northern post stable had that diffuse look that meant *I don't see anything or anyone* that Liere found secretly amusing, though the situation—a city of people divided against themselves—was troubling.

Summer thunder rumbled in the distance, the heat intense despite the sun vanishing. Liere hitched her carryall over her shoulder and took the sheathed rapier in hand as she breathed against the heaviness of fatigue in her limbs, then Andri reached for her free hand, his palm callused from a lifetime of sword work. He gave her a challenging grin. "Shall we make a run for it?"

A different kind of heat surged through her, and she laughed back, unaware of how enchanting he found that laugh. And how exhilarating it was to glance over to see her matching him pace for pace—vaulting walls, running along fences, and slipping through narrow alleys under leaning old houses, as the rain began pelting them.

Wordlessly they dared one another: a somersault through the air, a leap from a roof to a wall a hand-span in width. It wasn't that either of them were extraordinary in either daring or execution. It was the sort of game that those who trained long, and who were coming into the fullness of strength, exulted in. The charm lay in her tight grace as her long golden hair streamed, limning the curves of her body, and in his insouciant angles and careless strength, and the entrancing contours of strength within all those long lines.

As they neared the outskirts of the city they stopped more frequently, he listening and watching, and Liere scanning in the mental realm. Guards roamed in pairs instead of the old, ragged gangs. Though there were lights aplenty behind shutters, no one was out.

"Curfew," Andri whispered. "Not a good sign."

They made their way by a circuitous route to their hideout. It was empty, with an old sign out front claiming it belonged to a brewery, and inside were stacks of barrels, and a yeasty smell that must have been accomplished by spilling an entire barrel.

Andri looked satisfied as he stood in the doorway; Liere was going to ask what he saw when he murmured, "The stacks are a code. They've dispersed to the third hideout. Gared is by the river."

It took them a while to cross the lower part of the city, but at last they entered the linen-makers at the very southmost part of the city, off the river; even with the intermittent rain, the smell of retting flax rose from the ditches that in turn would drain off to an old ravine, where the ground would filter the water before it made its way back to the river.

The house was a low, ramshackle affair, unprepossessing at best.

Andri ducked under the low eave, Liere at his heels, and tapped lightly at the door in a quick pattern.

Two breaths later, as thunder rolled across the sky, Gared yanked open the door. "There you are," he said. "We've bean soup waiting."

As soon as they stepped in inside, a cacophony of voices rose, everyone with complaints and reports and questions speaking at once.

Liere sensed Lyren-Sartora's presence directly above. Knowing that she would be no help to Andri now, Liere mounted a steep staircase that led to a narrow loft under the roof.

Here she found Lyren-Sartora, Jaydi, and the other orphans in the middle of an elaborate game of Cards'n'Shards, markers ranged in a complicated pattern as the cards riffled and snapped. They ignored the clamor of adult voices below; Liere sensed that the orphans were inured to it, and that Lyren-Sartora was making a point of being casual.

Lyren-Sartora glanced up. "Have fun?" she asked, her tone a bit too bright.

"Some. Did you?"

Lyren-Sartora looked left and right. "Did we have fun?"

Jaydi looked up, blinking behind his shaggy hair hanging over half his face. "Lots," he croaked, his voice hoarser than ever. "We peppered Talipin's bully-boys with horse apples."

"And the traitor who led them to the old hideout," piped up one of the other orphans.

They seemed to want to brag about their exploits, so Liere listened and put in murmurs of amazement and horror when appropriate. She sensed that Lyren-Sartora was proud of her exploits—it was she who suggested loosing all the horses of a stable master who mistreated the animals—but beneath that was worry about what was to come.

When they ran out of brag, Jaydi demanded they return to the game, and Liere went back downstairs to discover everyone seemed to feel that Andri's Letter of Credit was the triumph of the night.

It was late by then, and Liere was more than ready to sleep. Once again she felt very grown up as she waited to see what the cues were. How did they arrange such things? But she forgot. He didn't stay in a bed all night with anyone.

Gared said, "We should go now."

Andri turned to the group. "Well done, all of you. We'll be back by morning." He flashed a tender smile Liere's way, and then he and Gared slipped through a narrow door, the rap of their bootheels diminishing. Liere noted that her rapier had been put in the rack with the other weapons. Was that a sign that they counted her one of them?

She would have to get Lyren-Sartora alone, and ask if she wanted to return to Bereth Ferian, or even to Atan in Sartor, to await Liere. Because Liere knew she was going to stay, to see it out, whatever happened.

She turned, to find Fronsa waiting. "We've got an extra hammock in here," she said.

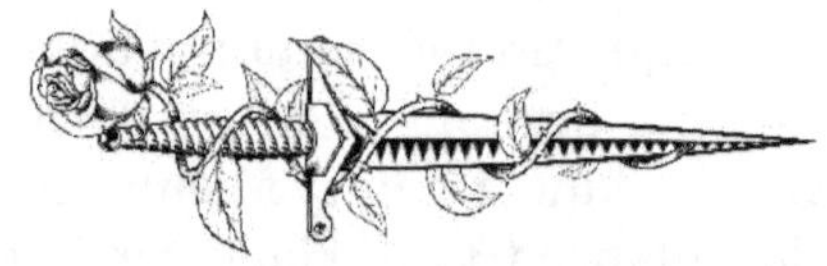

FORTY-THREE

Liere didn't see Andri again until Midsummer Eve, when they all met for Gillor's wedding. But she located him on the mental plane.

She'd sensed people all her life, beginning with her mother when she was an infant. She'd learned to sense her father's moods, so that she could be elsewhere whenever possible when the sourness turned purple-green, like thunderclouds. Sensing Norsundrians during those terrible days when she was on the run had saved her life. And it had been useful when Lyren-Sartora was an infant, for Liere always knew why the babe cried, until it became worrisome when Lyren-Sartora began to walk, but she didn't talk. Why struggle with sounds and language if you didn't have to? Liere had to put up the shield, and endure the tears of frustration that all parents do while their child learns language.

She'd sensed friends from continents away, and at times had walked in the dreams of the friend she knew best, Senrid Montredaun-An. Since her return, she'd had to learn to firmly shut that door and keep it shut because it was intrusive, the mental realm version of creeping up on people when they expected to be alone.

So being aware of Andri's proximity was nothing new in itself. The entrancingly new part was the warmth, like the shimmer of beeswax candles, when she thought of him. Sometimes he was aware of her, or perhaps thinking of her, and she sensed that, too. No words. He was clumsy at contacts unless he sat down and concentrated, which he had no time for. But he still maintained that imperfect mind-shield, which she never trespassed. She could feel the pressure of the burden he carried, and she never ceased to wonder at it, but to be trusted meant being trustworthy. He would tell her when he was ready. Or not.

What disturbed her most was that fear did not leak through often, mostly late at night, though all day he was talking about Adon-Marsael. That meant Andri's fear did not have the would-be king as the cause.

Everyone else had jobs to do, racing in and out, sometimes crimson-faced from the heat, sometimes tense, or laughing breathlessly at near misses. Liere, with no assigned tasks, remained at the linen house with the tailor couple, Devea and Banisa, who were busy making wedding clothes along with their regular work. Both were in their twenties, Banisa nearer to thirty. Liere hadn't understood that they were bonded (Liere picked up that they thought marriage was for rich people who had property to sort out), and that men were little to Devea beyond an occasional distraction. Learning that made her feel that at last she was on the inside of the mysteries of adult relationships.

She voluntarily took over the cooking while Marten running messages between Bassl among the nobles and Andri in the city below the ridge. There was something satisfying in being able to sit people down to food she had made, and then to restore the kitchen to order, though it seemed the rest of the world was uncertain at best. In this, she began to understand the quiet Marten.

Liere didn't bring up Andri, as she could sense him, but it appeared that the others were concerned on her behalf, for Banisa took her aside on the second day, saying earnestly, "Kizka says all Andri talks about is you. It's just that we've this wedding on top of everything else. He promised Gil a year ago."

Devea reappeared, her arms full of fabric. "Also," she said, "Midsummer is our traditional time for weddings."

Liere did not want to point out that it was that way most of the world over.

Devea scowled. "But! I still don't see why it has to be this year, when those two have been essentially ring-bound since they were sixteen. They just didn't have rings, or say their vows before family and friends."

Banisa shrugged without missing a stitch. "Andri says we deserve something normal the last night, rather than sitting around chewing our nails down to the elbow."

"I don't like it," Devea stated. "Something's going to go wrong. For one thing, we've got too many people all saying they have to be there."

Banisa sighed. "Gared won't refuse them. He says that Andri says we have to begin seeing ourselves as one kingdom. Which begins with those dockside rowdies, and Vec's wastrel of a brother."

Into the silence that followed, Liere said, "Who was Old Invor? And Valdon?"

"Which Valdon? It's such a common name," Banisa began.

Devea caught her by the wrist, shaking her head.

"Oh," Banisa murmured. "That Valdon."

To Liere, Devea whispered, "They were two of Andri's earliest followers, one a noble. They were murdered, along with those freedom people, and the—"

"All of which we don't talk about," Banisa sang under her breath.

"—and anyway, Andri caught the blame, but we all know he didn't do it. And no, we don't know what happened. Gared does, but try to pry a word out of him, he's worse than a hundred-year-old oyster." She shut up at the sound of footsteps.

Marten entered, carrying a bag of flour. "This is the last they had. I don't dare go into the market." He turned to Liere. "Could you do that stage illusion trick and fetch some currants? The last of mine went bad in the heat, and they want a currant cake."

Liere set aside the biscuit bowl she'd been stirring, threw a cloth over it, and picked up a basket.

She used her Ones skills without being asked, never taking the same route twice in a row. As she headed toward the Lower Market, she eyed the stiff postures, the sidled glances in knots of people, outward signs of the tension that gripped the city; it was easy to imagine the same tension up in the palace, as the servants decorated for the Midsummer Ball, and readied the bunting and banners for the grand balcony from which Adon-Marsael would make his first official speech as prospective king.

It seemed reckless to plan a wedding the night before a revolution. But no one had asked Liere's opinion, so she kept her questions and comments to herself, just as she kept to herself her wish to ask why the knuckle-gnawing, passionate Ratface had that nickname, but the one who resembled a rodent most strongly was Gillor.

Mindful of roaming guards and unseen watchers, Liere paused between an old chestnut tree and a fence and sketched an illusion over herself, using Gillor's features to replace her own, and altering her posture to a listless shuffle.

It did not take long to make her purchases. No one seemed to want to bargain more than a token exchange or two. She returned to find Martan with his hair tied up high and sleeves rolled above his elbows, beating an enormous bowl of batter. "Just in time," he said with a smile.

She washed the currants, dumped them into the batter, and from then on a ceaseless flow of activity, punctuated by brief naps rather than true sleep, wheeled the hours by until word of the just-chosen wedding site passed in whispers from lips to ears. They gathered along the riverbank, some carrying food to contribute.

The sun had set. The afternoon thunderstorm was a jagged line heading eastward over Sles Adran, leaving a faint breeze smelling of wet grass. As twilight deepened from blue to a rain-washed purple, people turned to silhouettes, quiet except for the rustle of movement, and here and there a whisper. Once, a laugh.

Out of the gathering mass a tall form appeared, and though Liere only saw the shape of a shoulder, and the soft, pale glow of emerging starlight on a lock of long hair, she recognized Andri, and shivered at her inward burst of delight and want.

"We settled on this site not two hours ago," he said. "We should have long enough before some snout calls down the hunt onto us."

"It seems so risky to do it today," she couldn't help murmuring.

"I know. But they need it."

"They," it was soon apparent, took in the entire gathering, not just the two who stood awkwardly in the center of a ring of well-wishers, as bits of candle or tiny oil lamps were lit and passed from hand to hand.

Faces emerged out of the darkness, ruddy-lit, candle flames reflecting in eyes. Andri reached for Liere's hand and gripped it once, then he made his way around the circle, clapping this one on a shoulder, clasping two hands of that one. A couple of women he kissed, amid laughter and soft crows, "Woo!"

Then he walked into the circle to face the pair, and Liere thought she understood why it had to be now. The world over, most marriages were officiated by an older married couple, or by a guild chief or a noble. Peers made their vows before kings and queens. Those marriages usually involving the legal disposal of land. (Like clothing, she thought, ownership of land being a fiction we all agree on.) After tomorrow, assuming they were successful, he was going to be swept into the work of rebuilding, and it would be a while before he'd be able to officiate again. And kings usually didn't preside over common weddings, or they'd end up doing nothing else but that.

Whispering rose briefly, then died away after a few fierce "Sh-h-h-h!"s.

Andri spoke. "Whether this is my first act as king or my last, what could be better than to seal the vows made by Gillor and Ranasal?"

Someone began to cheer, to be muffled by someone else.

Then, in thin, high voices, nervous yet full of emotion, the two in the center gave their promises to one another. Each produced a ring for the other, and it was over.

There could be no true music, lest it attract roaming guards. But a small group hummed softly, in counterpoint, and the newlywedded pair led the dancing.

Now Liere understood the real reason for the gathering. Her throat hurt, and tears stung her eyes as she watched the ruddy light paint over the celebrants dancing with desperate abandon — the quick, hard hugs, the upward-turned faces, the breathless laughs that teetered on the edge of ragged sobs, but never quite fell.

This was what Andri had foreseen: a celebration that bound them together, and for a joyous occasion that, for this moment, had nothing to do with politics or greed or the prospect of the worst happening. Except that it was important enough to sneak here to the riverside, and speak in whispers, and dance without music. It was important to be together, and meet in joy.

She wanted to embrace them all, to shout out their

gallantry: she twirled about, laughter fizzing inside her as she grasped the fact that she had fallen in love not just with a person, but with a kingdom. Here was where she could make a home!

They danced until everyone was thirsty, and most had been hungry all day. Devea took charge of the food, which had been set on two blankets laid side by side, and Liere was surprised to see that big, hulking Vec in charge of the drinks. Andri was indeed serious about binding everyone together, not just the nobles.

". . . lemon cake," the bride Ranasal exclaimed. "My favorite! Tal, did you make this behind my back?"

"Not I," a woman said. "I told you true I couldn't afford what they were asking for lemons, even the bad ones."

"Did someone say lemon cake?" Andri had been approaching Liere, but at this, he stopped dead and whirled around. "My favorite."

Gillor's voice cracked. "Ran's, too, so back off, you're not a king yet!"

Muffled laughter surrounded them as the bride, wearing a new blouse over an old skirt, held the cake close, then a knife flashed as Gillor cut a huge piece out for her.

Liere, looking on, reveled in the laughter, her senses wide open—and so she caught the sour note in the thrum of happy voices: a gloat.

Her head turned as Ranasal took a huge bite. And then began to choke.

"Ah, being married isn't that bad," Gillor said as people chuckled and snickered, she began to keen on a high note, clutching at her throat. The laughter broke uncertainly as Liere darted forward, and in a swift move, jabbed her stiffened fingers into the spot between the bride's ribs and stomach in the spot she had learned from a crisp, stern One.

"Whoop!" The poisoned cake came up again, leaving Ranasal sobbing, as Liere turned her head, and pointed at a hunched figure slinking away, triumph a glowing red fire.

"There!" She pointed. "He brought it."

Gared and Vec converged from opposite ends and brought down the slinker, as everyone burst out cursing, questioning, commenting. Making noise. Many turned to Liere in wonder, awe, and even fear.

"Disperse," Andri said, "disperse. Take what you

brought. It should be safe. That cake was for me. Disperse!"

Gared and Vec dragged their captive forward. Andri put his hands on his hips and stared down at the broad face of a young man his own age. "I don't even know you."

"Ten thousand gold," the assassin muttered. "Ten thousand gold just to snuff you. You don't even realize how hard it is to—"

"Be poor? Wrong," Andri said softly. "Wrong. I know exactly how hard it is. But there's no time to argue with you now."

"Shall I slit his throat?" Vec asked, flicking out a knife.

"No. I'd be tempted by ten thousand, too. Tie him up and stash him somewhere. Either I'll be dead or king by this time tomorrow. He can reflect until then."

As the would-be assassin was led off one way, and the bride's friends crowded around her as she gulped down water to ease the burning in her mouth and throat, Andri came to Liere. "That was well done, but word is going to spread," he said urgently. "I figured it was worth the risk of infiltration, but now we're going to have to break it up."

She nodded. "Is there anything I can do?"

"Go back, will you? Marten is going to take the orphans to the place we set aside for them." He glanced around. The wedding party was dispersing in haste. "Someone knew we were here from the start. That cake appeared with all the rest of the food, at the outset," he said. He looked up at the peaceful stars. "A change in plans."

"I wish I could help you," Liere said, the words wrung out of her.

"You did. You saved Ranasal. You'll have to teach me how you did that." He was backing away as he spoke to her. "But your description is surely going out right now, and I need you to be safe."

Then he turned and vanished into the night.

Liere ran back through yards and alongside vegetable patches until she reached the linen house. She paused, scanning. She found no inimical minds. She ran upstairs.

The orphans stood in a tight group under Fronsa's hard eyes. "Is Marten coming?" she addressed Liere.

"I believe he's on his way."

Liere turned to Lyren-Sartora: *I can send you to Bereth Ferian.*

Lyren-Sartora tossed her head: *Do you think I'm scared?*

: I am.

Lyren-Sartora's answer came a lot less belligerently: *I promised Jaydi I'd stay. Are you going anywhere? You're not attacking the palace, are you?*

: No, and no. But I don't know what's going to happen. You have your butterfly clasp in case.

Lyren-Sartora touched her braid, and Liere nodded. Marten appeared then, and the youngsters filed down the stairs after him.

Liere went back downstairs. For something to do, she tidied the kitchen. Then she sat down, her mind racing, her body trembling with reaction. With fatigue. She knew she couldn't sleep—

And woke with a snort. The weak, blue light of early morning highlighted Gared's worried profile.

"Liere. Andri He says you have that mind . . . thing."

Liere shut her eyes, sweeping the mental realm: Lyren-Sartora asleep and dreaming, the whisper of minds in restless slumber.

And there—Andri. Shock. Pain.

"He's hurt," she breathed.

They ran. Not three streets away the tramp of boots: a patrol.

"Roofs." Gared swarmed up a rain pipe. He turned to reach down, but Liere was already beside him.

Liere took the lead as she scanned and ran, wincing against the threat of vertigo. Once she nearly panicked, till she realized Andri had not shut her out. He was fighting for consciousness.

Proximity was easy, precise location more difficult. They ran from wall to roof and from roof to wall as the morning light slowly began to strengthen. Liere made two false turns, but on a third try, they dropped down into an alley, where Andri stood against a wall, fingers spread, blood blackening his white shirt. "Ratface," he said. "Street of Crows . . . Trap."

Liere and Gared had not taken two steps when he toppled like a felled tree.

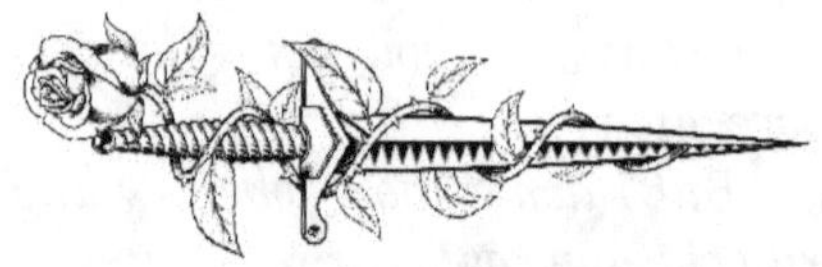

FORTY-FOUR

Liere reached him first.

Gared tried to shake him awake, but when Andri's head lolled, he turned a panicked gaze to Liere, who said reassuringly, "He's unconscious."

"How can you . . ."

Rather than get into an explanation of "the mind thing," she said, "Feel his pulse."

Gared put a finger to the side of Andri's neck, and let out a ragged sigh. He looked as tired as Andri ever had.

The sound of tramping feet registered with them both. Not close, but coming. Methodically searching.

Liere said urgently, "Go to the Street of Crows. It was clearly important to him. I don't even know where that is."

"But you can't—"

"I can," Liere said. "I'll get him safely to the linen house." And when Gared looked uncertainly from her to Andri lying there, she said, "I promise. Go!"

Urgency won over questions. Gared straightened up; as Andri had said, he was fast in action when he had orders that made sense. He vaulted to the fence, to a roof, then vanished.

Liere bent over Andri and pictured the bedding she had been sleeping on as a Destination. She checked Andri's pulse once more. His heartbeat was strong, and this was not a long transfer. She murmured the transfer magic, then dashed around a corner to give the air between here and there a chance to clear.

The patrol reached the alley, and someone exclaimed, "Look, blood all down this wall."

"Still wet," someone else said

"Break into pairs, line of sight search—"

Liere transferred herself.

She staggered, swayed, and dropped to her knees beside Andri. A couple of breaths and the transfer reaction dissipated. She did a mental sweep, ignoring a mild head pang. Marten was not back yet. No one else was in the house. She ran to fetch the box of bandages and salve and medicines that they shared, and brought it back. Andri was still out cold.

She hesitated, then ripped his already torn and bloody shirt open, revealing a gash across his ribs. It was shallow, bleeding steadily. She wadded up a clean towel and gently began mopping him up, then pressed a wad against the wound.

She had never actually seen his body. They had always come together in the dark. She had attributed it to reluctance to expose his scars. Her gaze roamed over the contours of his chest and halted, shocked. There over his heart, a gray-white "scar" like a slug trail, neatly and deliberately made. Chill gripped her viscerally.

"Bloodknife," she whispered.

"You know what that is?"

She started. He was awake.

She hesitated, and gave herself a mental shake. This was not the time to hide crucial information. "I do."

"I thought . . ." He laughed hoarsely, then coughed.

"It's not healed," she said.

"Wondered. I—" He gasped as if stabbed by an invisible knife. His eyes widened, their expression stark and blind.

She reached on the mental plane, and once again recoiled. Here, at last, was what he had so desperately hidden all along: a bloodknife attack through dark magic. Was that Yeres? Liere had never seen Yeres, who emerged from Norsunder very rarely.

Liere cautiously extended a tendril, and for the first time, breached Andri's imperfect mind-shield. Then she recoiled again, at the violence of the emotions and the onslaught of memory: faces, threats, death.

Her gaze fell to that ugly slug trail. She knew how to break the bloodknife spell. Arthur had taught her years ago, and though she could not do magic in those days, she'd never forgotten it. But if she did it now, she would give her presence away.

She did the next best thing: holding Andri's hand to make

the contact easier, she slipped into the nightmare visions, hiding herself easily, and spoke to Andri be-neath the magic-driven noise: *Build a wall. Brick by brick.*

In the realm of the spirit, she demonstrated. Andri did not argue, or question. With the desperate focus of one pushed nearly beyond endurance, he built the wall — and the noise stopped.

He turned to her, struggling to verbalize, and fell back into physical awareness. "How . . ."

"I'll tell you everything, but first: shall I take this thing off you?" She pointed to that slug trail wound. "It will start bleeding immediately, just as if it was made today. But my guess is, it's not that deep."

"She said she wanted me alive," Andri muttered. "Do it."

Liere extended her hand over the wound, and brought the spell to mind. It was dark magic, which built power fast, and internal heat. Her hand glowed — the wound glowed — then the binding snapped. Blood began to well up.

Andri gasped. "Oh. So much better."

When pain from a cut feels better, that is a measure of just how terrible a burden one has been bearing. She said, "Hold tight. This will hurt."

It did. He winced and grunted through the cleaning and bandaging process, grimacing and grunting with such verve that in spite of everything laughter fluttered behind her ribs. When she sat back, he opened one eye. "Done?"

"Yes."

He sat up. She began to protest, but gave up. He was far too pale from blood loss; she figured nature would force him to lie down again if necessary. "How did you do that?" he asked. "No, what did you do?"

"The bloodknife spell is like a poison. In your blood," she said. "Norsunder used these all the time. Clearly they still do. Some of them. I was taught the antidote. Yeres put that one you?" She remembered Cath, and all the humor was gone, leaving her sick and shivery. "She seems to be collecting princes, or young men known for their martial prowess."

"Yes," Andri said grimly. "She told me right off that if I won, it would prove that I was worthy to join her merry band of pretty kings. I turned down the offer. While her minions held me down she stabbed me, and said we'd revisit the question once I was ready to surrender. She also promised that if I told anyone at all, she'd begin killing random people in my life. And she made that threat come true."

"Valdon and . . ."

". . . and others. Eight, all told, including two from the freedom movement. She always attacked me at night. Not every night, but randomly. I never knew when. It could be once a week, then four nights in a row. But always near midnight. This, attacking me now, is new."

"You were wounded," she said carefully. "They wanted you to drop." Should she define that "they" or not? Not until she was *sure*.

"The killings happened any time of day. I wasn't always there. But it always happened after I saw one of the victims. Usually within a day. I'd told the first two what happened, and they swore to keep it secret. I still believe they did. The next ones, I didn't tell anything. The last two times I slept with someone all night, they ended up dead the next day—neither at all interested in kings or politics or even sword fights. Just laughing, and loving." He briefly closed his eyes, residual pain a bruise on the spirit. Tough his had not been the hand to take their lives away, he felt the guilt of it just the same.

He moved restlessly. "That's why I asked about magic. What you knew about it. *She* has to be stalking me by magic, for I've been very careful, moving constantly, never sleeping next to anyone. Vigilant, always, and yet, somehow she knew my people."

Liere took his hands. "Yeres doesn't stay but a couple hours at most in the physical world," she said tentatively.

"Yeres? She said her name was Iris. You know her?"

"I know *of* her. She lives in the heart of Norsunder."

He stared at Liere. "Norsunder? But can't they spy . . . Wrong question. What is the limitation of their magic? Any magic?"

Liere shut her eyes, sorting the impressions she'd been bombarded with. It was soul-wrenching. She tried to imagine being tormented like that for a couple of years, never knowing when she would strike. She?

He. The driving mind behind that attack had been masculine, and she was fairly sure she had winnowed out the identity. She needed to be absolutely sure.

Andri's hand was hot and dry. Fever was already setting in. "Liere, does Sartor really teach envoys that kind of magic?

And familiarity with the heart of Norsunder? Who *are* you?"

She opened her eyes. "I will tell you, though I'd hoped to live just as myself. But I guess that never really is possible, is it? Our past is no easier to shed then our shadow on a sunny day. However," she said, "There's a . . . a question I need to resolve first."

"I can't. Cousin Adon's about to give his speech, but then there's the signing of the treaty with Sles Adran."

"Treaty?"

"You're the one who told me about sovereignty. It's supposed to be a peace treaty that Bartal sent over. I've got to stop it . . ." Andri made an effort she could feel—and red bloomed on both bandages as he swung to his feet. He managed two steps, faltered, and once again fell flat on his face.

"And there is nature," she murmured, just as Marten burst into the room, his face distraught before his gaze lit on Andri.

Horror widened his eyes. She could see tears on his lower lids.

"Marten?"

"Is he—?"

"A faint. Help me get him covered up."

The two of them got Andri into the bed again, then Liere said, "Do you know what happened?"

"Everyone was in place. Maybe still is. But they got Ratface and Kizka, and let the word spread that the dockside gang was holding them hostage and wanted a deal. Andri went. He would never leave any of us. And he walked straight into a trap."

Marten swallowed. "I don't know what happened, exactly, except that I had just got Jaydi and the rest settled when I saw Ratface and his little brother Radri, hand in hand."

At Liere's puzzled expression, he flushed and said, almost too low to be heard, "Their ghosts."

Liere, unlike everyone else, did not laugh, or give him a skeptical eyebrow lift, or back away as if he were diseased. "I don't think I know Radri," she said softly, compassionately.

"He was killed along with Ratface's family. The man holding the title did it himself. Stabbed Ratface, too, and left him for dead. Their elder brother Yanji, who wasn't there when Arbanion was taken over, is in the mines. We think. Andri promised Ratface that, first thing, he'd free the miners forced . . ." Marten shook his head. "You believe me?"

"You are not the first person I've ever met who perceives spirits among the living. Andri was upset about a treaty. What exactly is going on, do you know?"

Marten sighed. "The Adrani ambassador is strictly neutral. She's been around since Andri's father was king. She's been the only means of communication with Bartal, such as it is. She has no power of her own, of course."

Liere bit back impatience. "Understood."

"It's her aide — they've been partners for years — who tells us things. He's related to Andri through Andri's mother. Distant, but family seems to count, anyway, he warned us two days ago that the treaty, which has been in negotiation for months, was agreed on. After Adon-Marsael makes his speech, there will be a treaty signing. This treaty, supposedly one of peace and alliance between the two kingdoms, promises that should anything happen to the acknowledged monarch, the Adranis will come over to his aid. And if Adon-Marsael signs it, that makes him king in Sles Adran's eyes."

"I got it. Andri can then be blamed for any further attempts," Liere said. "if he even tries. All right. I see what I can do. I have an errand to run."

Marten looked worried. "Liere, stay off the streets. There are patrols everywhere."

She said soothingly, "I promise I will stay off the streets."

Marten bowed his head, hiding his grief over Ratface.

Liere flitted downstairs, and paused on the warped, worn, bare floorboards inside the back door. She closed her eyes and brought up a picture of the hallway outside that white and gilt library Adon-Marsael had used as an office.

She transferred, and to her relief, found it empty and dark. She laid her land on the library door and listened by Dena Yeresbeth. No one inside. She turned her back to the door, and widened her perception. Ah, there was Adon-Marsael. Of course. Was this not the royal suite? He was down one floor.

She fled down the grand staircase at the side, and halted before a long hall with only four doors that opened onto what had to be sizable suites.

The door opened and a servant came out, bearing a heavy

golden tray with breakfast things stacked on it.

Two guards on either side of that door turned quickly, hands going to weapons. Liere held up her empty hands, saying, "May I speak to his excellency?"

"His majesty," one guard growled.

The door opened wider, and Adon-Marsael himself appeared. He said, lightly enough, "Not until New Year's." He glanced up the hall, and his eyebrows rose in surprise. "Our intrepid envoy has returned, I see. Or did you ever leave? Let her pass."

The guards eyed her as she followed Adon-Marsael into the room, then he shut the door in their faces. He wore a long silk tunic of Elsarion midnight blue, cut up the sides, over trousers and blackweave boots. The tunic was embroidered with golden twined kingsblossom. His trim waist was sashed in gold and white.

"I ought to have guessed that you'd join the unending line of Andri's harem. But I thought you would have less, ah, common taste. Live and learn." Then, seeing her completely unmoved by this attempt to put her on the defensive, he eyed her. "Where do you come from, anyway? Are you really a shopkeeper's daughter, as Thadara Otobris insists?"

"I am," Liere said.

"Interesting," Adon-Marsael said. "She'd have it you're some connection of the Dei family, disgraced as so many of them end up being, usually after power plays that failed. But the name still would get you somewhere in Sartor, no doubt?"

Liere said, "My grandmother always claimed we were related to the Deis of Everon, but she was a notorious snob. In any case, it means nothing to me." And to get the subject off of her and onto the topic of Norsunder, where it belonged, "Did you know that Yeres, the pretty mage with the long dark curls, is a Norsundrian?"

Adon-Marsael perched on the edge of a beautifully carved desk, the morning sunlight outlining his form. In spite of his words about New Year's, it was apparently that he had been gathering kingly furnishings to fill this vast room. "What," he drawled, "would you say if I told you I have no idea who you are talking about?"

"She might have called herself Iris," Liere said. "But she is from Norsunder, and from what I hear, she has never yet kept any promise, except when it suits her hunger for power."

"Isn't that true of everyone?" he retorted with unimpaired good humor.

"What I'm trying to say is, she might have helped you. Did, one respect. But there is always a cost."

"How do you know who has or has not helped me?" Adon-Marsael left the desk. Liere's heart raced, and she shifted her stance, but he only strolled to a cupboard set into a wall, pressed it, and cast a glance over his shoulder. "Join me in a glass of wine, Honor Feriadar?"

"In the morning?"

He lifted a shoulder. "I find it soothes the nerves whatever the hour. Do you know, I loathe making speeches? But needs must."

She was going to refuse, then remembered that she was stalling him. "An envoy," she said, "is required to bow to all kinds of customs. This one seems easier than many."

He turned to reach into the cupboard. She could only see his silk-covered broad back, bisected by his long silky dark braids fixed with golden clasps. Hiding the pouring of wine. Did he really keep poison or sleep herb or the like ready to be used, right there in his soon-to-be-kingly cupboards?

He turned, a spun glass goblet in each hand, and brought one to her. She reached for it, her mind racing through Sister Sunflower's lectures on Diplomatic Deceptions. *To look real, it has to be real,* she had said.

Adon-Marsael raised his glass in salute. She bowed deeply, holding the wine carefully, but when she came up she put a foot forward and stepped on the hem of her robe. As she straightened, it yanked her off-balance. "Ulp?" she squeaked, staggered, and the wine went flying.

Adon-Marsael sidestepped, but not quite fast or far enough; the wine caught him on one side.

"Oh, oh, oh," Liere twittered. "Oh, no, your excellency, I am so very sorry. Here, let me — oh no, I came away without a handkerchief . . ."

He eyed her, the humor fading for a heartbeat. She continued to blither apologies until Adon-Marsael turned away and slipped through a side door. Liere let her voice fade as she shut her eyes and sent a tendril to seek Andri. He was awake.

"As it happens," Adon-Marsael said, reappearing with another garment in hand, his sashes over his arm, "it seemed prudent to have the tailor make several of these." He shrug-ged the new tunic over his fine shirt, and fastened the two jeweled buttons at mid-chest. "You were going to tell me how and why you came here to accuse me of meeting with . . . Iris, was it?"

Liere remembered Marten's tear-stained face, and what he'd said about Ratface. "Her name is Yeres. And her biggest fear that I know of is aging. She never spends longer than an hour or two, if that, in the world." A pause.

Adon-Marsael regarded her steadily, his slight smile one of patience. Humoring her.

"I felt it only just to warn you off someone very, very dangerous."

"Norsunder's inner workings are common know-ledge in Sartor?" Adon-Marsael drawled. "Who does your queen keep company with?"

Keep talking, Liere willed him. What time was it? When was he supposed to be making his speech? "Yeres stayed around long enough to try to seduce Andri."

"Ah, now you are implying that *he's* aligned with Norsunder? Will it disturb you if I admit that I'm not at all surprised?"

Liere began to wonder who was delaying whom. Yes, he *was* toying with her! Rage churned in her stomach: she'd wanted to be fair, to assume ignorance in preference to evil, but the fact was, whether or not he knew who Yeres truly was, she was fairly certain that she had sensed his hand driving the bloodknife magic. Which was entirely possible. She knew from past experience that once the magic was set up, any minion could be put in charge of it.

Liere tried one more time. "Yeres cut him with a bloodknife when he refused her. But she would not have stayed long once she did that."

The last of his smile disappeared. "Where is Andri?"

"I don't know. I do know that he didn't die in your trap at the Street of Crows." Her voice hardened. "She might have begun the torments, but it was you running them. Like last night."

Adon-Marsael had begun to wind the white sash around his waist, but at that he tossed it aside and came at her. She whirled out of his grasp. Three quick exchanges, her evading his grasp as she worked toward the door, then he blocked her off. When she turned toward the window, he caught the end of her braid and yanked her off-balance.

She made a praise-worthy attempt to land in a roll, but he was too fast. A short, sharp struggle, with him using his heavier weight to advantage and got her pinned. He said, panting with effort, "You're a lot stronger than you look."

Since she'd lost, she regarded that as less a compliment than a gloat.

He cast his eyes about, leaned over, and grabbed the spilled silk. With quick efficiency he bound her wrists behind her, and her ankles together. He straightened up as a bell rang in the distance.

"Just in time," he said and wiped his hair hack. Then frowned. "I think, all things considered, we'd better have a long talk as soon as I get back. Let's not have you shouting the place down."

So saying he reached into a pocket and pulled out a handkerchief. "It's clean," he added, holding it up — and then gagged her.

She utterly despised looking weak, but she made herself wriggle futilely and whimper as he stood up, straightened his cuffs, smoothed his hair back, and then regarded her there on the floor.

She wriggled helplessly then let her head fall back as she sagged. *See how defeated I am? You don't have to tie my wrists to my ankles, or put anyone in here to guard me.*

He walked out, shutting the door firmly behind him. "No one is to enter or leave," he commanded the guards outside, loud enough to be heard.

The single advantage to being scrawny, Liere had discovered when doing prisoner of war drills with the older girls, was how fast she could work wrist bindings under her butt. The silk chafed mercilessly at her skin, but at last she succeeded. Then she got her feet inside the circle of her arms and pulled the bonds up over her knees.

The knots had pulled tight. They would take an hour of hard work with her teeth. She had been taught, along with the best of the elder students, a kind of muscle contraction that gave one a margin. The girls had called it "butterbones." She contracted twice, painful as it was — it felt like a sharp cramp — but that succeeded in getting an edge of the silk over the joint at the base of one thumb.

That was all she needed. She soon worked her hands free, got rid of the gag, and freed her feet. She flung the sashes to the floor, hesitated, then picked them up again. *Leave no evidence* had been drilled into her; she stuffed them into her pocket and looked around the room.

There was a narrow door. For servants? Let's see where it goes, shall we?

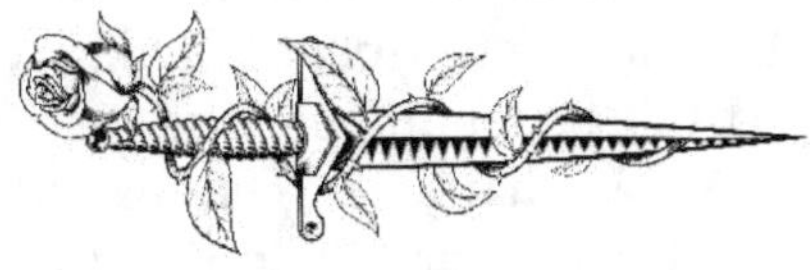

FORTY-FIVE

Gared and Andri felt their way along a narrow, spiderweb-draped passage. Its twists and turns, in total darkness, confused Gared, but Andri pushed on, muttering, "I'm sure it's past here."

"Not arguing," Gared muttered. "Just noting you've said that twice."

"I was five when I was in here last," Andri retorted over his shoulder. Alismira had shut him in what she'd thought was a forgotten closet, which he'd discovered was actually a passage—to the royal bedchamber, which was far scarier than any mere spiderwebs. But at least his father had not been there.

"It seemed even longer then. But it only goes the one way, once we got past that second door back there. At least, if Cousin Adon hasn't discovered it. Judging by these webs—ah. Here. Dead end. I told you." He grunted with effort. He suspected the wounds were bleeding again, but he hoped the bandages would hold him together, just a while longer . . . "Uhn. Latch is stuck. There."

"Let me," Gared said quickly.

"I'm fine," Andri said. "Great! Having that damned spell off me is like an anchor lifted from around my head. I could take on a patrol."

"Leave patrols to me," Gared said dubiously, not liking the breathiness in Andri's voice.

Gared shouldered against the much-painted-over door. It finally gave way with a protesting creak. Gared gripped his sword, expecting Adon-Marsael to leap at them, but the royal bedchamber was completely empty. Both breathed in relief; though Andri talked tough, it was partly to keep Gared from worrying, and partly in hopes that if he talked tough, he could somehow make it real. As it was, the light sword he'd slung through the baldric felt like an iron mace the size of a horse. At least the baldric hid the terrible fit of Gared's best tunic.

They crossed the bedchamber, and paused outside the door to the interview chamber. The sound of the crowd packed in the vast courtyard below muffled any nearer sounds. Both glanced toward the long windows, then Andri gave a mental shrug. They were as ready as they'd ever be, no matter what was on the other side of that door.

Gared opened it. They stopped, face to face with Adon and two big guards in Marsael livery.

For one endless moment, everyone stared. Then Andri leaned back against the wall, and a laugh escaped him. "Ah, this is convenient."

"Convenient indeed," Adon-Marsael said, his hand going to the gold-chased hit of his dress sword. "Make sure they are alive," he suggested to the guards, who drew their blades.

"Wait!" Andri said. Had that servants' door on the opposite wall cracked? He kept his gaze on Adon-Marsael's face.

Adon half-lifted a hand, relishing his win. "What now, Cousin?'

"The treaty," Andri said, desperate for something to talk about, anything, because he was not going to look away from Adon's face, and (he hoped) neither were the two Marsael guards gripping their swords and poised to attack. Andri had his own sword, but he knew that he had maybe two good blows in him. However . . .

"What about the treaty," Adon-Marsael said, a hint of impatience in his voice—judging by the growing noise, the crowd was getting restless and rowdy.

"Just that it's mine," Andri said.

At that moment Liere, who had ghost-footed through the servants' door, picked up a bust of Alored Elsarion, first king of Enaeran. Her sandals noiseless on the beautiful Bermundi carpet, she thought of Adon-Marsael torturing Andri by magic *while eating breakfast,* and swung from the shoulders.

Thok! Adon-Marsael dropped like a stone.

The guards pivoted, the one on the right swinging his sword, but Liere was faster. The guard and the bust collided on the backswing, and his sword spun away as he fell. The second guard leaped at Andri, completely losing his head.

Andri had ripped his sword free. He warded two attempts to skewer him before Gared reversed his blade and clubbed the guard down.

Liere glared at Adon-Marsael, her lips a white line. "I hope he's dead. No, I don't." She set the bust carefully on the table and looked worriedly into Andri's face.

He was pale, but when their eyes met he managed a smile. "Marten said you had an errand?"

"That." She pointed at Adon-Marsael. "There's more, but I'll tell you later." She pulled out the sashes, tossing down one and keeping the other. "Turnabout is fair," she said to the unconscious Adon-Marsael. "And by the way, this is the way to tie someone up." She bound his wrists efficiently with one end, using a knot that Sister Rose had taught the girls, and then bound his wrists to his ankles. "Let's see you break out of that."

Gared had silently picked up the gold sash, which he used to bind one guard, who groaned as he came around. Gared's own cotton sash took care of the unconscious one.

"Go," Gared said to Andri.

Andri took a step toward the double doors that led to the proclamation balcony, then he looked back, his expression one of hilarity and horror, accentuated by those dark marks under his eyes. "They expect a speech!"

"And you will give it," Liere said. "I was taught that if you must make a speech, begin by telling your auditors how excellent they are, tell them what you're there for, and then keep whatever promise you make."

"That's right, make it *sound* easy. I notice you are not volunteering to do the deed."

Liere's mouth was perfectly serious, but her eyes betrayed laughter. "I," she said, "am not a king."

Gared leaned on his sword. "We can always make a run for it. Get over the border. Hire out as tavern guards."

"Well-diggers." Liere patted the top of Alored I's marble head.

"Neither of you is helping," Andri observed, as the crowd noise intensified.

Andri opened the balcony door, and stepped through.

Exclamations, questions, and shouts dissolved in a shrill

cheer from the very back, other voices catching on. Bassl at a side balcony, began to cheer. The other young nobles who secretly (or not so secretly, as in the case of Thadara Otobris) had been on Andri's side also cheered, as did a few young nobles who didn't care who sat on the throne, but wanted handsome Bassl 's attention.

The crowd, catching the mood, joined in.

Andri looked out over the sea of upturned faces; though his Dena Yeresbeth had never been reliable, it was somehow a little easier without Yeres's evil magic drilling into his head. He sensed word passing from one to the next among his followers, each keeping faith with their promises.

Then this was where he must begin making, and keeping, his own promises.

"People of Enaeran," he said, and waited for the mutters to die down to a susurrus of whispers as people shushed each other.

Silence at last.

He cleared his throat. "From the time our ancestors faced off Mathias the Conqueror at our eastern border, Enaeran has been a strong and independent kingdom."

Cheers. It had sounded pretty fatuous coming out, but Liere was right about beginning with a compliment. Though he didn't recollect his father ever complimenting anyone. Ever.

"A lot has gone wrong since the civil strife began. I intend to shore up what we have, and to make Enaeran stronger. Beginning with this treaty."

He turned to find Porganal, the Adrani ambassador's aide, helpfully holding out a fine steel-nibbed pen. Having been warned about the treaty's content, Andri scanned it hastily and found what he sought. He dipped the pen in the dark blue ink, and made two cross-outs. Above Adon Marsael's name he wrote his own, and above the clause that said Sles Adran would be invited in to restore peace if anything threatened the sovereign, he wrote, *will remain on its side of the border, except in trade.*

He signed it with a flourish, and held it out to the Adrani ambassador, who looked back impassively, as from behind the door Gared said in an undervoice, "I'm off: Talipin is trying to seize both docks."

Andri suppressed the instinct to vault over the balcony

and run to direct the defense and add his sword to it. Before he fell flat on his face. He was close enough now; that brief exchange with the Marsael guard had definitely started the cuts bleeding again.

But he was here. And Adon Marsael wasn't. As he watched the Adrani ambassador take her time signing the treaty, he was aware that this is where sharing power—the ability to act on behalf of the kingdom—begins.

She stepped back.

Feeling that something else was needed, Andri picked up the treaty, and brandished it on high.

Cheers!

Someone bellowed, "What's it say?"

Should he read it? Why not begin with a summary. "It says—now—that Sles Adran is not allowed to cross the border, except in trade."

They cheered that.

"What about the mines?" another man yelled.

A woman added, her voice strident with fury, "Both my sons were snatched right off the streets. If they still live."

"I made a promise to address the mines before anything else," Andri shouted. "I'll be doing that this week." *As soon as I take the treasury back.* "From now on, I'll look at every judgment before anyone is sent."

Another cheer, but more voices broke out, trying to outshout one another, then a deep voice boomed, "What about Navor Mandracar? They say he's lined along the border, ready to invade."

Navor Mandracar? Andri knew that name. Mandracar was Bartal of Sles Adran's latest army commander.

Andri turned to the ambassador. She said, "It had been arranged for by his excellency Adon-Marsael n'Elsarion."

"I rescind that arrangement," Andri said distinctly. "Please inform your king."

The ambassador bowed, and behind her shoulder, Porganal dipped his head in a tiny nod.

From inside the room, Liere listened, white-knuckled with tension. So far it seemed Andri was finding his feet. But she saw his arm pressed to his side where the two wounds were the worst. He was wearing something of Gared's, which was dark enough to hide bloodstains. It also happened to be the Enaeraneth midnight blue, though without any gold or white embellishments.

A noise from the doorway to the hall caught her ear. Liere turned as Fronsa slammed her way in, leading a few of Andri's people, all brandishing weapons. Their eyes widened when they saw the two guards, one awake struggling futilely against Gared's knots, and the other, like Adon-Marsael, out cold.

"Is there somewhere to stash them?" Liere asked.

Fronsa's sword point lowered. "We hold the garrison now. Why not use the lockup?"

Liere said, "The guards outside?"

"Ran off." Fronsa twirled the sword. "Some have thrown off their liveries and come over to us."

Liere said, "Gared said that Talipin is fighting at the docks."

Fronsa scowled. "We heard. He's fighting to kill or be killed. He knows he hasn't a chance now, after all he's done. Ah, our job is the palace."

She and her party picked up the three and bore them out.

Liere turned back to the door. The questions were still coming, it seemed.

". . . duel squares?"

Andri was getting hoarse. "Not all the recent laws are bad. This law, meant to limit Enaeraneth killing one another, I won't rescind, but I will amend. Dueling squares are traditional. That privilege will be restored—"

"*Yay!*"

"—but! Not duels to the death. Murder is still murder. If you need to fight, join the royal guard. We'll need to patrol the border if Mandracar is looking for an excuse to start something."

A ragged cheer at that, which gained strength as people hotly debated the right to slaughter each other, according to established rules.

Andri began to roll the treaty, saying, "The coronation will be at harvest time. That means a feast day for the entire kingdom, at crown expense."

At that, the cheer was loud and hearty, especially from the new faces crowding in from the city below.

"I'd better get started. There's a lot to do," he said, wondering if he would faint before his vocabulary entirely fell out of his head, or the other way around. "It's Midsummer.

Go and celebrate!" he shouted, backed up, waved, then entered the royal interview room, which previous to today, he'd last seen when his father disinherited him.

The image faded when he saw Liere there. The sight of her was so reassuring. He sank into a chair, light-headed with relief, blood loss, and fever. All his tired mind could think was: she was there.

He smiled. "Fine work with Alored the First. I like to think he'd approve."

"Thank you. That was impressive for a first speech."

"Short. But no one seemed to mind short. You were right again." He drew a painful breath. Now that the euphoria was dissipating, the pain was back, more insistent than ever. "I think I'd like to invent some more crises, just to see you surprise me. Oh, to have an army of you!"

"I'm not an army," she responded. "But you can have the one."

He blinked, completely at sea.

"Me," she explained. And at his still looking bewildered, "I love Enaeran. I love riding side by side with you, and laughing with you, and sharing joy as well as sorrow. I want to make your home my home. Unless you don't want me. Was that a joke that I didn't catch?"

"Not want you?" They stared at each other, both tired and exhilarated and overwhelmed by the moment. Yet despite being exhausted and grimy and overwhelmed, the sweet fire burned as bright as it had the day they first laid eyes on each other.

He held out a hand, and she put hers in his, as he said huskily, "How could I not want you? Even if I still don't know who you are."

"Liere Fer Eider," she admitted. It was time for the truth. "I'm not Sartoran. I'm from Imar. Originally. Though I haven't ever been back since I left at age ten."

"You left at *ten*?"

"Well, it was special circumstances. I'm sure you don't want to hear it—"

"Who just promised to tell me everything?"

"I was being chased by Siamis. Well, his Norsundrians. Senrid and I, which is how I know the king over the mountain, and by the way, he wouldn't take over here. Unless he's changed in the five years I've been away."

"You're—you can't be—that Liere?"

She sighed. "There are times I wish I couldn't be. But I am. Further, Lyren-Sartora isn't actually my cousin. She's my daughter."

Andri stared helplessly at her. "I don't know what to say. Not about your little scribe. I can understand why you might want to keep the closer relationship to yourself. But you—being you. It is like, I don't know, asking for a candle and being given the sun."

"That's exactly why I didn't want anyone to know. Because I'm not a sun. I'm just a candle."

"You are a sun to me," he said, his voice thready. "You were before you told me you were that Liere, the Worldsaver. A candle wouldn't know what to do about that . . . what did you call it? Bloodknife spell? Or sweet-talk my sister in perfect Sartoran. Or do any of the amazing things you do."

"But that's all just training. I've had very good training. It so happens it was on Geth-deles—"

"That's another *world*. I've never even been outside the kingdom. Except one morning, by magic, to see my sister. Was that true about just happening to have those coins with the transfer spell on them?"

"I'm trained in magic," she admitted.

"Of course you're a mage." He uttered a laugh of sheer amazement.

She looked unhappily at him. "Please don't make any of it out to be . . . more than it is. I didn't tell you before. Maybe I could have helped sooner."

Exhilarated as he was, Andri could see how the subject upset her. They both had hidden a lot of themselves, for what had seemed very good reasons. He tried to think of something reassuring to say. It seemed of primary importance, though his body clamored *pain, pain, pain* and then there was the matter of securing the capital.

At that moment, the door banged open, and Thadara Otobris stalked in, trailing three of his teenage followers who had been assigned as runners once the palace had been secured. They were trying unsuccessfully to stop her.

"Andri," she stated, "you may begin by telling your rabble to respect orders—"

Andri raised a tired hand, the edge of his palm bloody. "My rabble is now palace staff," he said.

Thadara checked, her eyes widening. "Andri, there's blood on your hand."

He pressed it to his side, wincing. "There's a lot more here, I assure you."

Liere whirled and ran to the far room, which she remembered as a linen storage, and beyond it a private dining nook off the personal library. She snatched up a pile of clean cloths here, and a pitcher of fresh water from there, then ran back.

Thadara was mid-rant. ". . . begin as you mean to go on. I am happy to take over Trade. I already have a staff in mind, but I'll need a place in the palace until I can arrange for my own home. Father will be intolerable until you exile him to Otobris. But first, and more important, you must establish the tone of kingship, which means assuring . . ."

Andri had leaned his head back, his eyes closed. Liere knelt by his chair and gently unfastened the tunic, her breath hissing in when she saw the deep crimson of her bandages.

"You're going to need to lie down," she murmured beneath Thadara's steady lecturing.

"Can't. Bind it tight," he whispered.

". . . to be by your side as long as I can, to oversee these tasks that I know you do not wish to trouble yourself with — Andri, are you listening to me?"

"Ow, ow, ow," he said as Liere eased away the sodden bandages. "Ow!" he added as she poured water over the wounds. "I should have left Yeres's mark."

Liere whispered, "You will sleep tonight."

"Or not." A flash of his old smile.

Thadara took a step nearer, looking from one to the other. "Girl, wrap him neatly and take yourself off. This is the beginning of his reign, and it's important to establish — "

Andri spoke over Liere's head as she carefully bounded three layers of folded cloth over the wounds. "Thadara, you will be the kingdom's best Minister of Trade. For which I'm grateful. It ought to keep you very busy, especially now, so you can safely leave my tasks to me."

"I already have a list of actions to be taken, in order of urgency. The top three will need edicts, beginning with reclaiming the — "

"Treasury," Andri said. "I'm with you there."

" — but equally important are these other matters I've

been telling you about, which I —"

"Can leave to Liere," Andri cut in once more.

"What?"

Andri lifted heavy eyelids. "Thadara, this is Liere Fer Eider."

Thadara frowned. "That simply means 'from the Eid,' which is a respectable enough name for a family of shopkeepers, though the Eid no longer exists — it was taken from the Dei family when Everon and Imar broke apart, and —"

"Liere Fer Eider. Better known as Liere Worldsaver. Liere, all things considered, I think you ought to wear this, and not I."

To Liere's astonishment — exponentially more intense in Thadara, judging by her rounded eyes — Andri produced from his pocket a signet ring. "I don't know why I brought it. I've never worn it. Until I swiped it back, I only saw it on my father's hand. Not a good memory. But . . ." He held out a peremptory hand, and when Liere laid hers in his, he put the ring on her palm. "Speak for me."

"Speeches can wait," Liere said, dropping the heavy gold question of her entire future into a pocket, to be dealt with later. She eased her finger under the knot she'd just made, to make sure it wouldn't press tender flesh.

Andri's laugh was no more than a puff of breath. "I realize you don't like titles. But it's been said that titles are like underwear —"

" — an agreed-on fiction that doesn't muffle farts," Liere finished. "Lasva Sky-Child to Emperor Mathias of Colend."

Thadara had fallen silent, looking from one to the other during this quick exchange; she heard the shared intimacy, the tenderness, surprised at how much it hurt. But then she scrutinized Liere's golden hair, the glint of gold in her eyes, and remembered her earlier guesses. Liere was a little too pale to be a Golden Dei, she argued mentally. But it would be useless to argue with Andri, because he didn't give a spit about the Deis. Or the Landises of Sartor. She wasn't even certain he properly respected his own royal blood. Victory had come at a personal cost: though she had been thoroughly outflanked, at least it was by a somewhat worthy opponent. If that was even true about Liere being *that* Liere, she did believe in the Dei connection.

But that did not mean she'd lost the war. (Because everything in her life was a competition.) She said with icy dignity, "I will speak to your royal steward for an appointment. I take it you do have a royal steward in mind?"

Andri's eyes were still shut. With the other hand, still clutching the treaty, he said, "Steward, yes. Thanks for the reminder, Thadara. Where's Marten?"

"Marten brought us."

Liere and Thadara turned at the new voice, as Lyren-Sartora danced in, golden threads glinting in her dark curls, her rough-woven undyed tunic that most city children wore somehow graceful on her. Thadara stared, stunned: she could try to convince herself that Liere's pale skin meant diluted blood, but this girl was definitely a Golden Dei. It wasn't just the gold-colored eyes or the mane of gold-touched dark hair, or even the grace. There was an inner luminescence to her. This girl would one day storm the world if she so chose.

Lyren-Sartora jerked a thumb at Andri as she said to Liere, "Did you tell Poopsie Face who we really are, *Mother?*"

"I did," Liere said. "I can go find Marten," she offered, straightening up.

Lyren-Sartora eyed the pile of sanguine bandages next to Liere, and all the guise of affront leaked out of her: so far, everything could be regarded as a game, the most important players Liere and Lyren-Sartora. Even the shocking news about Ratface hadn't disturbed her unduly, as she'd scarcely known him.

But all that blood shocked her.

She said in a very different voice, "I know where he is. And we're supposed to be running errands."

Andri held out the treaty still gripped in one hand. "Here's his first task. After he gets his heralds in place. Find somewhere to put that."

Thadara was thinking, Martande Eldias? He was actually a very good choice. And he, at least, would listen to sense. Liere had taken the treaty and was about to pass it to Lyren-Sartora, but Thadara snatched it away, then bowed to Andri, very deliberately, and exited, leaving Lyren-Sartora glaring after her. She was about to deliver her opinion of Thadara when she caught Liere's eye.

Liere gave a tiny shake of the head, and Lyren-Sartora sighed and rolled her eyes.

Here was another aspect of finding a home, Liere thought as she piled the bloody bandages onto one of the golden trays: compromise with difficult personalities.

Andri opened his eyes and grunted as he swung to his feet. "Let's get down to the dock before they set the entire city on fire."

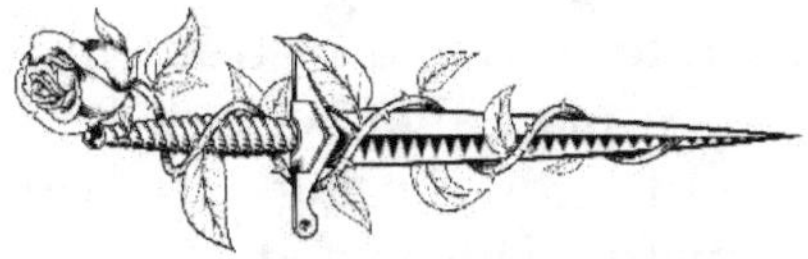

FORTY-SIX

Alsais, capital of Colend

The afternoon thundershowers in Enaeran usually rolled over Sles Adran late in the evening, and if the mountains at the eastern border did not scatter the clouds, they would reach Colend by late the next day.

Because of the series of storms that had come through for the past week, the guilds discussed the matter, then petitioned the newly-arrived king to begin the Music Festival.

Ordinarily all attention was on the winner from the year previous, whose presence this year was paid for by the crown. It had become a tradition that the last winner of the Silver Feather would present a new piece to begin the week of the festival.

This year, all the attention was on their handsome young king, who at last had truly come into his power, and already life was better, the people of Alsais assured one another.

This was not the first time he had presided over the Alsais Music Festival's opening day. He'd done it every year since his father's death, with the regency council lined up behind him (and always assured of the best seats, especially as they had either served as judges or selected them).

But this year, they were noticeable in their absence from the places of prominence. They had to obtain seats at the more formal stages like anyone else. Further, the judges were, once again, anonymous, chosen by the king. No one could be sure who they were. They might be anyone, from a canal poler to a count.

Shontande had been making speeches all his life. Though he no longer repeated the words he'd been told to say, he knew the rhythms that graced a happy occasion. He gave a brief, graceful speech of welcome then introduced last year's winners.

This was a group of wind instruments. They gave the entranced listeners a piece that began with sounds evoking the mating dance of birds chasing and flirting through the sky, then all the instruments joined, swelling into a melody that celebrated youth, and life, and the dance. Half the young people on the edge of the crowd twirled and stepped and leaped on the grass by the end, a perfect beginning.

It ended in a deafening rattle of applause, then a voice rose from the canal, and another. People began spreading out to take in the performers wandering the streets or boating down the canals: the festival had truly begun.

Shontande went around to the chiefs of the guilds, thanking each personally for their efforts this past week. He did not rush, but he had an end in view: there was only one guest whose opinion truly mattered to him today. Hidden in a private court screened by aromatic ferns and shaded by awnings, sat none other than Jilo, a Chwahir.

In the two strategy meetings in Remalna that Shontande had attended, he had observed that the quiet Chwahir was sensitive to art. It was more than a sensitivity. It was a thirst, almost a craving, the more intense for being completely unspoken. Shontande might never have known, except that he had twice caught Jilo gazing on a set of carvings, and then on a trumpet lily vine trained over an archway with the rapt focus of someone committing a precious sight to memory.

He'd waited until they were walking to the Destination, then took Terry Larensar aside to ask if the Chwahir had their own art. "Forbidden," Terry said shortly. "Along with everything else in life. Except serving Wan Edhe."

The night Shontande returned to Alsais from Sartor, the first thing he'd done was write a note to invite them both to the Music Festival before the next meeting at Remalna.

For Jilo, that week was like living in a dream. He had not been prepared for how Alsais was harmoniously balanced no matter where you turned your eye. This kind of living art took generations to create.

Painfully self-conscious, he shuffled from shadow to shade tree to unobtrusive corner, looking and listening, as music was everywhere. Singers and players strolled back and forth over the pretty arched bridges, or sailed along the canals, or drifted in and out of pavilions and stages of various types; some stages offered more formal programs. These were invariably the established performers, most having won awards here and at home, for they came from as far away as Goerael.

He listened so hard and so long he almost forgot to eat, except when he smelled something so delicious that his appetite roared to life. This, too, was new: food as art.

The only plaintive note was the occasional exclamation overheard, "Is that a Chwahir?" "There are even Chwahir here!" "Ah-ye, do the Chwahir even know what music is?"

Thoughtlessness such as this he could look past. Most wasn't even cruel in intent. But beneath it all was the deep regret that the Chwahir, who had slowly begun finding their way back toward the greatness of Chwahir music, had been silenced again except for Wan Edge's minatory drum beat, pounded out for executions and punishments, and meant to keep everyone in lockstep obedience.

Late the last day of the festival, Terry found Jilo crouched under a shady willow, listening to a choir whose polyphonies were echoed by higher voices unseen in the rafters of the stage, which (it was whispered around the group rapt below) emulated the echo singers of the cave-dwelling morvende.

"Sorry, Jilo, this is the last song. Everyone else is packing up. We've got to head for the Destination. They'll be looking for us in Remalna."

Jilo mooched along with many backward glances.

"Shon said we can come back next year." Too late Terry saw that reminding Jilo of Chwahirsland under the grinding heel of the mad king Wan Edhe was not exactly cheering. "Hiya, I wonder what Senrid will have for us today."

Shontande was waiting for them in the palace. He'd changed from his fabulous embroidered, fluttering silks to more sober colors that matched the steel blue paint on his nails.

One by one they transferred to Remalna. Shontande was glad to see that Senrid was early. In fact, Senrid had made a point of arriving early so that he and Shontande could talk a little.

"How's it feel to be regency-free?" Senrid asked.

Shontande hesitated, not wanting to sound like a

complainer. The truth was, he'd returned to a mountain of labor, and the awareness that from now on, bad decisions could not be blamed on the former regency council. Most of whom, he knew, still got together to criticize him. Severally and singly they had come to him, offering to guide him through a smooth transition. It might even be well-meant, but such was his lingering resentment he'd been hard-put not to shadow ward them with a sharp gesture.

He met Senrid's gaze. Senrid was not exactly expressive, but Shontande in these brief meetings had become aware of the subtle shifts in the tiny muscles around eye and mouth that revealed shades of irony. That irony, with his steady and understanding gaze, was a reminder that he'd been there once, and at a much younger age. Learning to rule people who tended to register complaint with steel.

"Splendid," Shontande said. "Everything is splendid," he added, grateful that his mistakes would bring no worse reaction than oblique mockeries at the Hour of the Bird, or perhaps a hilarious bit in a play, with a foolish character masked in royal Colendi colors.

Senrid flashed a grin, and Shontande said, "One of my first conversations was with Donais Altan. Perhaps you will not be surprised to hear that he repeated much of what you said: they can withstand small groups of marauders, but not a large army. He also pointed out that small bands of mounted marauders who break the Covenant by using arrows would effectively double their numbers. I gave him permission to drill the herald-guards in archery, with the understanding that these weapons would only come out if it is Norsunder invading."

Senrid said, "I'm afraid that the Covenant, which was a fine idea during its day, won't last long if and when they come."

Shontande hid the chill these words gave him, that bleak sense of helplessness at the knowledge that a war no one wanted might be forced on them anyway. "It is an irony I cannot quite assimilate that the turning point in the regency council's withdrawal, according to Bee, was interference by one of Detlev's followers."

"Curtas?" Senrid said knowledgeably. "He was your friend once, wasn't he?"

"Can it ever be friendship when one is ordered to

infiltrate and spy?"

Senrid turned up his hand, remembering his own first meeting with Leander Tlennen-Hess, which came about because his uncle expected him to spy out weaknesses and exploit them. It had been his first mission on his own. And it had taken some time afterward to overcome a very natural distrust. "That's a question only you can resolve. But I will say. Of that gang, Curtas was one of the least harmful. No one ever had anything bad to say about him, or Adam."

Terry broke off a conversation with Jio and Vidanric, saying, "Adam? Curtas? Is there word from Detlev?"

"Not that I know," Senrid said.

Atan arrived then, with Rel behind her. "Have you heard anything from Detlev or his people?" Senrid asked.

"I have not." Atan took them all in at a glance. "My apologies for us being late and last. A day I don't have to hear Detlev's name, or think about him, is a good day." She raised a quick hand. "Though I realize he's likely to know Norsunder's strategic situation better than anyone."

If he isn't part of it, several were thinking.

They settled around the table, and Atan said, "We've been using the time to organize the archives. So much has been left generation after generation, with the attitude that what the previous people in charge thought acceptable should be fine now. The most important records are being relocated into the white tower, which as you probably know, is the only undamaged building left from before the Fall. Norsunder can't get inside for some reason the mages still cannot figure out."

They accepted that, Senrid thinking that actually there were two complete buildings left over, and parts of at least one more, north of him in Larkadhe. But he said nothing, for he was certain that that strange castle in Mearsies Heili was far older than the seven hundred years the Mearsieans so blithely assumed. Far older.

Atan went on, "This relocation isn't as simple as it might sound, as there is already so much stored there. And we don't know whether there will be an attack tomorrow, or in ten years, or if at all. This affects planning."

"We can hope they are so busy fighting each other they don't have time for us," Vidanric murmured. "Though I would not count on it."

Everyone agreed; Shontande thought of the meeting he had had with the mages who ran the banks, the most secretive of all of the guilds. They had made some mutual agreements too grim to describe casually.

Atan turned to Rel, who said, "The city guard has been drilling ways to deflect an invasion from the south long enough for those who can't fight to get out."

"Which brings us to today's topic: resistance," Senrid said.

Everyone else there understood the context: defeat.

"Let's discuss your strengths, even if you've been forced to surrender. You know the territory. Your opponent doesn't. You can make their win costly for them, in such a way they cannot take their losses directly out on you. Then there are hit and run tactics, what we call lever resistance, in which a small force can be as effective as a large one. It begins with being maneuverable . . ."

Everyone, thought Shontande, prepares for the coming thunder in different ways. Some sleep. Others perform their daily tasks with a desperate precision, as if that will restore order. Someone like Senrid, it appeared, used those long watches of the night poring over histories and maps, and preparing useful suggestions for other people: he had something for each of them, taking into consideration very different terrains, populations, and readiness.

He came to Jilo last. "I know your situation is the most dire of anyone's, before the first Norsundrian is sighted. But there are some things you can do with your people."

Jilo's hands flexed, then he looked up, and in a thin, bleak voice, he said, "I cannot say they are 'my people' because you're talking about kings. I'm not one. Whatever I accomplished is being undone day by day. And I am not stopping it. My fellow Chwahir would be perfectly justified in regarding me as a cowardly traitor who ran to save himself."

Rel interrupted here. "Jilo, I know differently."

Though he was the only one at that table not a king, he was aware that Jilo knew the blood tie that would terrify Wan-Edhe if he were to find out. Jilo's desolate gaze met his, and Rel said, "You are the Chwahir ideal king. No, hear me out, and deny this if you dare: to the Chwahir, you are the one who restored, bit by bit, the honor of work. Is that not true?"

Jilo opened his mouth to gainsay, but he remembered his uncle saying something to that effect. *To us, meaningful work is honor,* Uncle Shiam had said. *The magic you have removed from Narad is important, but this is your true gift, and everyone knows it. Everyone.*

Rel went on, "I know it hurts, thinking of your work being undone by that madman Wan-Edhe. And there are undoubtedly those who will blame you for not warding him, for not coming back with fire and sword to get rid of him. But most people are more realistic, this Mondros insists on, and he listens to the Chwahir, as you know. He says that even in the army, which was resisting your changes the most, those who survive Wan-Edhe's latest purges would be reminded of how much better life was when you were in Narad."

Shontande was studying Jilo. He had no idea how old Jilo was. He looked no older than sixteen or so. He knew from Senrid that Jilo had risked his life attempting to dismantle eighty years of lethal magic, all on his own, beginning with a pocket Norsunder which bent time as it sucked out the lives of the people in the city to fuel that lethal magic. Jilo had never done the Child Spell that some of the other alliance members had had for a time. His lack of aging was due entirely to the poisonous effect of that magic. That he chose to endure so that he could dismantle it from the inside.

Was that not the essence of heroism? Yet to Jilo such terms were meaningless, because he had not been able to succeed. And the people suffered.

But there might be something he could say, something true.

Shontande spoke. "One thing is granted a powerless king: plenty of free time. My busy regency council had no objections whatsoever to my delving into the oldest archives, those even older than the kingdom of Colend, when the counts of Kifel were vassals of Sartor. Ah-ye, I suspect some of those dusty and much-copied records are older than that, especially the ones in your own language, still untranslated until I found them."

Jilo lifted his eyes. "You know Chwahir? You didn't tell me that?"

"We spoke so much of music this week! Yes, I learned some. And what I discovered is that my ancestors stole most of what they know about our famous silks, and linens, and linden honey . . ."

"Dyansha," Jilo whispered.

"So many claim that the silk that is the heart of Colend, before it was Colend, is actually Chwahir in origin. Whatever occurred in your history to lead you to the present crisis, I do not know. These were mostly trade records. But I wish you to understand that I believe circumstances could easily have led us the same way. It might even lie in our future, though I'll resist as long as I can. But in the future. If we both should survive what is to come. if you have no wish for war — if your desire is to reopen trade — you will have my full support."

"That is exactly what I want for the Chwahir," Jilo whispered.

Shontande reached over, both palms up, Colendi-style.

As the two clasped hands, Senrid thought, this would be a fine moment for the balladeers, if any of 'em were present. I just hope the three of us survive to tell someone eventually.

"The Chwahir had begun to taste freedom," Jilo said, his thin cheeks flushed, but his voice marginally stronger. "For three generations Wan-Edhe has convinced them they're hopeless. That to resist him will earn instant death for everyone and his twi — his peer group. My hope is they understand that together they can act."

"Ah," Atan exclaimed. "Exactly why I want to thank you, Senrid. Whatever comes next. Isn't that a summary of what we've been learning here? It is for me: that no one person can resolve what is to come. But together, we can act."

Senrid flashed his toothy grin at her. "If we're moving onto the compliments, let me say I wish you could dump your throne and crown and join Commander Keriam's command class, which is where I've been doing my own learning. You might still be skimpy on tactical know-how, but you've got great strategic grasp."

Atan shook her head. "I don't see much difference between this and the sorts of problems Tsauderei used to set me all the years of our tutoring, on problem solving."

Senrid's brows shot up. "You know. It hits me that that old geezer could probably have taken the world if he'd wanted to."

"But he never wanted to," Atan said. "Bringing me to something else I intended to say. When the subject of maps came up once before, some of the visitors who have never returned were offended by old Sartoran concepts of honas and selas: the latter being the countries often centered in maps, and honas, being those around the edges, sometimes not completely depicted."

The only ones there whose kingdoms could be defined as honas were Vidanric, who knew Remalna was barely a blot next to the kingdoms of these others, and Terry, who thought that Erdrael Danara's size was perfect.

Atan had paused, and seeing no resentment in the circle, turned to Rel. "You know the most. Will you explain?"

Rel said, "Roy pointed out that Norsunder's military maps center around kingdoms with armies they consider the biggest obstacles to conquering. Selas to Norsunder is just that: the biggest challenge. Honas is everyone else."

"I don't see any argument here," Senrid said, glancing at the others. "Your point?"

"Along with not knowing if, or when, Norsunder will attack, we don't know if they will pick off leaders, or try to capture them and force them to comply. Maybe even enchant their brains out and put them back in as puppets."

"Arthur made a suggestion: if kingdoms are overrun, meet somewhere in a honas country, to coordinate recovery."

Senrid sat up straight. "I assumed I'd be alone, if I survive. Have to say, I like your idea."

"So do I," Terry said.

Shontande nodded, though with reserve. He had never been part of the alliance.

Jilo said softly, "Where?"

"Nalisse, Thad's friend, comes from Lisdan, a trade town in Melire," Rel said. "I knew the place from my travels. It's small, militarily unimportant, but used to seeing strangers coming and going along the trade routes. Arthur and Roy suggest that if the worst happens, and you rulers decide to run, we meet there."

"I'm in," Senrid said.

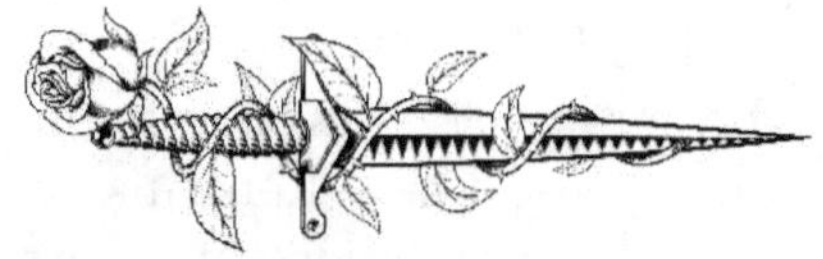

FORTY-SEVEN

Adon Marsael (no longer claiming to be The Elsarion) sat in the prison waiting for some muffled figure to come in the middle of the night and slit his throat. That was certainly how he'd dealt with problems in the past, only he'd been the one sending the muffled figure as he disliked the mess, the noise, the smells of killing. But there was always someone willing to do the deed, for gold, for revenge, or for the fun of it.

The first night dragged on, hour by hour, and no one came near.

The next morning one of Andri's followers appeared with a host of armed youths. Adon Marsael braced himself. The door was unlocked, and Gared approached with a knife, his mouth set.

Here it is, Adon Marsael thought, heart racing.

Gared yanked his head forward by the hair and cut the bonds. Adon's limbs flopped apart. His circulation had not been cut off, but being bent for so long caused the sense of a thousand bee stings in his joints. "Who tied me up?" he asked.

Gared said shortly, "I'm for slitting your throat, but Andri doesn't want to. I don't know why."

Adon laughed mirthlessly.

Someone dumped down a bowl of water and some sort of food, and the door clanged shut. When Adon Marsael could move again, he ate, drank, and began formulating plans.

He was still at it three nights later (one bowl of water and food per day) when he woke to the sound of someone's throat being slit. The body fell with a thud. Adon sat up, rapidly reviewing his arguments, if Andri himself showed up.

A shadowy figure unlocked the door, and reached to haul Adon roughly to his feet. "She wants you," said the newcomer.

She? Adon Marsael had wondered if Iris would show up again.

Yeres herself waited outside the prison in the company of two of the Black Knives who followed her brother Efael. Moonlight flattered her loose white garment worn over one shoulder, tied by a cord under her breasts and crossed at her trim waist. The draping was not a style Adon had ever seen, but it flattered her.

She looked around the back end of Brydon with distaste, unmoved by the dead guards, then said, "Come along. We'll have to transfer to Norsunder Base in order to get back to the Beyond."

Adon said, "Thank you for the rescue. I'd rather stay. At least until I cut my cousin's heart out."

Yeres laughed and gave her bare shoulder a coy shrug. "Let them play at housekeeping for a little while. It'll be that much more fun for you when you come back and take it all away again."

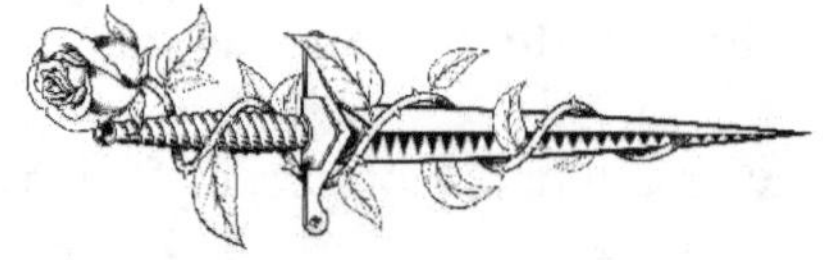

FORTY-EIGHT

"Andri, I realize how advantageous your connection with so famous a person could be, but you've only known her a month. What if she gets tired of mucking about in our backwater of a kingdom?" Thadara had just put a stack of reports on Andri's desk, but instead of going away, she stood right by his chair, her arms crossed.

"You think Enaeran is a backwater?" Andri began to twist around in order to look her full in the face, but the wound pulled. "Ow."

Thadara flushed. "I do not. But she might."

"Have you heard her say such a thing?"

"No, but . . ."

"But you haven't spoken more than ten words to her. I have, every day for most of that month, and I've yet to hear anything at all from her on the subjects of rank and birth."

His tone was even, but that didn't lessen the sting. "You've only known her for a month," Thadara repeat-ed, irritated enough to retort. "Yes, anyone can see the hot eyes you two give each other every chance you can get. Why don't you go somewhere and bunny for a solid week, and get over it? Such things never last."

"That's true enough when the only quality is hot eyes. But every day with her, I discover something new."

Lyren-Sartora, listening avidly from outside the door, decided that the "hot eyes" turn in the conversa-tion was all she could stomach. She banged the door open, jerked her thumb over her shoulder, and said, "Andri. Marten says don't forget—"

"The ambassador," Andri exclaimed, starting up; he still

did not understand why Bartal na Shagal would recall the ambassador after her decades in Enaeran. She'd done nothing wrong. Or maybe he was going to send someone younger? "I didn't forget her. I forgot the time." He charged out of the room with almost his old speed, after ten days of healing.

That left Lyren-Sartora alone with Thadara. Who stared at Lyren-Sartora with the oddest expression on her face, as if she'd taken a bite of her favorite cake, but discovered a bug in it.

"A princess," she said, "does not bang into a room like a cow-hand in a barn, if she is to be respected."

"I'm not a princess," Lyren-Sartora said airily.

"But I understood that Liere is your mother —"

Lyren-Sartora cut in, "I'll probably go back to Bereth Ferian."

Thadara's eyed widened. "Bereth Ferian?"

"That's where we live. Well, I live. Liere's lived a lot more places."

Lyren-Sartora sensed that Thadara was equally fascinated and mortified. Liere had said not to bait her, that she worked hard for Enaeran, and that repairs were already in process, and people settling down, was due in large part to Thadara's scrupulous honesty and attention to the recovered treasury.

Lyren-Sartora suspected that Thadara was not working for Enaeran, she was working to get Andri's attention. And though Lyren-Sartora found the whole matter irritating, she also felt that if Liere wanted old Poopsie Face, she ought to have him instead of someone who made snide comments about Liere.

"Liere's supposed to be Queen in Bereth Ferian, but it's just an honorary title. A presiding title," Lyren-Sartora said. "Liere's lived there, and in Marloven Hess with Senrid — that would be the king — ""

"I know who King Senrid is," Thadara said, disbelief gathered in a line between her brows.

" — and Vasande Leror, and Tahra of Everon is al-ways inviting her, and before we came here, we were with Atan of Sartor. That would be Queen Yustnesveas the Fifth." As Lyren-Sartora finished, she was aware that she was beginning to sound like a far worse snob than this Thadara. If only it wasn't so much fun!

All right, *one* more. Only one. "That was after she went to Geth-deles, our sister world, to study magic." There. Last one, Lyren-Sartora promised.

Thadara blinked twice, then her lip curled. "It al-most seems a shame she didn't stay there to straighten out that world's problems, as no doubt she could," she drawled, and walked out.

Lyren-Sartora stuck her tongue out at the door. That had definitely not gone the way she meant it to, and Thadara was sure to be complaining all over now about her bad behavior, when she'd promised to be good. Especially as Marten had been specific about being polite about the ambassador.

Lyren-Sartora sighed and left the interview chamber. If only Thadara wasn't so irritating with her nasty little comments about Liere in the guise of compliments. "She's so famous she probably finds us amusing." And, "I wonder how long before she gets bored with queening over our poor country." Those were the two Kizka had overheard just yesterday, when Lyren-Sartora brought in bandages for him.

Perhaps it was time to leave the adults to the adults. Lyren-Sartora had spent the past week being a page. It was fun, sometimes, but mostly tedious. Still, tedium was far better than those first couple of days when Liere stayed by Andri's bedside day and night after he collapsed.

Lyren-Sartora had heard how he walked right through the fighting, then looked down at Talipin's dead body, and said, "We'll make sure his family gets the death duty." Then he'd said, "Anyone who lays down arms now will start afresh. Join the royal guard, exile, do something else. No fighting; save it for Norsunder."

Norsunder! Vec, telling the story later, said that the word whispered through Talipin's people like an evil wind.

"Adon Marsael is one of them," Andri said. "There may be others. That's for me to find out. But we need to be united if we're to survive. If Norsunder doesn't come, Sles Adran is ready to. So what's it to be?"

Exchanges of looks, then one dropped his sword. When he wasn't skewered, another did. And another. Leaving two distinct groups of glowering warriors. "Gared, get them situated," Andri said. "Peaceably."

And then, privately to Liere, "I'm done."

They made it to the linen house, where he collapsed.

Liere had shared her memory rather than describe it. For a couple of days he'd been in and out of consciousness. Lyren-Sartora had had to fetch new bandages and carry the gory ones to be washed. Liere and Gared had executed Andri's orders, claiming he was always somewhere else, so that no one knew he'd collapsed.

That was when Lyren-Sartora had volunteered to join the orphans in being a page, since she was already fetching and carrying. They were all so proud of their new liveries, made by the tailor couple, that they were complaining less than usual about being forced to do school in the mornings.

Lyren-Sartora could see that Andri wasn't bad as kings go, and she'd met her fair share of them. And it wasn't as if he was claiming Liere's attention. She was giving it to him. Marten, who was still grieving over Ratface, had said to Lyren-Sartora just the other day, "Let them have their happiness. Life is sometimes so very short." His thoughts were so clear, so sad, and even sadder his memory of the luminescent outline of Ratface with another little boy. That glimmer, so eerie in the mental realm, had made Lyren-Sartora's neck prickle. She knew she was seeing, through Marten, her first ghosts. But she couldn't contact them, the way she could contact living people.

She ran back downstairs to wait for the others to finish morning school, all easy stuff she'd learned long ago. Ah, most of it, she admitted, a little unsettled. There were two orphans, both a year or two younger, who tackled math problems that Lyren-Sartora found difficult. Maybe it was time for her to study again; another year or two and Jaydi and the rest, who she'd thought so ignorant, would catch up with her.

The bell rang, and Jaydi led the pack racing out. Lyren-Sartora joined them, and shrugged off the grownup stuff.

That night when Liere came at last to the suite they'd been given, she said, "The wagons and supplies Andri sent to the mines ought to have arrived by now. I'm going to take him by magic so he can keep his promise."

"Why does he have to go?"

Liere's expression turned pensive, even a little sad, and Lyren-Sartora regretted her pettish tone, and muttered, "Oh, I know he has to. He kept mumbling about his promise to Ratface during that fever."

"Exactly. And I intend to go with him. But after we return, I wanted to talk over plans with you."

Relieved that "talking over plans" didn't sound like "have a talk about how you've been baiting Thadara Otobris," Lyren-Sartora said, "That sounds fine," and promised herself she'd be good no matter what that person said next.

Liere had arranged a Destination pattern on one of the wagons. She used it to send Andri and then herself. When she arrived, it was noticeably cooler, smelling of wet rock after a heavy rain. Andri leaned against the wagon, the greenish cast to his face rapidly fading.

He turned to face a milling crowd of mostly men and boys, all ragged, covered with the dull gray grime of mines. All coughed hoarsely, too weak to fight, but pushing against one another to get closer to the wagons.

The lead driver, one of Andri's gang, said, "The keepers ran off as soon as they saw us." He tipped his chin toward the armed escort, who had been looking forward to a scrap.

"We'll catch up with them."

"The miners all came out, those who could walk."

Andri could see that, but he dipped his head in acknowledgment and climbed up onto the wagon. He still favored a loose lace-up shirt under a long vest-tunic that he wore open while the weather was warm. It was sashed, over loose trousers stuffed in boots. Devea and Banisa had summarily replaced his wardrobe with nice things that they had been making in secret over the past few weeks, and caused the shabby old clothes to vanish.

He would probably never, Liere thought fondly, look like the eastern half of the continent's idea of a proper king, with all their fuss about manners and fashions, but he had presence as he said, "Adon Marsael is gone. We think Norsunder took him. I know all of you consider yourselves innocent, and a lot of you are. Some aren't."

A pause. No one spoke, though there was plenty of side-eye.

"Those who are here as the result of heinous crimes, I'll remind you that people remember. And I listen. That said, we're going to do two things. One, repair and shore up these mines so that they're not so dangerous to work in. Second, miners will now get paid. Anyone who wants to stay, this will commence tomorrow. Today, we sort you out, you get some clothes, and the feast we brought in these wagons, as I heard that the eats here would barely keep a squirrel alive."

He waited for the comments to die down. "The rest of you who have somewhere to go, or did before the troubles, line up. I'll talk to each of you." He climbed down, murmuring to Liere, "I want to find Yanji Arbanion first."

He had explained that Yanji, the heir to a duchas, had been in court when the troubles broke out. He and a lot of other heirs whose families were targeted had either been killed outright or bundled off in chains to the mines, something that Andri had been unable to stop.

From the crowd emerged a gaunt figure who strongly resembled Ratface.

"Yanji," Andri said.

"You remember me," Yanji said flatly, unspoken accusation simmering below the watchfulness of his thoughts.

Andri had told Liere he had given up explaining how he'd been on the run himself during the troubles. Survivors willing to listen, he'd found, asked. Others believed what they wanted to believe, or came around on their own.

"Arbanion is yours again," Andri said. "If you want it."

Yanji stilled, his mouth compressing.

"Renge also took a good part of the treasury, after killing Presined, who led the raid on my father's vaults. Renge is dead."

"He killed my family, that's what I heard," Yanji said, the words spilling out of him. "I've tried to stay alive so I could get justice. Radri was seven! How could seven be a threat! Or thirteen? Ivor was thirteen."

"Ivor survived being stabbed, though he always had trouble eating," Andri said. "He didn't survive Adon Marsael, I am sorry to say. But it was to him I promised that my first action would be to find you."

"Did you kill Renge?"

"No. I was in the capital recovering from a wound taken in the same fight that killed Ratface, ah, Ivor."

Yanji's expression tightened to anger, and Andri said, "Ratface was his name for himself. He said that Arbanion was lost and his family all but dead, and we were to call him Ratface. So we did."

Yanji's anger lengthened into grief. "It was I who taught Radri to call him Ratface. It was just a joke. Radri's little voice was so funny piping up. Ivor thought it was funny, too . . ." He clenched his teeth.

"I know. I think 'Ratface' was his way of staying close to you both."

Yanji broke then, leaning one thin hand against the wagon. Liere ached to hug him, but his entire body stiffened. He did not want to be touched. It was hard enough to wait there while he sobbed, his sharp shoulder blades and the knobs of his spine poking against the ragged, grime-dark shirt he'd been wearing for five years. But then he looked up, and the total desolation in his face hurt Liere far worse.

Andri leaned close and said, "I need you to take Arbanion back."

Yanji stood unmoving. Liere clinched her fists behind her back, sensing that right now Yanji saw no reason to keep living

"It's still there below the southern pass, which is why every king with any wit knows that he needs someone trustworthy at his back."

Yanji stared at the ground, mumbling, "The Marlovens haven't come over for centuries. Not since one of *your* ancestors poked the hornet's nest."

"It's not the Marlovens I'm worried about," Andri said softly, and Yanji looked up at that. "Adon Marsael allied with Norsunder. One of 'em tried to get at me. All the records say that they don't come in ones, like rats. If there's trouble, I need you below that pass. I also need a good home for some of Ratface's friends he'd been living with these past years. Some were Radri's age when I took them in. They all knew him. Are missing him--want to talk about him."

Yanji's bleak gaze shifted to Andri's face and away. "How did Renge leave Arbanion?"

"Good, overall. Hard taxes raised every year, as he never had enough wealth, but you'll know how to straighten that out. We've dispersed his gang. The worst of them are on their way to these mines."

Yanji breathed hard once, twice, and then he dipped his chin in the tiniest of nods.

"Go get something to eat. You'll plan better with a decent meal in you," Andri said.

The second wagon, full of stores, had been emptied, and the volunteer cooks had set up a fireplace to begin frying up pan bread with cheese melted on it, cut from a huge wheel. The Healer had said, "If they've been starved, keep it simple at first."

Liere turned away to help distribute the food, and Andri continued to speak to those who needed an interview, though none were as rough as Ratface's brother.

The third wagon was full of donated clothing that Weavers Row had gathered, added to the well-made but out of fashion donations that Bassl had sweet-talked from the court.

Andri had earmarked Alismira's donation specifically for the mines and miners, which enabled him to pass out coinage to all who wanted to leave, with very few exceptions. (Most of the hardened criminals who had survived the guards' brutal treatment had run when the guards did.) A few were too weak to leave, and were more or less resigned to staying to live out their sentences, while knowing that at least life would be somewhat better.

By nightfall, things had been settled. The two empty wagons were full of former miners who wanted a ride to the nearest trade town to hire horses for going home, or wherever they were going. Yanji had been one of those, coughing raggedly, as did they all.

Andri looked after him worriedly, until Liere said, "If he goes to a healer, he will be given herb steam to lift the dust from his lungs. It'll be a nasty couple of weeks until it's all gone, but then he'll thrive."

"It's not his lungs that bother me. It's his head."

Liere said, "He was listening when you talked about the southern pass, but the turning point was the orphans needing a home."

"You heard that?" Andri regarded her in the gathering darkness. "Not just saying it?"

She knew he believed her, but she sensed it was important enough to him to repeat. "Not just saying it."

"I wish I could use Dena Yeresbeth like that. Instead of getting skull-struck with images and too much emotion. It's like sticking your head inside a bell." He looked around at the circles of people sitting, and the wagons disappearing in the distance. "We're done. Let's go." He made a face, like Jaydi when being told to brush his hair, and added plaintively, "Do you ever get used to this transfer kick in the gut?"

"No." She laughed.

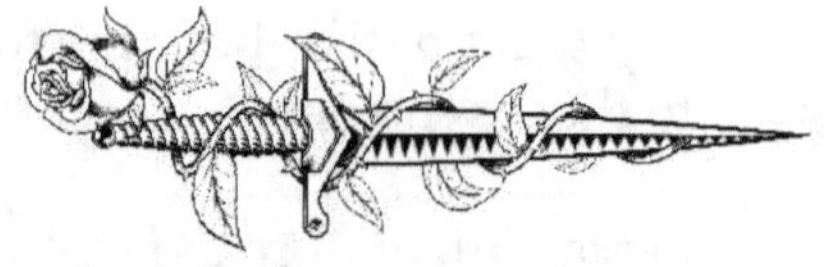

FORTY-NINE

It was late at night. Liere and Lyren-Sartora sat alone.

Liere clutched Andri's ring tightly behind her back. She could not settle her future until she and Lyren-Sartora understood one another.

She said, "Andri's coronation will be at Harvest Time, which they celebrate the first of Ninth-Month. "Then I'll be living here. Do you want to stay—where you know you are welcome—or go back to Bereth Ferian?"

"You're really going to stay?" Lyren-Sartora repeated. "Why?"

"Do you want my reasons?" Liere asked.

"Without being disgusting," Lyren-Sartora said, her face turned away and a hand out as if to stop a horse in its tracks.

"To begin with, I've found happiness. A place I truly belong. I've found someone who accepts me as I am, even knowing all the stupid things I've done. As well as the successes."

Lyren-Sartora knew that if she said, "You had that with Senrid, and Clair of the Mearsieans, and Roy, and Arthur," it would start an argument she didn't want to have. She didn't really know Liere's relationships from the inside with any of those people, and anyway, those relationships had been five years ago. People changed. Everybody said so.

What she truly wanted to say was, "You aren't happy with me?" But she couldn't get the words out. She knew they were more dramatic-sounding than true. She didn't want Liere's attention all the time. Attention all the time is reasonable when you're two. She wanted it only when she wanted it. But that isn't reasonable when you're twelve and telling everybody that you deserve independence.

She also knew that she had been a brat ever since Liere laid eyes on that poopsie-faced scarecrow Andri Elsarion. But even before that—five years ago—Liere had had to go all the way to another world, because Lyren-Sartora and Mac had been brats.

Useless for Arthur to say, *You were just little children.* Siamis had said, with that cursed reasonableness with which Lyren-Sartora couldn't argue, *There is a strong difference between abandoning you and not being able to cope. And you know how much she loves you.*

Lyren-Sartora did know. But she'd taken that love for granted, which again you can do when you're two.

She swallowed hard, though her throat ached, and her eyes stung with tears she would not let fall. Remembering what Marten had said about happiness, she made her mind-shield tight as she said, "You're really popular here. They seem to respect you. Even that cactus-person Thadara does, though she doesn't want to."

"Thadara will get used to me. And I hope she'll find her own happiness. I don't think she had much growing up."

"That's true." Lyren-Sartora made a face, thinking of that horrible Baras Otobris. But even he seemed to be less obnoxious since Andi gave him command of the King's Guard. Gared had said, *Baras Otobris was sent to Khanerenth to study military subjects when he was young. When he returned the king didn't trust him. Along with everyone else. So he was reduced to raising horses and being spied on, until the troubles. Now he gets to do what he was trained to do.* Lyren-Sartor thought resentfully that they would all find happiness except her.

"I'm learning to love the people here," Liere said, studying her. "But not like I love you."

Lyren-Sartora fought against a sob. "I love you, too, and I don't mean to be a brat. I know you can't be around all the time, watching everything I do. I don't even want it. But . . . " *Not here,* she wanted to say. Though she couldn't define why.

"I'd be happy if you chose to stay, and learned to love them, too," Liere said, and Lyren-Sartora wondered uneasily if Thadara had blabbed their earlier conversation all over. "But I know you value your independence, and that people your age do go on the Wander."

There she went, being fair again. Lyren-Sartora wanted to stamp and scream and throw things, but she'd learned when Siamis started her on window cleaning that tantrums got all the wrong kind of attention. She'd demanded to be permitted to make her own choices, so she had to let Liere make hers.

"I can see that that doesn't appeal to you," Liere said slowly. "You do know you're welcome. Everyone wants you to stay."

"I know. I did promise Jaydi and the others that I'll visit," Lyren-Sartora said carelessly as she could. "But the truth is, I miss everybody in Bereth Ferian. I never got a chance to go ice skating, my favorite winter thing, and the lake ice won't be safe soon, and we'll have to wait."

Liere said, "I want to tell Arthur myself that I'm leaving and why. I also need to tell Atan what happened. I really don't want to write it all down on those tiny pieces of paper." She tapped her inner pocket, where the golden notecase lived.

"What about visiting everybody? You said you would. Just you and me."

"We'll do that, too. Now that Andri's so much better, and things are settling down, you and I can continue our visits before I return. How's that sound?"

"Just you and me?"

"Just us."

Lyren-Sartora agreed, secretly hoping that once Poopsie Face was out of sight, he'd slide right out of Liere's mind — while Liere was hoping that a month together would be enough time for Lyren-Sartora to accustom herself to the change in Liere's life.

She waited until the following morning, first looking into his face before she spoke. He looked rested. He had been sleeping well ever since she'd removed the bloodknife mark, and last night he'd eaten his dinner without stopping halfway through, or a quarter of the way through, and dashing off to address some urgent thing he'd forgotten.

He saw what she was doing, and flashed a quick grin. "I'm not going to drop dead any time soon. I feel great. Not just these cuts healing up. Getting Yanji Arbanion on his way home feels like I've come out of a crowded alley full of dangers into the clean air. There's still had a long road ahead, but it's day, and clear. Ah, make sense?"

"Yes," she said, rejoicing in the thought that she would be beside him. Strengthened inwardly by that resolve, she said, "Unless you need me for something, I think it is time to take Lyren-Sartora back to Bereth Ferian. She's eager to resume our visits to old friends, after which I can return with my belongings."

Andri looked into her steady gaze. She was more like the sun all the time, including in the way it never stayed in one place. Was that a good thing? He didn't know anything anymore. "I wondered how much of your life you put on hold to help me," he said. "My biggest regret, you already know."

"I know," she said. "Let's promise each other, no more secrets."

"I promise," he said, and sealed it with a kiss. "On your return, you will get a full report, right down to how often I changed my socks."

He'd said the words *On your return* with confidence that she could feel, but some of the old uncertainty made her want to hold tighter, as if something had already separated them. She looked down at the signet ring that she wore on her thumb, her other fingers wrapped tightly around it.

Andri blinked at that, then gave her a look full of question. "I really will be safe. Or is there some threat out there worrying you? I thought you could reach me anywhere in the world." He tapped his skull. "If not through that letter case you said you'd send me."

"It's not the same," she said, but couldn't define why.

He leaned forward and tapped the ring. "On one of those rare occasions when my father spoke to me without ranting, he told me that that ring had belonged to Uncle Thunder — that is, my great-uncle Trevor Elsarion. That can be your bit of Enaeran, if you like. Till you bring it back."

And he knew by her smile that it was, somehow, the right thing to say. That this wonderful person, so smart, so amazing, so knowledgeable, felt the same uncertainties that everyone else did.

She held it up to admire it. Central was a cobalt blue stone, the color no surprise. At either side, worked in gold, two tiny shields, surrounded by diamonds. One was the Enaeran flag, the other the old Elsarion family crest, which Marten had drawn one rainy night. He enjoyed explaining the origin and evolution of symbols, especially lilies: how they could be daggers or crowns, yet also symbolize hope and peace, depending on how they were shaped and colored.

Kingsblossom had been named that because of the way it resembled crowned lilies.

She turned the ring over, liking the heavy, solid feel. It was a masculine ring. Even though Andri had worn it only one night, it reminded her strongly of him. "I'll bring it back," she said.

"Devea and the others want to give you a party," he said.

"No, no. So much better to go as quietly as we came. Parties should be reserved for those who like them. I found them trying when I was small. Too much bombardment here." She touched her head. "By the time I learned to close crowds of people out, I'd already gotten into a solitary habit."

"We'll work on parties when you get back. Catch up on the fun you missed.'

They smiled at each other, each feeling the imminent parting painful. She kissed him hard, and went out quickly, before she could say "I changed my mind."

She had promised Lyren-Sartora, and anyway, she was not going to be the old weak Liere, afraid at things that never had actually happened.

She went around to her particular friends to say a quiet farewell. Gared was surprised that she was going, but accepted it as he accepted everything. "Have a good time. We'll make things ready for your return."

Marten startled her by bowing low. "Thank you," he said.

Liere's emotions surged as she studied his face. His mind-shield was shuttered, but she sensed no irony. "It will be good to see you back."

"That, I can promise," she said.

Banisa gave her a rib-cracking hug, and Devea whispered, "Don't worry, we'll all take good care of Andri." And winked lasciviously.

Liere laughed. "Do. Please." She loved the way Andri's favorites made her feel a part of them, and wondered if she would find her own favorites among Andri's male friends. Though she could not imagine sharing a bed with anyone but Andri. But she had all the time in the world to figure that out, a thought that filled her lighter than air.

She was smiling when she rejoined Lyren-Sartora. "I should report to Atan. Think about where to go from there."

Lyren-Sartora liked being asked. "We'll go back to Bereth Ferian, and dump off these clothes that I'm thoroughly tired of. Then we'll decide."

Liere had remembered that the best time to catch Atan was early in the morning, before her complicated schedule took her away. As it was, the sun jumped a finger's breadth into the sky between Shiovhan and Eidervaen: not so early in Sartor now. They were conducted to a pretty room and offered breakfast, and then it was Rel who came to them first. He nearly took a step back when he saw Liere; if anything she was even more intensely eye-catching than she'd been weeks ago.

"You're back," he said easily. "Atan will be glad."

"And we found Norsundrians," Lyren-Sartora stated. "I want to tell Julian she was right! Is she here?"

"No, she went off with some friends from Sarendan," Rel said apologetically. "But it so happens Hinder is here, as there is a morvende concert as part of a new play being offered. And they were asking for locals under the age of fourteen who know how to dance."

Lyren-Sartora gasped in sheer pleasure. "Am I too late?"

"Why not go and see?" Rel gave her directions, and she pelted off without a backward look.

Atan showed up moments after Lyren-Sartora vanished. She, too, had to suppress the instinct to stare. Liere had almost changed as much between the last visit weeks ago and this one as she had in the five years she'd been gone. Her smile, her gaze, her posture signaled a self-reliance that had never been there before. The effect was stunning. "Liere?"

"I know you're busy," Liere said. "Briefly, Yeres did her best to add Andri Elsarion to her collection of young men. But this is more serious: Adon Marsael knew it. We're fairly sure he was rescued from prison by Norsunder."

Atan flinched. "I will let Tsauderei know. And I do have a pile of things I cannot postpone much less put off. Can you stay till evening? I have it completely free, and I want to hear everything."

"Everything it shall be." Liere flashed a tender smile that made Atan catch her breath. "Lyren-Sartora ran off to find Hinder, so we probably won't see her back for hours. I'd like to do some exploration in the archive, if I can get permission?"

"I'll give you a scribe pass," Atan said, going to a beautifully carved desk with a lot of drawers. "Here. I'd better run."

Liere accepted the wooden token with the scribe guild

sigil carved in. Magic tingled on it: from that, Liere guessed she would be able to access records not open to everyone.

Eidervaen was a city of records. There was not one archive, but many. However, Liere had an entire day to fill. She ventured into the huge chamber with the world map on the outside, where she found very little about Enaeran after the first century of its existence. During that century, she was found references to the Marlovens, and to trips across the continent.

But after the dark days of Ivandred Montredaun-An, Enaeran, as well as the Marlovens, had closed inward, mistrusting mages and magic. They had even cut off connections with one another, according to Sartor's traveling envoys.

These readings only took a couple of hours. She then gave in to curiosity and looked up the Dei family, and discovered an entire archive dedicated just to them.

Where to begin? She went to the modern section where she should find descendants, and tried to find Fer Eiders, to discover exactly nothing. No surprise again. She'd probably have to go to Everon, or more likely Imar, which she was unwilling to do. What would that furnish but listings of births, deaths, marriages, and taxes? The real story behind whatever had happened to cause a Dei to either adopt over or change names outright to Fer Eider (or Eider, or whatever it had been) would not be found in city records.

She tried going back to the Dei family's beginnings, but here she found that the oldest records were in the Sartoran form that was so difficult to read, the language full of outdated words, and names she was unfamiliar with.

That search could wait for someday when she had a lot of time. There was no urgency. After all, she had four grandparents from whom she might have inherited traits, not just one, however famous one set of ancestors might be.

She then got sidetracked into mages and archivists and heralds' debates on inherited traits, specifically the theory that the Birth Spell might be responsible for the persistence of recognizable traits through generations; everyone knew that the Birth Spell was likelier than physical birth to produce throwbacks. But it was not solely responsible.

Now, there was a question! When did that "everyone knew" begin, and who proved it? Not that she doubted that there was some truth to it. One only had to take a look at

Atan's eyes, and at tapestries and paintings of her ancestors, to glimpse those eyes over and over. She recollected being startled to see those same eyes in the mad Prince Kessler the one time she met him, and later discovered that the Chwahir royal family and the Landises had had a marriage long ago.

But there was just too much to wade through. It seemed that mage students, and herald students, and scribes, and healers all had delved into the subject for mastery works through years and years, no one agreeing with anyone else completely.

In the distance a bell clanged, and a page appeared to say that the archive was closing. Liere flitted, not wanting to keep Atan waiting.

She found Atan alone. "Lyren-Sartora insisted on staying for the concert," Atan said.

"A concert?"

"Just for tonight, a dance concert with morvende music as theme. First an actual performance and then the court will get their chance. I hope you like what I ordered for dinner. It's all light, summer fare. Or, light for Sartor. I recently learned that the main ingredient of Colendi food seems to be air. A dash of wine, aromatic herbs, and then tiny amounts of other ingredients, chosen for their visual appeal as well as taste and scent."

"I've never been to Colend," Liere admitted. "That is, after I met the strange king. I know he's gone, but I've never been back."

"It's a very mannered society," Atan said. "Very."

Liere suppressed a private shudder, and then, when Atan asked for her report, she gave it.

She began in the approved style taught the Ones: summary of findings, and steps leading to the conclusion, with proofs ordered by priority. But as the light Gyrnian wine sank in the carafe and Atan's questions circled more and more around Andri Elsarion, everything came out in a rush.

Atan listened in growing amazement. Of all the people in the world she would not expect such a drastic change in, Liere was near the top of the list, Tahra Delieth of Everon perhaps being second. Though if Tahra met a woman half as attractive as Liere seemed to find Andri Elsarion, even she might change her *I will never marry* stance. But the most distracting thing was the change in Liere herself, a smiling, clear-eyed brilliance that brought Shontande Lirendi unexpectedly to mind, though it would be difficult to find two more different people.

"We ended by promising we will always tell one another everything," Liere finished. "I understand completely why he wouldn't tell me about Yeres. He figured out fairly soon that I was not sent by her, but he still feared that I, as well as others around him, would turn up dead if he did. He did not know the reach of magic, whether they could spy on him day and night, and whom could he ask, as I did not tell him I was a mage?"

"That's horrible."

"Especially in those last days, when Adon Marsael was torturing him by magic most every night. But I? I had no excuse beyond my own comfort. If I hadn't been so selfish, I might have saved lives. Certainly would have saved him days of misery. Though he's never given me a hint of regret."

"I think there is a natural instinct," Atan said, "to spare a beloved what can only be termed bad news, which one believes helps no one."

"Except sometimes we don't *know*. What we keep might be the key to figuring out a mystery, or a trap, or some such," Liere said in earnest, the diamonds in the ring on her thumb flashing as she picked up her goblet.

"It sounds like events changed so rapidly there is no surprise you were not able to consider as deeply as you might wish."

Rel entered on Liere's smile as she said, "Everything feels new. Everything," she admitted. "New, and changing as fast as a horse can gallop. It's wonderful—I understand why people and horses love a good gallop—but for reflection, not idea."

"How about this?" Atan suggested. "If Lyren-Sartora gets back late and you don't want to endure the transfer to the other side of the world, spend the night. I will show you the Purrad in the morning. This will give you an opportunity to reflect in quiet and utter peace."

"I'd like that," Liere said.

"Then we shall regard that as settled," Atan said. "The Purrad being a constant when everything else seems to change around us. And peaceful, though too often these days we have to plan for war, bringing us back to Norsunder getting its evil fingers in places like Enaeran. I'm wondering how many kings that terrible Yeres has been successful in putting her mark on?"

"Considering that she won't come out except rarely," Rel said calmly, "likely not that many. If you're worried that that is Norsunder's grand strategy, Tsauderei thinks it unlikely. We can bring it up at our next Remalna session."

"Remalna session?" Liere repeated.

"I neglected to mention it before, though it's no secret, exactly," Atan said, and explained.

At the end, Liere nodded, "Just what I'd expect of Senrid. I'm glad he's sharing what he learns."

"It's helpful, and intimidating, as well as frightening," Atan admitted. "I wish it was all theory. But one has only to look at Senrid to know that he doesn't consider it theory at all."

"No," Rel said. "There's a fatalism there that I think many find difficult to deal with, which might be one reason there have been fewer attending than we'd expected."

"There's also prejudice. Not just against the Marlovens, but also against the Chwahir," Atan added with a sigh. "Though I suspect most of the prejudice is against Senrid himself. He's very intimidating, though he doesn't mean to be. Though he hasn't changed a jot in how he talks, or thinks, it was somehow easier to overlook before he released the Child Spell. He wasn't intimidating while he was shorter than anyone else."

"He did release it, then?" Liere asked.

"Oh, yes," Atan said. "Long ago. I think even before you left. He's no longer a boy. If he ever was one. I can't imagine him playing."

"He played," Liere said. "We played with building blocks, and chase games. Those had been his cousin's favorite games, before she ran away. He'd kept the blocks, and we had fun with them when I used to stay there."

"You saw a side of him that no one else did," Rel observed.

"You know he had a girl cousin, who ran away," Liere said, feeling wise in her new adulthood. "He was used to girls. I was a cousin substitute, or a sister, as well as a friend."

Rel nodded. "That makes sense. He accepted the Mearsieans' idiosyncrasies, which not many did."

"I'm glad he had you during those years," Atan said. "He

always seemed so lonely—"

"What fun I had!" Lyren-Sartora exclaimed, twirling in. "Oh, it was such fun. Until the grownups started their kind of dancing. I came away. My feet got tired, after rehearsing all day."

The conversation switched to morvende echo music and the dance styles that evolved around it, and—Lyren-Sartora having eaten long before—she and Liere were conducted off to guest chambers.

Before dawn, Liere rose to a light tap on the door. She soon joined Atan out in cool air, the first hint of impending autumn, though the actual season was still weeks away.

Atan took her to the Napurdiav's starting place, and Liere set out, reveling in how right it felt. With a rush of elation she closed her eyes and paced one full loop, amazed that instinct knew exactly how many steps before the turn. Everything about this pattern was in balance: body. Mind. Spirit.

She opened her eyes westward toward the last grand promenade of stars vanishing in the vapors that overhung the horizon. To the east the sky had lightened to an airy effulgence of silver; the thin-shadowed light rendered distances as dimensionless, nearly timeless. Turn. In this direction the light strengthened, and toward the west the darkness finally lifted, limning the five-pointed leaves of summer trees, nature's coinage.

Stillness, except for the rising light beckoning toward infinity: she almost, almost heard something like music. No, not music. It was too vast, too deep, too sustained for instrument of wood and wind and string. Distraction: here, close by, the sweet warbles of morning songbirds. Off to the right, left, right, sang a stream, its descant the contented croaks of unseen frogs.

It was the giddiness of joy, that was all, joined to the perfect summer day, and the great arcs of nature reflecting these triple arcs she stepped.

Then a bell tolled, and the timeless sense gave way to the demands of daylight: Liere had come to the end of the pattern. High-hearted, refreshed in spirit, she ran inside and up the stairs to thank Atan, collect her daughter, and transfer to Bereth Ferian.

Atan and Rel both escorted them to the Destination.

When the two vanished, Atan said, "Why do I feel the sun dimmed a little?"

Rel waited until they were upstairs again, and said, "I don't think I've ever seen that dramatic a change in someone."

"She says it's love. Can it be love, when it's only been a month?" She searched Rel's eyes, suddenly doubting the careful years she waited between each tentative step in their own relationship—which she, supposedly so powerful, did not dare to make permanent with marriage. Oh, she could, but what would be the consequences? So many of her ancestors had nearly wrecked the ship of state on the rocks of what they thought was love. Or it might have been love, to the exclusion of everything else. "I think I'm jealous of her freedom. Yes, I know most think I have perfect freedom to do what I want."

Rel shrugged his massive shoulders. "If they say it's love, then it's love. Until it isn't." He frowned in perplexity. "Though might there be an element of self-love, for the first time in her life?"

"Now that makes sense, far more than a sudden discovery of lust transforming someone so thoroughly," Atan said, rolling her eyes at him. "When she first turned up, it was just after she'd taken a knife wound. Which she neglected to tell me at the time, typical of the Liere we know. And she was worried about that Geth boy that Yeres got hold of. So I didn't see the five years' changes, except the superficial ones. Maybe her month . . . completed the changes?""

"What happened?"

Over breakfast she summarized what Liere had told her, finishing, "What a luxury, to know you can tell one another everything. Or is that possible?" She eyed Rel. "Do I tell you everything? I think I do, then I remember I haven't."

"Oh?" he asked, unperturbed.

"The night you returned. When Shontande gave me that dinner. He very nearly gave me a lot more than that. A lot more."

Rel waited.

"You're not upset?" Atan asked.

Rel said, "Not about something that didn't happen. I'd be upset if you decided to end your vows. But I think I'd understand. That last night, before he left, during the regatta, when he got up and showed that bit of dance, and no one could look away, I couldn't either. And I'd thought myself indifferent to other men."

Atan shook her head. "Just as well he's now king over there in Colend, which means he and that aura of his is confined to the land of airy cakes and pretty fans. Well, that's my confession for the day. The year, I trust."

Rel hesitated, then said, "Don't you want to ask me if I have a confession?"

She sank back down, giving him a startled look. "Did someone tempt you during your recent wanderings? I thought you were with the guard, and then Mondros."

"I was. This isn't temptation. It's . . . different. But perhaps it's time to admit it, lest it seem as if I'm ashamed when I most assuredly am not."

The bell toned. Atan waved off the page who came to the door. It shut again, and she crossed her arms. "Oh, no. You can't drop that and expect me to last all day wondering."

"I told you that Mondros is my father."

"Mage, disinherited noble, from Ralanor Veleth. Fought for the king and queen of Everon at one time."

"I did not tell you about my mother."

"Only that you discovered she is dead."

"My mother was Gwasan Sonscarna. Princess of Chwahirsland," Rel said.

Atan's jaw dropped. "I want to hear that story, later. All of it. But Rel, that makes you royalty."

"Which is why I kept it to myself. I am arrogant enough to want to be accepted on my own merits," he said.

Atan nodded two or three times, then smiled. That smile widened until she gave a whoop of laughter.

"Atan?"

"Don't you see? How absolutely floored the likes of certain courtiers would be to find that out. Oh, Rel, it would be priceless!"

He held out a hand.

"But that is your life, to share or not share. I know. It goes under the seal of our vows, then, unless you choose to reveal it. But you're going to have to forgive me for letting loose an evil chuckle now and then when I think of Irza and her like sniffing over your low birth. And how chagrinned she'd be to discover you are technically a Chwahir prince." A questioning look. "You are a Chwahir prince."

"Jilo is safe from me. Even if Wan Edhe is defeated, I'd defend Jilo to the death, but never replace him."

"I love you so much." She hugged him, then went off laughing.

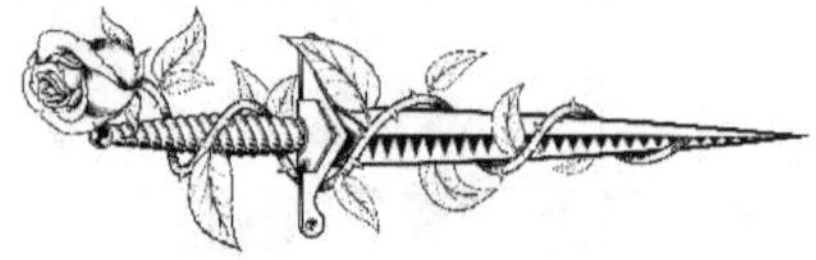

FIFTY

I f anything was needed, Liere thought later that day, to prove how fundamentally different she and Lyren-Sartora were, that would be their respective rooms in Bereth Ferian's palace.

Lyren-Sartora greeted her many belongings with a glad cry, flinging her carryall into a closet, then declaring that she wouldn't look at it for at least a year. In the days that followed, she changed her clothes morning, noon, and evening, just to be wearing something new and pretty again.

Whereas Liere had left little when she went to Geth-deles, and of course came back to furnishings that had always been there. It was a guest room. It had always felt like a guest room. Liere remembered how long it had taken before she dared to touch the beautiful bureau at the one wall, or the trunk, lest she somehow damage them and her father would know and come roaring up from Imar at the other end of the continent and scream at her for not respecting other people's property and for her presumption in stepping out of her proper place.

Even after she got used to the room, it never felt like hers. Less so now. She slept through the first day, then napped and read through the rest of the week, until she had regained all her strength. The morning after she ran around the entire palace complex without stopping, she pronounced herself ready to face the world.

She looked at the two outfits airing on the clothes rack, which she had made herself. She thought of the lovely robe she had bespoke for the Envoy Ball—which she had left in Enaeran. She certainly wouldn't need it before she returned.

There was one thing she relished being back with: cleaning frames. That meant she wouldn't have to think about clothes at all.

She left the room, stopped by the scribe desk to order a golden notecase made for Andri, then she went in search of Arthur, as Lyren-Sartora ran out to skate on the lake.

At the sight of Liere, Arthur set aside his never-ending archival matters. Liere caught him up on her version of events. At the end, he smiled. "What a change! I'm all for good changes, and I'm glad you're happy. You know I've felt bad for years that you were never happy here."

"Not your fault," Liere said. "Most of the problem was within myself, and of course my being unable to learn magic because Dena Yeresbeth got in the way, only none of us knew it. But even if I'd been able to learn magic, I was too anxious for happiness."

He accepted that with a gesture.

"What has happened here in the time I was gone?"

"Here in Bereth Ferian, or here in the rest of the world?"

"Both. Atan didn't say a lot, except I sensed an underlying tension. She talked about strategy sessions, and though I was not trying to hear in the mental realm—they both forget mind-shields—I sensed both her and Rel thinking 'If we get the chance to hold another meeting.' That feels like they think the Norsunder attack is imminent?

Arthur's smile faded. "Part of the tension is not knowing. When we finished cataloguing the Venn donations, Roy went off to Detlev's house. Every time that happens, I wonder if this is it. In the meantime, did Atan or Rel tell you about Lisdan?"

Liere nodded. "Lisdan, in Melire. Apparently Rel bought a house there, and established a false identity as a labor broker, so he can come and go, and strangers can show up and leave, and the townspeople will think they know why. That really feels like preparation for imminent trouble."

"It's preparation," Arthur said. "We don't know how imminent. I hope Rel will own that house for years and years. Meanwhile we have to live our lives."

"We have to live our lives," Liere repeated, suppressing an urge to flee back to Enaeran.

No, she'd made a promise. If Lyren-Sartora changed her mind, that would be different.

Lyren-Sartora turned up when the sun vanished, and a wintry wind rose. "You've come out of hibernation!"

Liere squashed down the worry that wanted to boil up. Live our lives, she repeated to herself. "Have fun?"

"Yes. It's so good to be back. Except I forgot how much I hate being cold."

The following day, Lyren-Sartora flounced into Liere's room just after Liere finished her old Ones drills. Her shoulder only twinged now.

"Mac is gone, and Yanli is busy studying, and even Siamis is gone off somewhere. There's no one to skate with, and I hate building snow forts alone. Let's go visiting, as you promised."

"All right, where to first?"

Lyren-Sartora eyed her, but decided not to say how annoying she found that big, gaudy ring on Liere's thumb. "Are you over your argument, or whatever it was, with Senrid?"

"Not an argument." Liere had forgotten her resentment over the news about Senrid having a child. What a silly reaction! Senrid was free to do what he wanted. Of course. "Not even a disagreement. More of a misunderstanding, that can be fixed in two heartbeats."

"Good, because I figured out the time. It's afternoon in Choreid Dhelerei. Perfect!"

"Perfect," Liere echoed, reaching for transfer tokens to fix the Destination. "Let's start with Senrid."

About the Author

Sherwood Smith writes fantasy, science fiction, and historical fiction. Her full bibliography can be found on her website at https://www.sherwoodsmith.net

About Book View Cafe

Book View Café is an author-owned cooperative of professional writers, publishing in a variety of genres including fantasy, science fiction, romance, mystery, and more.

Its authors include New York Times and USA Today bestsellers as well as winners and nominees of many prestigious awards such as the Agatha Award, Hugo Award, Lambda Literary Award, Locus Award, Nebula Award, RITA Award, Philip K. Dick Award, World Fantasy Award, and many others.

Since its debut in 2008, Book View Café has gained a reputation for producing high quality books in both print and electronic form. BVC's e-books are DRM-free and distributed around the world.

Book View Café's monthly newsletter includes new releases, specials, author news, and event announcements. To sign up, visit:
   https://www.bookviewcafe.com/bookstore/newsletter/